The Lonesome Road

Originally from County Galway, Eire, the author emigrated to London in the early 1960s. He found work in the construction industry, where he remained until arthritis forced early retirement in 1998.

The author now resides in Hereford.

James Farrell

The Lonesome Road

Olympia Publishers
London

www.olympiapublishers.com
OLYMPIA PAPERBACK EDITION

A CIP catalogue record for this title is
available from the British Library.

ISBN: 978-1-84897-271-1

(Olympia Publishers is part of Ashwell Publishing Ltd)

First Published in 2013

Olympia Publishers
60 Cannon Street
London
EC4N 6NP

Printed in Great Britain

Dedication

This novel is dedicated to the men and women who ventured to join the tide of humanity that swept eastwards across the Irish Sea in the nineteen-fifties and sixties, the vast majority of whom settled and put down roots, a resolute classless generation now almost forgotten whose generosity to their homeland and to the families and friends they left behind knew no bounds, many of whom I have the good fortune to number among my friends.

'You'll never go back', a catchy saying among the London-Irish, has stood the test of time, inasmuch as it's as veritable as it's droll, for only one in a thousand of the immigrants realize their dream and return to settle. Nevertheless, for all that the odds are stacked against him, Jack Daly is determined to prove the forecast as absurd as believing a favourable forecast could change the weather.

Author's Note

After World War II, to counterbalance the vast influx of immigrants from its colonies in Africa, Asia and the Caribbean, the British government came to an agreement with the government of the newly-declared Irish Republic to allow right of entry without passports to its citizens provided they were of good behaviour. As a result, in the period between nineteen-fifty and the end of the nineteen-sixties it's estimated that a million of Ireland's youth crossed the 'duck pond', as the Irish Sea was referred to derogatorily, all carrying with them a dream of returning someday to settle when fortune smiled their way. However, it turned out to be a dream too far for all but a few, the dreams foundering on the rocks of reality. A million dreams, a million stories, this is but one.

Part 1

Chapter 1

It was one of those wet days in the west of Ireland when the rain was falling with such persistence that it seemed the gods were trying to empty the heavens of water, a day in a succession of similar days which could easily have coined the phrase: 'as long as a wet week', another day of frustration, another day of pacing the kitchen for Jack Daly, a loose steel tip on one of his boots striking a discordant note on the concrete floor, while outside, the downpour, whipped up by a gale-force wind, lashed against the windowpanes, shivering them in their frames. To compound his misery he hadn't a penny to his name, not even a cigarette and, when his craving for a smoke became unbearable, inspiration born of necessity sent him striding to his bedroom to search the top pocket of his Sunday suit for a butt. Probing with an index finger through the accumulation of ticket stubs and other dross he fished out an obtuse-angled, half-smoked cigarette with a slight colouring of pink lipstick on one tip.

Taking infinite care in case it came asunder in his fingers he straightened the dog-end and hurried back to the kitchen and, as matches were a commodity not to be wasted, he picked up a small red coal from the open fire with the tongs and lit up. "You saved my life, Mary O'Hara," he muttered to himself, taking a long satisfying drag of the stale smoke, his thoughts returning to the Sunday night dance at the Phoenix and the rather demure manner in which the glamorous Mary had handed him her lighted cigarette to dispose of when he asked her to partner him in the last waltz. In a dither that she had assented instead of resorting to the timeworn and most incredible of excuses: "I have this dance promised," instinctively he had topped the cigarette, and from force of habit stuffed it down his top pocket.

Now, as he sat savouring the reward of his unwitting prudence, the scene reconstructed itself in his mind: Mary, as light as a feather in his arms as they floated round the dance floor to the lilt of THE MOUNTAINS OF MOURNE, the all-pervading scent of her perfume overpowering his senses, the impetus of each whirl gently propelling her closer, their cheeks brushing lightly, touching but not intimately, and finally the shock back to reality when the music stopped and the compere called: "That's all for tonight, ladies and gentlemen! Now let's have your attention please for our national anthem!"

If only she was poor like the rest of us, he thought, as her father's disapproving face peered through the window of his reverie, blighting any pleasure he might have gleaned from the memory. For a brief moment both faces, one smiling, the other scowling, crossed swords with each other, the scowling one winning the battle and bringing home the raw reality that he was smoking someone else's leaving. The thought prickled his pride and, with a flick of a thumb, he sent the dog-end arching into the fire. Disgruntled at the unfairness of the system to which he was bound and chained he returned to pacing the floor, while the repetitive tick-tocking of the wag-o'-the-wall (a clock with weights and chains) marked off the time in separate atoms of monotony, its ponderous tones when it struck the hour as desolate as the pealing of a death bell.

Contrary to the belief that Jesus Christ was the only true six-footer Jack was spot-on six feet tall. Broad-shouldered, lean and muscular, his angular features, high forehead, straight nose, hard jaw, and the determined set of his chin, a physiognomy crowned by an unruly crop of raven-black hair, gave his face a somewhat truculent cast, which made him look older than his twenty years. However, this was offset by the twinkle of humour in his grey-green eyes, cynical humour that seemed to be deriding himself and his impecunious portion, a lack of means which was translated in his dress: navy-blue woollen trousers, drooping at the knees and girdled at the waist by a black leather belt, striped flannel collarless shirt, tweed jacket which, like the rest of his attire, showed random mending and patching, and brown FCA boots.

Jack was startled out of his reverie when the pot of potatoes for the pigs boiled over, splashing water on the fire with an exploding hiss of steam and ashes and, spurred to speed, he lifted the huge three-legged cast-iron pot off the fire and moved the pothanger up a notch on the crane. Just as he was banking the fire, a lump of soot dislodged by the rain came thundering down the chimney and, when it rebounded off the pot and smashed into smithereens on the hearth, scattering in all directions, the black cat, Jack's only companion since early morning, had a few anxious moments before judiciously seeking higher ground on the hob, which was part of the fireplace.

It took a few moments for the disconcerted cat to settle in his new seat, and Jack, for all that he was in the doldrums, managed a laugh. "That shook you, cat, clever and all as you think you are. Well, make the most of it today, because you won't be in here tomorrow, and all the rats that's in the barn eating the oats – scarce and all as it is. Out there you'll be – earning your keep," he said, in scolding tones, scowling at the cat, and when the cat just stared back at him sullenly through drowsy lids, he shrugged forbearingly. "This rain'll see the end o' me – talking to myself and talking to the cat," he muttered. "It's a sure sign that a man is going soft in the head."

Jack's dialogue with the cat was interrupted by the sound of footsteps outside and a failed attempt at shouldering open the front door, which was swollen from the rain. "Go round the back, Murt!" he called, just loud enough to carry outside, and when he heard the retreating tread of the man's hobnailed boots, he swore under his breath: "No matter how many times I tell that ludramawn if I open the front door I mightn't be able to close it again, it goes in one ear and out the other." And, some moments later, when he heard the latch lifting on the back door, followed by the clanking of empty buckets as the man stumbled about in the back-kitchen, he shook his head in exasperation. "He'll fall and break his next someday, as if I hadn't enough troubles as it is," he went on, his muttering trailing off when an elderly, stoop-shouldered man stepped out of the gloom. "Come down to the fire, Murt – you must be drownded," he greeted, faking a smile. "I knew it could be nobody but yourself on this unearthly morning. It's even too wet for the tinkers to come begging, and that's wet."

Murt Burke, the intruder on Jack's hopeless thoughts, gave himself a dog-like shake and, shedding his overcoat, he draped it over the back of a chair and turned it inside out to the fire. "It's a terrible mornin', surely, Jack," he said at length and, with his back to the fire, he stood silently flexing the stiffness from his bones, the overlap of his belt, which was hanging down almost to his knees, making a queer shadow on the wall. Finally, when steam began to rise from the legs of his baggy-arse trousers, he shooed the cat from his warm perch with a smack of his cap and took up a crouching position on the hob, his palms spread over the flames.

"This weather isn't suiting at all, Murt," said Jack, when his neighbour was comfortably ensconced.

Ignoring Jack's comment Murt embarked methodically on the process of filling his pipe, knocking out the dottle, blowing the stem, and packing the bowl with fresh tobacco, which he cut from a two-ounce plug with a penknife and kneaded in the palm of his left hand with the heel of his right. When there was still no reply from his visitor, Jack went on: "I was just saying to myself that it'd remind you o' the time o' the Deluge with all the rain it's making and, if it keeps up, we might be needing an ark ourselves. At least, we have two of everything to put in it – two cows, two calves, two pigs and two of anything else you care to mention, and there's nearly enough water outside to sweep us away to the top o' Croagh Patrick."

Murt, his wizened face set in an expression of complete unconcern, was in a world of his own, and when he had the pipe prepared, he brought a lighted strip of newspaper to the bowl and gave a few preliminary puffs.

After another unsuccessful overture at broaching speech, Jack turned his eyes pitifully to heaven to emphasise his perseverance and, taken by a fit of irritation, he asked bluntly: "Did you ever smoke dried cowshite, Murt? I heard they used to mix it through the tobacco during the War to make it more plenty."

When there was still no response, Jack felt like throwing the cat at him. Nevertheless, he kept on dauntlessly: "Well, it'll be soon time to feed the pigs, rain or no rain, and put on a piece o' bacon for the dinner. Eileen, as you know, is over at Quinn's keeping an eye on young Rita – the baby is two weeks overdue as it is. There's always trouble with the first one, or so they say – can you throw any bit o' light on that for me?"

As if he was just awakening from an anaesthetic, Murt raised his head and looked at Jack, as though he was seeing him for the first time. "Huh – I know nothin' about them kind o' things, Jack – a farmer I am, not a midwife," he said and, as if to give more emphasis to his words, he expectorated loudly and spat so copiously on the fire that the flame flickered.

At this point Jack threw in the towel, and for the next half-hour, save for intermittent explosions of tobacco spittle and the grate hissing back in protest, they sat silently staring into the fire.

When the clock struck twelve, both men hurried through the motions of making the sign of the cross, murmuring the Angelus prayer in double-quick time as though there were extra indulgences for speed, and shortly afterwards Murt eased himself stiffly to his feet and flexed his spare shoulders. "It's time I was tendin' to me stock, Jack," he said, and though there was steam still rising from his overcoat and it had shrunk somewhat, he made a spirited effort at shrugging into it, while Jack, with one hand on the collar and the other gripping the material at the back, heaved up so vigorously that the collar almost came away in his hand. Then, as if he was purposely trying Jack's patience, Murt made straight for the front door and, with the effort of forcing it open, he broke wind loudly in a succession of sharp raspers.

"Fair play to your ould arse, Murt! At least that part of your body has plenty to say for itself – it just goes to show what talking through your arse means," Jack called in his wake, although the remark was smothered in the wind howling through the open doorway.

Alone again save for the cat, Jack turned to the pigs' pot and, with a deftness that looked like sleight of hand, he flipped the lid aside, leaned his head back to avoid the sudden gush of steam, and prodded a few of the piping-hot Aran Banners with an index finger without seeming to touch them. Satisfied that they were cooked he swung the crane on its pivot away from the fire, lifted the pot off the pothanger, and dragged it along the floor to the back-kitchen. As the back door was on the sheltered side of the house, he opened it fully and, standing the pot on the threshold, he gradually tilted it sideways for the water to drain. When the potatoes were fully strained, he mashed them with a wooden pounder and ladled them into four galvanised buckets – three for the pigs, one for the hens.

While he was waiting for the mash to cool, he leaned a shoulder against a jamb of the door and looked out on the dismal day. "If water was even a ha'penny a barrel, we'd all be millionaires around here," he said to himself, as he listened to the rhythm of the rain changing notes from galvanised roofs to water-barrels, tin cans and saucepans until his impatience to have done with the feeding got the upper hand of him. "Hot or not, good or bad for them, they're getting it now!" he swore and, with an old coat thrown over his head, he sped across the farmyard with the buckets, hop-stepping to avoid the puddles, until he reached the shelter of the pigsty.

The two pigs were almost fully grown, and he watched speculatively as they wolfed down the hot mash. "I'm going to eat you, and I'm going to have a good day's drinking out of you when I sell you at the fair next month – that is, if those spuds don't give you stomach-cramp and kill you first," he said aloud, addressing the pigs, as though the hapless animals could understand. "And the day for the drinking can't come soon enough."

When the pigs had licked the trough clean, he returned to the back-kitchen and mixed the remainder of the mash with Indian meal for the hens, which were converging on the back door from all directions, their feathers awry from the rain. "Will you look at them!" he muttered. "Standing like the Israelites in the wilderness waiting for the manna from heaven – everything is waiting to be fed around here, and I hardly able to feed myself."

The words had hardly left his lips when Charlie, his horse, stuck out his head through the open top part of his stable door and whinnied, as if he too wanted to be included in the feeding. "There's nothing for you, Charlie – I fed you this morning, you greedy guts, you," he called, giving the V-sign to the horse. Nevertheless, he selected a carrot from the bag behind the door and, shaking his head as though he was going against his better judgement, he crossed to the stable.

When Jack held out the carrot by its tail-end, Charlie snapped it to within a hair's breadth of his fingers, nodded his head in an equine thank-you, champed it, and then nuzzled the remaining particle from his open palm. As black as his master's hair, Charlie was part racehorse, and though he measured just over fifteen hands, he made up for his lack of stature in spirit and intelligence, and an uncanny telepathy passed between horse and master in their three-year association, for Charlie had come as one of God's rare gifts, or so Jack believed.

The partnership had come about one Easter Monday at Milltown point-to-point races when Charlie, running under the name Black Narcissus, fell in the novice event, injuring a fetlock. The vet was on the point of putting him down when Jack came on the scene and, after pleading with the owner to give him a chance to save him, he had paid a little above the knacker-yard value and taken him home. Over the following weeks, showing a knowledge and perseverance that belied his years, he treated the injury with every available remedy, and against all the odds nursed the four-year-old gelding back to fitness.

As the horse was beginning his second life, like Lazarus after coming from the tomb, Jack had thought it proper that he should have a new name and, as Lazarus wasn't a suitable name for a horse, he re-christened him Charlie, after Charlie Sootdrop, the travelling medicine man who had supplied the recipe for the poultices, the healing balm, the liniment, and the advice, without which the horse would never have recovered.

After a half-hour of horsey talk Jack gave Charlie an armful of hay and ran for the shelter of the house. Shutting out the rain he returned to the fire and resettled the coals, poking them into flame. "You don't have to look at the mantelpiece when you're poking the fire – that's for sure," he smiled grimly and, somewhat cheered by the philosophy, he set about preparing his dinner. Ever since Sheila, his widowed mother, passed away six years earlier, Eileen, his sister, and himself had a hard struggle on their hands trying to eke out a living from their nine-acre farm, a never-ending drudgery which was presently being hampered by the torrential April rains. Reluctantly he had to admit that if for nothing else he missed Eileen for her culinary capabilities and, sick to death of his own cooking, he hoped that Rita Quinn would drop her bundle of joy soon so that some normality would return to their humble home.

When he finished his tasteless meal, he turned to the wireless in the embrasure of the front window and cursed profanely when he found that the dry battery had come to the end of its tether. Quickly disconnecting the leads he stood the battery on edge on the hearth, hoping that heat would inject enough life into its bowels so that he could hear the weekly episode of *The Kennedys of Castleross* and, when heat did the trick, he was allowed the fifteen minutes

21

listening time to get an update on the changing fortunes of the popular radio family. Afterwards, at a loss for something to do, he spent the remainder of the afternoon staring morosely into the fire.

When dusk descended, lengthening shadows began to creep out from the corners of the kitchen, stealthily claiming back the ground they had lost at daybreak and, shaking himself out of his lethargy, Jack took down the lamp from the wall and topped it up with paraffin, ready for lighting. Having neither the inclination nor the patience to do the milking he hoped that Eileen wouldn't be late, although a glance out of the window put paid to his fears when he spied her approaching, head down over the handlebars of her bicycle, pedalling against the rain. When she stepped into the kitchen, breathing heavily from her exertions, he smiled a greeting, a bleak smile that had a hint of derision in it. "I was just saying to myself, Eileen, that the *Hunchback of Nôtre Dame* is never dead when I saw you through the window, humped over the handlebars of the bike," he sniggered. "But that aside, did ye have any luck over there today – good luck, bad luck, or no luck at all? Anyway, you're back just in time to do the milking."

Eileen Daly wasn't short in stature, but in flat heels, her shoulders hunched, her headscarf soaked, her raincoat dripping, she looked shrunken, almost tubby. Hanging her coat and scarf on a crook on the wall she turned her back to the fire, running her fingers through her short fair hair and smoothing her grey woollen skirt over her hips and rump which were stretching the seams to bursting point. Her high cheekbones, full lips, straight nose, and general good looks were redeeming factors for the lack of sparkle in her blue eyes, a sparkle that work and worry had dimmed over the years and, completely ignoring her brother's sarcasm and question, she continued to stare vacantly while her body absorbed the heat.

"Well, did you, or did you not?" repeated Jack impatiently.

"Yes – a fine baby boy she had this afternoon, God bless them both," returned Eileen at length, in a tone devoid of any elation or sense of accomplishment.

"For that news alone I'll do the milking for you myself," said Jack, a mischievous smile flickering between his lips and eyes.

The suggestion brought a scowl from Eileen. "Are you going soft in the head or something with the rain? You, is it – do the milking? You know well the cows always get sore elders after you, whatever kind o' hands you have at all," she snapped, staring at him in utter disbelief, as if the idea of a man milking cows when there was a woman in the house was heretical and, without further comment, she shook off her fatigue and set about the twice daily chore. As though 'milk' was part of the feline vocabulary, the cat suddenly showed interest, and when he heard the milking pails clanking, for the first time that day he left the fireplace and followed Eileen to the cowshed, miaowing at her heels.

The usurping of a woman's province by a man was always a source of amusement for Jack and, as he sat staring into the fire, he searched for some reason other than the bleak future for his sister's lapse into dowdiness, for not many years ago she had made a pretty picture sauntering down Castleford's main street, her gleaming crop of hair bouncing in rhythm with the natural swing of her hips, her high heels clacking on the pavement, her lips set in a smile like a screen goddess. Although he was six years her junior he still remembered some of her boyfriends, and one in particular, Jimmy Murphy, brought a sardonic smile to his lips. "Lock up your daughters, Jimmy Murphy is in town," the children used to whoop like a nursery rhyme every time he passed by, as if he was the big bad wolf or some other roguish animal from Disneyland. Although the chaffing was just childish chatter it contained an element of truth, for not only the single girls, but many of the comparatively younger wives of the rich businessmen of the town had succumbed to his charm, and the earthiness of some of their trysting places down Poke Lane, the sinning side of Castleford, was oddly at variance with the silk lingerie and expensive perfume of his rather prim conquests.

Eileen and Murphy had been going out together for over a year, and she had been living under the misconception that he intended to marry her. However, the plug was pulled abruptly on her aspirations when he ran off to London with Peggy Wilson, a well-to-do shopkeeper's daughter, and the contents of her father's safe, although Peggy returned alone a few months later. Looking at Eileen now, it was hard to picture her as she had been then, bubbling over with vitality and full of banter, and harder still to put her lack of enthusiasm for life down to a broken heart, or perhaps it had something to do with the conversation he had eavesdropped on one night in the Royal Hotel.

Meanwhile, the flowing tide of emigration was taking its toll on Knockrush, the village where the Dalys lived in their two-bedroom cottage, and on the town of Castleford two miles away and, like a scythesman cutting a swath through a field of corn, it was reaping a bitter harvest on the youth of the community, leaving those remaining pushed to the pins of their collars to keep up with the farmwork. To counterbalance the labour shortfall the village pooled its resources and worked in a rotary system, which entailed forming 'mehels', groups of workers to help one another at the potato-picking, haymaking and harvesting. Although the aftermath of the War had brought increased mechanisation, horses and donkeys were still the main beasts of burden, and the only tractor seen in Knockrush was the one towing the threshing machine at harvest time.

One after another Eileen's admirers had left without her, and now that the mantle of spinsterhood was hanging inauspiciously on her shoulders, perhaps she didn't see any need to look attractive, for facing them was a future that bore no immediate hope. It was a no-win situation, for if he pulled up stakes himself and followed the well-trodden path eastwards, Eileen would never manage on her own, they couldn't sell the farm because the title deed, which was in his late father's name, was missing and, in all optimism, if some man took Eileen off his hands, no woman worth her salt, least of all Mary O'Hara, would marry him and expect to raise a family on such scant acres unless he had a regular job as well. But jobs, like other luxuries in the locality, were for the chosen few, a case of who you knew, not what you knew and, save for a miracle occurring, he was stuck with Eileen for better or worse.

After tea, when Eileen had cleared the table and lit the lamp, she sank wearily into her armchair by the fire and, completely ignoring her brother as if he wasn't there, she took up her knitting. In an attempt to break the monotony, Jack tried the wireless again, and when he failed to resurrect a murmur, disgruntled he returned to staring into the fire. "Murt Burke called again today," he ventured finally, hoping to get a conversation going after his day of talking to himself.

Eileen slowed her needles just long enough to ask: "Did he have any news?"

"News, is it? – will you cop yourself on!" returned Jack, a sarcastic ring in his tone. "You know yourself what he's like. He nearly talked the clock down off the wall and, as for spitting – I thought he'd quench the fire with all the spitting he done. And what's more, he's heedless, and a heedless person is twenty times worse than a thick person."

When Eileen failed to comment, Jack went on: "What a silly question to ask, 'Did he have any news?' You know yourself he never goes to town from one end o' the week to the other except to go to Mass on Sundays, and where would he get the news? – unless he got it from one o' them tinker women that keep calling. I've got my own ideas too about the tinker women – it looks suspicious. An ould bachelor living on his own and young Maggie Sheridan or some other woman of her tribe calling twice a week or more. If it's just for begging they're calling, how is it they never bother to call here? And, if that's not proof enough, I noticed too that he's scratching his ould grapes o' wrath a lot lately. Then, when he was going out the door, he let a few raspers go – I could feel the wind o' them down here by the fire. So, now you have it – the highlights of my morning."

Frowning at her brother's outburst, Eileen eased into a more comfortable posture in her armchair, stretching her legs and making a footstool of the hob. "I don't know what's the matter with you at all – you haven't a good word to say about anybody," she scowled. "Murt, the poor ould craither, is the salt o' the earth, and I don't believe all that tattle about the tinker women either – it's all in your own filthy mind. If you ever go to England, I'll have to depend on Murt and the rest o' the neighbours to give me a helping hand."

"The neighbours – the neighbours! That's all I hear, morning, noon and night!" interjected Jack. "If you ask me, the whole country is governed by what the neighbours say – nobody seems to have a mind of their own anymore and, as for giving you a helping hand, well I'll tell you – they'll help you into the world and help you out of it, especially out of it. They'll wash you, lay you out, dig the grave, put you in it, and straighten up the coffin if it's crooked – that's the only helping hand you can ever depend on from those neighbours you think so much of. Still, when you come to think of it, it's marvellous how gently they'll handle you when you're dead, as if they could hurt you, and they're very forgiving too, always looking for something nice to say about you, no matter how bad you were. But changing the subject, where did you get the idea I was going to England?"

"You're always on about going, that's why!" snapped Eileen. "If I got a shilling for every time I heard you saying you'd be better off over in England, I'd be a rich woman today."

"Yes – and if you got another shilling for every time you had a go at me, running me down, you'd be rolling in money," countered Jack. "Just say for instance I did go, you wouldn't last six months here on your own without a man about the place, or maybe you have some man in mind? Well, if you have, you'll frighten the life out of him for sure if he sees you with your skirt up like that – showing it all off," he went on, drawing Eileen's attention to her skirt, which was riding up, exposing the backs of her bare thighs all the way up to the elastic on the legs of her knickers. "And besides, I could lay claim to half the place. We could partition the house down the middle and have four and a half acres apiece. Then, we'd soon see who needed who the most."

Jack's remark about her skirt brought a blush to Eileen's cheeks and, quickly correcting her pose, she smoothed the garment into more modest alignment with her legs and thighs. "Oh, shut up, you – you're always picking on me just to upset me!" she hissed. "Anyway, it's me that's keeping the place going. If it wasn't for me, you'd have it strapped and drank in a year, and I'll have you know that I spent the best years of my life, here in this house, looking after you, ever since Mother passed away, God rest her."

"The best years of my life – I like it! Well, if them were your best years, I shudder to think what's to come," returned Jack, shaking his head as if at the horror of the thought. "But you're right – you're right – women are always right. Yes – I'd strap the place and drink it, not that I'd get much strap, seeing as we've no deeds to it. But since you drew down drink, is there any fear you might have the price of a few pints stashed away somewhere, or even the price of a smoke, and I'll pay you back double when something turns up? It's this blasted weather that's getting me down and making me peevish, but if it's fine tomorrow, I'll make a start at cutting the turf. Someday, when I'm rich –"

"Someday is the day they forgot to put on the calendar," Eileen cut in, the faintest trace of a smile softening her features into something of their former comeliness, for she always found it hard to sustain her irritation with her brother. "There isn't a ha'penny in the house, nothing till tomorrow when I sell the eggs to the travelling shop, but if there's anything left after I pay for the groceries, I might manage ten fags. This is the worst year we've had yet. We could do with another calf badly, seeing as we've plenty o' milk to feed it on. So, maybe if we sell both pigs instead of keeping one for killing, we could buy a calf – it'd be a great help," she went on, anxiety creeping into her tone. "It's our turn to have the Stations in October, and we'll have to sell the big bullock to cover the cost."

"For the love o' Christ, will you shut up about the Stations!" Jack snapped. "It's six months away – we could all be dead by then. I keep telling you and telling you that it's no good worrying about a problem until it's time to face it – let tomorrow take care of itself. You know yourself something always turns up. You never can tell, we might win the sweep, and then all our troubles'll be over."

"Win the sweep, is it – whatever will you dream up next? We could hardly afford a ticket – things are so bad. You never take anything serious, you! You don't give a shite as long as you can get your belly full o' porther, and come home here drunk, annoying me."

"Belly full o' porther, is it? – chance'd be a fine thing," countered Jack. "All I'm trying to say, if you'll just listen for a minute, is that worrying never solves anything – it just makes it worse. And now that you drew down again about me being drunk – as if you'd ever let me forget – I've only got this to say, a drunk will someday be sober, but a fool will always be a fool!"

Jack smothered a grin as he watched Eileen's bosom heave with silent wrath, and the sudden change in the rhythm of her needles spoke volumes of meaning before she finally exploded: "You're calling me a fool now, a fool for hanging on here looking after you!"

"Not exactly, but if the cap fits –"

The slanging match was cut short when they heard footsteps outside, and the front door shook open in spite of the canvas sack on the floor keeping out the rain. "I'm sick o' telling that eejit to go round the back. We'd be just as well off if we left the front door open altogether and put a bush in it. I keep telling him and telling him –" Jack swore, his tirade trailing off as his visitor of earlier came within earshot.

Chapter 2

Daly's kitchen was a popular nightly meeting place for the people of Knockrush, and Eileen was hearty in her welcome as the first of the visitors stepped into the glow of the lamplight. "Sure, it's yourself that's in it, Murt," she greeted. "Come down to the fire and have a warm – you must be famished with the cold."

Grunting a goodnight Murt went through his ritual of disrobing before taking his usual seat on the hob, while Jack, muttering profanities under his breath, slammed the bolt on the front door in case others had the same idea.

Shortly afterwards, one by one and in groups, the villagers arrived: Peter Costello, Michael Joyce, Mick Moore and Kathy, his teenage daughter; Tom Kennedy, Paddy Keane, Tommy Fogarty, old Granny Mulhaire, the village matriarch, and many others and, with each new arrival, the semicircle of chairs, settles and trestles around the fire fanned out until it almost touched the walls in places. Soon, general conversation took a back seat, and emigration and the best way of tackling it became the main topic.

Tommy Fogarty, the local thatcher, a lanky, hollow-cheeked man in his mid-fifties, was the first to comment. "Dillon, the TD, has the answer, at least according to himself," he stammered, pausing to catch his breath which was coming on hoarse whistling sounds, the effort of raising his voice above the chatter bringing a touch of colour to his consumptive face. "He's goin' to deepen all the rivers and streams in this new drainage scheme he's havin' for the county. To put it in his own words: 'I'm goin' to take the water from under yeer beds'. This, he believes, will drain the bogs and turn it into grassland where cattle can graze to the knee."

"Drain the bogs and turn it into grassland, is it?" Murt Burke cut in, a scowl screwing up his weathered features. "Grass to the knees, you say? Well, grass to the knees, my arse! Coz all you'll ever get to grow in that stretch o' bogland that's surroundin' this village of ours is rushes, and I've yet to hear tell of cattle eatin' rushes, not to mind gettin' fat on them."

"Well said, Murt!" echoed round the kitchen, more for his uncharacteristic outburst than for the reality in his words, until Peter Costello called for attention with a silencing motion of a gnarled hand. "I'm sure most of ye heard Dillon's speech on emigration after last Mass on Sunday," he said. "But in case ye didn't, I'll give ye the gist."

When the cocked ears of his audience gave him the cue to continue, Costello, a stocky young man with a fresh face and a mop of ginger hair, took a political stance in the vacant area between the fire and the semicircle of seats, and went on in deep guttural tones, mimicking Dillon's style of oratory, pausing and spacing out the words for effect. "Says he: 'We'll get rid of the dog – and – the herdsman, and we'll bring back our young men from the beetfields of Lincolnshire – and – from the coalfields of Lancashire, and go in more for arable farming. In the last century our beloved country supported eight million

27

people, and now it can't support half that amount. Why? – because we're not making full use of the land. So, the answer must lie in compulsory tillage, which will put an end to emigration and bring both employment and food, and eventually prosperity'.

"This is Dillon's recipe for our problems – force us to grow more crops and no market for what we're producin' at the moment. I know we could produce enough to feed another million or two, but just feedin' them isn't enough, and what does he mean, 'bring back our young men', and the *Princess Maud* loaded down every night with men, women and shilder. The way things are goin', we could be soon joinin' them ourselves, not to mind bringin' them that's over there back."

Everyone had heard of the *Princess Maud*, a British Rail converted cattle boat which was fast becoming synonymous with emigration to England, although no one believed their turn to board her would ever come until they were walking up the lonesome road to Castleford station and later up the gangway of this ill-omened ferry at Dunlaoire docks, no more than the French nobility believed their day was done until they were in the tumbril on the way to the guillotine.

There was a round of applause for the mimicry, for Costello, more than anyone in the village, had already one foot on the gangway of the emigrant ship. Living in a rented cottage he had no land and an invalid mother to support on the pittance he earned working on a day-to-day basis for his small-farmer neighbours, people almost as hard-up as himself, which made it somewhat ironic that even in the hardest of times the survival of the poor should depend on the poor.

Paddy Keane, a newly-married man, one of the younger generation, was next to have his say. "I suppose ye all heard about the hecklin' ould Jack Diskin gave to Dillon, when Dillon promised that Ireland'd soon be a self-sufficient country?" he asked, his snipe features wrinkling in a grin. "He said that the only self-sufficiency Ireland'll ever have is in pipe-lids, and what Castleford really needed was a soap factory, and by the looks o' some o' ye, says he, it wouldn't go astray at all."

Others too added their tuppence worth until Michael Joyce, a middle-aged man who had his large family almost reared, struck a bitter chord. "You couldn't trust Dillon as far as you could piss, and the crooked eye o' the bastard – and sharp. He'd see a pimple on a midge's bollocks, so he would. They say you should never trust a man with a crooked eye or a crooked arse. But you can take my word for it, Dillon is only out to feather his own nest, nothin' else, and the only time you'll see him around these parts is at election-time when he's lookin' for our votes. He'll buy drink all round him then all right. But I seen the day when he was glad to talk to us, and his ould father too. Poor as a pothanger his father was when he came to Castleford first," he went on, pointing to the crane of pothangers above the grate, a grate big enough to roast an ox.

"You're right there, Michael," cut in Fogarty again. "Sure I seen the day when they had to sell the big spuds and eat the small ones and the black ones themselves to keep body and soul together – they were that poor. But that's all behind them now. Them days are gone and forgotten. It's all drinkin' with them now and pissin' it up agin the wall, and not a murmur about it when his son ran off to England with the rates' money, only to give the rate collector's job to the other son. All swept under the carpet, it was. It makes me sick every time I think about it, so it does."

When it came to Jack's turn for comment, it was obvious from his pathetic shake of the head and roll of the eyes that he was fed up listening to the same spiteful chatter every night. "You have to take into consideration that a politician doesn't have to know anything as long as he's a hypocrite – he could even be blind," he said, a cynical note in his tone. "And you know what it says in the Bible about the blind leading the blind. But it's the party the people vote for, not the man, and in most cases the civil servants do their work for them. Even if you put a piece o' dogshite up for election and stuck a Fianna Fáil or a Fine Gael flag in it, there are people who'd vote for it. So, being a hypocrite is part of the political game – that's the only qualification required. A good politician, besides being able to waffle for hours, has to develop the knack of answering a question by asking a question and give the impression that he can see into the future, and he has to be able to turn on a smile, a frown, and laugh or cry whenever the occasion demands it, and most of all, he must have a thick skin. He has to walk the fine line between lying and not telling the truth, and he has to be able to tell the truth cleverly, and you can take it from me, the truth cleverly told can be worse than any lie."

After Jack's contribution to the debate the knives came out again, someone saying this, someone saying that, all in derogatory tones, until they had compiled a damning dossier on Dillon, the source of their problems, or so they believed.

Now that the kitchen was filled to capacity, the lamp on the wall was competing with the fire for the lighting of the shadowy area between the semicircle of seats and the hearth, and for all that it was a homely scene, outside that cosy gathering of tobacco smoke, snuff, thumb-twiddling, scratching of heads beneath ragged caps, patchwork clothes, frayed shirt collars, hobnailed boots and wellingtons lay all the uncertainty and hardship of the world. Although all age groups were represented, it was the grey heads, stooped shoulders and wizened faces of the elderly, interspersed here and there with the glowing cheeks, bright eyes, and the impatience of youth, that stood out, for there was scarcely a soul from the prime of life to temper the stark contrast between the old and the very young, which was a grim but true reflection of the dwindling population.

A lull in the conversation gave Ann Kennedy, a pretty, dark-haired sixteen-year-old, a chance to get a word in. "I'd love to go to England just to try it out, and if I didn't like it, I'd come home again," she chirped up, rather naively. "They wear such lovely clothes over there, like you see in the films. Even our own people when they come back for a holiday are all dressed up to kill."

Ann's enthusiasm was supported by Kathy Moore, who was a year younger and much prettier than Ann and bore all the hallmarks of blossoming beauty, from her flaxen hair and blue eyes all the way down to her neatly-turned ankles, although she was more sceptical in her outlook. "Oh, I'd love to go all right, just to see what it's like, but it's strange that none of our people ever come back to settle no matter how much they promise to do so," she pointed out, a frown puckering her brow. "It seems to me that England is for keeps – there must be something over there that holds them."

Granny Mulhaire, the oldest woman in the village, who was well into her eighties, was equally sceptical. "Don't be taken in by all the fancy clothes they wear over there. I think meself that most o' them are bought on the Kathleen Mavourneen system of payin'. It may be for years and it may be forever, if ye get me meanin'," she said, a rasping cough shivering her frail frame, which she soothed with a brown lozenge from the crumpled paper bag she drew from the bosom of her long black dress. "I hardly have to remind ye that all me own fourteen skedaddled, one after the other, and the boss himself above in the cemetery this many a year, God rest him. And as young Kathy said, if one o' them or their shilder don't come back soon to live, I'll have no one to put me down – none o' me own, that is."

Jim Madden, the local horse doctor, poteen-maker, sage and shanachie, also condemned Ann's impetuosity. "You might be over there sooner than you think, and you should know from your history that England is full o' thieves, cut-throats and renegades of every description. All that finery they have was stolen from other countries – India and the like. If everyone had their own, they'd be penniless, and didn't they strip this country bare of every stick o' timber that was in it, as if it wasn't bare enough as it was – robbin' bastards. Those of us they couldn't starve to death, they tried to bring up illiterate, and let's not forget the Black and Tans. It's not many years ago since they were drivin' round the countryside with their hostages tied back to back in their lorries, cock-shottin' at the farmers in the fields, and at the kids comin' home from school, and didn't they burn Castleford to the ground –"

"We don't want to hear all about the Troubles again tonight!" Jack cut in. "The needle is worn out on that record, and all the men who're still getting pensions out of it, especially the ones who jumped on the bandwagon when it was all over," he went on, hinting at Madden, who was one of the latter. "This freedom we won doesn't seem to have made much difference considering that most of the youth of the country still have to emigrate to make a living and, as Granny said, if the trend continues, there'll be no one left to put anybody down, morbid and all as it sounds. And what's here for them if they stay? – unless, as Murt said, they live on rushes. The only fact in the matter is, we're sitting here with hardly a copper to bless ourselves with, and the rain is pouring down outside."

The reality in Jack's words brought silence, for despite his easygoing nature, his knowledge was uncanny for a man of his years. He seemed to be endowed with the gift of knowing things without being told, of sensing things before they happened, as if God had put a special word in his ear when he was born. He could separate his observation from his preconception, and he relied only on the evidence of his eyes, not what he expected or wished to see, and anything he didn't understand, he didn't pretend to understand. His education had come from nature and books rather than from the schoolmaster and, as he had been forced to leave school when his mother died, he made up the lost ground by reading almost every book in the library, from novels to volumes on medicine, law and science. This knowledge he put to good use, which solved many problems for his neighbours and himself. He had learned to generalise, and take enlarged views. He believed there was a way out of every difficult situation if it was diligently sought, and there was a saying he adhered to, which he had picked up from a travelling man; there is a path which no fowl knoweth and which the eye of the vulture hath not seen.

When as a boy he had first caught adults out, that they did not have divine intelligence, that their judgements were not always wise, his world fell into panic desolation, and from then on he began to rely more on his own logic and natural astuteness. Although he gave every impression to the contrary he wasn't lazy, only that he didn't like doing things for the sake of doing them, no matter what they said about idle hands. He liked to leave well enough alone, and he believed it was senseless to struggle against fate.

Now, as he glanced around at the silent faces, he laughed, a laugh that contained both humour and cynicism. "I'm right, if you think about it, and all of us might be eating rushes yet. I'll have to get Eileen to make a rushes' stew just to try it out, and maybe she could throw in a sprig o' heather for flavourin'," he went on. "But joking aside, I think the day of the small farmer is over. If you took all the land in this village of ours and put it together, it'd just about make one decent farm. Industry is what we need. Only then will we have full employment, and it'll put an end to emigration and all this arsing about we're doing at the moment. If you ask me, I think the man who said England was a nation of shopkeepers should also have added that Ireland was a nation of small farmers."

There was a bout of uneasy throat-clearing before all heads, as if they moved on one muscle, turned to Jim Madden, mutely asking him for a comment that would ridicule Jack's opinion. But before he had a chance to take up the gauntlet, Kathy Moore interjected: "Tell us about the time you were over in England, Jim?"

Settling himself in his chair Madden pushed back his cap, revealing more of his snowy hair and taking out of shadow the red and purple pattern of capillaries cobwebbing his cheekbones and bulbous nose, which bore silent witness of a lifetime of drinking his own poteen. Licking his lips as if he didn't know where to begin he quickly found his stride and went on to relate some hair-raising stories, from knife-fights with gangsters to earthy escapades with the fair sex. Although only the very gullible would believe his twaddle it was a case of the tale being in the telling, and the night sped by on the wings of yarn after yarn.

"How is it you never got married, Jim, and all the women in England traipsing after you?" asked Eileen, betraying a woman's curiosity, for all that she was in the slough of despond.

Taken somewhat aback by the question Madden hesitated and cleared his throat, as though he was hoping a good lie would spring from his memory, and then he began, shakily at first: "It was like this. I was courtin' this lovely lass, one of the gentry she was – a daughter of Brigadier Fitzroy-Parker. I hardly have to tell you that she fell madly in love with yours truly here, fine man that I was at the time, as I did with her, fine lady that she was. They used to say I was a Valentino with the ladies, and she a Garbo with the men. But to make a long story short, we were out huntin' one day, me in me huntin' pink, and she in a black ridin' habit, sittin' a side-saddle, and just as we were comin' to this ditch, her horse's bit snapped and he took off across the field. She was thrown heavily, poor girl, and I don't have to say more. I can still see her pale face as she lay on the ground, her neck broken," he went on, more confidently now and, as his imagination swung into top gear, he even managed to squeeze a tear from the corner of his eye to lend more credibility to the tale. "There, on that lonely field, ended my hopes of happiness, and from that day to this, I never looked at another woman."

There was a brief interlude while Eileen dished around tea and bread and jam to the company. "Just a sup in your fist," was her encouragement to the bashful, and when everyone had partaken, there was a litany of commendations for her proficiency with the teapot: "Lovely tea, Eileen – the nicest cup o' tea I ever drank – nobody but yourself could've made it so nice, not too weak, not too strong – the knack must be in your hand."

When the conversation resumed, emigration again forged its way to the fore. "What's goin' to happen at all?" asked Michael Joyce, concern in his tone as he lifted his cap in a practised motion with a forefinger and thumb and scratched his sparse grey hair with his remaining fingers. "Like Granny, most o' mine are gone. I've only two left at home out o' the twelve, and they're itchin' to go as well. They're only waitin' for one o' the others to send the fare and they'll be off. I don't know how in the name o' Jasus we're goin' to put a stop to it."

"Birth control!" Jack cut in. "Like the small farmer, the day of the big family is as ould-fashioned as the donkey and cart. What Ireland needs is family planning, like they have in England."

"But that's agin the teachin' of our religion, Jack," countered Joyce. "The Lord said: 'increase and multiply' – it's in the Bible."

"Did He now?" returned Jack. "But I don't remember reading that you're supposed to have one every year, hell or high water. Big families bring poverty, and poverty brings famine and emigration. How is it that you never see a rich man with twelve or fourteen children?"

"The Lord save us, Jack – don't let anyone hear you talkin' like that, or you'll bring Father Hennelly down on top of us!" interjected Paddy Keane, who was among the many who believed that if they stuck resolutely to the religion of their forefathers everything would turn out for the good. "What you're sayin' is next to blasphemy."

"Most of Father Hennelly's fire and brimstone sermons are aimed at the poor, but he's hand in glove with the rich, like the rest o' the clergy – the man with the red cap included," Jack parried. "They're all for the rich, buttering up to them and turning up at their funerals in all their regalia – like they were canonising saints. Nothing at all for the poor, save to say that the poorer you are, the nearer you are to God, that God ennobles the destitute. And, if the government suggests anything sensible, they're up in the pulpit preaching against it and threatening to put asses' heads on anyone who doesn't agree with them. Everything is sinful according to them – jazz, the music of the Devil, as they call it, dancing too close, drinking, the pictures, unless it's a film about the life of some saint, even a roll in the cock o' straw – you name it and you'll find they have some sin attached to it. And I don't believe all that shite about the Devil turning up at Toureen dance hall either, no more than I believe that Saint Patrick said that Ireland'll sink into the ocean seven years before the end o' the world. If you ask me, religion is all about money."

"Christianity is all about givin', and lovin' your neighbour, Jack," returned Keane. "It's one of the commandments of the Church that we contribute to the support of our pastors."

"Yes – us giving and they taking, and besides, contributing to the support of our pastors isn't one o' the original commandments – that's something they made up themselves," countered Jack. "There's nothing whatsoever in any o' the gospels, either Matthew, Mark, Luke or John, the basis on which our religion is founded, commanding us to give money to the clergy. If anything, it's the other way round, because Christ said to Saint Peter: *'feed my lambs, feed my sheep'*. But you know yourself that the sheep and the lambs, meaning us, would have their bellies stuck to their backs with hunger if they were waiting for the clergy to do anything in the line o' feeding. I'm sure if Christ meant them to beg off us, He would've said: 'milk my lambs, milk my sheep', or perhaps fleece them, because that's what they're doing – fleecing us and milking every shilling out of us."

"According to the clergy 'feed my lambs, feed my sheep', means feed their minds with the doctrine of Christ," Keane pointed out. "He also said that the Lord will temper the wind for the shorn lambs."

"I know they do, Paddy," Jack agreed. "But no matter what stretch of interpretation you give it, the word 'feed' means give food. I'll put it like this, if some poor man asked you to feed his starving children, you'd give them a dinner or a meal of some description. The last thing you'd do is give them a sermon on the evils of the flesh – you'll have to agree with me on that point. As for tempering the wind for the shorn lambs, it could easily mean that the clergy, Christ's representatives on earth, are obliged to supply shelter as well as food for the impoverished ones of their flock."

It was plain to see by the contradictory shaking of heads and restless shuffling that Jack was on his own in his belief, but no one was prepared to argue the toss, until Michael Joyce rallied: "It's a mortal sin to talk like that, Jack. It's part of our religion to believe. We've got to have faith – for blessed is he who has not seen and has believed. I know there's a lot in our religion we can't understand, but we're not supposed to understand it – that's why they're called mysteries."

"If it's a case of being blessed for not seeing and believing, it could also be argued that cursed is he who has seen and has not believed," returned Jack. "What I mean by that is, the clergy are living it up and eating the best while the rest of us do without. We can see it, and yet, we don't want to believe it or do anything about it. He who has eyes to see, let him see, and he who has ears to hear, let him hear, that's in the Scripture too. As for the mysteries, the only mystery I can see is that they have us bamboozled, not by what Christ said, but by the meaning they say is hidden in the words Christ said. If you listen to the clergy, they'll tell you everything'll be all right when you're dead. But it's the bit in between then and now that's worrying me, and why shouldn't we have our cake in this life as well as in the next life like the people who are always mouthing about it? So, we're back where we started. And don't be looking at me like that, Michael," he went on, addressing Joyce. "You were the one who asked what were we going to do at all. So I say, if we carry on the way we're going, it's either emigration or poverty – take your pick."

When she saw that the conversation was sailing into controversial waters, Granny Mulhaire coughed meaningfully. "Isn't the divvil stuck in you now, Jack – arguin' about religion," she said reprovingly and, perhaps hoping to close out the argument, she turned to Eileen, saying: "It's yeer turn to have the Stations in October, Eileen – you won't feel the time comin' round once Galway races are over. I suppose you'll be whitewashin' the outside o' the house and the stables."

There were sighs of relief all round for Granny's timely intervention, and the conversation rambled back to the Stations of long ago, the nights of revelry, the good old days when porter was tuppence a pint and cigarettes fourpence for twenty. Finally, when the clock struck eleven, Eileen yawned, an unspoken curfew for everyone to be on their way, and in a matter of minutes, amid a flood of 'goodnights' and the tread of hobnailed boots on the concrete floor, the visitors took their leave, save for Jim Madden and Murt Burke. When Eileen yawned again, Madden took the hint, and finally Murt, reluctant as it seemed to leave his warm roost, hoisted himself up from the hob with his hands and followed the shanachie through the door.

When the door closed behind them, Eileen took down the lamp from the wall and set it on the table, bathing the table-top in light as the ceiling receded into shadow. Lighting candles for each to take to their bedrooms she turned the full glare of her accusing eyes on her brother. "You! – and your arguing about religion again tonight," she snapped. "If you keep on like that, God'll strike you down! It'd be more in your line if you suggested saying the rosary like other families do, or we'll all go to hell when we die. Prayer in this house seems to have gone out the window ever since Mother passed away, God rest her – no rosary, no grace before meals, no mention of the Novena, or the First Fridays."

"God strike me down, is it!" interjected Jack. "Well, if He didn't strike down the Black and Tans for all the murdering they done, or Hitler either, what makes you think He'll strike me down – for telling the truth, is it? Anyway, God could no more strike you down than a priest could put an ass's head on you – that doctrine is only for frightening children and gobshites like you. As for saying grace before meals – they had no need to say grace before meals during the Famine. When they prayed for food, God turned a deaf ear, and when they went to the priests for help, they found the presbytery gates locked against them – there was no share and share alike then no more than there is now."

"But you're always running down the clergy in front o' the neighbours, as if Father Hennelly was talking through his hat. I get ashamed sometimes."

"Tell me then, what d'you want me to do?" snapped Jack. "Go down on my knees, is it, and give thanks just because we have barely enough to eat? – something I had to slave for. No – if there's going to be any kneeling and giving thanks, let the rich do it – they have something to be thankful for. And don't be looking at me like that, as if I was some kind of an anti-Christ – I'm not stopping you from saying the rosary, now or ever. If you ask me, the Lord stopped thinking about us the day we were born and, as for going to hell when we die, it could hardly be much worse than this, could it? You'd need some imagination to believe all that shite about demons sticking red-hot pokers up our arses, all day, every day, no more than you could believe we'll have wings if we make it to the place where all the good people are supposed to go – the bigshots, the clergy, the nuns, and all those who repent their wicked ways and by way of atonement cough up their hard-earned money to the Church."

"But why d'you always have to be different from everybody else?" returned Eileen angrily. "We can't ignore prayer altogether, and you've only got to look at all the miracles down through the years to realise that there's something in what the priests say."

"Grow up, Eileen, for Christ's sake! – it's high time you stopped dreaming that prayer and miracles can solve the problems of the world," countered Jack. "You can pray till your arse turns blue, but nobody is going to walk in that door there and give us the money to pay the rates. It's up to ourselves to find the money, otherwise we'll have the bailiffs calling, and don't be getting carried away with all this bullshite about miracles. Just say for instance that a man lost both his legs in a car accident, he could go to Lourdes, Fatima, Knock, or any other place of pilgrimage you care to mention, and there isn't even a ghost of a chance that he'd grow two new legs. If he did, it'd definitely be a miracle."

When Eileen made no further comment, Jack stretched and went outdoors, slamming the door behind him just loud enough to register his irritation. Now that the rain had stopped, a dull wrack was drifting across the sky and a star or two twinkled faintly. The dim shapes of his neighbours' houses were coming alive as a watery moon appeared through a rift in the clouds, and in the distance the glow from the streetlighting over Castleford was forming a giant halo on the horizon. A hopeless life, he thought, wondering if Eileen was psychic when she mentioned England, for the idea of emigrating kept invading his reverie of late, too many times to pass it off as a mere whim. Still, it was a big step to take and, like most people contemplating an unknown future, he was afraid, for if it didn't work out, he would be worse off than ever.

Shrugging off what he felt was an encroachment of pessimistic thought he returned to the kitchen where Eileen had the lamp quenched and the fire raked and, taking one of the lighted candles, he grunted a goodnight and retired to his bedroom. Stretched out in his high double bed with its feather mattress and full-length bolster, the blankets pulled up to his ears, his FCA greatcoat across his feet acting as a buffer against the cold draught whispering under the door, his thoughts returned to Mary O'Hara. Closing his eyes he tried to make-believe that she was lying snuggled beside him, a consummation he would trade any day for heaven.

Chapter 3

Next morning, a shaft of daylight cutting through a gap in the curtains played on Jack's closed eyes and, arms outstretched, he yawned into wakefulness, his sweet dreams of Mary O'Hara which he had taken to his pillow the night before quickly fading in the face of reality. Eileen was already bustling about in the kitchen and, as he reluctantly abandoned the warmth of the bed and swung his feet to the cold floor, an idea was forming in his mind. The travelling shop usually called in the afternoon, and if he played his cards right, it might be possible to talk Eileen into parting with a half-crown out of the egg money. There was music in Grogan's Bar in Castleford on Thursday nights which always drew a crowd and, as the cattle and sheep fairs were taking place on the following week, there was every chance of picking up a day's hire, droving for one of the bigger farmers. The half-crown would lift the latch for him, and if Grogan was in an amiable mood, he might let him put a few pints on the book.

Although everything depended on the uncertainty of the words 'if' and 'might' it put him in a more optimistic frame of mind and, quickly pulling on his shirt, trousers and socks, he picked up his boots from under the bed and hurried to the warmth of the kitchen. "Good morning, Eileen," he hailed, a cheerful ring in his tone as he took up his armchair and plonked his stockinged feet on the hob. "Whatever else we may disagree on, you've got to agree that having a good fire is half the battle, and after that comes a comfortable bed and a comfortable pair o' boots, because if you're not in one, you're in the other."

Jack's fake good humour and philosophy was lost on Eileen, who was hovering over the fire, waiting for the kettle to boil and, when finally it spouted steam, she laid his breakfast on the table – a boiled egg, a mug of tea, a couple of thick slices from one of the cartwheels of brown bread she baked in the pot oven, and a pat of home-churned butter.

As Eileen's mood was anything but encouraging, Jack put the matter of the half-crown on the long finger and applied himself hungrily to the simple fare, the silence between them broken only by the ticking of the clock, the sound of his munching, and the slurp of hot tea cooled in transit to the tongue. When he had all but finished, to his surprise, Eileen asked: "What's the weather going to do at all? After all the trucking back and forth to Quinn's I'm left with two weeks' washing to do, and I'm wondering if I should risk it."

Straight away Jack rose from the table and, with the air of a practised meteorologist, viewed the morning from the open doorway. "It's hard to tell with all the mist," he said, after a few moments of feigned deliberation. "But later on, if you see a bit o' blue in the sky big enough to make a trousers for a sailor, it's going to be a fine day. I'm off to the bog myself to make a start on the turf, but if I was you, I'd take a chance – it can't very well rain every day."

Now that they were back on speaking terms, Jack didn't push his luck by mentioning the money. An opportunity was sure to present itself later and, leaving Eileen to get on with her chores, he finished his breakfast and went outdoors.

Outside, the farmyard was boiling over with animation: calves were wailing plaintively at the pasture gate, waiting to be fed, single files of ducks were waddling off to the pond, their quack-quacking somewhat overwhelmed by the more clamorous can-canking of the geese, which were making stealthy advances towards Eileen's flower garden, only to be thwarted by the surrounding chicken-wire fence, the hens were clucking faintly as they pecked and scratched on the dunghill, and Jack took time out from his preparations to watch as big lady Rhode Island Red hypocritically protested the horror of being lustfully pinned to the ground and threaded by a young bantam rooster. "Any time is cocoa time," he grinned, the mismatch reminding him of Mrs O'Regan, the bank manager's portly wife, and the relentless, almost brutal shagging Jimmy Murphy had given her down Poke Lane, which he had inadvertently witnessed, although he quickly blanked out the picture his memory evoked when he realised that Eileen too had been on the receiving end of the same earthy treatment.

The mist shawling the countryside was lifting and mingling with the smoke spiralling lazily from the chimneys of the village houses, bringing into light the green expanse of small fields and the criss-cross pattern of stone walls and blackthorn fences. The air was heavy and cold with dew and, as he crossed the paddock to tackle his donkey, the mass of wet grass rustled like silk underfoot, the dampness finding his feet through the porous leather uppers of his worn boots. Earlier he had decided to rest Charlie before the more strenuous work of cultivating the land, but now, after loading his turf-cutting implements and backing the donkey under the cart, he regretted his decision, for the donkey was the most unwilling animal.

"Proceed, Edward – proceed!" he commanded, in peremptory tones, as if he was a sergeant major barking orders on parade and, with one hand gripping the crosspiece between the shafts of the cart and the other controlling the donkey, he jerked the cart into motion and they set off down the rutted boreen to the bog, the cart rocking to and fro, the hawthorns arching overhead turning the track into a dim tunnel. The balminess of spring encompassed him sweetly, the moist smell of new-ploughed earth mingling with the scent of fresh greenery piquant in his nostrils, the hedge sparrows were chirping blithely, the jackdaws were squabbling among themselves for possession of the chimneys, while the rooks building nests in the trees were adding their discordant notes to an already unharmonious chorus. Shortening his stride to keep pace with the donkey, which was plodding along with less enthusiasm than a man on his way to the gallows, he was still cursing his decision when Peter Costello stuck out his head through a gap in the bushes.

"The top o' the mornin' t'you, Jack!" he hailed. "You're abroad early."

"Yes, Peter, I'm off to the bog while the weather is in my favour – that is, if I ever make it. As you can see for yourself, ould velvet lugs here is as slow as constipation."

"I agree with you, Jack – he's the sorriest poor ould animal God ever put on the face of this earth. He was never meant for farmwork – more for givin' rides to kids at the seaside, or for drunkards to drink the cross off his back," returned Costello. "What was Saint Joseph thinkin' about at all, gettin' such an unfortunate beast for the flight into Egypt? Wouldn't you think with all the gold and the other stuff the three wise men brought them that at least they could've afforded a pony and trap."

"How d'you mean 'flight', Peter? – the crawl into Egypt'd be more like it – a one mile an hour crawl," said Jack. "Still, it's a good job it wasn't my Edward they were depending on, because I could never see them getting there at all, not to mind getting back again in time for the crucifixion."

"As you said last night, Jack, it's hard to believe some o' the things you read in the Gospel, raisin' the dead, or turnin' someone into a pillar o' salt – it defies imagination," returned Costello. "Even though I agree with most o' what you said about the priests, to come out with it openly'll do you no favours. You know what the people are like yourself where the clergy are concerned – see no evil, speak no evil. As a matter o' fact, it's the first step on the road to Blighty, coz nobody'll want to know you or give you a day's hire if they hear you runnin' down the clergy."

"Whatever about turning someone into a pillar o' salt, raising a man from the dead'd cause pandemonium, especially if the family had the insurance policy cashed and drank," said Jack, smiling at his own imagination. "Worse still, if the wife got married again or ran off with someone else – that'd definitely put the cat among the pigeons."

"I never looked at it that way, Jack, but it makes sense," returned Costello. "Anyway, I'll leave you to it and get back to me work. We have a big contract on today; washin' sheep's daggin's – meself and Jimmy Kennedy. But it's worth it all the same – the price o' wool is goin' sky-high at the moment."

"Yes, Peter, every penny helps. So, God bless the work, and I'll see you later."

At the end of the boreen the terrain opened out into a vast expanse of turbary and heather which stretched endlessly to the horizon, the very type of land that Dillon was planning to turn into pasture, and it wrapped round the village like a giant curving arm, embracing it on three sides and isolating it from the village of Aughamore scarcely a mile away. Directly ahead, a range of high turf-banks, which had troughs of dark water beneath them, jutted up in a zigzag line, cutting across the heather like a long black scar. Each of the fourteen homesteads in the village had its own turf-bank, reachable by a communal track which could just about bear the weight of a horse and cart.

When he reached his allocation, Jack unharnessed his long-eared companion and tethered him on a long rein so that he could graze on the scant croppings. The sun had now broken through the mist and, shedding his jacket and woollen jumper, he began clearing away the top part of the turf-bank, digging out the heather and clay with a spade until he reached the peat, the three lorry loads of the commodity he expected to have for sale for Galway races his only incentive. As the sun climbed the sky, he kept on doggedly, the scene coming alive in his mind: the horses, the cheering crowds, the bookmakers shouting the odds above the din, the busker music, the tinker women begging, and the charisma of the trick-o'-the-loops and their recipe for easy money. For those two days he would live like a king, dining in the Imperial Hotel, touring the bars, betting on the horses, jaunting on the bumpers at the funfair in Eyre Square, dancing into the small hours of the morning, and lastly, if there was to be any icing on the cake at all, a date with one of Galway's pretty colleens – something to look forward to – enough to make him stop from time to time and rub his palms together in anticipation.

The hard work was conductive to thinking, and unwillingly his thoughts took a turn down memory lane, a memory trail that carried him back to his schooldays where the misery of life had begun, and for all that they were being acclaimed as the happiest days of one's life, the only memories he could recall were bitter and fraught with anger.

No other words in the vocabulary other than cruelty and ignorance could describe the modus operandi of the Sisters of Mercy who used hat pins as a means of inflicting punishment on children barely out of the cradle, especially on the hapless orphans from the county home, pricking them, not to maintain discipline, but for the sadistic pleasure of making them cry, or the Board of Health dentist yanking out carious teeth without an anaesthetic, and the biannual visits of the ghoulish *cigera* (inspector), with his handlebar moustache and plus-fours, whose image alone was enough to frighten the life out of a child, not to mind assist it in achieving academic success. Still, the cruelty of the nuns had turned out to be the hors d'oeuvre before the main course when they ascended the educational ladder to the Christian Brothers' school, a modern-day torture chamber where every lesson was stung into them with the constant encouragement of the cane until they were frightened into automatons, reciting text by heart which was as incomprehensible to them as the Holy Ghost would be to a man from another planet.

His anger was further inflamed when his thoughts moved on to the clergy who were using every artifice to pluck clean their already impoverished flock so as to maintain their own lavish lifestyle, ploys which went as far as inciting competition among the parishioners by reading out the names of the contributors and the amounts of their donations from the pulpit, and by continually harping on their favourite parable – the widow's mite. "Yes – no matter how small the donation, it's better than nothing! Give us your last ha'penny like the widow in the parable. Do without yourself so that bishops and priests can live in luxury – parasites!" he cried out, so passionately that the donkey pricked his ears and, unable to contain himself, he drove the spade down to the maker's name with the added strength that only anger and frustration can induce. "And me here without a fag!"

The sun was on its return journey when Eileen arrived with his lunch – a bottle of tea, a slice of cold boiled bacon between two wedges of home-made bread, and two hard-boiled eggs. However, before he had a chance to open a conversation, she had wandered off towards Patcheen's Lough, a depthless pool of dark water which was said to be haunted by the spirit of the eponymous character who had drowned himself there. While he was eating, he kept her in his sights, for now that she had seen the industrious start he had made, there was no better time to put the hammer on her for the money. Still he needed something to break the ice between them, for she was in a world of her own, staring dreamily over the landscape, as if she was recalling childhood memories when the bogland was a place of intrigue, a wilderness where the ghosts of their dispossessed ancestors were said to roam, their voices supposedly discernible in the melancholy piping of the curlews that nested there, although now it was only a place of desolation, and a place of despair for those trying to eke out a living from its marshy sod.

Finally, when Eileen returned from her faraway places, Jack wiped the crumbs from his lips with the back of a hand, swilled out his mouth with the residue in the bottle, and spat out on the heather. "I've something to ask you, Eileen, if you can spare the time to listen," he said, faking a smile.

"You must want something badly, otherwise you wouldn't be so polite to me," returned Eileen. "But whatever it is, I'll have you know I won't be soft-soaped."

"I'm not trying to soft-soap you at all; I'm only trying to say that you can forget all about the fags when the travelling shop comes round today," said Jack, allowing the words to hang in the air until the expression on Eileen's face changed from suspicion to incredulity. "Instead, you might see your way to lending me a half-crown so I can go to town tonight," he went on, a note of appeal to her better nature, mingling with a note of appreciation in his tone. "You never can tell, I might hear of a day's hire, droving, and then I can pay you back double out o' what I earn."

Eileen's blank expression gave nothing away. "We'll see," was all she said, after a few moments' deliberation and, without further comment, she gathered her bits and pieces and trudged back towards home, Jack's eyes following her progress until she was out of sight, and then, with renewed enthusiasm he returned to his work, certain that the seed he had sown had fallen on fertile ground.

Later that night, when Eileen agreed to lend him the money, Jack set about shaving himself with a blunt Mac's Smile blade, aided by a basin of boiling water and the thin lather he managed to rouse from a hollowed rectangle of red soap. "This blade wouldn't cut shite!" he cursed, as he scraped again and again over the toughest of the stubble. "For the love o' Christ can't you buy a few blades, or are we that hard up that I haven't a blade to shave myself with?"

Eileen, who was sitting in her armchair by the fire, behaved as if she hadn't heard, and continued with her knitting until Jack finished his ablutions. "Here you are now – ten Players and a half-crown – for all the thanks I'll get," she said, forcing a scowl. "I must be going soft in the head in my old age."

Jack pounced on the cigarettes like a cat on a mouse. "I don't know what I'd do without you at all," he said, his tone full of flattery as he lit up and took a long satisfying drag. "But you'll not be sorry. When I'm rich, I'll never forget the people who helped me when I was down – not like some people I know."

Ignoring the blarney Eileen emptied the basin after Jack and, as she was wiping the mirror, she laughed bitterly. "I suppose I'd better not look too hard at it in case it cracks," she muttered. "Twenty-six and an old maid – who'd ever have thought. But saying that, I've had my good days too."

The hint of self-pity in his sister's mumbling wasn't at all to Jack's liking – she was looking back. It was no good looking back, for if she kept looking back, she would do nothing else but look back. It still wasn't too late to pull herself together and shake off whatever was ailing her, and though his natural instinct was to say something to cheer her up, he felt that a kind word might be detrimental, for the only help for Eileen lay within herself. Dismissing her despondency to an inner chamber of his mind where it could mull with his other problems he smoked his cigarette in silence, and then, flicking the dog-end into the fire, he donned his overcoat and cycled to Castleford.

When he reached Castleford, the streetlamps were lifting their feeble glow to a white moon which had thin shreds of cloud fleeing across it, and a bitter blast was blowing stiffly through the streets, eddying dust particles and sweet wrappings at the intersections and rattling loose galvanised sheets on hoardings and sheds. Yellow gleams of light from the shop fronts and undraped windows were spilling on to the pavements, which were deserted save for a group of corner boys who were standing with their backs to the town hall, while the church tower, grey in the background, looked down like the ghost of some monstrous giant. Shivering as the wind penetrated his threadbare overcoat he parked his bicycle against the church railings and walked the remaining distance to Grogan's Bar in Broad Street.

When he lifted the latch and entered the smoky glare, he was greeted by the usual muttered goodnights from the scattering of men seated on high stools along the bar, their flashlamps, bicycle pumps, and gloves on the counter at their elbows. Shuffling into room among them he nodded to Mick Grogan, the proprietor, calling: "A pint o' stout, Mick, when you get a moment."

Grogan, an ex-wrestler and fairground fighter, was thickset and hunched, and to give credibility to every picture telling a story, his crouching stance, scarred face, and flat nose told the tale of his earlier career. Bald, save for a few grey strands which were fighting a losing battle at screening his cauliflower ears, he had sharp knowing eyes that missed nothing, although the permanent grin on his face did much in the way of softening his rugged features. Acknowledging Jack's request with a nod he turned to a row of barrels which were seated in wooden cradles behind his back, spigots turned out, and began the slow process of filling the pint, tipping the frothy porter from one glass to another and allowing it to settle.

Grogan's, a spit and sawdust establishment of the old-fashioned mode, was one of the few public houses in Castleford that didn't sell groceries or hardware. It was basically furnished with an assortment of wooden tables, chairs, and high stools, and a rough-hewn oak counter ran the full length of the wall facing the door, its hollowed top, which had been saturated over the years with spillage, showing the circular imprints of the many glasses left down in different moods. At one end of the room, an open fireplace, which had an oak surround and mantelpiece, stuck out imposingly, and at the opposite end there was a low stage, fitted with a microphone and speakers. Over the years tobacco smoke had turned the walls from magnolia to a dull brown, and the only embellishments were a framed photograph of a younger Grogan in fighting regalia and the usual miscellany of prints advertising beverages and cigarettes. The goodly display of wines and spirits on the shelves behind the counter were interspersed with cartons of matches, packs of playing cards, and a box of Mrs Cullen's stomach powders and, hanging from the ceiling on the hooks were a string of pipe-lids, a fly-blown card of penny-tinker pot menders, and two storm lanterns in case of a power cut.

When Grogan had the pint topped up to his satisfaction, he set it on the counter in front of Jack. "That'll be one and tuppence to you, Jack," he said, smiling a greeting. "Rotten ould weather we've been havin' lately, but it's promised to pick up from now on accordin' to the forecast."

Jack didn't need to be reminded of the weather, or that drinking wasn't any fun when you had to watch every penny, and when Grogan turned to serve another customer, he pocketed his change and supped down quarter way on the pint, wiping the froth from his lips with the back of a hand before stepping back to allow access to the counter to three men who had just entered. On the bandstand, two musicians, one with an accordion, the other with a fiddle, were tuning up, the man on the fiddle whanging with his bow, the other calling: "Testing, one, two, three – testing," into the microphone in monotonous repetition, each over-pitch of the amplification sending icicles shivering through Jack's teeth. Behind his back at one of the tables, five men were engaged in a sixpence-a-deal poker game and, when one of the players motioned for him to make up the six, he declined with a negative shake of the head.

Turning away from the card table he scanned the crowd for anyone who might require his services and, provided that there was money at the end of the day, he was prepared to do any type of work, however menial. He had almost given up hope when the sound of the latch lifting brought his head around, and when a young man appeared in the doorway, squinting against the glare, he called a greeting.

"Over here, Tim!" he hailed, just as the duo on the bandstand broke into a selection of reels and, when the man came within earshot, he added in an undertone: "I'd buy you a pint, but I've only got the price of another, and what's more, I'll have to make it last till closing time unless Grogan lets us put a few on the book."

Gangling and slightly bowed Tim Kelly was taller than Jack by an inch. He had sharp features, a long sallow face, thin lips, and his lacklustre grey eyes held a gentle melancholy, as if he had already accepted that he was one of life's losers. He was clean-shaven, and his short fair hair, which was parted at the side and combed back in waves, was showing the first signs of thinning on top. His double-breasted grey jacket, which almost reached down to the knees of his navy-blue serge trousers, was limp and buckled at the shoulders and looked as if it had come off Jack Cheap's stand on market day, his blue cotton shirt was frayed at the collar and worn thin from too much washing, and his brown brogues, which were at least a size too big for him, were scuffed and down-at-heel, the uppers faded for the want of polish.

"It's all right, Jack – I know the feelin'. I'm in the same boat myself," returned Tim, grinning and putting on display a gapped set of uneven top teeth. "But you're the very man I wanted to see – are you interested in a day's work?"

"It must be the Lord Jesus Christ Himself that sent you – what's the job?"

The furtive manner in which Tim was treating the matter, a finger to his lips for caution, his eyes darting in all directions as if for eavesdroppers, Jack thought he was planning to rob a bank, until finally, bringing their heads closer, he went on in an undertone: "There's two paupers after dyin' in the workhouse and Father Tierney asked me to make the graves. Even though he didn't say so, I think some of his own cronies let him down. But no matter how much I haggled, all I could knock out o' the tight ould bastard was three quid – that's thirty shillin's apiece, but you can be sure he's gettin' twice that himself from the Council. They're buryin' them tomorrow evenin' at seven, just before it gets dark. So, we'll have to get crackin' early in the mornin', hail, rain or snow. You know yourself how rocky the new cemetery is, 'specially on the paupers' side."

"That's the best news I've had since Christmas," returned Jack, his eyes alive with enterprise. "And it just confirms my belief about being in the right place at the right time."

By now, the music had the ear of the crowd and, when some of the customers began to drift towards the bandstand with their glasses, Jack and Tim made a beeline for two vacant high stools at a corner of the counter. Quickly dispensing with the next morning's arrangements Jack broached the subject that's never far from any young man's mind, "Any luck with the women, Tim?" he asked.

Tim, his eyes fixed on the mirror behind the bar, ran a hand over the quiff of hair that kept falling on his forehead. "To be truthful, no," he replied. "But I'm chattin' up young Sadie Doyle, a nice young thing, if you don't mind me sayin' so myself. She's only sixteen and she's just startin' off, and you never can tell which way she'll turn – will she or won't she? But it's promisin', if you know what I mean, and I've had my hand up already, nice and soft it was, just like a foal's nose. Maybe when the weather picks up in the summer, I could take her down by the river some night, or maybe down Poke Lane for a knee-trembler. But it's a bit too soon yet to be thinkin' o' Poke Lane – frightened the girl might get. I've got to build up her confidence first – take a leaf out o' Jimmy Murphy's book."

"That would be something Tim – to follow in Murphy's footsteps – to harrow all he ploughed," Jack agreed. "He had a way with the fair sex, and that's for sure – he had only to leave a hand on a woman's shoulder and her knickers fell down. Married or single, old or young, pretty or plain, rich or poor, it made no difference, he rode them all."

"You're right in what you say, Jack – there was no class distinction in him whatsoever. He'd get up on a tinker woman just the same as he'd get up on a duchess, and you know what Father Hennelly said about a woman's chastity bein' a stye in the Devil's eye? Well if it's true, he wouldn't have many while Murphy was around. But how about yourself – anythin' blossomin' in your garden?"

Although he had plenty of admirers around the town, and young Kathy Moore called at his cottage more times than neighbourly goodwill warranted, Jack kept his infatuation for Mary O'Hara to himself. The O'Haras were in a different league, and John O'Hara, Mary's barrister father, would go into convulsions if he knew that his only daughter was even on speaking terms with a man of such poor means. Nevertheless, she was a dream, an island to sail to in the sea of make-believe, something bright and clean to cling to and bring a touch of glamour into his drab existence. Every time he saw her in the street or heard her name mentioned, it was like a summons to all his foolish blood, and her image accompanied him everywhere, even in places hostile to romance. Although a relationship was beyond his wildest fantasy he was at liberty to look and long, as a poor boy who has no money can look in a sweetshop window, and now, as Tim waited on his reply, he decided to keep his phantom courtship to himself for fear of ridicule. "I'm on the loose at the moment," he said finally. "But who knows, I might have a bit o' luck at the Phoenix on Sunday night."

Tim was his only companion and confidant and, as he was from the town, it had taken longer for their friendship to develop, for the unspoken mistrust between country people and townspeople had discouraged boyhood association, even though they had been in the same class at school. However, now that they were among the few remaining of that class of sixty boys, necessity had brought them closer, and presently they were struggling together against the same uncompromising enemies – poverty and emigration.

As the night advanced, the magic of the music and the hope of jam tomorrow wafted them into a more carefree mood and, when Grogan tipped them the wink that the book was open, they drank more liberally, yet sparingly. "It's better on the book than in the barrel, eh Mick – at least it's sold," Jack remarked to Grogan as he was logging the transaction in the dog-eared ledger he kept under the counter.

"That's debatable, Jack," countered Grogan, stifling a smile. "What'll happen if you drop dead tonight – I'd never get paid, would I? I'd have to let the dog go – it'd be no use holdin' on to him then."

Leaving a dog tied, a popular saying in the locality, had been coined when a con man promised a publican that he would pay for his drinks when he returned from the bank and, as a guarantee of his good intentions, he left his dog in the publican's charge, tied to a stool. Needless to say the man never returned, and Jack, seeing the funny side, laughed. "I suppose that's one way of looking at it, Mick," he said. "But all the booze you'd sell at the funeral would more than make up for it. Still, you'll have to admit that I look a picture of health, not like the two ould fogies over there I saw you giving strap to."

When Grogan went about his business, the conversation rambled from who had dogs tied and who had to let them go, to weddings, wakes, and funerals, bordering on every topic, and when closing time came round, they had righted most of the country's problems, in wishful thinking they had dated all the desirable women in the town, some economic miracle had brought full employment, and overall, they were optimistic for the future now that summer was just around the corner.

"It's marvellous what a few pints'll do, Tim," said Jack, as they braved the air outside. "This evening I was down in the dumps; now I feel like a million dollars."

Tim's attention was focused on the crowd spilling out of the Odeon cinema across the street, perhaps searching for his new girlfriend among them, and he held fire on his reply until they had dispersed. "You might feel like a million dollars now, but you won't feel like a million dollars in the mornin'," he laughed. "More than likely you'll feel like one o' them ha'pennies we used to put on the railway line when we were kids for the wheels o' the train to flatten so we could pass it off as a penny."

"I suppose you're right, but what about tomorrow? You know it's Friday, the day we draw our few shillings dole, or the 'free beef', as some people are still calling it."

"I'll have to let mine go till Monday in case someone reports me if they see me workin', and they'd be bad-minded enough to do it too – they can dock me a day out of it if they like," returned Tim. "It's different for me bein' from the town – I've got to sign on twice a day, mornin' and afternoon, while ye unemployed country lads have only to sign on once a week on Fridays, the day ye collect. I'm not sayin' you, Jack, but there's well-to-do farmers' sons rollin' up in cars every week, drawin' it, while they're still workin' on their ould fellas's farms – it makes me sick when I think about it, so it does – no wonder the country is in the state it's in."

"I agree with you, Tim," said Jack. "When it was first introduced, it came as an allowance of free beef for the unemployed with no means of support, and later, they changed it to cash to suit the farmers, and it's being abused by them ever since. But what can we do about it – all the politicians are on the side o' the farmers. I'm entitled to it because the deed of our land is still in my later father's name, but I have no qualms about drawing it. I know thirteen shillings a week is a contemptible sum, but it's better than nothing."

"Only just, Jack, especially when they dock a day out of it," returned Tim. "But let's not argue about it or we'll be here all night."

"D'you know, Tim, I've got a feeling our luck is about to change for the better. I've got this idea, a great idea – you'll be in on it too. But it's going to take capital –"

"How much capital?" interjected Tim. "As you know yourself, we've got nothin' between us only the three quid we hope to earn tomorrow – minus the strap we got off Grogan."

"It's going to take a lot more than that – at least four hundred to get me off the ground."

"Stop, Jack – you have about as much chance of raisin' that kind o' money at Hitler has of sharin' one o' the many mansions with Moses in the life hereafter."

"You can scoff if you like, but I'm going to the bank to see if I can raise it on the few acres," returned Jack. "This is the only chance, as I can see it, of getting us out of this poverty trap we're in, and I'll have to get operating soon before someone else gets the same idea."

"What's the idea anyway?" asked Tim. "It'll have to be a good one for the bank to lend on it, seein' as you haven't full title to the land."

"I'm keeping it to myself until I see the bank manager, because if he doesn't come up with the money, I'll have to put it on the long finger."

"There's another way you might get the money, but you'll have to raise at least a hundred quid first."

"How?"

"You're a good poker player, Jack, second only to Ray Power and, if you could raise the stake, you could sit in that big game they play behind closed doors in the Royal Hotel every month when the Northern-Irish cattle jobbers come to town for the fairs," returned Tim. "If you play the percentages, over a period of time you could win what you need without bein' too conspicuous. But, as I said, you'd need a hundred quid stake."

"Leave it out, Tim! I'd have a better chance if I tried singing for the money than winning it playing poker. Anyway, I thought playing poker for high stakes was the priests' pastime, but as you say, it's worth considering if the bank manager doesn't come across."

"And gamblin' on horses at the races with the parishioners' money is another o' their pastimes, but you still haven't told me what the idea is."

"You'd probably laugh at me if I told you, but I'll let you in on it someday soon if you promise to keep your trap shut," returned Jack. "But it's time we were off home now, and I'll see you in the morning, bright and early."

Chapter 4

Next morning, when Jack awoke, his head felt numb, as if it had been kicked about like a football. There was a late look in the light streaming through the undraped window and, when it suddenly dawned on him why he had left the curtains undrawn, a stab of painful recollection pierced his stupor, reminding him of his commitment. Sweeping the blankets aside he vaulted to the floor, struggled into his trousers, and hop-stepped to the kitchen. A glance at the clock showed that it had turned seven – he was late.

When Eileen, who was returning from the henhouse, the morning collection of eggs in the fold of her upturned apron, saw Jack blundering about the kitchen, making his preparations, she stared at him bewilderedly. "Did you wet the bed or something?" she asked derisively. "It's not your usual caper to be up so early, darting around like a sparrowhawk."

In no mood for wisecracks Jack shut her up with a scowl. "Hurry up and get my breakfast. I've got a day's work to go to and I'm late!" he snapped, his hangover not helping his temper. "And while you're at it, fill two bottles o' tea and ready a bit to eat to take with me – and a bit for Tim Kelly too. I won't be back till late tonight."

Leaving his sister to the task Jack dashed to the barn and sorted out a crowbar, a pickaxe, a shovel and a spade, bundled them together, and tied them on the crossbar of his bicycle. Back in the kitchen, he gulped down a mug of tea and a slice of bread and, when Eileen had his lunch packed, he set off for Castleford, the bright sunlight, which was usually a bad sign for rain later, giving him cause for concern.

When he reached the cemetery and trudged through the long grass and thistles to the paupers' side, Tim had the graves pegged out. "Good mornin', Jack," he greeted. "I suppose I have no need to ask how's the head, if me own is anythin' to go by. As you can see, we're facin' a busy day's work, and I was just sayin' to myself before you came that we'd be better off singlin' out and attackin' a grave apiece, otherwise we could easily run out o' time, and if the worst comes to the worst, at least we'll have two shallow graves."

"Mentioning hangovers, Tim – I'll bet there's many a man lying under the sod here who'd be glad of one," returned Jack. "But I agree with you as far as the graves are concerned. So, let's get the show on the road."

Without further comment they went to work, hacking, shovelling, and levering out the larger stones with the crowbar and stacking them against the wall, and they kept on without respite until the Angelus bell rang at noon. Murmuring a quick prayer they retreated to an alcove in the high perimeter wall for their lunch break.

For all that the bottles were swaddled up to the neck in woollen socks the tea was cold, although cold tea was the least of their grumbles as they made short work of the hard-boiled eggs and home-made bread of Eileen's providing.

When he finished eating, Jack stretched out on the ground, his overcoat spread beneath him, his back propped against the wall, and lit one of the three cigarettes he had saved from the night before. Blowing a few thoughtful puffs in the air he passed the cigarette to Tim. "D'you know, Tim, I think it's backwards this ould country of ours is going, in spite of what they say about times improving," he said. "Take the time o' Christ for instance, they had wine, loaves and fishes for their lunch, and that's just the poor. And what have we got today, two thousand years on? – home-made bread and cold tea. You can add eggs if you like, but that's only because the hens are laying."

"Talkin' about wine, Jack, the only wine I ever drank was altar wine when I was servin' Mass," returned Tim. "I used to get at the cupboard when the priest's back was turned and have a good guzzle for myself, and then top the bottle up with water so he wouldn't notice. Sure you know yourself it's only the clergy and the upper classes who can afford wine with their meals."

"That's what's wrong with the country – the wealth isn't evenly divided, and the more I think about it, the more I feel like getting out. How about yourself, Tim – d'you ever give a thought at all to pulling the pin and hitting for Blighty?"

"Loads o' times," returned Tim, without deliberation. "I've got four sisters in Manchester, two brothers in London, and another three in Bernyham. Although it's seldom we see them, they always send a few quid every time they write, otherwise we'd never make ends meet. But if I go, I'll be leavin' mother and young Julia on their own. I know I haven't a regular job or much chance of gettin' one, but the crowd across the water'd feel better if I stayed at home – to keep an eye on things – to cut the turf and all that."

"You're right, Tim – they expect you to keep the home fires burning so they'll have a place to come back to in their old age or, if they happen to break a leg or an arm, they'll have a place to rest up, till it's healed."

"But what about the future? I've my own life to lead, and you can see for yourself that prospects aren't exactly rosy when we're over the moon at gettin' paupers' graves to dig," said Tim. "It's not just me and you I'm talkin' about. It's the same all over the town – the able-bodied going forth, and the youngest, the lame, and the lazy stayin' behind, somethin' like the story of the pied piper. They can say what they like about England, but the whole country'd be in dire straits if it wasn't for the money comin' from our people over there. Nothin' at all comes from the crowd in the States, except maybe the odd parcel of cast-off clothes – rags, if you know what I mean – no dollars."

"I'll have to agree," returned Jack. "Prospects are bleak surely, and there are people comparing it with purgatory. They say 'Ireland is a state or place of punishment where some people suffer for a time before they go to England'. Still, they don't take kindly to people going to England, because no matter how much money they send or how much money they spend when they come home on holidays, there's no more welcome for them than there is for Ward, the tinker. Taking their money is as far as it goes, and you know the saying they've coined – the best son stays at home, the next best goes to the States, and the sweepings go to England. I'm in the same boat as you, Tim. I'd go too if it wasn't for Eileen – she'd never manage on her own, poor craither."

Tim pulled hard on the cigarette, tapped it with an index finger, and handed it to Jack. "Yes, they never stop runnin' down our people in England and, to put the boot in, the gobshites who come back after a few months with their tails between their legs help to spread the poison, sayin' that they met better Englishmen over there than Irishmen."

"They say it behind their backs too," interjected Jack. "They haven't got the guts to say it to their faces in case they get a few skelps. Still, it doesn't stop them from guzzling down all the booze they buy them when they come home at Christmas."

"I don't know what's the matter with the country at all," said Tim. "There isn't a job to be got around the town unless you know someone, not even a job sweepin' the street. They have it all sewed up, so they have – the bigshots and the clergy. There's no winnin' with them if you're not in the clique, even if you went cap in hand, like poor ould Happy Gaynor when he went to the bishop, threatenin' to change his religion if he didn't get him a job."

"And did he get him one?"

"Cop yourself on Jack – don't ask such silly questions! You know what them people are like yourself, the man with the red cap and his crowd – they wouldn't give you their piss to drink if you were dyin' o' thirst, not to mind put the word in for you for a job. But he fed Happy some kind o' bullshite about God bein' good and, if he prayed hard enough, God'd see that he got a job – and he's down on his knees ever since, the big eejit."

"So, you reckon praying'd do no good?"

"Stop – stop, for Christ's sake, and don't be talkin' *shauffoid*," Tim laughed. "But seriously you could walk any o' the four roads out o' town, as far out as you could go, and there isn't a day's hire to be got anywhere, not even from a farmer. Then, you have the likes o' Mike Cullinane takin' young lads out o' the industrial school in Letterfrack and workin' the daylights out o' them on his farm, doin' men's work for no wages. Some o' them are no more than children – locked up coz they have no parents or for stealin' – stealin' somethin' small – sweets and the like. Cullinane is supposed to be rehabilitatin' them, if that's the right word, and givin' them a good Catholic home. Good home, my arse! Beatin' them with a stick, like you'd beat an ass, if they step out o' line, and Ireland boastin' about bein' a republic – freedom for all. I know Cullinane is one o' the richest men around, but he shouldn't be let get away with it."

"He'd got influence with the powers that be – that's all that matters around here, and there's nothing me or you can do about it, Tim," returned Jack, bitterness creeping into his tone. "Besides, it's going on all over the country as a means of cheap labour – child labour. I think myself we're gradually going back to slavery days – and they have the cheek to run down the English. What we really need is another revolution – but who's to lead it when all the good men are already gone – or going!"

"A revolution is just a dreamer's talk, Jack – even if there was a revolution, we'd still have the same rich and the same poor. What we need is jobs, permanent jobs."

"But there'll never be full employment unless we change the system – that's what I'm trying to say," interjected Jack. "Look at the system today – it's all in favour of the likes o' Cullinane, well-to-do farmers, so much so that they don't even have to fill out an income tax form, not to mind pay tax, and miracle of miracles, if one o' them gave you a day's work, you'd need a revolver to get the wages off him. The last time I worked for Cullinane, he tried to pay me in spuds, and I swimming in them myself."

"I agree with everythin' you say about the farmers – and the richer they are, the tighter they are," returned Tim. "Then, if they gave you somethin' to eat, heaven forbid – you know yourself the kind o' grub they'd give you – a big hunk o' soggy home-made bread with runny butter on it, and the butter full o' cowhairs – well that'd be the dearest bit o' bread you'd ever eat in your life. For that, they'd try to knock a few bob off the day's hire, and it sickenin' you to eat it – ugh. And, lo and behold, if they gave you an egg for your tea! The Lord save us – they'd expect you to burst with the feedin', too rich like givin' fresh milk to a jobber's calf. They have great faith in the boiled egg, the farmers have – good as a pound o' steak, they tell you."

"Then, when it comes to paying up – they'd hold on to the few shillings for as long as they could," added Jack. "Or else they'd have you hanging around outside the church after last Mass on Sunday."

"That's enough!" cut in Tim. "I won't have any more of it – me! It's bad enough to let them shite on you, but when they try to rub it in as well, it's time to call a halt."

"We could always join the army – at least we'd be sure of three square meals a day."

"Stop, Jack! Join the army, is it? I'll let on I didn't hear that – that's as bad as runnin' off with the tinkers. Goin' to England'd be a hundred times better than that."

"How about tapping Bull Paisley for a start? I heard he's building two terraces of houses on the Dublin Road."

"You sure are a glutton for punishment, Jack. Workin' for that thick bastard is as near to slavery as you can get," tut-tutted Tim. "Besides, he wouldn't start the likes o' me or you – we're too independent. Married men, he wants – men who have no choice but to knuckle down and kiss arse, or otherwise it's the boat for them, and any o' them that has a good-lookin' wife had better look out."

Jack took another pull on the cigarette and handed it to Tim. "Talking about England, Tim, most o' the lads we went to school with are over there now. Remember the old days, and all the fun we used to have? It's hard to believe they're all gone – Tom Reilly, Digger Nolan, Christy Fox, Mick Carroll, Tom McHugh, Seamus Dooley, Kevin Burke –" he ran on, telling off the names like the litany of the Virgin Mary, Tim adding a few at each pause, until finally Jack asked: "I wonder what would've happened if they'd all stayed at home? Would there be a revolution or another famine?"

"You've got revolution on the brain, Jack, but tell me this, Digger Nolan used to be a great buddy o' yours, if I remember rightly – d'you ever hear from him at all?"

"I only heard from him once, shortly after he left – I was all set to go with him at the time if it wasn't for Eileen. It's some kind of a curse, this emigration. All our friends –"

"Don't think about it, Jack! It'll only make you lonesome, and it won't bring anybody back," interjected Tim, rising to his feet and stubbing out the cigarette. "Let's get this job out o' the way. That sky up there is like a baby's arse – it's hard to trust it."

Not long afterwards, just as Jack had feared, the heavens opened, and they were still two feet short of depth in each grave. The deeper they went, the rockier the ground became, and Tim cursed profanely. "Whoever let Father Tierney down knew well what they were doin' – you'd need blastin' powder to get this ground out. He's as sly as a fox, Father Tierney is, all for the bigshots, a pity there isn't a tail on him and maybe the hunt might get him. He's a typical case of the practical priest with an eye for the bulgin' purse, and all that prayin' he does and tryin' to be nice to poor people is all a sham – at the back of it all he'd swap his shite for sweet cake, so he would. Look at the two of us, for Christ's sake – drenched to the skin," he went on, turning up his palms to the downpour. "We'll catch pneumonia if we're not careful, and we'll be lucky too if we're finished on time."

Nevertheless, they kept on doggedly, and when the Angelus bell rang again at six, they were throwing out the last few shovelfuls. Wet through they returned to the alcove and finished the last of the tea. "What a way to earn a crust, Tim," Jack remarked, when he felt the rain reaching his skin. "It looks as if we've just reached a new low, and it's hard not to grumble when you think of all the people in cushy jobs who don't appreciate them."

Tim laughed harshly. "Still, we shouldn't be grumblin'. You know the sayin': 'If you don't like it, there's no barbed-wire fence round the Princess Maud'. Anyway, we'll soon forget all about this when we're blowin' the froth off a few o' Grogan's pints. Yes, Jack – a crust well-earned is sweeter than a feast inherited."

"Are you taking the piss, or something?"

"No – all I'm tryin' to say is that tomorrow we'll have some jingle in our pockets when the ould priest comes across – the ould playboy himself, and the snipe nose o' the bastard. If it was up to me, it'd be open season on all priests with snipe noses, just as it is on birds with hooked bills. But I'll have to be careful, because he's sure to beg some of it back off me for the foreign missions."

The change in the conversation to the crack in Grogan's and the dance at the Phoenix on Sunday night was an intoxicant in itself and, as they sat in the alcove sharing a cigarette, they had to admit that they had seen worse evenings and the money was worth getting wet for. The interim waiting for the funeral was interminable, although not long after the church clock had struck seven, the faint rumble of an engine reached their ears. When they looked to the gate, they could just about make out twin headlights, barely penetrating the rain, advancing towards them, immediately followed by the lights of a smaller vehicle, which they presumed was the priest's car.

"This is it, Jack," said Tim. When he identified the first vehicle as the workhouse van, and when it stopped at the end of the track, two men jumped out and dumped two plywood coffins on the ground. "Let's give them a hand and get it over with before it gets really dark – lookin' at all them headstones gives me the willies."

When the coffins were lowered into the graves, the elderly Father Killeen, in cassock, surplice and stole, his manservant holding an umbrella over his head, murmured some Latin invocations with bored celerity, sprinkled holy water on the coffins, and hurried back to his car, followed by the workhouse men, leaving Jack and Tim alone.

The rain, heavier now, was coming down with a measured intensity, hammering on the coffins, as if it was driving new nails into the wood. "Rattle my bones over the stones, only a pauper nobody owns," Jack soliloquised, anger in his tone, his eyes following the priest's car until it was out of sight. "Is this going to be the end for me and you too, Tim – no hearse, no mourners, no Mass, no flowers, no marker?" he asked. "Wouldn't you think at least they'd have rang the dead bell."

Tim was strangely silent, and when he failed to comment, derisively or otherwise, Jack looked long and hard into the open graves. "I think we should say five decades o' the rosary for the repose o' their souls before we fill them in," he suggested. "It's the least we can do – whatever good it'll do them now."

When Tim nodded, they dropped to their knees and bared their heads, Jack telling off the Hail Marys, Tim responding: "Holy Mary, Mother o' God, pray for us, sinners, now and at the hour of our death, amen." As if the Almighty was looking down benignly on that very spot, the rain stopped before they were halfway through the first decade, and Jack, sensing that He was near, prayed that He would send down a Messiah, someone who would sweep aside the feudalism that had his country in a stranglehold and instil for once and for all in the minds of the clergy the doctrine of Christ in its full literal meaning – feed the hungry; give drink to the thirsty; clothe the naked; harbour the harbourless; visit the sick; visit the imprisoned; and bury the dead.

Back on his feet, Jack was still fuming at the priest's lack of compassion for these, the lowliest of his flock. "They should bury the dead with respect, and not throw them into a hole like an ould dead sheep just because they have no money," he said, bitterness in his tone. "It wouldn't cost that much when you come to think of it – a few ould candles, a few shakes of that canister thing with the smoke to keep away the evil spirits, and a dropeen o' drink – it should be every man's entitlement."

"I agree," said Tim, with equal bitterness. "But look at it this way, if them two in the coffins were bank managers or shopkeepers, hell's bells wouldn't keep the man with the red cap and his cronies away. How quickly they'd pounce if there was money to be made, even if it's out o' other people's grief, but as you say yourself, what can me and you do about it."

"Anyway, let's get cracking and fill them in," returned Jack, and they set about the task in the darkness, the clods hopping on the coffins with a dull woody accent adding eeriness to the desolate scene, although he gleaned a few ears of satisfaction from the grim lines of Death the Leveller, a school day poem, for death was indeed a leveller, inasmuch as rich and poor were destined to decompose in the same manner regardless of spiritual or temporal influences.

It seemed bizarre that as soon as the graves were closed the heavens opened again. "At least the rain kept off while we were filling them in," said Jack, as they trudged back towards the gate. "Maybe there's someone up there looking down on us after all."

"Or maybe there's not," returned Tim. "Maybe this is all that's to it. Considerin' the Gospel is delivered in parables all those headstones around us could easily be the many mansions Christ was preachin' about, one for each family – the big ones in the centre for the rich, the small ones for the poor, and nothin' at all for the paupers – your external reward, whatever about your eternal reward. And didn't He say: 'I will go and prepare a place for you', just like we prepared a place for the two quare fellas from the workhouse?"

"Stop, Tim, or you'll have me doubting too," interjected Jack, and though he wanted to believe there was a world beyond the one they lived in, a world untouched by corruption, sorrow and pain, to which he might go when his time came, the facts seemed to be stacked against it. "Whether there's another world or not, I think we should put this episode behind us – it's best forgotten. So, I'll say so long for now and I'll call for you in the morning when it's time to collect."

Leaving behind the hauntingly silent cemetery Jack cycled towards home, his mind torn between anger and sorrow, anger at the priest's indifference, sorrow for the nameless corpses they had just buried, and he was so engrossed in his reverie that he was oblivious of the chilly needle-like drops of rain driving into his face. It took the lamplight spilling out of the undraped windows of the village houses to bring him back to reality, and when he lifted the latch and stepped into the kitchen, Eileen came quickly to her feet.

"What kind o' work did ye get at all?" she asked, plainly puzzled, as Jack, cold and wet approached the fire, the drops of rain sliding down the loose strands of his black hair making him look all the colder.

Jack, his mouth drawn tight, had a strange light in his eyes. "Digging two paupers' graves, myself and Tim," he said, turning his back to the fire. "It's terrible the way they treat the poor craithers – no Mass, or nothing, just straight into the grave, gone and forgotten like last year's lambs. But I'd better change before I catch pneumonia – I'm wet through."

When he returned to the kitchen in dry clothes, Jack was still in a sombre mood. "I hope this never happens to me and you," he said, wrapping an arm about Eileen's shoulders to reassure her of his support. "But never you mind, I earned thirty shillings, and I'll get a new dry battery for the wireless so you'll be able to hear the top twenty on Radio Luxemburg on Sunday night."

Jack's uncharacteristic show of brotherly affection touched the soft spot in Eileen's nature that was never far from the surface. "Sit down there now at the table and I'll put up your dinner," she said, feeling closer to him than she had ever felt before. "I got another ten Players too from the travelling shop that I was keeping for next week, but you can have them now and have a good smoke for yourself."

On Friday nights most of the villagers went to Castleford to the pictures or the public houses and, as there were fewer visitors, the conversations were less animated. Jack's distress over the paupers gradually gave place to the greater influence of money and, making a mental assessment of his finances, he reckoned that after paying for the battery and clearing his slate at Grogan's, he could still afford a few drinks and the dance at the Phoenix on Sunday night.

Next morning, when he cycled to Castleford to collect, Tim pulled out all the stops to entice him into Grogan's. "Just for one," he persisted. "I think we earned it after the drownin' we got yesterday."

"No – I can't afford it. As you know yourself, all my good intentions for tomorrow night could vanish like a gambler's lucky streak, as it says in the song, once I got even a sniff of the booze," returned Jack, his thoughts on the possibility of a dance with Mary O'Hara. "No," he said again, shaking himself loose of Tim's grip when he tried to bundle him through the door. "I'll be off now, but I'll meet you there tomorrow night without fail."

As Saturday night was a time for bathing in the long aluminium bath, polishing shoes, starching and ironing shirts, and general preparation for Mass next morning, the neighbours kept to their own homes, and Daly's kitchen was so quiet that the crickets chirping behind the fireplace sounded as noisy as jackdaws in the chimney. As the night advanced, with no one for company save for his morose sister, the boredom was getting to Jack, and in between spells of pacing the floor he sat restlessly, staring into the fire.

Daly's kitchen, compared with others in the neighbourhood, was roomy and airy, and its low ceiling, from which a flitch of bacon, a storm lantern, and an old carbide lamp were hanging, made it look longer and wider. Above the fireplace the mantelpiece was casting a pencil shadow across the floor and up the wall like the line of a sundial, bisecting the face of the clock and throwing one half into gloom. Immediately to the right of the clock, an oak dresser, shining with bright rows of crockery, stood out imposingly, a decorative display of porcelain plates taking pride of place on the top shelf. On the opposite wall, directly above the table, the oil-lamp was bracketed, and round the walls, the rows of chairs and settles were interrupted only by the doors leading to the back-kitchen, parlour and bedrooms.

Nodding in her armchair Eileen was plying her needles to a piece of knitting as monotonously as an hourglass pouring its sands and, hoping to vex her into conversation, Jack drew her attention to the cat, which was sitting on the hearth, washing his face and the fur behind his ears with graceful movements of his paws. "Keep an eye on the cat, Eileen," he said. "Because the first one he looks at when he's finished washing himself is supposed to be the first to die."

Baiting his sister, ripping the lid of her gunpowder temper, firing it, and then enjoying the blast, was one of Jack's favourite pastimes. "It's true," he went on. "A cat is clairvoyant, and besides, he's very independent. He's so independent that he even kisses his own arse and feet, not like some people I know – mentioning no names. It's a wonder more people don't die of boot-polish poisoning from kissing boots, or from diseases of the lips from kissing the other thing. If it was up to me, I'd have an arse-kissing contest every year in the fair green on Saint Patrick's Day, and run a book on it."

"Oh, shut up, you, and don't be getting on my nerves!" interjected a scowling Eileen. "You never take anything serious, do you?"

"I don't – do I not! Well, tell me this, who cuts the turf and works the land? What d'you want me to do – start feeling sorry for myself, is it?" countered Jack. "I was just saying to myself the other day that maybe it's you that's bringing the bad luck on us, because if you let life get you down, your luck goes too. Look at the two of us, for Christ's sake! – between us we can just about rake up the money to go to Mass on Sundays. Whatever are we going to do at all, Eileen, or will poverty be our last companion in this life?"

"Oh, the Lord only knows what I've got to put up with in this house!" snapped Eileen.

"But seriously, we've got to think up some new way of making money."

"Money, is it! If you had money, I wouldn't see you for dust, drinking in town every night, and then when you're broke, you're stuck here under my feet, getting on my nerves – I don't know which is the worst."

"Changing the subject, Eileen, but did you ever give a thought at all to joining the nuns and giving up all this drudgery? Still, it's usually ugly women who get the vocation, and by any standards you haven't reached that stage yet, but you're getting there."

"Yes – I could join the Kerry order – two heads on one pillow!" retorted Eileen, her hackles rising. "The silly things you come out with, and how many times have I to tell you not to be slagging off the priests and nuns!"

"The life o' Riley, you'd have in the nuns, although this would mean there'd be nun today and nun tomorrow," Jack went on, as if he hadn't heard. "Or you could always be a priest's housekeeper – that's the next step down from being a nun. You'd get a ride every day – in his car, I mean, when you're out doing the shopping. But saying that, I often wonder why priests don't have nuns as housekeepers. There'd definitely be nun for them then, and it'd put paid to all the gossip. But while we're on the subject, I wonder what'd happen if all the priests in Ireland married nuns. This way, we could produce the perfect child, all conceived in virginity on both sides, or maybe someday we'll all get a chance to go back to the Garden of Eden and start fresh. But if we did, would we do Adam and Eve on it again, or would there be enough apples to go round? Would the women say: 'Begone Satan', especially if Jimmy Murphy came along?"

"The Devil roast you and Jimmy Murphy! Whatever possessed you to draw his name down – is it taking the piss out o' me you are?" cut in Eileen, although the faint trace of a smile that flickered on her lips suggested she was enjoying the banter.

"Adam has a lot to answer for," Jack went on, sure of his audience now. "It was all Adam's fault. If only he'd kept it down, he'd have saved us all from this valley of tears. Still, I can't understand it myself, all the fuss about Adam and Eve, when a couple can give a few bob to a priest for a marriage licence, and this entitles them to taste the forbidden fruit, morning, noon and night, till they're disgusted with it – like Paud McHugh. Did I tell you the latest I heard about Paud?"

"No – and I don't want to hear about Paud either, because if I know you, it's sure to be something filthy."

"I'm going to tell you just the same – it'll do you good to hear it," Jack went on. "Well, a few days after he got married, while he was spraying the spuds in the garden, the wife brought him out a jug o' tea and a sandwich and, just as he was finishing the tea, the wife's skirt blew up around her waist, showing it all off. The temptation was too much for Paud, God help us, and he got up on her there and then on the ridge o' spuds with the can o' spray still strapped to his back. But it wasn't a mortal sin, because Paud paid the priest for the marriage licence. It's something like having a dog licence just to keep within the law. So, how can we blame Adam and Eve after that, just because they hadn't got that piece o' paper to make it legal, or perhaps it could be backdated? But to me, it was too harsh a punishment to lose everything, just because he lost control for a few minutes."

"Oh, shut up, and turn on the wireless or we'll miss *The Balladmakers Saturday Night!*" snapped Eileen. "And, if I was you, I'd keep my mouth shut about Adam and Eve, the nuns and priests, or you'll bring Father Hennelly down on top of us."

"But it's still puzzling me how someone can write all about Adam and Eve being the first man and woman – taking a rib out o' one and all that, unless he or she was there to witness it. Also, it contradicts nature, because all mankind was born of woman – even Christ Himself," Jack went on unperturbed. "So, where does that leave us, and they say in the next life we'll be doing exactly the same as we were doing in this life, which means that you and I, Sis, will be together again forever and ever and ever."

"Not if I die first, because I'll come back and haunt you."

"You don't have to die to do that –"

"This kind of talk'll drive me to drink!" interjected Eileen, cutting Jack short. "Can't you ever think of anything sensible to say?"

"That's what's wrong with the country – they won't listen to anything sensible. If it was up to me, everything'd be different, I'd bring in new laws. Any parents who had no fortunes for their daughters would have to put fancy names on them – film stars' names like Lana or Ava, 'specially if they were plain. At least, a fancy name'd set the men's imaginations alight. It'd sound better than Maggie this or Biddy that. Just imagine if you were called Doris Daly. You'd be walking down the street someday and all the men'd start whistling, and saying to one another: 'Well, what d'ya know – there goes Doris Daly'."

"Less o' the Doris out o' you!" snapped Eileen, and she was just launching a scathing attack when Jack turned on the radio for the *Balladmakers*. Appropriately, as if the presenter was in step with the conversation, the first song was 'COME BACK PADDY REILLY TO BALLYJAMESDUFF'.

"See that!" said Jack, as he mimed the first few lines with the singer, drawing Eileen's attention to the part about The Garden of Eden.

"Even the man on the radio agrees with me."

Chapter 5

On Sunday night, as Jack was preparing for his trip to Castleford, he noticed that Eileen was more morose than usual, which confirmed his belief that something other than the uncertainty of the future was troubling her, some dark secret that she was unwilling to share. Earlier he had attributed her depression to their mother's untimely death, or Jimmy Murphy's equally sudden exit from her life. Yet, scarcely twenty-four hours ago, she had laughed without bitterness at his snide reference to Murphy, and it could hardly be that she was still in mourning for their mother.

Another question too kept cropping up for which he could find no feasible answer: how had they got by so easily in his childhood on just their mother's widow's pension and the paltry annuity from the letting of the land, while presently with the land fully utilised, they could just about keep the wolf from the door, or was there a bigger picture, possibly connected with the whispered conversation he had eavesdropped on one night in the Royal Hotel?

At the time of his mother's death he had accepted as gospel Doctor Cosgrave's confirmation that she had died in her sleep and had felt no pain, and Father Hennelly's assurance that she had gone straight to heaven. Such authority was enough to satisfy the concerns of a boy of fourteen, but lately, in the light of more adult reasoning, unwillingly his thoughts kept returning to that fateful morning – the bloody sheets, the pool of blood on the floor, and his mother's face, which had been waxen in colour and contorted in what seemed pain.

He had no fond memories of his mother, and the lyrics of such sentimental songs, 'A MOTHER'S LOVE IS A BLESSING' and 'MOTHER NO CHROI', roused not the slightest flutter of emotion in his breast, and for all that most boys thought romantically of their mothers he had perceived at an early age that she despised him, as if he was an encumbrance she could have done without, and for maternal affection he had turned to Granny Mulhaire.

There was something puzzling too about his father's disappearance and death. According to his mother he had deserted his family, joined the British army, and died at Dunkirk, although she gave no explanation as to why he should be carrying the title deed of his land with him. Considering the outspoken hatred his country still bore for England and the poorly-concealed contempt they bore for the people who were forced to seek employment there, joining the British army was doing Judas on it in no small way, and if so, why hadn't his mother been entitled to a War-widow's pension from the British government? Even his neighbours seemed to be in a close-lipped conspiracy on the issue, and any time he drew it down, they clammed up, as if there was something about it that they were oathbound not to disclose, which was enough to convince him that there was another side to the story, and that his father might still be alive.

One day, while he was painting in the sacristy, in that holy of holies out of bounds to all but the clergy and their trusted disciples, he had secretly checked his parents' marriage certificate, which revealed that had they waited another four months to tie the knot, Eileen would have been born out of wedlock. There was something sinister about the whole affair that was beyond his comprehension, and though part of his logic accepted the facts as they had been explained to him, another part was sceptical, the part that kept knocking on the door of his mind looking for answers, and his instinct suggested that it was in some way connected with the gloom enshrouding his sister. Sister? – he often wondered, for they bore no resemblance whatsoever to each other in physiognomy, hair colour, mood, or manner.

Never one to allow such disturbing thoughts to trouble him for long, especially on Sunday night, Jack pushed the matter into a cubby hole in his mind and slammed the door on it. Giving his full attention to the mirror he scraped off his stubble and brushed his teeth with a solution of soot, salt and cold water, which he used as a substitute for toothpaste. After a brief adjournment to his bedroom he returned wearing a single-breasted grey suit, starched white shirt, and black brogues which Eileen had polished to the sheen of army leather. Back at the mirror, he knotted and re-knotted his maroon tie and, when it was the right length to fit inside the vee of his jacket, he embarked on the finicky task of grooming his hair. When he could do no more to enhance his appearance, he took a step back from the glass so as to squeeze in his full reflection, pulling several faces in an attempt to perfect the Tyrone Power look.

All the while Jack was under the silent observation of his sister and, when he turned away from the mirror and shrugged into his overcoat, she sniggered, saying: "You must be expecting to meet someone tonight with all the fuss you're making."

"It wouldn't do you any harm if you tidied yourself up now and again, and maybe you might be meeting someone!" Jack retorted. "It's not the end o' the world, you know, or maybe you're looking forward to winding up an old maid, wearing black clothes, and doing the First Fridays with the other ould women."

Jack's riposte brought the hot blood of anger to Eileen's cheeks. "Mind your own business, you!" she snapped. "You don't seem to be making much headway yourself in the marriage stakes and, if by some miracle, you did find someone soft enough to have you, where would you bring her? In here is it –"

The rest of Eileen's tirade fell on deaf ears, for Jack was already through the door and on his way to Castleford. Pedalling along in the darkness, the lamp on his bicycle sending out a cone of dim light before him, he tried to justify himself to himself. "I'm right – there's no excuse for moping and making everyone else miserable. Someone had to tell her – better hearing it from me, her own brother," he argued with his conscience, until finally, like the wringing of a dishcloth, he squeezed the matter from his mind and his thoughts returned to the likelihood of a dance with Mary O'Hara.

The night was dry and the stars were shining coldly in a cloudless sky and, as he quickened past a huddle of deserted cottages which were said to be haunted, he discerned an eerie moan in the wind soughing through the trees, as if the whispering of ghosts was borne on its wings, although on its breath was the last sting of winter mingling with the milder flurries of spring.

When he reached Castleford, he parked his bicycle inside the double doors of Forde's forge, a popular stopping-off place for the people of Knockrush when they came to town, and hung his overcoat on the wall over the blacksmith's apron, for not only would it save the thrupence cost, but it would save any embarrassment should Mary O'Hara see him checking such a wilted garment in the dance-hall cloakroom among the crombies, cashmere scarves and kid gloves of the town's affluent set.

When he stepped into the smoke and glare of Grogan's bar, he was greeted by an uneasy hush that smelt ominously of trouble, and at a glance he singled out its source – Bill Paisley, Castleford's loathsome building contractor. Well in his cups, Paisley was nodding on a high stool at the bar, his head slumped forward and six feet of vacant counter space at either elbow. Usually Paisley wouldn't be caught dead in such a mundane establishment as Grogan's, but perhaps in the stupor of drink his conscience had prompted him to return and mingle again with the men who were once his friends.

Hesitating for a moment Jack stepped into the gap on Paisley's right and waited until Grogan acknowledged his presence. "I'll have half o' the hot stuff, Mick," he called. "And be filling a pint as well."

Jack knocked back the whiskey in a gulp and, while he was waiting for the pint to be topped up, he slipped a pound to Grogan. "When you're taking for the drinks, let the dog I left tied the other night go too," he said, in an undertone. "And Mick, thanks for the favour."

The close proximity of the voices roused Paisley out of his stupor and, as if a resistless force was revolving his thickset frame, he turned on his stool until he was facing Jack, his shoulders hunched, one elbow on the counter, a huge jewelled ring that even a bishop would kiss gleaming ostentatiously on one of his fingers. Blunt of feature, he had a heavy face, round bovine eyes, cavernous nostrils, and a thick mop of dark hair, which was flecked with grey and receding before the tide of time. His straggling mouth lay open in a leer, exposing a strong set of yellow teeth, and even a man with two glass eyes could see why he was called Bull Paisley, inasmuch as he looked like a bull about to charge.

Nevertheless, the source of his soubriquet was a matter of dispute, some claiming that it had inadvertently come from the Northern-Irish cattle jobbers, whose pronunciation of 'Bill' sounded something like bull, while the hard core of his detractors argued that it had come about when, in his puberty, he had been caught trying to bugger a young bull. But whichever conjecture was true, the nickname stuck, much to Paisley's annoyance.

"How're ya gettin' on, Daly?" Paisley greeted, his thick lips curling in a sneer, the reek from his boozy breath forcing Jack to take a step backwards. "I heard yerself and Kelly are goin' into business together – diggin' paupers' graves. I can already see the shingle out: 'Kelly and Daly – paupers' graves dug, hail, rain, or snow – keen rates'," he gibed, his guffaw setting his heavy jowls to quivering. "This time o' year usually sees a lot o' them off, and by this time next year the two o' ye could be millionaires."

Although Paisley's sarcasm cut like a whip Jack refused to be drawn into the slanging match and, ignoring the slight, he stood silently contemplating his glass.

It was plain to see that Paisley was in one of his aggressive moods, and when he came unsteadily to his feet, he looked down arrogantly and contemptuously on Jack in the manner a rich man looks down on a poor man. As he was about to continue pouring out his scorn, the sound of the latch lifting attracted his attention, and when Tim Kelly appeared through the fog of tobacco smoke, he turned his derision on him. "Another paupers' gravedigger – how low can you stoop. I thought washin' sheep's daggings was the pits – but it's always thick work for thick men, that's what I say –"

"Less o' the thick, Paisley, if you know what's good for you!" Kelly cut in. "You might be a bigshot builder, but no one talks to me or my friend like that and, talkin' about bein' thick, what about yourself, because I'm sure they didn't call you Bull for nothin'."

"Why, you –"

"That's enough o' that, lads!" interjected Grogan, who had purposely stayed within earshot. "Everyone is welcome in this bar as long as they behave, and that goes for you too, Paisley – comin' in here throwin' your weight around. You're tryin' to pick a fight with these gentlemen, so my advice to you is, go across to that table over there and sit down – you've had enough to drink as it is."

"Gentleman, is it! Well, how do, gentlemen!" snapped Paisley, his nostrils flaring, and he was about to continue with his diatribe when Grogan's menacing stare stilled the words on his lips. Although Paisley had a fighting man's name and plenty of drink on board to bolster his courage a flicker of uncertainty crossed his eyes. After a moment's deliberation his scowl broadened into a half-smile. "Forget it, Mick – I was just havin' a bit o' fun, and just to show that I meant no harm, I'll buy the two o' them a drink."

"You can stick your drink up your big fat arse, as far up as you can put it!" Tim cut in, scowling at Paisley and, as he was bracing himself for the inevitable retaliation, Grogan came quickly from behind the counter and pushed them apart with his outstretched arms. Reprimanding Tim with a hard glance he turned to Paisley, shoulders hunched in a crouching stance, left foot forward, ready for action.

For an instant Paisley appeared to be in two minds, but perhaps recalling Grogan's earlier career he nodded an apology and tottered across the floor to a vacant table.

Grogan quickly poured oil on the troubled waters and the bar began to hum again, although Tim was far from placated. "I wouldn't work for that thick bastard if he gave me twenty quid a week!" he swore bitterly. "And, if any man deserves a pauper's grave, he does."

As the night advanced and drink spread its mantle of joviality over the scene, the two companions drifted into a less discordant world on a frothy black tide and, as closing time neared, Tim, all agog about his date with his new girlfriend after the pictures, excused himself, leaving Jack to fantasise on Mary

O'Hara. "You're a fool, Jack Daly!" he chastised himself, but like all star-crossed lovers, wild horses couldn't keep him away from the Phoenix, if only to catch a glimpse of the lady he had put on a pedestal in his heart. When he reached the street he dallied awhile watching the crowd spilling out of the Odeon cinema, hoping to catch an eyeful of Tim's latest flame and, when his curiosity was satisfied, he set off for the Phoenix, the music blaring through its open windows in the distance putting extra spring in his step.

The Phoenix, situated between the marketplace and the railway station, blazed lights from every window, and the sign 'Phoenix', which was encircled by revolving coloured lighting, had its letter N hanging lazily like an Z, so that it read: Phoezix. As the dance was well into its second half, Jack was reluctant to part with the full three shillings' admission, and he hung around outside, hoping to get a pass from someone leaving early. When there was no such luck, he shot an appealing glance at Kevin Douglas, the bouncer, on the off chance that he might let him in for nothing, for unlike most bouncers, Douglas's sympathies lay with the underdog. Douglas quickly read the situation, and when the manager's back was turned, he gave Jack the beck to slip past the box office.

Inside the long rectangular hall a quickstep was in full swing, and the lead singer of the Stephen Garvey Orchestra was straining his vocal chords to reach the high notes of the Doris Day hit, 'THE DEADWOOD STAGE'. Picking his way through the static group of men standing along the aisle at the back, which was part of the furniture of every dance hall, Jack squeezed into room in the slightly-elevated area leading to the tea bar and immediately set his eyes to searching for Mary in the merry-go-round of couples dancing towards him, whirling at the corner, and then floating away into the overhanging cumulus of cigarette smoke like giant marionettes in a fog.

When there was no sign of her on the floor, he waited until the music stopped, and when the dancers split, he scanned the round-the-wall seating through the gaps in the crowd. Somewhat disappointed by her absence he crossed the floor and stood among the hopefuls waiting for the next dance to be announced, facing Ann Flynn, an old friend from his schooldays and, when the band struck up for another quickstep, she read the intimation in his eyes and stepped forward to partner him.

As the trumpets, clarinets and saxophones blared out the tune, the maple floor began to vibrate beneath the hundreds of swishing feet and, with Jack's eyes fully focused over his partner's shoulder, they quickly covered a lap of the hall. Whirling whenever a space appeared, huddling and marking time in the crushes, they were on their second circuit when his heart suddenly missed a beat and, without actually seeing Mary, he sensed her presence. Weak at the knees, tingling sensations coursed through his body, and in the next instant, when a gap appeared in the dancers, he caught a fleeting glimpse of her standing near the door of the ladies' cloakroom, conspicuous among her lesser luminaries like a real diamond in a cluster of false stones. It was agony to look, and agony not to look, and the more he tried to ignore her, the more he lost control of his eyes, which kept returning to her at every opportunity until he felt as tormented as a man with a sore thumb who keeps knocking it against the wall. Finally, when the music stopped, the compere calling: 'next dance please!' startled him out of his stupor.

When the tempo slowed for the next dance, the overhead lights dimmed and, when the revolving coloured lights on the walls began to spin and reflect on the glitter balls suspended from the ceiling, the hall was transformed into a romantic palace. Taking courage from the darkened setting Jack eased through the crowd until he came face to face with the lady who, in his opinion, was the epitome of an angel. "Would you like to dance, Mary?" the hesitant words from his lips asked, but his faculties were in another land – dreamland.

"Yes – of course, Jack," said Mary, smiling her assent, her full lips broadening over her gleaming white teeth, her brown eyes sparkling in the rainbow of lights, her nose, which was slightly retroussé, enhancing rather than detracting from her allure. Not too tall, not too short, her stature was perfect for a woman, and though her figure was slim, it was nicely rounded at bosom and hip. She was fashionably turned out in a dark-blue taffeta dress, its narrow straps exposing the milky-white skin of her bare arms and shoulders, and her short auburn hair, which was smoothed back from her forehead and tied with a white ribbon, highlighted the graceful curve of her neck and the attractive jut of her collarbones. Still, for all her blossoming beauty, it was her smile, which was warm and sincere, that held the most appeal, and for an instant it flashed from her lips to her eyes as if she was pleased to see him.

When they reached the centre of the floor, Mary eased closer, stretching her body upwards until her firm breasts were tight against his chest, their cheeks brushing lightly in a tender caress. Dizzy in a heavenly world Jack felt as if he was gliding into the mists of some strange land, and, with Mary's perfume and feminine fragrance overpowering his senses, he wished that the music would go on and on and the night too. Round and round they crept, each press of Mary's body a separate sensation of bliss, each brush of her cheek an ecstatic thrill, until the music stopped and, when the overhead lights blazed down, the romantic world of a few moments ago vanished as if by the wave of a conjuror's wand.

Standing in a no man's land just outside the gates of paradise a thousand words shot through Jack's mind, and yet, in spite of all his rehearsals on the long lonely mornings when he had sat staring into the fire, he failed to grasp any of them to mould into an appropriate sentence, a cryptic sentence that would convey his feelings without putting Mary under obligation to respond. Barely conscious of her saying: "Thank you, Jack" as she eased away, he finally blurted out: "And thank you too, Mary," before she disappeared in the smoky haze like a lady in a mirage.

Standing sheepishly in the centre of the floor reality came back with a rush, reminding him that he would have to wait at least a week before he could ask Mary to dance again. In the unwritten dance-hall code every man was entitled to one courtesy dance from the lady of his choosing, but to ask the same lady again on the same night would be a declaration of more amorous intentions. So, it would be presumption of the highest order if he continued his pursuit, especially in the light of the reproachful stares he was attracting from her clique of wealthy admirers scattered around the hall, as though he had already committed a mortal sin by stepping out of his class.

As the night was drawing to a close, the compere announced a lady's choice, and again the revolving lights and glitter balls spun their magic. Never an optimist at the best of times Jack was about to turn away when he spied Mary crossing the floor in his direction, her smiling eyes boring down on him. Instinctively he looked to his left and right and then behind him to see if it was someone else who had attracted her attention, and yet, when she stopped before him, her eyes turned down demurely, asking in a hoarse whisper: "Would you like to dance, Jack?" less than a feather could have knocked him down.

Jack could have sworn he blushed, and before he was quite aware of it, he was back again in dreamland, dancing cheek to cheek with his dream woman, the lights fluctuating from one colour to another keeping pace with the fluctuation of his emotions, for it was turning out to be one of those rare nights when everything is possible and everything succeeds in the crazy world of romance: soft lights, soft skin, soft music, and the song, 'STRANGER IN PARADISE', could not have been more appropriate. Drifting into an entrancement from which he hoped he would never awaken, he drifted into the paradise of the lyrics.

Completely absorbed in the rapture of the moment Jack responded to each press of Mary's body, to each caress of her cheek, savouring every second of the heaven in which he suddenly found himself. Following the lyrics of the romantic melody he was soon in a state of suspended bliss, so much so that he wished he could grab the hourglass in his hands and stop the sands from running. But running they were, and much too quickly, for somewhere far back in his mind a warning bell rang, reminding him that the singer had reached the last verse. It was up to him to do something, say something, otherwise the opportunity would be lost forever, and the voice that barely breached the shell of his hypnosis, asking: "Would you like something cold to drink, Mary?" he could scarcely identify as his own, but the soft voice that whispered in reply: "That would be nice, Jack," was more recognisable.

When the music stopped, without hardly breaking from the embrace, they walked in tandem to a vacant table in the tea bar, and when Jack returned from the counter with two bottles of Golden Orange, straws projecting from the necks, again he was lost for words. He had already reached this stage in his daydreaming, although now that the daydream had become reality, his mind went blank, his oft-rehearsed lines deserting him, save to offer her a cigarette. Sitting somewhat uneasily, staring at each other across the table through the blue wreaths of smoke curling up from their cigarettes, Jack finally broke the deadlock. "It's stuffy in here, Mary – it could do with better ventilation," he stuttered uncertainly, and no sooner had the words left his lips than he wished he had swallowed them.

"It is stuffy, Jack, I agree," returned Mary and, perhaps sensing his discomfiture, she laid a reassuring hand on his, her smile suggesting that no small talk was necessary.

Time too seemed to have borrowed wings and, believing it was more than just by chance that they were sitting at the same table, stealing admiring glances at each other, Jack took his courage in both hands. "Is it all right if I see you home, Mary?" he asked, bracing himself for some form of refusal.

"But of course, Jack – that is, if it's not too much out of your way," returned Mary, without deliberation and, patting his hand as if she meant him to wait, she flitted across the floor to the cloakroom.

When they reached the street, the cold night air came as a cleansing benediction after the smoke, sweat and cheap perfume of the dance hall. The usual clique of hangers-on were loitering outside Smith's fish and chip shop, backs to the wall, taking everything in with their wily street-corner eyes, and the sudden explosion of their whispered conversations suggested that the gossip of the coming week would be Mary O'Hara walking arm in arm with Widow Daly's son.

When they were clear of the crowd, Mary tightened her grip on Jack's arm. "It's so nice of you to see me home, Jack, but it seems to me, except for the odd dance, that you've been avoiding me ever since I came back from boarding school," she said, a slight huff in her tone. "I don't know why this should be – we used to be such good friends."

"I assure you, Mary, it has never been my intention to avoid you, it's just –"

"It's just that you think I'm a snob! Say it! – everybody else thinks so."

"You were never further from the truth; if only you knew –"

"Knew what?"

"Knew of all the times I've lain awake at night thinking about you," returned Jack, determined to play the game to the end now that the ball was in his court. "And, as I was going to say a minute ago, we live in different worlds – you should know that."

"It doesn't make any difference to me what you are, Jack," said Mary reassuringly, affection replacing the earlier huff in her tone. "You were always my knight in shining armour in our schooldays, ever since the day you dragged me out of the river when I fell off Ballinderry Bridge."

The half-mile walk to Mary's secluded home on the outskirts of Castleford had never felt shorter for Jack, and before he realised it, they had reached the high wrought-iron gates at the entrance. Unsure of his next move he lingered in the shadowy darkness until Mary, perhaps sensing his uncertainty, moved closer and began to fidget with his tie. "I'm sorry for cutting you short earlier, Jack," she said, a note of apology in her tone. "But you've been so distant with me, like a stranger – we usen't to be like that. What was I to think? Six Sunday nights one after another you gave me one lousy dance and then disappeared, until tonight when I had to take the initiative myself. Did it ever cross your mind that I only keep going to that – to that rat hole of a Phoenix hoping you'd be there, when I could be dancing in Seapoint or the Hangar in Salthill where all the top bands play and where all my friends go – well now you know."

Without knowing how they got there, Jack found his hands inside Mary's coat, and before he was quite aware of it, he was kissing her tenderly, her upturned lips responding with the correct blend of delicacy and passion. In a moment of ecstatic bliss, something vital, something electric, leaped from her to him, something that caressed his whole body thrillingly. However, the moment she eased away, the hopelessness of his position assailed him. "This'll never work, Mary," he said, incredulity, anxiety, and a little hope all discernible in his tone. "Whatever will your parents say when they find out?"

"I don't care what they say. These aren't the dark ages when parents manipulated their daughters' lives – this is nineteen fifty-three," she countered haughtily, tossing her head like an unbroken filly, as sure of her ground as any nineteen-year-old. "I've got my own life to lead – and I'm going to lead it."

Mary's passionate outburst did much in the way of relieving Jack's anxiety about her parents. Together they would prevail, although the scowling spectre of old O'Hara still hovered in the background of his mind like a villain from a horror movie. When he kissed her again, he felt her breasts coming alive with tension, and the thrill of her response as her tongue probed his mouth provocatively sent the blood bounding along in his veins, dispelling all rational thinking from his mind, but when he allowed his hands to drift below her waistline on to her buttocks, she eased away.

"Where do we go from here, Mary?" Jack asked, holding her at arm's length. "I hope you don't think I'm too forward, but I'd like to go on seeing you, if you have a mind to. And I must say this, if anyone told me earlier tonight that I'd be standing here kissing you goodnight at your gate, I'd have said: 'Yes, and the sun'll rise in the west tomorrow morning and the trees'll sprout pound notes instead of leaves'."

"Yes, I'd like to go on seeing you too, Jack. But you're right about my parents – they are prudes, and when you mentioned them, I knew you were only thinking of me," returned Mary, anxiety creeping into her tone, yet smiling that warm smile that always sent his heart fluttering. "But my parents don't have to know, at least not right away."

"The parents are always the last to find out," said Jack sardonically. "I'll hardly have left this gate when a little bird –"

"Oh, Jack – don't say such things!" interjected Mary. "We could meet secretly until I get the opportunity to break it to them gently."

"It's getting late, Mary, and I know you'll have to go indoors soon. But maybe, if you happen to be strolling towards Ballinderry Bridge on Wednesday night at about eight, we might just bump into each other."

"Oh yes, Jack – Wednesday night about eight," said Mary and, in an abandonment which blindly sought his lips and embraces that broke off only to be renewed, she kissed him again and again, long and lingeringly, tenderness struggling with passion, and in all his life Jack had never known anything a millionth part as sweet as that moment. "Goodnight, Jack, until Wednesday night, and thank you for seeing me home."

"Wednesday night can't come soon enough for me," returned Jack waving in her wake until she disappeared in the darkness on the other side of the gate.

On his way back to collect his bicycle and overcoat Jack was walking on air until the cold wind wrapping his scant clothing about his body brought with it just as chilling a dose of reality. It was hard to see it working out no matter what

Mary said about having a mind of her own and, as pessimism dogged his steps, the cloud began to drift from beneath his feet, and by the time he reached the forge his earlier high spirits had all but vanished under the weight of his gloomy prospects. So near, yet so faraway, he thought, although later, as he lay in bed reliving every second of his entrancing night, again he felt the wings of hope take flight, and in his reverie he followed ever note, every word of STRANGER IN PARADISE miming the last verse over and over in his mind.

Now that fate had lent a hand, it couldn't possibly go wrong, and then sleep came, the dark starless night of wonderful sleep, which is thought by some to be a premonition of eternity.

Chapter 6

As the cold rains of April passed into the balm of green May weather, now that one of his birds on the bush was in his hand, Jack turned his attention to the other – to shake off the shackles of poverty and get ahead in the world. His plan was to have done with his present method of farming and concentrate entirely on pigs, a piggery which could turn out dozens of pigs a month on contract to the new bacon factory that was presently under construction in nearby Ballyglass. Initially, his nine acres would be ample to grow their feed, although the next step was the stumbling block. He needed a whole new layout – separate pens for the breeding sows, pens for the shoats after they were weaned, pens for fattening the barrows, a pen for the boar, and an automatic feeding system. He had already formed a picture of the end product in his mind and, after sketching it out in detail, he estimated the cost down to the last nail.

Considering he would be doing most of the labour himself and by skimping to the bare boards he would need a thousand pounds, which was approximately the price of twenty-five good-sized cattle, and presently he had only one, the one that Eileen kept reminding him would have to be sold to cover the cost of the Stations. Alternatively, four hundred would get him off the ground, and once the enterprise started to produce he could complete it in stages.

Unknown to Eileen he had seen the bank manager, although the meeting had turned out to be as unfruitful as the seed in the parable that had fallen on stony ground – no money without collateral. Later that night when he met Tim in Grogan's, he explained the situation. "You were right about the bank, Tim – they'd lend me nothing without having the title deed of the land," he went on, after giving a brief synopsis of the meeting. "So, I'll either have to abandon the idea altogether, or try to raise the hundred-pound stake for the poker game as you suggested, which is about the same as asking the sky to fall."

"I wish there was some way I could help," returned Tim. "But it's like everything else in the country – the rich have it sewed up tighter than a cod's arse, and the more you're in want, the more you'll go without. But for Christ's sake, don't give up on the idea altogether. Winning the money playing poker might be the stuff that dreams are made of, but if you could manage to put a little aside every week, especially when the turf-cuttin' season starts, who knows."

"I guess you're right, Tim – I shouldn't give up hope."

Dismissing the setback to a far-off country in his mind Jack set about tilling his clapped-out acres, and afterwards he had a free hand for a few weeks cutting turf on hire. Although the rate for sleaners was thirty shillings a day Jack only charged a pound, as it was mostly Castleford's poor who required his services, people as hard up as himself. Nevertheless, little by little he began to build up his stake, although he badly needed a miracle to turn the slow process of addition into multiplication.

Now that he was meeting Mary regularly, mostly on strolls in the countryside and at the Sunday night dance in the Phoenix, he didn't feel quite as fulfilled as he ought to be, and he found himself living between two worlds – one grey, one golden. Over the weeks he had noticed a change coming over her, as if the novelty of their secret courtship was wearing off and the upshot of what it might entail was coming home to her. His ambition she dismissed as pie in the sky, and one night, when he mentioned eloping to England as a last resort, she was anything but agreeable. England was too uncertain a future, she had said, and she was quick to point out the disgrace Peggy Wilson had brought on her family, which left him in no doubt that she had already considered the option. Still, nothing could shake his belief that fate had meant them for each other, and in her passionate kisses he found ignorant hope.

Mary wasn't just a pretty girl, not merely a bright one with character, but a girl born with that particular something that brought excitement to every man who looked at her, and definitely not the type to take down Poke Lane for a knee-trembler. That others had their sights on her was only to be expected, and one night at the Phoenix he felt the first septic pricks of jealousy when he saw her dancing cheek to cheek with the suave Gerald Cronin, a hotelier's son. Still, for all that she had the reputation of a virtuous young lady whom the tongue of scandal could not touch, he sensed that it was there for the taking if he caught her in the right mood, for too often in their passionate moments when he slipped a hand inside her knickers, her efforts at fighting him off lacked resolve, as if her desire was getting the upper hand of her virtue, and her somewhat repetitive protest: "You don't think I'm that kind of girl," almost convinced him that she was, although in his heart of hearts he didn't want her to be: 'that kind of girl'.

One night in Grogan's, when he aired his anxieties with Tim, he took it as good news. "Now is your chance to get ridin' her – consolidate you position, for Christ's sake," he said supportively. "Once you start givin' her a rub o' the ould relic she'll be yours, for a while at least, because if you don't, someone else will, and the beauty of it all is, if you put her up the stick, she'll have to marry you. That's a much surer way of gettin' your pig-farm, for once you tie the knot her ould fella'll have to cough up – he can't very well see his son-in-law strugglin'."

Tim's words: 'if you don't, someone else will', gave Jack cause for concern, for Cronin, like Jimmy Murphy, had a way with women, and gossip had it that one of his recent conquests had to depart hastily for England before her pregnancy became noticeable. Nevertheless, he felt that such pursuit was too callous, too calculating, and against all the rules of the love stories and films he treasured and his dream of lifelong happiness. In his own romantic world he felt like a ploughboy elevated from the peasantry to the gentry, and he was determined to live in that world rather than drag Mary down to his own bog-trotter status. However, as more of her character came to light, he felt as if he had caught a tropical bird, all flame and colour, when a thrush would have been more suitable.

Still, like all men besotted, he found excuses for her haughtiness, her lack of consideration for his means when she proposed expensive nights out, and for hurting his feelings when she apologised, and once he thought he detected derision in her encouragement for his venture, derision in the word 'pigs', as though pigs detracted from his social standing. Her unspoken words seemed to say: 'Why couldn't it be horses or cattle?' and yet, to be in love wasn't an ignoble emotion, even if he got nothing from it but anxiety, jealousy and pain. It was hard to expect Mary, who had never wanted for anything, to understand what it was like to do without, and he accepted her shortcomings as the price he had to pay for happiness.

Once upon a time in his fantasy daydreams, when he had courted Mary in his imagination, he had cast her in the role of some of fiction's heroines, one of the Bathsheba Everdenes or Lucie Manettes of the literary world, casting himself in the role of its unrequited lovers: Sydney Carton, Gabriel Oak or Diggory Venn. Then, in the light of Mary's ardour, he found himself playing more swashbuckling characters, rescuing maidens in distress, and in all his castles in the air Mary was the only occupant. Now his love had reached such a stage that he was beginning to be unhappy, to be desperate, and for some unexplainable reason the wheel of his fantasy had begun to rotate in a reverse cycle and he found himself playing the William Dobbins of the world again.

One sunny evening, as he strolled out of town for his rendezvous with Mary, try as he might, he couldn't shake off the downbeat feeling that dogged his steps. His route took him past terraces of drab houses where scores of ragged children, some barefoot, were kicking a rubber football up and down the concrete road, their shrill clamour drowning out the blithe choruses of the songbirds. Oblivious of the prying eyes peering out from behind curtained windows he walked on, the houses growing farther and farther apart, until finally he reached a ballustraded bridge where a path, arched over with rhododendron and other shrubbery, meandered along by the river.

The evening, chill with lots of sunshine, bore an air of gloom that matched his mood and, leaning over the parapet, he dallied awhile, watching the water below, with its flowing leaves and spots of froth, stealing away like time under the dark stone arches. When the church clock struck eight, their rendezvous time, his despondency deepened, not at the prospect of being stood up, for on several occasions Mary had found it difficult to keep the date, but at the thought of it all ending. The feeling persisted and, after a decent interval had elapsed, he retraced his steps, hoping to bump into her on his way back. He had scarcely gone a hundred yards when he noticed a tall man approaching with deliberate steps and, as the distance closed between them, he recognised the grim features of John O'Hara, Mary's father.

The impact of recognition momentarily stopped Jack in his tracks, and his first impulse was to turn on his heel and hurry away from the tirade he felt certain was in store for him. However, as if some rebel ancestry was stiffening his spine, he reminded himself that this was Ireland, a country for which brave men had shed their life's blood so that all men would have equal rights and, with his face as blank as a poker player bluffing the game with a pair of deuces, he waited for O'Hara to state his business.

The message in O'Hara's frown could hardly be plainer and, dry-coughing to clear his throat, he began: "Jack – it is Jack, I believe. I'd like to have a word with you on a matter of the utmost importance – my only daughter, Mary. It has come to my attention that you have designs on her – or am I using the correct phrase? – as she has on your good self. In this matter I'm speaking as a father, and I hope you'll allow me a few minutes of your time."

Jack didn't need a crystal ball to see what was coming next and, with a half-apathetic expression on his face as if he deemed anything possible in the unequal society in which he lived, except perhaps fair play, he nodded for O'Hara to make his point.

O'Hara's erect bearing and solemn countenance epitomised his years of courtroom drama, and his grey hat and pinstripe suit added a shade of severity to his sharp saturnine features, which he tried to soften with a stereotyped smile. "First of all take Mary; she's nineteen, impetuous, idealistic, and attractive – not taking after me in the latter, I assure you," he went on, laughing hollowly, a laugh that contained more sarcasm than mirth. "But I'm sure you can see what I'm getting at. She's at a very impressionable age, and I'll add, very susceptible to handsome young men – men like yourself for instance. Don't get me wrong – I don't doubt your sincerity where Mary is concerned. As a matter of fact she spoke very highly of you in a tête-à-tête we've had, so highly that it prompted this encounter, but like all parents I worry about my children's future.

"As you are no doubt aware, I have two sons ready to be ordained in Maynooth and another in law school, and naturally I'm concerned about Mary and how you intend to provide for her should the occasion arise. I'm not here to ask, I'm here to beg for your kind consideration in the matter, for you'll have to agree that your prospects are anything but propitious. Admittedly you could elope as Mary is threatening to do if I don't keep out of the affair, but let's deliberate for a moment on such a move. You'd hardly consider taking her to your cottage in the bog, or perhaps you were thinking of taking her to England – to some room in Camden Town – to some hovel, to live the rough life of our emigrant brethren. It would appear that these are your only options, because if you carry on seeing her against my authority, I'll disown her."

Cornered by the reality in O'Hara's words Jack responded by playing the only decent card in his hand – the card of honesty. "Is there no other way, Mister O'Hara – has it to be so final? I agree with everything you say about my prospects, nobody knows better than myself, and on my honour I'd never ask Mary to share such a life, but don't take away our chance of happiness. I'll find a way – I'm already making plans –"

"Find a way – do you believe in miracles!" snapped O'Hara, cutting Jack short, his cordial expression changing first to one of anger then to contempt. "Well I don't, and I won't listen to any tommy-rot about love finding a way either! Mary will do my bidding – she's under my prerogative until she's twenty-one! That is the law, my good man, and by then she'll think differently! I thought I could reason with you, but I should've known better than to have any truck with a bog-trotter on the make, and I suppose you were counting on me throwing in a nice fat dowry to boot – you're all the same, you lot!" he ranted on, the anger in his tone increasing, his face turning pale, his lower jaw trembling. "And, I feel I should warn you, if you go on seeing Mary behind my back, I'll have Superintendent Dolan put the Guards on you – a good friend of mine, the Super."

Always at his coolest when his back was to the wall Jack listened silently until O'Hara's tirade fizzled out. "Is that it, Mister O'Hara – are you sure you have nothing else to add? But take your time and you might think of some other slight to cast on my character. After all, honesty and poverty are the two cardinal sins of the human race," he countered, making no effort to disguise the sarcasm in his tone, although he was in no doubt as to his position no matter what Mary said. The Super, as O'Hara had hinted, could make life difficult.

"No – that's not all I have to say on the matter," returned O'Hara, mopping his brow with a handkerchief, his expression changing again to one of cordiality. "First of all I must apologise for my outburst, for it seems that in such a delicate family matter I've taken a step too far, and I can see you're not happy with the situation in spite of your bland look. You think I'm doing you a great injustice, but who knows, you might thank me for it in later years. However, if you bear with me, you'll find there are two sides to me, and to show that I bear you no ill will I have here an envelope containing a hundred pounds. It's yours – and all you have to do to earn it is, give me your word that you won't meet Mary again socially until she's twenty-one. Think about it – a hundred pounds is a lot of money. So, what do you say? Let's shake on it and part on amicable terms."

Reading between the lines Jack perceived that O'Hara wasn't as sure of his ground as he had earlier expressed, otherwise he wouldn't have resorted to bribery, or perhaps he was doubting Mary's chastity, which might lead to a shotgun wedding, as Tim had suggested. Unwillingly his thoughts dwelt on the bribe until suddenly the hundred pounds took the form of a hundred devils in his head, urging him to accept it, for it seemed that fate was handing him a lifeline. For a timeless moment the philosophy of the gift-horse struggled with his pride. "You're right, Mister O'Hara – a hundred pounds is a lot o' money," he said at length, a wry smile on his face. "And I'd be a fool not to take it."

"It just goes to show what a great reconciler and sweetener money is," interjected O'Hara, taking Jack's words completely in the wrong context, a bleak smile registering his triumph as he held out the envelope.

Jack, his face set in firm lines of dignity and defiance, looked O'Hara straight in the eye and, with a lazy motion of a hand, pushed the envelope aside. "No, Mister O'Hara – I won't be bribed, though I am flattered by the large amount, considering Christ Himself only rated thirty pieces of silver," he replied. "But you've already made your point, and I'm prepared to abide by your request – until Mary is twenty-one. So, as you put it, we'll part on amicable terms," he went on, his words as clear and punctuated as if he was treading the boards in a Drury Lane drama and, leaving a somewhat bewildered O'Hara stroking his chin, he turned on his heel and set off walking in the direction of Castleford.

In the following days reality quickly dispelled any resentment Jack felt for O'Hara – it was all his own fault. He had built a palace of cards, and now that it had tumbled down around him, he was destined to live forever in its ruins, for what right had he, a penniless homesteader, to expect Mary to leave the protection of the golden circle of money for a life of drudgery. But what of Mary? – he would have to meet her somewhere and explain, although this issue was resolved for him shortly afterwards when O'Hara's unyielding attitude was confirmed in a short letter from her. The letter exuded apology, the gist of which said that she was obliged to conform with her father's wishes until she was twenty-one. Then, they could pick up where they had left off.

Swallowing his disappointment that Mary hadn't discussed the matter with him personally, again Jack's infatuation found excuses for her. A lot could happen in two years. Perhaps by then he would be well on his way to fulfilling his ambition, although he cursed a wasted chance every time his thoughts dwelt on O'Hara's hundred pounds, which would have given him the stake for the poker game. Yet, had he taken it, besides having to contend with his conscience, he would be kissing Mary goodbye forever.

On the last week in May there were fairs in Castleford – sheep on Tuesday, cattle on Wednesday, pigs on Thursday, and horses on Friday. Eileen was all for selling both pigs so that they could buy another calf, although Jack was against the idea. "You're right, Eileen, we need another calf to replace the bullock we're selling for the Stations and two shoats to replace the pigs," he agreed. "But in the meantime what are we going to do for meat?"

"We have enough bacon to last at least six weeks, and then it'll be only a matter of a few months before one o' the shoats is big enough for killing and, as soon as August comes, I'll have plenty of cock-chickens."

"So, in between, it'll be spuds and butter every day for the dinner!" Jack cut in. "If you ask me, it's backwards this ould country of ours is going – back to the days of the Famine."

"We can have fried eggs with the spuds and there's plenty o' rabbits. If you get out your gun and snares, we can have rabbit stew now and again."

"How exciting – something to look forward to – and now is your chance to try out a rushes stew, as Murt said, just in case times get harder," returned Jack, finally agreeing that both pigs should go, although his guilty conscience stirred when he realised that he could easily buy a calf out of the money he was saving for the poker game.

On pig-fair morning, when Tim Kelly arrived to help with the loading, Jack harnessed Charlie and led him under the cart on the cobbled part of the farmyard and, as Charlie disliked pigs, he called for Eileen to hold his head. The moment he heard the pigs squealing Charlie reared and tried to bolt, but Eileen kept him on a tight rein long enough for Tim and Jack to bundle the two eighteen-stone pork monstrosities on to the cart. When Jack took over at the bridle, Charlie relaxed, and shortly afterwards they were stepping out for Castleford, Tim following on his bicycle. When they reached Grogan's yard, they unloaded the pigs and stabled Charlie and, with a rope looped about a hind leg of each animal, they prodded them towards the marketplace.

The marketplace, encircled by a clutter of makeshift stalls, selling all types of merchandise: second-hand suits, harness, reject crockery, horse liniment, sweets, turkey eggs, old hens, clogs and other oddments, was bustling with enterprise, and all over the wide area in front of the town hall the pigs were on parade, ropes on their hind legs holding them in check like dogs on leads. Grim-faced jobbers, in their trademark trench coats and brown hats, ashplants under their oxters, were moving among them, rejecting the asking prices and making offers, while the cacophony of the hawkers peddling their wares, the pigs squealing, and the slapping of bargaining palms, mingling with the jangly renditions of busker music, added a vibrant hum to the scene.

When Jack and Tim found a pitch among them, at first the cagey jobbers just looked, shook their heads and moved on, until a thin, sallow-faced man, gaudily dressed in a beige check jacket, pink shirt, and yellow polka-dot tie, showed more interest. Running his shifty eyes over the pigs, then over Jack and his companion, his pencil moustache twitched speculatively. "What'll you take for them?" he asked cheekily, spreading his long talon-like fingers over the pigs' backs to evaluate their worth.

The man had 'tangler' written all over him, and well Jack knew the breed. "They're not for sale!" he replied sarcastically, casting a sidelong glance at Tim as if for support.

Taken aback by Jack's curt reply, it took a moment or two for the man to regain his composure. "Why did you bring them here if they're not for sale?" he asked indignantly.

"So they'll know you and your kind if they ever see you again – I don't sell to tanglers!" snapped Jack and, making no effort to hide his resentment, he spat on the ground, barely missing the man's scuffed brown shoes, for tanglers were shysters, usually without money, who weren't beyond doing a slick deal and absconding without paying.

When the disgruntled tangler walked away, they had an offer of thirty pounds for the pair, five pounds short of the asking price. "That means we'll get at least thirty-two," remarked Tim and, as the morning advanced and demand took an upturn, one heavy-jowled man kept returning, until finally, after a vigorous bout of slapping of moistened palms with Jack, they agreed on thirty-four pounds, the deal including a pound luckpenny for the jobber.

"That's two quid more than I was expecting, Tim," said Jack, as they walked the pigs to the railway station for shipment, and later, when the jobber paid out, he put thirty pounds in his inside pocket for Eileen for safekeeping until he bought the calf and shoats. The rest he kept for himself – what Eileen didn't know wouldn't trouble her and, slipping a ten-shilling note to Tim, which he reluctantly accepted, he steered him towards Grogan's.

Although it had just turned nine o'clock the bar was humming with farmers and drovers, and the whiff of pig-shite from their boots and wellingtons, mingling with the sizzling smell of mulled porter, beef tea, and the fresh ham from the sandwiches, was creating a stink-savoury odour that defied classification. "Good health, Tim!" Jack toasted, when Grogan served them two half-glasses of Power's Gold Label. "The two happiest days of your life – the day you get married and the day you sell the pigs."

The whiskey burning with fiery pleasantness brought a wave of warmth and mellowness to his stomach, a sensation that only the thrill of kissing Mary O'Hara's sensual lips could surpass, and for a brief while she was with him, smiling into his eyes. With great effort he put her back in her ivory tower and turned to his friend. "We can't drink on an empty stomach, Tim," he said. "So, I'll nip across to Brennan's and get something for Pudding Joyce to fry for us."

Pudding Joyce, the proprietor of a rough-and-ready eating house across the street from Grogan's, wasn't the adventurous type and, as bread and tea was the extent of his menu, it was up to the customers to provide their own meat, which he would fry for them for a few coppers extra. Leaving Tim in Grogan's, Jack picked his way through the busy streets to Brennan's butcher shop and bought steak, black pudding and sausages, which he left in the eating-house kitchen. Back in Grogan's, he kept a vigilant eye on the clock, the demands of his stomach more for food now than drink. "Twenty minutes, Pudding promised, but you know yourself Pudding's twenty minutes could mean an hour," he said, and when a decent interval had elapsed, they crossed the street to Joyce's.

The walls of the dingy dining room were bare and mildewed, and the fresh layers of newspaper covering the linoleum were already tattered and showing the print of dirty boots. The windows were grimy and fly-blown, their sills covered in cigarette ash and mouse droppings, and the half-drawn curtains, which were stiff with grease from the customers wiping their hands on them, were putting up a brave fight at keeping out the sunlight. Four long trestle-tables, which had backless benches on either side, made up the furniture, the unclothed tables swamped in tea-spillings and littered with crusts of bread and the crockery on the previous diners.

Pudding hadn't come by his nickname for nothing, and Maggie, his plump spouse, looked as if she had been cut from the same piece of cloth. As rotund as she was tall, she had a round fleshy face which made her piggy eyes look smaller, and her flat boxer-type nose was turned up in such a manner that her nostrils were staring. Her multiple chins almost reached down to her voluminous bosom, and her straggly red hair was so unkempt that it looked as if it had been through a winnowing machine. Her dress and smock were as greasy as the curtains, and the long-ashed cigarette that never left the corner of her mouth had once prompted Tim to remark: "I never saw a cigarette dangling from a pig's arse till now." Maggie administered on the tables and the redoubtable Pudding did the frying, the clouds of rancid smoke billowing from the open kitchen doorway bearing witness of his culinary proficiency.

Notwithstanding its shortcomings Joyce's was good value for money and popular with the farming fraternity, and for all the proprietor's lack of hygiene and initiative there were many in the community who wouldn't mind being a sovereign or two behind him. As it was up to the customers to make their own seating arrangements, Jack and Tim squeezed into room on one of the benches, and shortly afterwards they were wolfing down their food, washing it down with mugs of hot strong tea.

Mopping up his plate with a hunk of fresh bread Tim belched salubriously. "I'm full, Jack," he said. "Full as a priest's wallet."

"And that's full," returned Jack, passing the cigarettes. "It'll be hard to get the drink down us after that feed, so let's stand outside till it settles."

Outside, the sunlight was dazzling after the gloom and smoke of the eating house, and they loitered awhile at a street corner, taking in the morning air. Castleford, its four narrow streets converging at the marketplace, looked drab and bereft of warmth, although now that the sun had cleared the rooftops, it was coming more into light. The fair was all but over, and the last of the pigs were on their way to the railway station, leaving behind the stink of their earlier presence. Jack Cheap was at his most charismatic as he knocked down the last of his bargains (he wasn't there to sell, he was there to give away), while smoky tinker women, dirty babies inside their shawls which had to be pinched or pricked with safety pins to make them cry so as to highlight their privation, begged from the diminishing crowd, heaping such blessings on their benefactors that it would appear that further atonement was totally unnecessary to enter the kingdom of Heaven.

As Castleford went about its normal business after the hullabaloo of the fair, Jack took a long hard look at his home town and, as he recalled all his boyhood friends who had stepped up the long winding road to the station, he was taken by one of those queer shudderings which they say mean footsteps on one's grave. "What d'you think, Tim, now that there's just you and me left?" he asked, an aggressive pull on his cigarette paraphrasing his mood.

"I suppose our turn to hit the trail'll come someday too," returned Tim, whose thoughts seemed to be on the same frequency. "Even the railway station gives me the willies, as if there was somethin' haunted about it."

"Sure it's bound to be haunted when you think of all the men and women who were forced to go – and they not wanting to go. Every morning you can see it, that is, if you want to see it – some man or other with a suitcase walking up the street to the station, throwing the odd look back, the kind of a look an ould horse on his way to the knacker's yard'd throw back at his master, as much to say: 'What are you doing to me – what have I done to deserve this?' And they don't deserve it either – the horses or the people. Something constructive should be done by the government and the clergy to stop the rot, besides politicians talking bullshite and the priests trying to stuff it down our throats that Masses and prayer'll bring an end to it."

"Forget it, Jack – it's too depressin'. Let's go back to Grogan's."

"But I just can't forget it, and if nothing can be done about it, at least they should erect a memorial with all the names of the exiles engraved."

"Stop, Jack – you're makin' no sense at all!" interjected Tim. "If there was such a memorial, where would they put it? It'd have to be at least fifty foot high and fifty foot wide to fit in all the names. Come on – let's go back to the pub."

Back in Grogan's, when a banjo and fiddle struck up, rasping out a selection of reels, the ambience took a livelier turn and, as the day advanced, the combination of music and drink cleared the cobwebs from even the gruffest of throats. Big problems soon became little problems, and little problems were pushed into temporary repose until Castleford didn't seem such a bad town after all.

All too soon it was time for home and, bidding farewell to Tim, Jack made his way to the stable to harness his horse. "Come on, Charlie Sootdrop – it's time you and me were getting back," he laughed, running his fingers through Charlie's mane. "The tinkers are already on their way out o' town in their ass-carts, the cops chasing them," (the tinkers had to be outside the town limits by six o'clock in the evening).

Charlie let out a whinny of delighted recognition, and immediately began to prance and flick his ears, as if he was in full agreement with the idea. Perhaps only a horse whisperer can sense what is going on in a horse's mind, but Charlie's capering suggested he would be glad to be away from the squealing pigs which always upset him and from the smoky tinkers who kept opening his mouth and inspecting his teeth as if he was for sale, although he should have no fear that Jack would ever sell him, especially to the tinkers, or perhaps he was looking forward to a long drink of cold water from the trough and a roll in the turf mould before being rubbed down and stabled for the night by his young master, the man who kept him fed and shod, and his harness goose-greased and limber. On the other hand, perhaps he was recalling the day when he had fallen and injured a fetlock at Milltown races and they were getting ready to shoot him when Jack came on the scene, and how Jack had pleaded, how Jack had got to his way, how Jack had mended the fetlock and slept in his stable every night until he was fully recovered. Or perhaps he was just happy, like humans are sometimes happy.

Later, when Charlie was rubbed down and stabled, Eileen waited patiently until Jack had finished his dinner to hear the news. "I have thirty quid in my pocket for you," he went on, after explaining the highlights of the morning, his speech slightly slurred. "And, I know where there's a bull calf for sale – I'll pop over there tomorrow and take a peep."

"I suppose I have no need to ask if ye had a good day in town, because I can see by your gimp that you're mait galore [well on it]," said Eileen, scowling her displeasure. "You can never come home, can you? – not while you have a shilling in your pocket, and why have I got this feeling that you got more for the pigs than you told me, otherwise how could you afford to get into such a state? – and I don't want to hear any bullshite about the jobbers buying all the drink either," she ran on, her nagging falling more on deaf ears as Jack closed his eyes and allowed his head to slump forward.

Chapter 7

In the weeks following his meeting with O'Hara, Jack steered clear of the Phoenix or any other place where he might accidentally bump into Mary, and spent his Sunday nights at the pictures or in Grogan's with Tim. At first two years didn't seem so long to wait, but as the days went by, with no improvement in his prospects, he was beginning to have doubts.

"What d'you think, Tim – am I a fool?" he asked, one Sunday night in Grogan's as they sat on high stools in their regular corner.

"No – I don't think you're a fool, but you have a mountain to climb and not enough time to climb it," returned Tim, somewhat hesitantly, as if he was reluctant to be drawn out.

"How d'you mean?"

"It's none of my business, and I don't want to fall out with you over it, but if you must know, I think you're eatin' your heart out for nothin'."

"Go on, Tim – tell me. Tell me honestly what you think of the situation and I'll thank you for it," urged Jack. "No pulling punches – the straight truth."

"All right, if that's the way you want it," replied Tim, grimacing, as though he was going against his better judgement. "First of all take Mary – if you really believe she'll come runnin' with open arms when the two years are up, and ye'll get married and live happily ever after, ask yourself why the long wait – why not now, and the two o' ye can run off to England together, because England is your only chance. If you think it's not, just name one person of our station who ever married into that clique? Even Bull Paisley, who came up from nothin', can never be one o' them, and the only reason they socialise with him is because he has money. So you see, the odds are stacked against you."

"But when I get my pig-farm going, it'll be different."

"Let's face it; pigs'll be sprouting wings before you even get off the ground."

"Say, for instance, I went to England for a couple o' years, I might earn enough to start me off. I heard the lads saying there's piecework –"

"Stop, Jack!" interjected Tim. "You should know yourself that once you step on board the train at Castleford station there'll be no comin' back, no more than there was for the thousands who left with the same idea. Now my advice to you is, see Mary, and ask her to run away with you. The money you're savin' for the poker game'll get you to London, and then both o' ye can get jobs and start fresh from there – others have done it. If she loves you, she'll go, and if she doesn't, she won't – it's as simple as that."

The bald truth in Tim's counselling drove a knife into the heart of the little optimism Jack had left, but as always when he heard the truth, no matter how unpalatable, basic honesty forced him to accept it as the truth. "I suppose you're right, Tim," he sighed. "Damned if I do and damned if I don't."

"On the other hand, you could get over her, because she's not for you, and love makes us blind even to what we can see," said Tim. "Look at me – all them bullock notions I had about Sadie Doyle came to nothin', and I got over it. So, cheer up – it's not the end o' the world. I had a bit o' luck today at the pitch-and-toss school and we'll have a few for the road – my treat. Grogan looks as if he's in the mood to do a bit of after hours."

It was two in the morning when Grogan called time, and when Jack reached home, he was puzzled when he saw lamplight still showing in the kitchen window. Anxious in case anything had happened to Eileen he hurried through the door, only to find her sitting morosely in her armchair, staring into the dying embers of the fire. "What's wrong – don't tell me the radio packed in and you missed the top twenty?" he remarked jokingly, trying to kindle a little cheer. "Anyway, 'SECRET LOVE' is still number one – I heard it in Grogan's."

Eileen mumbled something incoherent under her breath, and when Jack asked again, she raised her head, saying: "I'm afraid sometimes here on my own if any o' the neighbours don't call. You're never here – always off gallivanting. Anybody could break in."

"Break in, is it – you mean a thief?" interjected Jack. "That should be the least o' your worries. Anyway, if someone broke in, you could give him a hand searching – he might know where to look. You never can tell, he might find something – gold maybe, hidden here years ago by some kindly leprechaun. Who knows what treasure we might be sitting on, and then ye could split it fifty-fifty. Break in – if anyone broke in, they'd probably leave something when they see how hard up we are."

"Oh, shut up, you! You don't care –"

"Who frightened you?" Jack cut in, sensing that there was more to the matter than her everyday gloom. "Tell me!"

"I was sitting here in the armchair on my own – Murt never came tonight – no one comes on Sunday nights any more – when I heard a car pulling up outside. The headlights lit up the whole kitchen, and then I heard these heavy footsteps. Frightened out o' my life, I was – I was so frightened that I forgot to run up and put the bolt on the door."

"Who was it?" interjected Jack, his impatience overriding his concern.

"Mike Cullinane."

"What did he want?" snapped Jack, immediately sensing the purpose of the visit, the very idea igniting the touchpaper to his temper. "What did Cullinane want?" he asked again, and there was no compromise in his tone – he wanted to know.

Eileen looked as if she regretted having mentioned the matter. "He just wanted to know how we were getting along. He was a friend of mother's years ago, and he thought you might be gone to England, and he said if I ever needed help –"

"Needed help!" Jack cut in. "What kind o' help – and what did he want in return?"

"He said if you ever went to England to let him know and he'd look after things. He said he looked after things when Father ran away. He was very nice about it."

"Nice, is it – Cullinane nice!" interjected Jack. "He's too nice, if you ask me. And I don't want that conniving bastard calling here behind my back with his sugar talk. Him – and he up at the rails every Sunday morning taking Communion, and giving money to priests so that his name'll be read out from the pulpit: 'Mister Michael Cullinane; twenty guineas' – all that kind o' shite. Outward show – that's all it is. It'd be more in his line if he gave some decent grub to them two young lads he took out o' the industrial school and forgot his sham piety. Half-starved they are, and he has them out working on the land from morning till night without a bite in their little stomachs, poor craithers – beats them too, so he does, if they as much as grumble. Two city lads is all they are, and they know as much about farming as a pig knows about a holiday. All one o' them done was steal a jar o' sweets and the black-baby box out of a shop, and for that he got five years in the industrial school."

"I don't believe it," countered Eileen. "The priests see to it that they're well looked after."

"You don't believe it!" snapped Jack. "You're just like everyone else in the country – you'd never see anything if it wasn't written in letters a foot high and stuck under your nose – 'oh, this couldn't happen in Catholic Ireland', and all that bullshite – bah," he went on, and unable to contain himself he felt like grabbing Eileen by the throat and shaking her until she woke up to the wrongs being done to children under the guise of philanthropy. "Everyone is being led to believe that the industrial schools are something like they saw in the film *Boys' Town* – Father Flanagan working his fingers to the bone for his delinquent children, the epitome of what a priest should be, and what's more, they want to believe it, yourself included. But can you imagine any of our priests doing Father Flanagan on it? – doing without themselves and giving it to the orphans and waifs. There'll be white blackbirds out when you see the day. Then, if any o' them run away, the cops bring them back and they get another hiding. They don't deserve that, the poor craithers, no matter what they've done. I've a good mind to give Cullinane a few skelps to straighten him out, but if I did, he'd probably have the law on me – and the priests."

Jack felt it would be a complete waste of breath trying to convince Eileen that Cullinane was an out-and-out lecher who preyed on the recently widowed and on gullible single girls with pregnancy problems, by first offering them a lifeline and then withdrawing it if sexual favours weren't forthcoming. His true character was cleverly concealed behind a benign front, and what Jimmy Murphy procured by charm and good looks, Cullinane achieved by cunning, duplicity, and even blackmail. However, whether it was nature striking a balance or divine disapproval of his depravity, it was calling him to account through the person of Trevor, his idiot son, who was costing him a fortune buying him out of bogus paternity claims, besides having to contend with the ignominy of his own wife's suicide.

Earlier Jack had sensed that there had been something going on between his mother and Cullinane, a suspicion that was further fuelled by a conversation he had overheard one Saturday night in the Royal Hotel. Although the bar was thronged and noisy, in one of those odd silences that sometimes falls on a crowd he had heard Eileen's name mentioned and, straining his ears, he picked up: 'Cullinane had the mother, now he's after the daughter – it'll be something for him to boast about, having the mother and the daughter –.' Once he had caught the gist of the conversation he supplied the rest from his subconscious, as one picks up the striking of a clock in the middle with only the rhythm of the first uncounted strokes lingering in the mind. At first he had dismissed the conversation as tattle, for he rarely took for granted what he heard about other people, as most gossip, he had found, was malicious or irresponsible and based on the most fragile of rumours. Although now, as it all came back to him, he looked across at Eileen and, feeling suddenly apprehensive, he waited for her to challenge his words.

Whatever Eileen was about to say, she left unsaid, and Jack, taking her silence for agreement, rounded off: "The next time Cullinane calls and I'm not here, bang the door in his face. I know we're poor, and it's only a few inches of wall and a roof that's keeping us from being tinkers, but we have our pride and we'll manage somehow. Even if we haven't the deeds to the place, we can still claim squatter's rights, but if we do, it'll mean I won't be able to draw the dole every week – as little and all as it is. So, for the time being I think we should leave bad enough alone until we see which way the cat jumps."

Next morning, when Jack appeared in the kitchen, Eileen was on her knees on the hearth trying to get a blaze going, smoke blundering everywhere but up the chimney. "I slept it out this morning," she explained, somewhat apologetically, rubbing her red-rimmed eyes. "I never got a wink at all last night whatever the matter was."

Although Eileen reigned unchallenged in the kitchen Jack grabbed the tongs. "Leave it to me," he said, and immediately pulled away the smouldering turf from the few small red coals. Then, laying some strips of newspaper on the coals, he fanned them with a piece of cardboard until they burst into flame. One by one he added some small *ciarawns* and, when he had a healthy blaze going, only then did he add the larger sods. "That's the way it's done," he said, smiling omnisciently, drawing her attention to the thin tendrils of flame creeping through the fresh turf.

Whatever had caused Eileen's sleepless night Jack scarcely gave it a thought beyond women's problems. It never occurred to him that the same enigmas from the past might be torturing her too, but whereas he could dismiss and resurrect them as he pleased, in Eileen's mind they stayed to roost, for Cullinane's unexpected appearance in the guise of the Good Samaritan had dispelled the last of her doubts as to his relationship with her mother. Years ago, even though she was suspicious, she had dismissed his frequent visits as neighbourly goodwill, notwithstanding the coincidence that he always happened to be leaving just as she was returning from school, a grin on his face like a cat after cream. Her mother, flushed and guilty looking, would thank him for calling, and for days afterwards there would be plenty of the best to eat: ham and fresh bread, cake and sweets. Now these visits were taking on a new meaning, a hideous meaning.

At the time, though it was as clear as crystal, she had turned a blind eye on it, believing only what she wanted to believe. But now, as her mind began to delve, she recalled an afternoon in her childhood when she had caught her mother and Father Fitzpatrick in a passionate embrace, which gave substance to the snide remarks of her classmates: 'Ye'll all surely go to heaven in yeer house with the priest calling every day'. Although time had long since weaned her thoughts from those memories Cullinane's visit resurrected them with sickening clarity, reminding her of her vulnerability if Jack ever emigrated.

There was something too about her mother's death that niggled, something bothersome, like a pebble in the shoe, not really severe but a constant source of discomfort. On that fateful night her mother had retired at the usual hour, and next morning when she failed to appear, she tapped lightly on her bedroom door. When there was no answer, she peeped in and, panic-stricken when she saw the blood, she dashed off to Moore's, returning with Mick, and Maggie, his wife. Taking the situation in hand the Moores had railed her off to Granny Mulhaire's and, for some days afterwards there was nothing but evasive answers until time gradually eased the subject into obscurity. Now, as more of life's realities unfolded, she was almost certain that her mother had died trying to terminate a pregnancy, and she didn't need any divine enlightenment to figure out who was responsible. But, as yet, she had no proof.

It now seemed that Jack had sensed Cullinane's intent and his nature was in revolt, and she shuddered to think of his reaction if he knew the full story, or perhaps he did. He had certainly hit the nail on the head when he hinted that he wasn't calling for the good of her health, and for the first time in her life she could understand her mother's plight – the living nightmare of insecurity and the likes of Cullinane taking carnal advantage of it.

Tall, erect, his silver-grey hair neatly groomed and glistening with brilliantine, his brown mohair suit and brocade waistcoat set off to perfection by a criss-crossing of gold chains and fobs, she had to admit that Cullinane looked trim for a man pushing fifty. Still, for all his outward show of concern, his lecherous eyes had made her shiver as they raked her from neck to ankle, as if he was visualising her with her clothes off, and he had seemed disappointed that Jack was still around. He had even mentioned that she would have squatter's rights on the property if he ever emigrated, which suggested he knew about the missing title deed.

The stark reality that she could easily end up laying for Cullinane revolutionised her thinking – it still wasn't too late to catch a husband if she wasn't fussy. Years ago, her torrid affair with Jimmy Murphy had made gossip headlines, and their frequent trips down Poke Lane had come under the peeping eyes of the younger generation which, although now grown-up, would remember her lost virtue. In their eyes she would always be a 'good thing', someone to take down Poke Lane, but not someone to marry.

Poke Lane, long, narrow and winding, its eyesore of derelict houses, stables and old warehouses, interspaced by vacant lots for parking, lay like a crooked finger at the back of Castleford's main street, and it presented as great a contrast as the front of a picture does to the back. During the day it was quiet, save for the deliveries to the shops that backed on to it, but at night its darkness came alive with the whispering of fingers on nylon, sighs of surrender, grunts of satisfaction, and the bouncing of car springs as nature took its course, earthy sounds which were punctuated from time to time by the slashing of piss against the wall and the odd fanfare of flatulent reports as drunks relieved themselves on their way home from the public houses.

Unwillingly she recalled her one and only affair, and the lustful ending of each date: pinned against the wall, her skirt hoisted up above her waist, her knickers around her ankles, her thighs apart, her knees trembling, Murphy in a half crouch, grasping her bare buttocks, his rugged and relentless thrusts, her brief moment of ecstasy, and finally, his quicker shorter strokes that brought an abrupt halt to his gallop, which was immediately followed by the quick buttoning of his flies and his haste to be away once he had got what he wanted. No matter how often she swore to the contrary, it had always happened again, as if it was addictive, and now, as desire stirred in her disappointed body, she wondered if 'once lost, always lost' was true of chastity.

Putting all thoughts of Poke Lane and lost chastity from her mind Eileen looked to her brother, as if for reassurance, saying: "I keep worrying about the future, Jack – d'you think we'll manage?"

When he saw the woebegone look on his sister's face, Jack wrapped a comforting arm about her shoulders. "Of course we'll manage, you silly ould *cheolawn*," he said, tenderness in his tone. "That is, if you shake a leg and get my breakfast – there's so much work to do this time o' the year."

It seemed that Jack's encouragement was the tonic Eileen needed, for in the following days she became noticeably dress conscious, spending every spare moment altering her old dresses and mending her frilly bits. On Saturday afternoon, when she returned from Castleford, her hair was permed and she had a brown paper parcel under her arm.

Jack eyed the transformation and parcel speculatively. "If my thinking is on the right lines, I'll bet a shilling that's a new coat you've got there. I know I said to tidy yourself up a bit, but this beats Banagher – the extravagance of it all, and the Stations just round the corner," he tut-tutted, feigning a frown of disapproval as Eileen opened the parcel and paraded up and down the kitchen exhibiting her purchase – a fashionable three-quarter-length beige coat. "That must've cost you a pretty penny."

"Twelve pounds, seventeen and sixpence, to be exact," returned Eileen, tossing her head haughtily. "It's about time I had something new. Anyway, I've been putting a penny under the bag o' flour out of the egg money, so the money is all my own."

"No wonder you were afraid someone might break in with all that money in the house. Still, fine feathers don't make fine birds," said Jack, a derisive ring in his tone. "But it's not the clothes really – it's the peg they're hanging on that counts. See me in my old –"

Jack's dialogue was cut short when Eileen reached for the tongs, making as if she might strike him with it, and for the first time in ages they both laughed heartily together.

On Sunday night Jack had another surprise when Eileen appeared in her bedroom doorway in the bright-blue dress she had altered and pressed the night before. Although the dress fitted perfectly at the waist and shoulders her fairly ample rump kept pushing it out at the back so that it was riding up, and her midriff was so tightly girdled that her bosom stuck out like the prow of a ship. Raising an eyebrow ever so slightly she cast a tentative glance at Jack. "Why don't you say something, or has the cat got your tongue?" she asked, making a quick half-turn which sent the skirt part of the dress billowing. "I'm off to the Phoenix tonight, and it's your turn to stay home and keep the cat company."

Although Eileen's new image was a big improvement and he was pleased to see her in such high spirits Jack couldn't let the matter go without its full measure of raillery. "A bit of advice for you now before you go," he said, pulling a serious face. "When you get to the Phoenix, look for the plainest woman in the hall and stand beside her. This way you'll stand out like a Grecian vase beside a pisspot, and if some man asks to leave you home, be careful, because it's the creaky gate that always gets oiled."

Instead of taking up the gauntlet, as Jack had hoped, Eileen just stared blandly into the mirror, putting the finishing touches to her make-up as if she hadn't heard.

Early June was the most pleasant time of the year for working in the bog, which was in full bloom, its raiment of new heather rippling resplendently in endless waves to the horizon like a green and purple sea. In the background lay the weathered stone walls of Knockrush and its huddle of houses, some slated, some whitewashed and thatched, peeping out through the foliage, smoke spiralling almost perpendicularly from the chimneys, while overhead in a vast dome of blue sky, clouds drifted lazily like giant bolls of cotton. It was a busy, yet peaceful scene of families saving the turf for the winter fires, the children playing hide-and-seek in the heather making a picnic of it all and, as if to add melody to their happy chatter, a lark sometimes soared, treating them to a chorus from its mellifluous repertoire. Later, as the long day drew to a close and the black bog-water almost seemed of fiercer flame than the sunset it mirrored, a Catty Odha, its wings outstretched, would rise from its nest and hover lazily, waiting to swoop down and carry away to its nest any little children who hadn't weighted down their pockets with stones, or so they had been frightened into believing.

The bogland's solitude went a long way in easing the frustration that was bottling up Jack's heart, and when the day's work was done, he would sit awhile watching the sunset until a shadowy dimness crept over the land and the stillness of rural twilight came down around him as calming as a prayer. The tranquillity had the effect of opening the eyes of his mind, although the reality it unveiled was unsettling, mainly the inequality of the system to which he was hopelessly shackled. It was a typical case of the many bowing without question to the will of the few who had money and power, a discontented coterie which couldn't enjoy comfortably what God had given them, because they could see and covet something which He had not given them and, with the country locked in endless recession, they were taking ruthless advantage of the situation, paying such paltry wages that it fell just short of serfdom. It seemed to undo everything that Christ had preached, whereas by giving a little here and taking a little there, rich and poor could live together in more harmony. However, it was the ones who were prepared to knuckle down and doff their caps who were encouraged to stay behind in the face of mass-emigration, never the defiant, like Digger Nolan, his boyhood friend.

Digger was a rebel against authority, and in their schooldays Jack had shared a desk with him. "It's like being on a train bound for nowhere," he had once said, "school every day to have the mind filled with useless information about this world, and church every Sunday to have the mind filled with useless information about the next." However, Digger had escaped from the torture chamber, as he called it, when he was thirteen by means of a crafty alteration to his birth certificate, and in the following summer they both found work washing bottles in Shaw's mineral-water factory, ploughing their first furrows in the workaday world of Castleford for a shilling an hour. True to form, Digger was forever at loggerheads with the management, although two years later, when they joined the FCA, he pulled in his horns – a little.

FORSA COSANTA AITUIL, Gaelic for Local Defence Force, was in reality a part-time army. Members were obliged to attend parade one night a week at the local hall, and a field day once a month on a Sunday. Every year there was collective training for a fortnight at a regular army barracks, for which army wages were paid, plus an added gratuity for all-the-year-round attendance. A free uniform and boots were issued annually which contributed enormously to its derogatory nickname, the Free Clothes Association, for without the boots, many of Castleford's young men would be walking around unshod.

A twinge of nostalgia prickled Jack's reverie as he recalled a memorable St Patrick's Day when both he and Digger had been chosen to take part in the parade and, with tricolours and flags of maroon-and-white projecting from upstairs windows flapping in the wind above the thronged pavements, they marched with a jaunty step down Castleford's main street to the vibrant strains of THE LOW-BACK'D CAR. As the scene rose again to his memory, he began to hum, the words springing to his lips like flame to kindling.

As one memory evoked another he relived his first trip to the army camp at Finner, which was ideally situated near the seaside resort of Bundoran, a trip that would forever be a milestone in his life's cycle. As money was in short supply, every evening Digger organised a pontoon school in the billet and, with himself as banker, he always came out ahead. At the dance, to further his chances with his trendy dance partners, he posed as a holidaymaker staying at the fashionable Great Northern Hotel, and to lend credibility to his tale of affluence he invited some of the doubters to dine with him there, his fingers crossed in case they called his bluff.

His reminiscence carried him back to the Astoria, Bundoran's famed ballroom where, under its bright lights, he had his first taste of romance. As the night was humid, the roofs on both wings of the hall were rolled back to allow the sea breeze to circulate and refresh the dancers and, casting his eyes around, he noticed a tall slender girl standing on the balcony stairs. There was something clean and fresh about her that held his interest, and before the pessimistic side of his nature had a chance to talk him out of it he crossed the floor and asked her to dance. The music was for a foxtrot, and while they were picking their steps to the centre of the floor, it was only then he noticed the sticking plaster on the bridge of her nose. Tongue-tied with embarrassment he had ignored it and concentrated on his steps in case he tread on her toes.

"Are you not inquisitive?" the lady had asked, in a huff of feigned indignation. "You're the only man here tonight who hasn't asked me what's happened to my nose – if you were a cat, at least it wouldn't be curiosity that'd cause your death."

You can meet a woman every day of the week and forget her, and then one comes along you see just once and you immediately know you'll remember her all the days of your life. Casting his mind back he recalled having blushed when the lady smiled at his discomfiture, and yet, from that moment on, as if by magic, his reserve crumbled, and life took on a whole new meaning. Although she had no more than the prettiness of youth Dympna Whyte possessed all the natural qualities of dignity and deportment that are admirable in women, and never as artful as Digger at telling lies, he blurted out his story. Now, as he watched the last rays of the sun disappearing below the rim of the world, he relived the thrill of their first kiss, a kiss that dispelled all Digger's artifices like chaff in the wind on threshing day.

During the following days their friendship blossomed into a tender romance, the type of romance associated with adolescence, and yet, one to treasure, one of the jewels of life that no thief, however cute, could ever steal, a short period in growing up when idealism overwhelms reality, when fulfilment can be attained by a kiss or an embrace, or by dancing cheek to cheek, with none of the prurience that creeps into later life. The more he reflected, the more vivid the memory became until the heather around him faded and he was lying in the shade of a leafy tree staring into eyes which held the still gleam of a forest pool in winter when brown leaves shine up through quiet water, and kissing tender lips that contained all the sweetness and innocence of girlhood.

It was just a brief affair, one of those bright joys of youth when love is all strange and new, when dreams have not yet got the wings to fly beyond the days and weeks, and the space from summer to summer seems measureless. Still, it had ended with all the heartaches when the Cinderella hour finally came, and though they were living scarcely a hundred miles apart, it might as well have been a million. But young hearts heal fast, and now that his first romance was just another memory to cherish, his thoughts sometimes lingered on the simple lyrics of a sentimental ballad *THE SPECIAL YEARS*.

On the following summer, when he returned to Bundoran, expecting to recapture the enchantment of the previous year, he came home a sadder and wiser man in the knowledge that romance is something that flashes across the sky like a shooting star, all sparkle for a moment and quickly gone.

Meanwhile, the everyday drudgery of washing bottles had continued until he was eighteen. Then, it was the sack, as it was compulsory for the company to pay adult rates, and rather than pay higher wages it was management policy to recruit among the younger generation. Around Castleford jobs were hard to come by, and walking to the railway station with Digger was the loneliest morning of his life. The platform had been crowded with expatriates returning after the Christmas holiday, a scattering of first-timers conspicuous among them, and the atmosphere was so solemn that it could easily have been a troop train bound for the front. After the handshake Digger reluctantly accepted the pound note which he had surreptitiously tried to slip into his top pocket and, with nostalgic tears burning their eyes and the frosty wind swirling the steam from the engine about their legs, they had stood staring at each other, until the final shrill whistle blast had sent Digger scrambling aboard.

Digger never returned after a few months as he had promised, although a scribbled letter with two pounds enclosed arrived soon afterwards from an address in Birmingham. 'A pound interest', the letter had said, 'and see you for Galway races', was its last line, and though he had written and thanked Digger, he hadn't heard from him since.

As the long days chased one another into longer days, the turf-cutting season came to a close, and when Jack searched for other work, he came against the old stumbling block – knowing someone, someone with influence, one of the clique who could sweep aside the red tape with a sly wink or back-scratch. Although the refusals were cordial the message was plainly written on the faces of every prospective employer, from factory managers to council gangers – why don't you piss off to England; you should know there's nothing for you around here and, if hypocritical smiles were gold sovereigns, there would be no need to work at all.

It was strange that no one ever mentioned America. It was always England, a stamping ground of the Devil where cunning evil lurked in every corner of its smoky and uncongenial environs, a place where souls were lost and corruption and debauchery were the coins of the realm. Two wars had only gone halfway in paying her back for her past evildoing, and presently she was in her last throes, living on her hump, her undernourished population reduced to eating fish and chips.

Still, it was expedient for the politicians to have a devil to blame for their failings, and so a new demon was added to the ranks of Beelzebub – England. It was used profusely in schools to frighten indolent pupils into making greater efforts in their studies, otherwise start preparing for a permanent trip to that Hades of cloven hooves across the Irish Sea. In the law courts, judges used it as a type of remission of sentence if the offenders pledged their immediate departure for her adulterous climes and, as a result, the disgruntled unemployed, radicals, intellectual dissidents, the dishonoured, men leaving the priesthood or the monks, women leaving the nuns, pregnant single girls, unrequited lovers, or anyone running from the law or shotgun weddings, sought refuge there – depart from me, ye cursed!

It was enough to make Jack wonder if the same system would prevail in the next life, or would the good still suffer and the wicked prosper, or was it all a sham about the camel and the eye of the needle just to keep the Church coffers brimming? Would it be the rich again in the pound seats and the poor fighting for the crumbs that fell from their tables? – for, contrary to the teaching of Christ, the Church's interpretation of the Gospel suggested there would be no 'come ye blessed of My Father, possess the kingdom prepared for you' for anyone who hadn't contributed generously to the support of their pastors.

Nevertheless, he drudged on, and when the portion of his turf he had for sale was dry, he shifted it to the roadside with his donkey and cart for collection. Earlier in the month he had struck a deal with Killoran, the baker, for its purchase, and on the strength of the sale he had a suit making, which he was promised would be ready for Galway races.

Chapter 8

The Galway racing festival was by far the most popular annual event on the local sporting calendar, and Jack wasn't on his own in putting a penny under the bag of flour for its enjoyment. All roads led to Galway and, as bumping into Mary O'Hara there was almost certainly on the cards, he felt that the occasion warranted a dispensation from their commitment. He had so much to say to her, lines that he had rehearsed over the weeks, which had earlier died on his lips in the face of the nightmare of being turned down. Perhaps, if she knew that he loved her, it would make their term in purgatory all the more bearable, and love always found a way, in spite of old O'Hara's claim to the contrary.

As the countdown to the races began, every day the one o'clock train into Castleford was crowded with expatriates returning for their annual holidays, as most of the factories in the Midlands and Northwest England where many of them were employed closed down for the last week in July and the first week in August. Although he was disappointed that Digger Nolan wasn't among them Jack was pleased to see so many old friends, some of whom he had almost forgotten. There was a cavalier air about his exiled brethren that appealed to his easygoing nature, and throughout their stay the public houses in and around Castleford were humming with their free-spending presence.

Still, for all the expatriates' generosity, envy and sour grapes found a home in the hearts of the people who were benefiting most from their open wallets, and a fly on the wall of their narrow minds might discern: 'It's not fair – they should come back with their heels bare the same way as they left, and it's hard to believe their money came honestly – ah, but here's the rub – they squander all they have and go back broke – back to the fish and chips, and maybe their new clothes were bought just for show on the Kathleen Mavourneen system'. Although this ill will was cannily concealed behind two-faced smiles and greetings it perhaps helped to justify their own choice of knuckling under the autocracy of Church and State, a semi-feudal system that would always keep the proletariat poor and indoctrinated.

When the morning of the big event dawned, the golden ball of the sun pushing its august head above the background hills was a good omen for a scorching day and, making his preparations under his sister's watchful eye, Jack was all enterprise, silently hurrying back and forth from the kitchen to his bedroom. Finally, when he donned his new blue-and-white striped shirt and single-breasted charcoal-grey suit, he felt like singing, as if the act of dressing in new clean-smelling clothes was a baptism, an orgasm, as though he was putting on wings. The thought of wings spurred him to speed in case he missed his promised lift to Galway with Tom Reilly, Shaw's lorry driver and, whistling tunelessly, he stood back from the mirror and regarded himself with something of approval.

Taking in her brother's sartorial elegance with a somewhat cynical glance Eileen laughed sarcastically. "Never before have I seen such titivating – you have a track worn in the floor going back and forth all morning, and all for what," she scoffed. "In a few months' time the suit'll be like every other suit you've had – full of cigarette burns and porter stains, and I suppose I don't know when I'll lay eyes on you again – off gallivanting to Galway and leaving me here to do all the work."

"How right you are, my dear," returned Jack. "As for doing all the work, all you have to do is the milking, put the cat out at night, and see that you rub down Charlie – he likes to be rubbed down every day, and you won't have to worry about the tinkers calling either, because they'll all be in Galway – begging."

"Charlie – Charlie – that's all I hear, morning, noon and night. If I wasn't here, I wouldn't put it past you to bring Charlie into the house at night and stable him in the parlour. You think more of him than you do of me – your own sister."

"How right you are again, my dear, and I'll tell you why, because Charlie is just as much a part of the family as you and me – he's like a brother, like the brother I never had," countered Jack. "But mind you look after him now, and don't be taking your spite against me out on him."

"What d'you take me for – you know well I'll look after him. But tell me this, is Tim going with you?"

"No – he lost all his money at the pitch-and-toss school last Sunday. I offered him some of mine, but you know Tim – there was no way he'd take it. So, I'm off now, and I'll see you when I see you."

If Jack was ever right about anything, he was right about the tinkers, for it seemed that every tinker in Ireland had gathered in Galway, their camps squeezed tightly together, donkey-cart to donkey-cart on the grass verges on either side of the main road leading to the city, their smoky fires, rags, goats, mangy greyhounds and general pollution adding its smelly contribution to the festival.

The tinkers were seen as a blemish on Irish society, and there was much speculation as to their origin. Some said they were throwbacks of the old Tutha de Danann, a race of sorcerers who had inhabited Ireland before the arrival of the Celts. Others believed they were the descendants of the old, dispossessed Irish royalty, although the only evidence of royal blood Jack had witnessed was at Ballinasloe annual horse fair where the leaders of the different tribes fought one another with ashplants for the title of king of the tinkers, while the more enlightened were of the opinion that it was their tinsmith ancestors who had fabricated the nails that had impaled Christ when the blacksmith refused, and thus, like His crucifiers, they had been condemned to their present nomadic way of life. But whichever conjecture was true, not even an atomic bomb could stop them from converging on Galway like a plague of locusts every year for the races.

These were bonanza begging days for the shawled tinker women (the men never begged), although later, when the festivities were at a high, some of them were sure to fall foul of their drunken husbands and get a good hiding as a thank-you gesture for their importunity. But as yet, it was too early to hear the tinker women's plaintive cries: 'Hit me now will ya, and the child in me arms', resounding through the throngs. This was all in store, a grand finale, something traditional for the visitors from abroad to treasure from their holiday, for the spectacle of the tinker flailing his spouse was one of the highlights of the festival, although woe betide anyone naïve enough to interfere, as they were sure to receive a salvo of profane language from both parties in this love-hate tangle.

As there were still some hours to go before race time, Jack hopped off the lorry in the build-up of traffic on the outskirts of the city and walked the remaining distance. The streets were already beginning to throng with the inflow of racegoers and, quickly absorbing the gaiety of their mood, he made his way to Fleming's Bar, a popular hang-out for the people of Knockrush when they came to the city. There was an excursion by train from Castleford, and Mick Moore, Tom Kennedy, Michael Joyce, Peter Costello, and others from the village had arranged to meet there.

When he reached Fleming's, it was humming with a high-spirited buzz, the chatter and laughter interspersed with the whanging of banjos, fiddles and some vocal, as the twosomes and threesomes of musicians touring the bars played awhile, collected and moved on. The Knockrush crowd had commandeered a corner round two tables, and Silver Walsh on the tin whistle and Phil Reilly on the mouth-organ were either harmonising with the groups or discharging a few tunes of their own, as neighbours appeared, shook hands all round as though they hadn't met in two years instead of two days, before drifting on to sample the wares of the other public houses.

Squeezing into a seat among them Jack postponed his drifting from bar to bar until after the races, for it wouldn't do to have too much drink on board when he met Mary, and he supped sparingly, striking up a conversation with Michael Joyce and Tom Kennedy. As the morning advanced towards afternoon, the steady shuffle towards the door was a reminder that race time was approaching and, as he was about to join them, another group, two men and a young lady, appeared and struck up a medley of popular tunes.

There was something familiar about the lady rattling a tambourine and singing *STEP IT OUT MARY*. As if he should know her, or that they had met in a previous creation. Although she was nothing out of the ordinary: medium stature, blunt of feature, her sallow face scrubbed clean, her dark eyes sparkled in an entrancing way, a sparkle that was enhanced by her bouncing gypsy-black hair which kept tumbling forward on her forehead, and yet there was something about her that made him look twice. Her figure was trim and well-rounded and, as her feet tapped out the rhythm of the catchy tune, she allowed her flowery black dress to swirl and wrap, exposing her bare legs all the way up to her frilly white knickers, as if she was obeying the command of the verse.

Unwillingly Jack's eyes kept returning to her, even when Mary's more angelic image, which had the power to vanquish all others, came between them. When she finished her song, she made a round of the tables, shaking out money-pouch, and when their eyes met, hers teasing, his somewhat bewitched, for a brief moment they held each other's stares. Then, without even a backward glance, she went swiftly through the door on the heels of her musician friends, only to return almost immediately. "I'll be at the Astaire tonight," she whispered in his ear, and before Jack had a chance to reply she was gone.

Dismissing the incident as a female prank Jack joined the hurrying throngs on their way to the racecourse, amid the cacophony of hawkers selling apples and chocolate from baskets, tinkers begging, and hard-faced Dublin women, shouting: "Racecards, sixpence – racecards!"

Inside the main enclosure the hum above the milling crowd was like that of a newly-disturbed hive of bees, a buzz which was stridently pierced by the choruses of the trick-o'-the-loops, sharpers, three-card-trick men and their jolliers as they set about relieving the greedy and the gullible of their cash. Full of blarney and fake good humour they used every artifice to pull the crowd, and their gimmicky calls: "Hairy Mary from Tipperary – me pocket tinks me hand is mad," and "give the woman in the bed more porther," had as an accompaniment the drone of the fiddle, the toot of the flute, and the tinny music of the banjo.

When the bell rang for the horses to leave the parade ring for the first race, the excitement intensified as punters rushed hither and thither among the rows of bookmakers, almost knocking them off their perches in their impatience to grab the best odds, while in the background a sea of more meditative faces studied form, their glances alternating between racecards, the displays of prices, and the tick-tack men, hoping to gain enlightenment from the drifting or tumbling odds, their ears alert for any weight changes or such coming over the squeaky public-address system.

Ignoring the bookmakers Jack had two shillings each way on the tote on Reuben's Glen, one of his favourite horses for Galway, and by the time he reached the top tier of the stand the field was circling at the starting gate, waiting to be called into line. At the announcement: "They're under starter's orders," snorting and prancing the horses edged closer to the tape and a hush fell on the crowd, a silence so profound that the croaking of a corncrake in a nearby field sounded as loud as a foghorn in the mist until: "They're off," sounded and an ear-splitting cheer sent the colourful spectacle on its way.

Amid the oohs and aahs of the spectators as some of the horses fell or stumbled and recovered at the fences, the commentator described the action in his faultless diction and, as they raced uphill and swept into the straight for the final time, Jack's heart was in his mouth as Reuben's Glen snatched the lead, lost it, regained it, and held on gamely in a close finish.

The moment the horses passed the post the cheering and suspense gave way to petty grumbling and disgruntled post-mortems and, as the crowd vacated the stand and dispersed in all directions, discarded betting tickets in a hundred colours thickened on the ground, blotting out the concrete and grass like confetti at a summer wedding. Over the moon, especially when it was announced that Reuben's Glen had paid over ten-to-one for a win, Jack made straight for the bar and shuffled through the loosely-formed groups until he reached the counter, which ran the full length of the stand, and yet, as if it wasn't long enough, he found himself standing at Bull Paisley's elbow.

"Leave it there, ould stock," Paisley greeted, stretching out his right hand as far as the press of the crowd allowed. "Now why don't we let bygones be bygones, and me and you have a drink together – after all, it's race week."

This was company Jack wasn't prepared for, and too stupefied to think straight he shook the proffered hand limply, cursing himself for not being more vigilant.

"Oh, come on, Jack – don't be like that," coaxed Paisley, obviously feeling the lack of fervour in Jack's grip.

Although he despised Paisley and all he stood for Jack forced a smile. "All right, I'll have a bottle o' stout – if you insist," he agreed, somewhat hesitantly.

"Forget your bottle o' stout, Jack, and have a glass o' whiskey," pressed Paisley, his generosity belying his true nature, and when none of the barmen came immediately at the snap of his fingers, he banged the counter so violently with a fist that all the empty glasses and ashtrays near at hand leaped in the air.

"Cheers!" returned Jack, accepting the whiskey, at the same time wondering what Paisley had up his sleeve, for usually on these festive occasions he supped in the members' enclosure with the gods of Castleford, a group of wealthy businessmen who were a law unto themselves.

A smile, crooked and hard, played for a second on Paisley's thick lips, and there was a cunning gleam in his eye as he raised his glass. "God spare you the health, Jack!" he toasted. "I hope you have a bit o' luck at the horses, and I shouldn't have to mention at the dance tonight in Seapoint. But I must be off now – I've got people to meet."

When Paisley disappeared in the crowd, Jack tried to make some sense of the encounter, and when it suddenly dawned on him that he should have told him to stick his drink, as Tim Kelly would have done, the whiskey turned sour in his mouth and anger dispelled his earlier elation. It was only when he reminded himself of the winnings he had yet to collect and the prospect of meeting Mary that his good humour returned and, with Paisley's image receding to a remoter corner of his mind, he turned to the exit. He had just reached the outside when he felt a light tap on the shoulder, and when he spun round, he found himself face to face with Mike Cullinane.

There was something of refinement and delicacy in Cullinane's bearing, and though he was no more than five feet six inches in height, his slim build added a fictitious inch or so which made him almost look as tall as Jack. His sharp features and thin lips agreed well with his build, although the fine network of crow's feet creeping out from the corners of his eyes was more noticeable in the bright sunlight and showed his age. His three-piece suit of blue serge, which was padded at the shoulders and tapered at the waist, was impeccably set off by a frilled white shirt and gold watch-chain and, with his grey fedora tilted back, exposing his narrow forehead to the hairline, he looked more of a dandy than a gentleman farmer. "Why, Jack – it's so nice to see you," he greeted, putting on a smile which never reached his calculating grey eyes, and round his mouth the curved wrinkle of the hypocrite was discernible. "I called at your cottage on my round of visiting some weeks ago, but regrettably you weren't home. So I sat awhile with Eileen talking about old times. It gets lonely for her there, she was telling me. But I must say, Jack, I'm pleased to see you looking so well."

"You are in your hole – pleased to see me looking so well!" returned Jack, letting Cullinane have a full broadside of the pent-up anger which he felt he should have exploded in Paisley's face. "I think you'd be better pleased if I was over in England – and don't look so shocked – you know well what I mean, as if I didn't know the cure you'd have for Eileen's loneliness. Now, Mister Cullinane, my advice to you is, steer clear of my cottage and my sister if you know what's good for you."

"I don't know what you mean. I only called as a good neighbour should."

"You know all right! And what's more, you know that I know – that's putting it bluntly. So, as I said – keep away."

Cullinane's brows rushed together in a frown and, as his jawbones tightened, he looked as if he might explode, but somehow he managed to keep his cool. "This is a nice way to treat an old friend of the family," he said, smiling crookedly, an edge to the smile, a knife-edge that carried a warning. "Still, it's a long lane that hasn't a turning –"

Cullinane's last sentence barely reached Jack's ears, for he was already walking away, and less repressed now that he had cleared the air between them, he locked Cullinane in the same cell of his mind as Paisley and turned towards the members' enclosure.

Leaning over the rail he ran his eyes over the scattered groups standing on the lawn in front of the reserved stand, most of whom were sipping from cocktail glasses, the ladies, in hats and summer dresses, looking colourful and gay beside their more sombrely-dressed partners. Fashionably turned out in bright blue with white accessories Mary was standing in a mixed group of a dozen or so, her parents among them, and the very sight of her after so long sent tingling sensations coursing down his spine. Hoping to catch her eye he stared at her intently for several minutes, but every time she looked in his direction her gaze went through him or beyond him until he was taken by an uneasy feeling that she was purposely ignoring him.

Feeling keenly his lack of station he slipped away, collected his winnings, and returned to the parade ring. Oblivious of the hullabaloo going on around him he tried to concentrate on picking the winner of the next race, but nothing, not even his passion for horses, could dispel Mary from his mind, and he dropped back to his old habit of making excuses for her. It could only mean that she was being watched too closely by her parents to acknowledge his presence, and after repeating it over and over in his mind, as if iteration would make it more true, he was forced to face reality even though reality was agony. It would be no different in two years or twenty years unless he produced the wealth which would enable him to cross the great divide between the haves and the have-nots of the world, and even then, there was a matter of respectability. The reality persisted, and even his old charm: 'there is a path which no fowl knoweth, and which the eye of the vulture hath not seen', never sounded more pathetic in the light of the almost insurmountable obstacles facing him.

Shaking himself out of his stupor he wandered aimlessly among the stalls, bumping into old friends and absently returning their greetings, until he found himself back again at the members' enclosure, gazing over the rail, as if some magnetic force had drawn him there. Mary was standing at a distance from her group talking to Gerald Cronin, and again he felt certain she was aware of his presence and was adding to his torment by making up to Cronin, running her eyes over him and picking imaginary bits of fluff from his jacket. As jealousy struggled with his love, something in his stomach curled up in a ball and wouldn't loosen, and like all lovers sensing a rival he tried to put all the blame on Cronin, shutting his eyes to everything good in the man and looking only for the bad. Still, somewhere deep down in the recesses of his soul, the seeds of despair were taking root, and the more he looked, the more despondent he became, and at the first sign of movement towards the gates as the horses paraded for the last race he turned away.

On the long walk back to the city his masculine vanity wouldn't allow him to believe that Mary had purposely ignored him, and he searched for a straw to cling to in his promise to her father. Perhaps by purposely ignoring him she was sticking rigidly to her part of the bargain, otherwise if it was over between them, she would have let him know and, allowing his love to overrule his common sense, he fell into the oldest conviction in the world – that the girl you love can't possibly be anything but honest and faithful.

When he reached the outskirts of the city, he booked into one of the modest bed and breakfast places which opened for race week and, after dining lavishly in the Imperial Hotel, he returned to Fleming's Bar, only to find that most of the Knockrush crowd had already left to catch the train, while those left behind were too drunk to hold coherent conversation. Missing Tim's company he moved from bar to bar, searching for what, he did not know, perhaps society of his own age and station, and even the whiskey he knocked back liberally failed to bring its usual cheer. As darkness descended, he joined the crowds converging on the funfair in Eyre Square, which was coming alive beneath its looping festoons of coloured lighting, the sparks from the bumpers shooting out into the night like galaxies of twinkling stars, while the overhead speakers blared out, *THERE'S A PAWNSHOP ON THE CORNER*, and other popular hits above the din of the barkers and the shrill screams coming from the swish-cars and the other breathtaking rides.

Apart from backing a winner he was having a lousy day, first Paisley, then Cullinane, and finally Mary and, as he wandered about the funfair trying his luck at roulette and pongo, his thoughts kept returning to the bewitching lady who had deliberately forecast her whereabouts for later that night. There was a ceilidh at the Astaire, and though it wasn't as fashionable as Seapoint or the Hangar, its Salthill counterparts, something kept prompting him to go there, if only to test the strength of the lady's invitation. The alternative was Seapoint – Mary was sure to be at Seapoint, but to see her making up to Cronin again would be too much for his aching heart to bear. Finally, taking up the gauntlet against the downbeat side of his nature, he turned his feet in the direction of the

Astaire which, for all its high-profile name, was no more than a converted loft in Galway's dockland.

When Jack entered, a half-set was under way and, mingling with the onlookers, it took him a minute or two to single out the dark-eyed lady in the four lines of couples beating out the rhythm of the, *BIRD IN THE BUSH*, a popular reel, on the maple floor, as they advanced towards one another, retreated, whirled and made arches of their arms. She was attractively turned out in a dress of black and maroon quarters, and her hair, which she had earlier allowed to tumble over her forehead, was neatly pinned and held together at the back by a maroon ribbon. It was quite obvious that she had seen him, for she kept tossing her head and looking everywhere but in his direction and purposely losing control of her dress's movements, allowing the skirt part to float up almost to her waistline. The fleeting glimpses he caught of her bare thighs above her nylon-tops sent desire coursing through his body, overpowering all other emotions, even the loyalty he felt he owed to Mary, and even under the threat of being turned into a pillar of salt he doubted that he could have torn his eyes away.

When the music stopped, without as much as a glance in Jack's direction, the lady flitted to the cloakroom, timing her return just as the compere was announcing: "Take your partners for an old-time waltz."

Second guessing her, Jack was waiting to pounce, and she came straight to his arms, a mischievous twinkle in her eyes, her lips pouting in feigned indignation. "What kept you?" she asked, looking him straight in the eye, impudently, yet searchingly. "Was it so hard to tear your mind away from the girl you think you're going to marry someday?"

The lady's intuition froze any retort that might have sprung to Jack's lips, and it took a few moments deliberation to take stock of her words, wondering if she had guessed he was in love, or was she possessed by some type of gypsy clairvoyance?

When Jack failed to reply, the lady moved intimately closer and whispered in his ear: "Talk to me – I'm not a witch."

"I think you are – I think you put the evil eye on me today with your singing, otherwise why am I here? So, let's buzz off after this dance."

"But I don't even know your name."

"That makes us even – I don't know your name either."

"Guess?"

"Veronica," said Jack, as she bore a slight resemblance to Veronica Cassidy, a singer he had once dated from McFadden's travelling show, although he was expecting anything but a truthful answer.

"Bull's-eye – right with the first guess," she laughed, just as Jack had anticipated, and when the music stopped, she disappeared in the dispersing crowd and returned some minutes later, a black stole draped across her arm. "Where to – whatever your name is?"

Now that she had called his bluff, Jack was unsure of his next move and, as she was already on her way to the exit, he had no choice but to follow her. When they reached the street, he introduced himself. "I'm Jack Daly, for what it's worth," he said. "So, where do we go from here – Veronica?"

"Home!"

"Where's home?"

"Home is where you find it," she returned and, taking the cue, Jack set off in the direction of Salthill, certain that if there was to be any deviation she would let him know.

There was something enchanting about the night, as if some fairy godmother had waved her magic wand, for the dockland's warehouses, which always appeared stark and sinister, seemed more mellow in the moonlight, and the water lapping against the quay wall had lost its lonesome hush. Arms about each other's waists they continued over Wolfe Tone Bridge and along Grattan Road, as though they were following a predestined path or a wayward star, and the banter passing between them, which was full of pointed remarks and repartee, never once bordered on the personal.

On and on they strolled, asking no questions of the past or future, but content with the little joy of the living present, until they reached Seapoint, which was all lit up like a pleasure cruiser at anchor, its neon lighting making rainbows on the ocean, the waves and waves of music blaring through its open top windows following one another into infinity. Stopping for a few minutes to listen they carried on past the Lazy Wall, Rockbarton and the Hangar, until they reached the end of the promenade where the terrain opened out into a vast expanse of silver strand and a high headland in the distance raised a rugged head which, in the moonlight, looked like a great crouching animal tethered to the shore.

Setting off in its direction they were out of breath when they reached the summit where a mossy hollow, which was heaven sent for the purpose Jack had in mind, beckoned invitingly. From the moment they kissed and lay on the ground he knew that there would be no inhibition, no virginal pretences peculiar to most women, not even the timeworn cliché: 'you don't think I'm that kind of girl'. His wandering hands soon found and fondled the soft white flesh that had earlier provoked him, and he continued probing and loosening until all that lay between him and a trip to paradise was a pair of frilly white knickers. While he was removing the last obstacle, a cascading torrent of desire swept through his body and, with only the Devil to guide them, together they plunged into the fiery pleasures of the flesh.

Time and again they made light of the sixth commandment, the never-ending rhythm defying nature itself, while the music floating out from the dance hall added an air of romanticism to their ecstasy. Rapt in a half-sleeping, half-waking dream, it seemed that some celestial being was giving them a premature taste of heaven, or the Devil was seeking their souls, and if Jack had even the slightest inkling that there was a greater reward in heaven, he would willingly spend the rest of his days in sackcloth and ashes.

They were still in the throes of passion when dawn stripped the curtains on the earthy scene, and a lone herring gull screaming overhead was the only living creature bearing witness of their sinfulness as they continued relentlessly, perhaps like the two in the Garden of Eden. Finally, as the new day began to manifest itself, the lady propped herself up on an elbow and ran her fingers through Jack's hair. Kissing him lightly on the cheek, she whispered in his ear: "I think we'll both remember this night as long as we live, and if we don't pursue it, we'll always have it – this way we'll always have each other."

Jack knew exactly what she meant – there was no need of endearments and, arms linked, they retraced their steps of earlier, oblivious of the stares they were attracting from both night owls and early risers, until they reached Eyre Square. In the shadows near Padraig O'Connaire's memorial they stood silently facing each other for a timeless moment, lost for the words that would surely have said: 'why couldn't it have gone on and on forever and ever?' Although the tenderness in the lady's farewell kiss was more eloquent than any words she might have spoken.

Postponing for as long as possible the inevitable parting, finally the lady turned towards the docks, Jack's eyes following in her wake. When she reached the corner of a shadowy street, she stopped in a glow of light and waved, and then disappeared like a vampire in the rays of the morning sun.

Returning her wave Jack trudged back to his lodgings, heavy of heart and step, fighting the melancholy that had suddenly gripped him, although later, while he lay dozing and awakening on top of his bed, his melancholy gave way to a feeling of supreme fulfilment and, as if to enhance his languorous slumber, the birds twittering outside his window changed their notes to softer, sweeter nocturnes. It was a feeling that all the money in the world could not buy, and never before had the cliché: 'better born lucky than rich', made so much sense.

Later that morning as he toured the bars, the music and drink combination lifted his spirits as the dark-eyed lady kept intruding on his reverie, this time as a memory to cherish, and it had the effect of stiffening his spine against his hopeless love, for why should Mary O'Hara be the be-all and end-all of his life?

Chapter 9

Galway races split the year in halves for Jack, the bad part and the very bad part, and the very bad part was just beginning. With no work in the offing and the torch he was carrying burning more forlornly by the day, his spirits had reached a new low. To make matters worse, Tim Kelly, down in the dumps over missing the races, decided he needed a change of luck, and a few days later he borrowed the fare from Mick Grogan and boarded the emigrant train. Everyone was pulling out, and no one in authority seemed to give a jot that the country was being bled white of its youth, the strong and resolute going forth, the weak-willed and the cagey stayed behind, hoping to benefit from the poor leavings. It needed something to slow it down, otherwise the next generation would have nothing to breed off, only the kiss-arse kind, hypocrites, tinkers, and tyrants like Paisley.

Standing on the station platform on a glorious August morning waving after his only friend Jack felt the last prop being knocked out from under his optimism for a better Ireland. Conditions would never improve if there was no one to challenge the system, for nothing was ever achieved by knuckling down, nothing without demand, and now that the tide of emigration was in full flow, it was hard to imagine an uprising of the proletariat. Perhaps he should go himself, if only for a few months, and if it didn't work out, he could always return to the same rut. He had nothing to lose. He was twenty-one and going nowhere. He could send a few pounds to Eileen from time to time to keep the place intact, and perhaps if he was out of the way, she might marry.

He had all but made up his mind when the bird of common sense landed on his shoulder and hooted in his ear like a wise owl, reminding him that once he boarded the emigrant train he would be going against the odds. Notwithstanding the vast flow of expatriates toing and froing between the two islands for holidays and funerals, there were ten times more who were never seen or heard of again. Even Digger Nolan's mother hadn't heard from him in two years, and for all she knew he could be dead. On the other hand, it might be better to struggle on and hope for an economic miracle, and while he had his few acres, he would never starve. There were families in far worse straits, living in council cottages and existing on a rood of garden, two pigs, and a cow grazing on the long acre (the side of the road). The realisation that there were people worse off than himself lifted his spirits and, with the uplifting of sprits, came resolution, although now that his last friend was on his way to London, he had never felt more alone.

One evening, shortly after Tim's departure, Jack nearly collapsed with astonishment when Bull Paisley called at his cottage, offering him a job at a pound a day. "I'm buildin' twenty houses on the land at the back o' the bishop's palace," Paisley went on. "Eight o'clock start – Monday to Saturday. So, what d'you say?"

"I'll be there," replied Jack, choking on a Desperate Dan size portion of humble pie, for it was too good an opportunity to turn down, and the wages would help to build up his stake for the poker game, but like the Greeks bearing gifts, there had to be a catch.

The thought had hardly crossed his mind when he noticed Paisley sizing up Eileen's fairly ample rump which was stretching her skirt to bursting point, his huge bovine eyes glued to the zip at the back where the material was coming apart at the seam. Now that the method in his madness at Galway races was clear, it quickly came to him that Eileen was the key to the situation, an asset now more than a liability, if only he could coax her into stringing Paisley along until he reached his goal. Opportunity was knocking for the second time, handing him a lifeline, and he would be a fool not to avail of it. The downside was that Paisley, a bachelor on the wrong side of forty, wasn't exactly God's gift to women, and it was hard to imagine Eileen falling for his charm. Still, it was impossible to tell with women, especially when it came to choosing a partner, for it seemed that wealth, social standing, and the provision of a soft nest were powerful persuaders when it came to winning their hands, whatever about their hearts.

So engrossed was Paisley in his fantasy that Jack's acceptance had gone in one ear and out the other. "What d'you say, Jack?" he asked again.

"I've already said, OK."

"Huh – that's right. See you in the mornin'," said Paisley, turning towards the door, his lascivious eyes flickering for a final time over the object of his desire, a cold-blooded sneer on his face that wouldn't look out of place on a pirate appraising a galleon he was about to scuttle.

The moment she heard Paisley's car spinning round on the gravel outside the front door Eileen was up in arms. "What's all this with you and Paisley?" she snapped. "Only the other day you were saying he was an anti-Christ, and now you're going to work for him. Well, if you are, he's not to put a foot inside that door there – d'you hear! Did you see the looking of him? – he hardly left a stitch o' clothes on me with them filthy eyes of his."

Jack could be very persuasive when the occasion demanded it, and it demanded it now. "You should never turn a kindness away from the door, Eileen, in case it never returns," he said gravely, so gravely that Eileen looked at him twice for any sign of raillery.

"Kindness – kindness it is? – I've heard it all now!" Eileen snapped. "How can you even talk to him, considering the way he treats his men? And remember the time Jack Keogh lost his arm? Well, he never got a ha'penny, and that poor man that got killed, the widow and children could've starved for all he cared."

Since irritation and impatience were emotions of no profit Jack immediately suppressed them and summoned all his cajolery to his aid. "You should never look a gift-horse in the mouth, Eileen," he said. "And sometimes you have to pocket your pride when necessity shakes the reins – and it's shaking them now. Think about the Stations just round the corner, the Stations you never stop nagging me about. And winter almost on top of us too. A few weeks work'd be a great help."

Eileen fumed into silence and then exploded again. "You work for him if you like, but if he ever calls here again, I'll bang the door in his face."

"Don't be like that, Eileen!" countered Jack. "All you have to do is, be nice to him if he calls. Make a sup o' tay for him, maybe. You've got nothing to be afraid of – I'll be here all the time. But saying that, he mightn't call at all – just if he does, that's all I'm asking."

"I've only got two words to say to that, and one o' them is 'off'. What are you trying to do at all – make a hoor out o' me, your own sister, so you can have a few weeks' work," returned Eileen, her brow lowering, her face darkening angrily, for it was quite obvious she had heard of the liberties Paisley had a habit of taking with some of his men's wives, a privilege he considered to be his entitlement for providing permanent employment for their husbands.

"No one is trying to make a hoor out o' you at all – just think o' the Stations. It's not such a big sacrifice to make, just to be nice to him for a few weeks – you can offer it up as penance for your sins. Look at me – I've got to work for the thick bastard and put up with his abuse. See the sacrifice I'm making – it's worth at least a plenary indulgence –"

Jack kept his argument on the same thread until he noticed a chink appearing in his sister's armour, although he felt slightly annoyed at the female mind which thought only of petty principles when broader issues were involved.

"All right – I'll be polite to him till the Stations are over, and then I'm going to tell him what I think of him," Eileen finally agreed. "And, if he tries anything on or as much as lays a finger on me, I won't even wait till the Stations."

Next morning Jack went to work for Paisley, and before the day was halfway through he noticed something false about the set-up, for in as long as it takes to say: 'contribute to the support of your pastors', Paisley had changed from Simon Legree to Little Lord Fauntleroy. From the outset he was singled out for preferential treatment and never felt the edge of his abusive tongue, an attitude which was immediately transmitted to Paddy Mannion, his tyrannical foreman, who purposely kept him away from the more strenuous end of the business. However, as the days sped by, Paisley's visits to Daly's cottage became more frequent, and though he always called when Jack was at home, his eyes and conversation were only for Eileen.

Any near-sighted magoo could see through Paisley's façade, and to keep him interested Jack jollied him along. However, as the weeks followed one another into autumn, another thought, an absurd thought which he had earlier dismissed as the rattling of a simple man, kept obtruding – it wasn't Paisley's intention just to ride Eileen, he wanted to marry her, and the more he watched the drama unfolding before his eyes, the more convinced he became. Paisley, who lived with his elderly housekeeper in a mansion on the outskirts of Castleford, was getting past the age for settling down and, as his pedigree was somewhat under a cloud, it would almost be impossible for him to find a wife among Castleford's sanctimonious set, especially a young wife.

Like the tinker's origin, there was much speculation as to Paisley's pedigree, although in the turn of events it was now supposed that he was the illegitimate son of the late Thomas Crawford, the man who had founded his business and who, on his deathbed, had made him his sole beneficiary. The rest of Paisley's story was well-known as the parable of the prodigal son – dragged up by tinker foster parents in Dunhallow, a rough suburb of Castleford on the other side of the railway tracks, and kicked from house to house until he was old enough to earn his living. As a result, he had grown up unruly, bullying anyone whom he could bully, a trait that became more obtrusive ever since he had come into his inheritance.

At first excuses were plenty for Paisley's boorish behaviour, most having a tendency to put it down to his rough upbringing, although these excuses quickly wore think in the light of his ingratitude to the people who had once been his friends – hard-up, honest people who had fed and sheltered him when he hadn't a pot to piss in or a window to throw it out. It was the proverbial case of putting the tinker on horseback and he rode roughshod over the timid, the more formidable he bought off, and though he had come up from the gutter, he never really left it. Still, for all his lack of education, he was nobody's fool, and he used his wealth to manipulate politicians and council officials until he became a more powerful man in the community than his late benefactor. It now seemed that he needed a wife, a young wife, and if Jack's intuition was on the right lines, he had his cap set for Eileen.

If only there was some way to give the relationship a nudge in the right direction, he would have matters more or less his own way for a while, but knowing his sister's temperament, even the slightest inkling as to what he was up to would blow his initiative sky-high. As the days advanced, more slowly now, he took comfort in the fact that each day was bringing him a step nearer to his goal, although he shuddered to think of the upshot when the pin was finally pulled on Paisley's aspirations.

One sultry afternoon, as Eileen was preparing to do the weekly churning, she dragged the table from under the window into the draught between the two open doors. Even then, the kitchen felt steamingly hot, as though it held in its walls all the heat of the noontide, and flies were buzzing everywhere, big, fat flies. Before embarking on the tedious task she slipped to her bedroom on the shaded side of the house and, casting the odd tentative glance around as though there were covert eyes peering at her, she stripped to the skin and stood in the shadows, allowing the draught whispering under the door to refresh her body. Somewhat revitalised she returned to the kitchen wrapped loosely in a smock and proceeded with the churning, taking infinite care not to turn the handle too quickly in case it spoiled the butter.

The air was as powerful as chloroform, and when she finished the monotonous chore, she dozed on the chair until she was startled into wakefulness by a shadow darkening the doorway. When she opened her eyes and saw that it was Bull Paisley, the shock brought her quickly to her feet. "Come in, Bill, and I'll put the kettle on," she greeted, dry-coughing to stifle the anxiety in her tone, for Paisley, his white shirt open to the waist, his hairy chest protruding, his powerful arms stretching his rolled-up sleeves to bursting point, was as frightening as King Kong and, with sweat dripping from his jowls and his fat belly overhanging his belt, she had never known him to look more repulsive.

In two strides Paisley was at the table, flopping down massively on the chair Eileen had just vacated, his whole body overflowing it. "I was just passin' the way, Eileen, and I thought I'd call and bid you the hour o' the day," he said, taking in her flimsy attire at a glance, a disrobing glance that made her shudder, for if the intent in his eyes ever became reality, it was goodbye yellow-brick road.

While she was waiting for the kettle to boil, she cast the odd nervous glance at the clock, although it did nothing to ease her anxiety, for it would be at least two hours before she could expect Jack. Gripped by a sense of foreboding she searched her mind for an excuse to go outside so that she could skedaddle to Moore's, but Paisley's staring presence froze all her guile and, feeling as helpless as a rabbit in the rays of a flash lamp, she tried to hold her nerve.

Cups rattled on saucers and milk slopped from the jug as she laid them clumsily on the table, overstretching to keep out of the range of his arms. However, in a careless moment as she was leaving down the teapot so that he could help himself, he reached out, grabbed her round the waist, and landed her effortlessly on his knee. Kicking out with both legs she tried to break free, but her exertions only helped him to get a better grip, by first releasing her and then grabbing her again, like a hawk with its prey. The more she resisted, the more it seemed to provoke him, and in a sudden whirling motion that was as deft as it was swift he spun her round, and before she realised it, she was sitting spread-legged on his lap, facing him, her bare thighs exposed.

Time blurred into a nightmare. Everything had happened so quickly that she had forgotten to scream, although now that Paisley's thick lips were covering hers and his arms were tight about her waist like the tentacles of an octopus, she was powerless and choked for breath. "Now, now, Eileen – no need to be afraid," he said soothingly, the first note of tenderness that she or perhaps anyone had ever heard in his voice. "I couldn't mention this before now because Jack was always around, but I think you'd make a good wife for a man. We could live in that big house o' mine, up among the best o' them, and then you'd never want for anything. We could have lots o' babbies too. So, why don't you give just one little kiss to poor ould Bill to seal the bargain?"

Slowly, as if she was awakening from an anaesthetic, Eileen's faculties returned, and the sudden realisation of her vulnerability kick-started her brain into action, while Paisley, perhaps taking her silence for assent, bounced her on his knees horsey-horsey fashion. "Ah, come on, Eileen," he went on, in the same wheedling tone, as one of his ham-like hands sought a new target between her thighs, while the other fondled the soft flesh of her bare buttocks.

Now that he had her under his control, Paisley became more forceful, and when she sensed the nature of the beast that was beginning to uncoil and protrude from his open flies, forcing its way upwards, almost lifting her off his knees, she struggled frantically, pushing his head back with the heels of her hands. Fighting a losing battle against the inevitable she felt it inching forward, and when she looked down and saw it insinuating enormously between her bare thighs like a hooded snake, every exertion bringing it closer to the cleft where Jimmy Murphy had so mercilessly deflowered her, any doubts she might have had as to how Paisley had come by his nickname were quickly dispelled. Once it reached its target, surrender was sure to follow, and then perhaps response.

In the heat of the moment the instinct of survival sent Eileen's hand blindly searching the table for the bread knife, and in the act of groping it brushed against the teapot, scalding the skin on her knuckles. Snatching the hand away a thought flashed like a comet through her brain – the teapot. Tentatively she sent the hand exploring again until her articulate fingers found the spout and then closed around the handle. Too heavy to lift with her outstretched hand she dragged the teapot to the edge of the table and, bolstered by the strength such as God only gives to the desperate, she tipped it over, sending tea showering on Paisley's lap.

The shock of the scalding tea on his exposed manhood brought a yelp from Paisley and instinctively he released his grip, giving Eileen the chance she had been waiting for and, with her limbs thinking faster than her mind, she bounded through the door and across the yard to the horse's stable. Charlie was in the paddock, and once she was inside, she slammed the bolt on the bottom section of the door, holding the top part open just wide enough to peep out. After a timeless time she heard the rumble of a car engine and the scrunch of wheels on gravel, and when the purr of the car had faded in the distance, tentatively she re-emerged into the sunlight, a pitchfork gripped tightly in her hands. When she reached the kitchen, she locked both doors, the mere ease after torment being delight for a while.

Later, when Jack returned from work, Eileen sobbed her way through her ordeal.

"Did he hurt you?" asked Jack, his expression changing from incredulity to anger.

Eileen showed him the bruises on her arms, "Look!" she said. "I don't mind them so much – they'll heal, but he frightened the life out o' me, and that's worse. D'you think we should report it to the Guards?"

"No – the cops wouldn't want to believe you."

"I think we should. What if he tries again?"

"You'd be wasting your time!" snapped Jack. "You know what the cops are like yourself when bigshots are involved – they'd twist the story somehow. They'd say you led him on – making tea for him and all that. It might be different if he broke in. Better leave it all to me, and rest assured Paisley'll never darken that door there again."

"You're a nice one to talk about Paisley never darkening the door again. If it wasn't for you telling me to make tea for him, I'd have banged the door in his face. I don't know what you intend doing, but I still say we should report him to the Guards."

"Guards! Guards – my arse! Just tell me what the Guards'll do – arrest Paisley, is it? Paisley'll deny it, and it'll be your word against his. And I'll give you just one guess whose word they'll take. So, count yourself lucky –"

Eileen muttered something incoherent under her breath, something disagreeable by all accounts, cutting Jack short.

"Oh, go to the blasted Guards then," said Jack, although he knew that Eileen would whinge and whinge and do nothing.

Next morning when Jack arrived on the job, Paisley was in a foul mood and, as if they sensed something out of the ordinary, men were rushing hither and thither in confusion, tripping over one another to keep out of his way. "Hey, you!" he bawled at a small, stoop-shouldered man wearing a tattered jacket and cap, in a tone only used by men who are certain that those they call will rush to obey.

Old habits of subservience die hard, and the man, Mouse Moran, croaked meekly, "What is it, Mister Paisley?"

Paisley was about to issue instructions when he saw Jack striding towards him, his features grim, his jaw set. Perhaps something in Jack's approach warned Paisley what was coming and, squaring his shoulders and balling his fists, he stuck out his chin defiantly, as if to say: 'come and get me'. Yet, the suddenness of Jack's attack took him completely by surprise as, without warning, he landed a left hook squarely under his chin, following it up with a right. The second blow caught Paisley flush on the nose, sending blood spurting all over his lips and chin, and when Jack unleashed another vicious left, his knuckles ripped a gash in the podgy flesh under Paisley's right eye. "Come on, Bull – let's see what you're made of!" he cried, hissing the words through his teeth. "Or maybe you got your nickname for frightening women, and not for buggering a young bull!"

A growl of anger erupted from Paisley as he charged, head down, in the manner that most people believed had earned him his sobriquet, aiming a roundhouse swing at Jack's head. Bending his knees Jack ducked under the trajectory of the flying fist and drove a murderous left into Paisley's guts just below the ribcage. Paisley's explosion of breath was close to a yell and, as compulsively his arms came down to protect his belly, Jack moved in and chopped down savagely on the exposed neck with a succession of rabbit punches until Paisley dropped to his knees. Although Paisley was only a gypsy-type of a fighter he was strong and powerfully built, and if the brawl came to close quarters, Jack knew that his formidable weight would almost certainly carry the day. So, before he had time to recover he kicked out with a hobnailed boot, caught him on the chin, and sent him sprawling against a stack of concrete blocks.

Paisley, his back contracted like an ass that had been struck with violence, struggled to his knees and, arse in the air like a cow getting up, he got one foot under him, then the other, and straightened, while Jack stood silently waiting, fists at the ready. However, it seemed that Paisley had shot his bolt, for he just stared sullenly, stemming the blood flow from his nose with a crumpled handkerchief.

Silently, almost tentatively, the men began to gather, astonishment on their faces as they stared incredulously, first at their employer, and then at Jack. When no one ventured a comment or looked like taking Paisley's part, Jack eased back out of danger, his eyes fixed on Paisley in case of a sudden charge. "In future, Paisley, I'll thank you to stay away from my house, and if you ever lay a hand on my sister again, remember what you got today was just the chaff off the seed," he warned, favouring him with one of the best-known obscene gestures. "Now that it's come to this, give me my few shillings wages and I'll be on my way."

When Jack reached home and related the outcome of his set-to with Paisley, it brought a glimmer of satisfaction to Eileen's worried eyes, although later, when she had time to mull over it, her pessimism returned. "I still think we should've reported it to the Guards," she said. "What's stopping Paisley from calling again when you're not here?"

"Guards – how many times have I to tell you that it'd be a complete waste o' time," returned Jack, shaking his head at her obstinacy. "Surely you know yourself that the ordinary flatfoot hasn't the brains for anything except directing traffic, checking dog licences and lights on bicycles, and raiding the odd public house for after-hours drinkers, or waiting to catch some poor eejit for having no shoes on the ass. After that, he has to do what the sergeant tells him, and the sergeant has to do what the Super tells him. And the Super is in the pocket of the likes o' Paisley and his cronies. They can buy the law just like we buy a loaf o' bread in a shop, and if they can't buy the Super, they'll buy the judge – money talks all languages. Can't you get that into your thick head – the law governs the poor and the rich govern the law. Another thing too – you might see the cops sooner than you think, if I know Paisley."

Jack was right, for the words had scarcely left his lips when Sergeant Driscoll and one of his men called to say that Paisley was considering pressing charges.

"He can suit himself – it was a fair fight, a fight that he started, and if you want proof, listen to what my sister has to say," said Jack, turning to Eileen for support. "Now's your chance, Eileen – you wanted the law, and hey presto, here they are, all two o' them."

Jack's sarcasm wasn't lost on the policemen, and when Eileen blurted out her story, Sergeant Driscoll scratched his greying hair meditatively, as if he was searching for a compromise or an easy way out. Finally, he rounded on Jack. "Why wasn't this reported right away – now it's too late to do anything about it, considering you've already taken the law into your own hands," he said, an authoritative note in his tone. "But I'll have a word with Paisley about this other little matter. In the light of what Eileen has just told me I can talk him into dropping the charges. But I'm warning you, Jack, if you as much as sneeze at Paisley again, I'll have you arrested."

Jack was careful not to bait the sergeant further. "What about Paisley and this other little matter, as you put it, this little matter of almost raping my sister?" he asked. "Does this mean she'll be protected from now on in case he calls again?"

"But of course – that's what the law is for, and I'll have words with Paisley to that effect," returned the sergeant. "I'll leave it at that for now, and if there are any further developments, I'll let you know."

When the policemen had taken their leave, to ease his frustration Jack banged the door and slammed the bolt on it, the violence of the action threatening the very security of the hinges. "There it is for you in a nutshell, Eileen," he sniggered, his earlier sarcasm back in his tone. "See how worried the sergeant was about you? – made out a big long report about it, so he did. It'll be in the headlines of the *Herald* next week, 'Read all about it – lone country spinster attacked by lecherous building contractor'."

Eileen maintained an offended silence, but as Jack had forecast, they never heard from the police again. As the weeks went by and the Stations neared, Jack was in the doldrums over his lost income. Fate, he believed, had dealt him a cruel blow just as he was getting ahead, while Eileen lapsed further into despondency.

Chapter 10

The Stations of the Cross, abbreviated to the Stations, was a biannual event, spring and autumn, which each household in the village held in turn and, as there were fourteen families in Knockrush, it took the Stations seven years to complete its cycle. The morning began with Mass and Holy Communion in the kitchen for the local community and their friends, and afterwards it was traditional for the priest to breakfast in the parlour with a few of the village elders which, owing to the importance of the guest, was a formal layout: white linen tablecloth, china crockery, silver cutlery, lump sugar, and grapefruit for hors d'oeuvre. An all-day hooley and dance followed, which usually ran into the small hours of the next morning.

As the Stations were scheduled for Monday, on Saturday morning Jack set off for Castleford with his horse and cart, his list of commands in his pocket. Stabling Charlie in Grogan's yard he crossed the street to McCale's grocery and hardware store.

"It must me yeer turn to have the Stations, Jack," Harry Cahill, the shopboy, remarked when he noticed grapefruit on the lengthy shopping list, for over the years grapefruit had become synonymous with the Stations, as only the clergy and the upper echelons of society were accustomed to such fare for breakfast.

"Whatever put that idea into your head, Harry – even the tinkers have grapefruit for their breakfast nowadays," Jack laughed and, leaving Cahill with the list, he crossed again to Grogan's and ordered two half-barrels of stout, a dozen bottles of Power's whiskey, port wine, bottled beer and minerals, shuddering at the cost as each item was logged. To supplement the regulation tipple he had two gallons of poteen on order from the Bradys, another family of distillers, passing over Jim Madden, whose brew of late was hot in the extremes, fiery almost, as if he was using too much corn and not enough sugar.

While Jack was loading up, Bull Paisley, who was standing at the counter with two of his men, kept throwing the odd sidelong glance at the proceedings, but save for a scowl when their eyes met he showed no hostility. Even so, Jack felt that it might be the calm before the storm, for Paisley was far more ominous in his silence than in his worst ranting and raving, although he hoped that he would have the common decency not to interfere in the merriment on the night of the Stations.

On the morning of the event Daly's kitchen was a hive of activity. The women of the village, flustered by the priest's presence, were getting in one another's way as they arranged the table in altar-fashion for Mass, draping it in linen bleached to clinical whiteness and laying it out with candles, crucifix, chalice and cruets, while Father Carney, in a makeshift confessional near the back door, sat solemnly, hand on brow, listening to the transgressions of the old-timers, the ones too old to make the monthly trip to the church for the sodality.

The absurdity of having confessions for people past the age of sinning was more to be laughed at than criticised, for Granny Mulhaire's petty sins could literally be heard in the next village as she rattled them off like a nursery rhyme: "I missed Mass on Sunday 'coz I'm too old to go, but I listened to the one on the radio instead – I cursed Maggie Ward, the tinker woman, for bringin' bad luck on me over the calf that died – I sold glugger eggs to the travelling-shop man, ones the clocking-hen had been sitting on that didn't hatch out, but he didn't notice 'coz I dipped them in cold tea to take the shine off them – I slipped in a few cocks among the pullets I sold to Jack Dowd when his back was turned, but that's no sin, 'coz I heard he's a crook and that he puts dabs o' paint on his day-old chicks and tries to pass them off as Rhode Island Reds –" ran the litany, while Kathy Moore, by whispered pleas and jerks of her skirt, tried in vain to get the old lady to hush.

It was almost noon when the priest took his leave, and afterwards neighbours and friends were taken in groups to the parlour to partake of cold chicken, ham and tomatoes, tea and fresh bread, a bowl of sherry trifle, and a thick slice of porter cake with a glass of whiskey or port wine on the side.

The bar, not the least of the essentials, was set up on a trestle-table in the back-kitchen, the whiskey taking pride of place in the centre, flanked by the port wine, the bottled beer, and the minerals for the children and teetotallers. The two sixteen-gallon barrels of stout were seated on chairs on either side, tapped and ready, while the two-gallon jar of poteen, which Jack had coloured with ginger wine in a vain attempt to disguise its character, was covered with a canvas sack under the table on the million-to-one chance that the police might call, perhaps on Paisley's prompting, and to make sure that gluttony didn't triumph over common sense, Paddy Keane, the thriftiest man in the village, was given charge of its distribution.

When everyone had eaten, Jack called Keane aside. "We don't want to be running out now, Paddy, like the wedding feast of Cana – so go easy on it – see that it lasts out the day," he said jokingly, and yet, with some gravity. "That is, unless you know someone near at hand who can turn water into porter."

"I don't know what you're worrin' about, Jack – there's enough here to sink a battleship," returned Keane, indicating the goodly display with a sweep of a hand. "But it might be a good idea to dish out the poteen first to get them in the mood, and keep the good whiskey and the porter for later, like the wedding feast o' Cana, as you say, keepin' the good wine till last."

"That's a good idea, Paddy – why didn't I think o' that," said Jack commendably, and when the poteen worked its magic, sooner than expected, the trio of musicians: a banjo, a fiddle and an accordion, struck up, and the party took a livelier turn. All through the day and into the night jigs, reels and waltzes, which were interrupted every so often for a song, resounded through the kitchen; feet swished, scraped and patted on the concrete floor in a 'round the house and mind the dresser' type of fling, the interjection of the occasional high-spirited yoo-hoo-hoo heightening the ambience. The tempo slowed when it was time to sing, and quickened again when it was time to dance, the old come-all-ye songs bringing nostalgic tears to the eyes of the old-timers, as though they were jogging memories of their lost youth.

The music and drink combination seemed to be an activating agent for sentimental memories, and for all that he had programmed his mind against looking back, Jack too felt the sad-sweet pain of reminiscence. Waltzing with Kathy Moore, who was rapidly flowering into womanhood, he closed his eyes, hoping that when he opened them again his partner would be transformed into the lady who was still torturing his soul and tearing his heart into little pieces without actually making it bleed, for never before had the cliché: 'out of sight, out of mind', seemed further from the truth.

Taking in the jovial scene of neighbourly goodwill and gaiety over Kathy's shoulder he wondered if drink was an anaesthetic against life's realities, a postponement of crucial decisions, a temporary escape into security from problems which someday must be faced. At times like these he envied the rich and the clergy who were free of the vicissitudes of life, inasmuch as if they had problems, at least lack of money wasn't one of them. It seemed that while the rest of the world was going forward, they were going back in time, back to the days of famine and exodus. "Why?" he asked himself. "Why – why – why?" There were so many 'whys' in life, never any certainty of anything, never any sense of security, and nothing to look forward to only a life of drudgery, darkened by the ever-present spectre of want, for all that emigration had swept a quarter of the population across the sea.

The gaiety continued unabated until finally, like a tide in full flow it reached a high point. Then, it began to ebb, slowly at first and later more noticeably as the villagers in twos and threes and in family groups dispersed, full of food, full of drink, and full of praise for the hospitality of the Daly's, leaving Jack and Eileen to face the debris.

"That's the Stations over for us for another seven years, Eileen," said Jack, as he bolted up for the night. "Seven years – seven years bad luck, I suppose, is all we can look forward to, like breaking a looking-glass. Still, it was a good day all the same, and by the looks of most o' them I think they enjoyed themselves. You can grumble all you like about the cost, but to me, it was worth every penny. Anyway, it's poor lookout for any family that can't throw an ould hooley once every seven years."

"I thought there'd be trouble," said Eileen, stoking the fire and putting on the kettle for a cup of tea before they went to bed. "I was expecting Paisley to send out a few roughnecks from the town to cause a rumpus."

"He knows better," returned Jack. "And another thing I'll say, if any man deserves a stroke or a heart attack he does, and the sooner he gets one or the other, the sooner the world'll be a better place to live in."

"Jesus, Mary and Joseph – don't say that, Jack! Curses always come home to roost," said Eileen, frowning her disapproval, a shiver running down her spine as she relived her ordeal with Paisley. "I don't know what I'd do at all if you ever go to England – in dread o' my life I'd be."

The worried look on his sister's face touched a soft spot in Jack's nature. "Oh, shut up, you silly ould *cheolawn*, and don't be always looking at the bad side o' life – you should count yourself lucky you have me to look after you," he laughed. "And haven't I always looked after you, even though you don't appreciate it, and remember years ago when we used to go round the town looking in shop windows and planning what we'd buy if we were rich. Well, we will be rich someday in spite of everything, and we'll do up this ould place like we once dreamed," he went on, waves of wistful expression chasing each other over his face, as if the scene of velvet curtains, wall-to-wall carpet, electric light, and a car outside the door was coming alive in his imagination. "The ould cottage doesn't look much at the moment, but it's a whole lot better than the ould house in the song. You know the song, Eileen, *This Old House,* Rosemary Clooney. Come on – let's have a go."

Before Eileen realised what was happening Jack had her on her feet, jigging around the kitchen to his own accompaniment of humming and singing, and he went on until Eileen was forced to laugh.

"You!" she said, shaking herself loose of his grip. "You don't give a shite, d'you? Can't you be serious just for a minute."

Jack behaved as if he hadn't heard. "D'you know, Eileen – if you weren't my sister, I'd marry you myself," he said, pulling a serious face. "I wonder how we'd get on as husband and wife, instead of brother and sister? Then, you'd have a licence to nag me – you could start off in the morning the minute I got up, and go on all day, which is accepted behaviour as long as it's within the confines of matrimony."

"Oh, shut up and go to bed, unless you want to give me a hand with all this clearing up."

The icy winds of winter quickly dispelled the community goodwill brought about by the Stations, and for the first time in his life Jack wished that Christmas was over, something he had never thought possible. It was as if he had suddenly stumbled on the real world, for in the current economic climate all he could see in Christmas was expense and debt, and the money he had saved so thriftily during the year had all but disappeared. Gone forever was the old excitement of the festive season, for which the preparation was almost as good as the event itself – decorating the kitchen with holly and ivy, polishing the brass, making the crib in the parlour, whitewashing the outside of the house and cleaning the chimney for Santa Claus. It was as if another chapter in the story of his life had ended, and now the masked mummers in their motley attire touring the village with their music, the Wren Boys with their ornate boxes and quaint little verses, and the St Stephen's night dance at the Phoenix brought no more excitement than a sudden attack of diarrhoea.

To add to his increasing burden Eileen was finding it hard to come to terms with her fear of being attacked again, and she was seeing Paisley's lascivious eyes peering out from every stable door and dark boreen. Worse still, it was all his, Jack's, fault for having anything to do with him in the first place, and now that she had stopped going to the Phoenix, her chances of catching a husband were fading fast. Besides the doom and gloom enshrouding his sister, something else was troubling his mind, something that had nothing to do with Mary O'Hara or the realisation that Eileen would be always a millstone about his neck, something he couldn't quite put a finger on as though some catastrophe lay ahead. The feeling was with him at every awakening and it perched on his shoulder all day like a carrion crow and, try as he might, he could not shake it off.

The winter wind always blows colder for a poor man, he cursed bitterly, as his ambition, driven back and crushed on every side, became a dream again in the face of the more pressing struggle of keeping the wolf from the door. Every day brought a new low, another obstacle to surmount. In January, when the hens stopped laying, his dole money had to go towards paying for the groceries from the travelling shop and, as the money they had got for the ducks and geese had gone towards the purchase of the Christmas shopping, they had nothing to sell until March, save for a few old hens which Eileen was culling.

They had just reached rock bottom when Jack heard in Castleford that flooding had caused a food shortage in Holland, and the market for rabbits was soaring. Later that evening he explained the situation to Eileen: "There's a fella coming to town every Friday for the next few weeks and he'll take all the rabbits we can lay our hands on at a half-crown a brace, and the ten shillings bounty is back again on foxes and otters."

"A fat lot o' good that'll do us," grouched Eileen. "There's hardly a rabbit to be seen or a fox either."

"What I like most about you, dear sister, is your overwhelming enthusiasm for all my ideas," returned Jack, a sarcastic note in his tone. "Even if we only got two rabbits, that's a half-crown more than we have at the moment, and I saw a big dog-fox a few nights ago howling at the moon. That's another ten bob in the bag when I stalk him someday with my .22. I suppose I'd be wasting my breath asking you to give me a hand – if I ask Peter Costello, I'll have to split the money fifty-fifty with him."

When Eileen muttered something under her breath that seemed to signal agreement, Jack went on: "There's a chap in town, Long Tom Burke, and he's giving me a loan of a ferret and a few nets. I've already mapped out where to go, and if we get started every morning as soon as it gets bright and follow a wide circle, we should be back early in the afternoon. We can get one o' the Moores to keep an eye on the place while we're gone, in case the tinkers come round."

"Whatever will you be having me doing next to get a few shillings – begging around the town, I suppose, like the tinkers."

"I could think of other things – more profitable things."

"Knowing you, I wouldn't put it past you."

Eileen finally relented, and in the following days they scoured the countryside. On Friday morning they counted forty brace of rabbits. "That's a fiver's worth, Eileen – money for old rope," said Jack, rubbing his palms together in anticipation of a few pints in Grogan's, the memory of the taste coming back to taunt his thirst. "Now all you have to do is give me a hand to get them to the Shambles where they're picking them up. If we hang them on the bars of the two bikes, and walk with the bikes, we should manage all right."

"How d'you know there'll be anyone there to buy them?" asked Eileen. "It might be all a big joke – what'll happen then?"

"If that's the case, we'll have to eat them before they go stink – won't we!" snapped Jack. "So, less o' your grumbling and get a move on. It's promised snow in the next few days – that is, if we can believe the weather forecast."

When they reached the Shambles, a walled-in enclosure at the back of the public toilets where years ago cattle were slaughtered in the open, Eileen stopped awestricken in her tracks, for never before had she seen so many rabbits, the sudden impact bringing back some sparkle to her eyes. "All isn't lost," Jack smiled to himself as he joined the queue that had already formed, looping round and round the yard like a trick-o' the loop man's cord, the loop ending at a canvas-topped lorry in the centre of the compound where two men, one counting and checking the animals for broken backs or other damage, and one paying out, were making short work of the business.

When the buyer counted out five single pound notes Jack turned to his still mesmerised sister. "There, what did I tell you, you big goose?" he laughed. "And he never copped on the one with the broken back either, the one I stuffed the bicycle spoke up his arse to stiffen him. Now, there's two quid for you, and remember, I'm being generous, because that's thirty-nine shillings and sixpence more than you were worth, and don't squander it. I'm off now to Grogan's to have a good drink for myself, and I'll see you later – and don't forget to feed the ferret."

Next day, the promised snow fell heavier than forecast, making the roads impassable, which regrettably put paid to the rabbit-catching. Housebound for almost a week Jack only ventured outside to feed his stock and, without company save for that of his morose sister, the lonely days and nights dragged by with nothing to do but stare into the fire, listening to the monotonous ticking of the clock and the crickets chirping behind the fireplace. When Pat Gormally, the redoubtable travelling-shop man, failed to brave the weather, on Friday Jack set out for Castleford on foot to draw his dole and buy the necessities.

The whole countryside was blanketed in white, a white so pure that the sheep looked cream-coloured in comparison, and for all that he was in the doldrums he took time out from his hopeless thoughts to admire the picturesque scene, taking cheer from the boundless energy of the children as they threw snowballs and buried one another in almost sadistic fashion in the drifts, their shrill cries knocking snow off the bare branches. Moving on, his hands thrust deep in his pockets, a shiver ran down his spine, and again he was gripped by the old foreboding that something sinister was in the air, his fear of the unknown a thousand times more apprehensive than his fear of the known.

When he reached Castleford, the weak sun had passed its zenith, and when he had collected his paltry entitlement at the labour exchange, he turned towards Grogan's, knocking the snow off his boots against the wall before lifting the latch. As building was at a standstill, Bull Paisley was seated at a corner table among a group of tinkers, and by the tone of his guffawing he was mait galore. The cold draught that followed Jack in from the street brought Paisley's head around, but on recognition, it stopped in mid-swivel and cranked back to centre on his entourage, who were full of sham adulation, as if he was a medieval king and they were his vassals, their homage stopping short of kissing his arse as long as he kept the drink flowing. As there was no sign of Grogan, Jack ordered a pint of stout from Tommy Foley, the young barman, which he mulled with a red-hot poker.

Although he had his back turned to Paisley, Jack sensed that he was seething with resentment, and the snatches of the chatter he picked up suggested he was bent on making trouble. Electing to confront the situation rather than ignore it he turned sideways-on to the counter and hooked a heel in the footrail.

The moment Jack turned Paisley shot a baleful glance in his direction. "Well, if it isn't the bog-trotter himself, Mister smart-alec Daly, in to draw his few coppers' dole," he sneered, the sneer dripping over the folds of his chin and, dragging himself to his feet, he crossed the floor with a lumbering tread until he was face to face with Jack. "I have a day coming to me, and you'll be sorry, yourself and that hoor of a sister of yours – you can take that as a warnin'! I'll have you know, I went to that ould shack o'yours with good intentions, big eejit that I was, for all the thanks I got. Her, and all her airs and graces, as if she was entitled to have any, considerin' all the times she was down Poke Lane with her knickers down around her ankles and Jimmy Murphy ridin' the arse off her. Yes – I know all about that too, or for that matter, who doesn't? It's no wonder she can't get a husband, 'coz she'll never be anythin' but a good ride!"

Speechless for a moment Jack just stared at Paisley, shock and anger running through him in ice-cold waves. Perhaps Paisley had gone to his cottage with good intentions, but no mitigation could quell the rage that was sweeping through him at his insulting remarks, a rage that only the sight of blood on his sneering face could assuage. Balling his fists tighter, his fingernails digging into his palms until he felt them piercing his skin, he tried to keep the lid on his temper, for it was as plain as the red cap on a bishop's head that Paisley was bent on goading him into a fight in front of witnesses, which was sure to result in his arrest. By heroic control he fought down his anger and, with a bland smile on his face, he said quite calmly, but loud enough for the tinkers to hear: "Go and hide under Sergeant Driscoll's petticoats, Bull, and let real men enjoy a drink in comfort."

"Say that again, Daly!"

"You heard me the first time!" retorted Jack, a harsh laugh that was cutting with contempt giving more sting to the words. "Don't tell me you're deaf too as well as thick."

"I don't know what you're so cocky about, Daly, and you hardly havin' a copper to bless yourself with," countered Paisley. "If it came to cases, I'll bet you could hardly afford the penny to shite in the public toilet."

"If that's the case, you could make one for the two of us – a big shite, but if you ever made a big shite, Paisley, there'd be nothing left o' you – because you're all shite."

As the slanging match became more heated, the tinkers at the table came slowly to their feet and, shuffling across the floor, they stood behind Paisley, making as though they were going to back his play, all five of them, big, unshaven and smelly in their piss-stained rags.

Jack, his eyes as clear and fearless as an eagle's, left down his glass and eased back from the counter so that both his arms were free, for he knew from past experience that tinkers, like snarling dogs, always put on an aggressive front, but when it came to the crunch were lacking in courage and backed down at the last second. "I told you to go and hide under the sergeant's petticoats and let real men enjoy a drink in comfort," he spat, staring Paisley straight in the eye. "And a bit of advice for you too – you'd be far better off if you paid your men a decent week's wages, instead of buying drink for that shower behind your back. Or is it true what they say that birds of a feather flock together?"

"Why you f –"

"Hold it, Paisley!" a voice shattered the tension, Grogan's voice from the foot of the stairs and, hurrying forward, he stepped between the would-be combatants. "I've warned you before about your conduct in this bar, Paisley, so I'm askin' you to leave," he said fiercely. "The only choice you have in the matter is which way you want to go – the easy way or the hard way. It's take-your-pick time, and if you decide to take the easy way, take the wild bunch with you when you're goin' – ye're all barred."

Paisley shot a glance over his shoulder as though for support, but the wild bunch, as Grogan had called them, were already slinking towards the door. Scowling his best scowl he stood for a few seconds facing Grogan as if he was in two minds, and then, turning on his heel, he stormed through the door after his tinker friends, the vehemence of his tread on the flagstone floor translating his rancour.

"That shook him," said Grogan, as he shut out the cold and returned to the counter. "He was so mad that he even forgot to bang the door behind him – he's always trouble when he has a few drinks. I was upstairs when young Foley here came up to fetch me," he went on, nodding his approbation of the sallow-faced barman. "But take it from me, that's the last time you'll see him in here. So, let's forget him and have a drop o' Power's with me to warm us up on this cold day – it'll make you feel good. Yes – a dropeen o' Power's – it cures all ills – more power said ould Power and when young Power was born."

Still struggling with his anger Jack tipped back the whiskey, and when he felt its warm fingers rubbing comfortably against the lining of his stomach, he called another round. "God spare you the health, Mick!" he toasted. "If one makes us feel good, two should make us feel twice as good."

When the barman was out of earshot, Grogan sidled closer to Jack. "You want to keep an eye out for Paisley, Jack," he cautioned. "Take it from me, he's a bad 'un."

"I'm not afraid o' the bastard – or the tinkers either."

"Nobody is sayin' you're afraid, Jack. I'm only warnin' you that he's treacherous, that's all, and besides, you're up against money, and money talks –"

"Yes, Mick – money talks all right!" Jack cut in, somewhat derisively. "But all it ever says to me is goodbye, and if it was a crime to be poor, I'd be in jail all my life."

"For Christ's sake, Jack, I'm serious – if you'll just listen," Grogan went on. "I'll put it like this, it took God six days to make the world, on the seventh day He rested, and on the eighth day He made the likes o' Paisley – the bad guys o' the world. Take it from me, and I've met all kinds in my time, Bull Paisley is bad right through, from his head down to his ankles – there isn't a decent bone in his body. So, keep your eyes open."

"Yes, Mick, I can see what you mean – perhaps when he was being baptised, the holy water didn't take," Jack agreed. "But why do people stand for the likes o' Paisley riding roughshod over them, working for starvation wages, and all that? And what's more sickening still is the way the clergy condone it, preaching from the pulpit that by giving employment these men are helping to stem the tide of emigration and are keeping Ireland aloof from the corrupt outside world, instead of telling them the truth, that they're being short-changed so their employers can afford the good life and send their sons to college and university."

"You've got to remember that the clergy are preachin' to the already converted, which means they can run with the hare and chase with the hounds as much as they like," returned Grogan. "But the reality is that the clergy are goin' against the teachin' of Christ. Accordin' to the Gospel, Christ preached poverty and love, so answer me this – did you ever see a poor priest or one who put his parishioners before himself? It seems to me that blessed are the rich, and not the meek, for it's the rich that are inheritin' the earth. But dare we open our mouths about it, because we're up against money and power, and when money comes up against the truth, the truth fares ill."

"I think what the country really needs is a dictator, someone of the calibre of Napoleon Bonaparte, a genuine man who wouldn't be said or led by the clergy or the men of money, a man who'd abolish the system of knowing someone and palm-greasing, and enforce the republican ideal of equal rights and equal opportunities for all."

"Nobly said, Jack," interjected Grogan. "But if such a man came along, ignorance'd crucify him, as it did Parnell and Collins. So, all we can do is make the best of it, because anyone who ever kicked the system around here always wound up on the train out."

After spending an hour putting the world to rights with Grogan, Jack returned to the slushy pavements and, as he trudged homewards, again emigration raised its head as an option. Torn between the impulse to go and the desire to stay he felt his reluctance to depart from the old sod winning the battle, as Grogan had said, dig in and make the best of it, sooner or later things were sure to change for the better. The closer he got to home, the more the idea of digging in asserted itself, especially when his empty stomach reminded him of the dinner of steaming-hot bacon and cabbage that Eileen was sure to have waiting, golden-brown praties bursting in their jackets and a mug of buttermilk to wash it down, and afterwards a blissful smoke by the fireside while discussing the promised improvement in the weather with his neighbours.

Chapter 11

On the following week the weather relented and, as the traffic churned the snow on the roads into slush and the countryside emerged as a giant grey patchwork quilt dappled with green and brown, Jack's determination to stay was given new roots, although devastatingly so. Tim Kelly was dead, killed on a building site in London. On Sunday morning, when he met a tear-stained Julia Kelly, Tim's youngest sister, outside the church after last Mass, he was lost for words to comfort her in her hour of grief. Wrapping an arm about her slender shoulders he led her away from the general flow of the crowd. "Is there anything I can do, Julia?" he asked. "I only heard the sad news this morning."

"No, Jack," Julia sobbed, ashen-faced and in tears, her black coat and headscarf accentuating her pallor. "What can anybody do now – he's being buried next Tuesday over in London."

"Are they not taking him home?"

Julia shook her head slowly from side to side, as if she was trying to shake away her grief. "No – it'd cost too much," she said. "Most o' the family are over there, and they'd all have to come across. They asked if mother and me would go over, but instead we're spending the money on High Mass for him here on the same morning. Will you come, Jack?"

"Of course I'll be there – that goes without saying, and Eileen too," returned Jack, embracing Julia again. "I'll call to see your mother tomorrow, but in the meantime if there's anything she needs, tell her not to be shy for the asking. Now about you – I can see you're taking it bad, but you've got to pull yourself together and try to get your mind on to something else, otherwise it's going to be twice as hard for you – life has to go on."

"Oh, Jack, I'm too upset to think about anything else," Julia sniffled. "I could never understand why Tim had to go in the first place – we'd have managed somehow – we wouldn't have starved. I knew we'd lost him the day he walked out the door, but I used to pray he wouldn't like it over there and come back. Now it's all over, and I can't even put flowers on his grave."

"Of course you can, Julia. All you have to do is build a little shrine in a corner of your back garden, and put some of his things in a box and bury them there. Then, he'll be always near you in spirit, and I can go there too to pay my respects," returned Jack, searching his mind for some distraction for Julia. "But you've got to do what Tim'd want. The Tim I knew wouldn't like to see you all distressed like this, and you've got to put on a brave face in front of your mother – God only knows what she must be suffering. So, let's dry up your tears," he went on, in a wheedling tone, and before Julia had time to reply, he picked up her chin with a finger and thumb and dabbed delicately under her eyes with a corner of his handkerchief. "Now blow your nose, and I'll walk with you as far as the marketplace."

Julia eased her chin away from Jack's rough palm, blinked her eyes clear, and blew her nose. "Thanks, Jack – I know you're for my good, and I'll do as you say," she said, and then they fell silent, the awkward silence of two people whose only link lay with a lost brother and friend, until they reached the marketplace and Julia turned away.

Cycling towards home Jack struggled to come to grips with the news. Although she was scarcely sixteen Julia wasn't far off the mark when she said that they had already lost Tim to emigration, and in her words he found the strength to persevere no matter how thorny the path. Perhaps things might pick up in summer, and yet – yet more than ever – the fear that had been with him since the Stations kept pervading his thoughts, stealthily closing in around him like a dark impenetrable mist, a sombre, frightening sense of foreboding that had nothing to do with Tim's death. Ever since he had reached to the use of reason his feet had been firmly planted on common sense, believing only what he could see and hear, but this eerie sensation persisted, as if he, a professed unbeliever in ghosts, had been frightened by a ghost story, and he had no weapons with which to fight it.

Nevertheless, grief passed with time until the confused beginnings of many birds' songs spread in the healthy air, and daffodils and snowdrops appeared as if by magic in the fields which nature was turning to a deeper shade of green. The hope that comes with spring had perhaps encouraged Eileen's hens to start laying again, and Jack found work for a few weeks repairing stone walls for the master of the hunt. His spirits lifted with each lengthening day, he was back on the rails, their debts were cleared, he was saving again, and summer was just round the corner.

It was one of those mornings in late March when winter wishes to resume its sway and scatters its last snows and storms with desperate fury, those last three days of the month which they say are fierce enough to skin an old cow. Jack was sitting at the table eating his breakfast when Eileen came hurrying from the cowshed, panic-stricken and speechless.

"What's wrong?" Jack asked, rising from the table, ready to face whatever had frightened her.

"The cows – the cows! Come quick –"

Jack hurried to the cowshed, Eileen at his heels. The two cows were lying on their sides, their bellies bloated, their eyes staring lifelessly, and Jack hadn't to look too closely to realise they were dead. Nonplussed, he stood staring at the swollen carcasses, Eileen by his side showing the same bewilderment. For a long breathless moment his mind stood still as if it was paralysed, and then, as it raced forward again, suddenly, like a flash of summer lightening throws for an instant the whole countryside into unnatural brightness, a thought flashed through his mind, a thought too horrendous to even contemplate. Pushing Eileen out of his way, on winged feet he sped to the horse's stable, and when he flung open the top part of the door, his worst fears were founded. Charlie was on his back, his legs in the air.

Jack's face didn't change, but his lips went white, like a person who has received a stunning blow without warning and who, in the first moments of shock doesn't realise what has happened. For a brief while there was a merciful dullness of mind, a dullness that he knew would soon give way to sharp pain, just as severed tissues shocked by a surgeon's knife have a moment of insensibility before the agony begins. Turning away he looked like one who had seen the inside of hell, and it would be many a day before he laughed again.

Part 2

Chapter 1

Stricken to the very soul at the sight of his horse's lifeless eyes staring up at him Jack's stupor gradually gave way to grief, and then to anger, an anger so burning that he could scarcely think beyond putting a bullet in Paisley, for who else hated him so much to do such a dastardly deed? Every time he collected his thoughts fresh gusts of rage shook him until Eileen tugging at his coat sleeve brought him back from his angry world.

"I think we should go for the Guards," she urged through her tears. "I warned you about having anything to do with Paisley, but no – you knew best, and now he's got his revenge."

"Shut up about the cops and let me think!" snapped Jack. "If you want to do something useful, go and fetch Jim Madden and I'll have a look around. Maybe they left some clues – footprints or something."

When Madden arrived, he gave the dead animals a quick examination. "If you ask me, Jack, I'd say they were poisoned. But I can't prove they were, though. Even if I could, my word wouldn't hold water in a court o' law. The only man who can say for sure is Fluke Walsh, the vet, and you know what Fluke charges – he'd make a big thing of it –"

"And it wouldn't bring them back from the dead or point a finger at anybody!" Jack cut in. "I had a look around before you came and I found a set o' footprints crossing the potato field I ploughed the other day, and there were some loose stones knocked off the wall where someone climbed on to the road. So, if it's not too much trouble, Jim, could you go to the Guards' barracks and report it, while I have another look around. Maybe it might give that detective they have in there, what's-his-name? – the Brylcreem Kid everyone calls him – a chance to earn his money for a change, besides standing with his back to the town hall every day, shining the stonework with his overcoat.

Later in the morning John Mahoney, alias the Brylcreem Kid for the hair-oil he plastered profusely on his sleeked-down black hair, arrived on a bicycle. Alighting at the gate he removed his bicycle clips, smoothed down his trousers with a few brisk slaps of a hand, and followed Jack, arms swinging, first to the horse stable and then to the cowshed. "You're right – they're dead," were his first words of investigative enlightenment. "But how d'you know they were poisoned? Only a vet could tell you that. So, what am I doing here – cycling out all this way? Unless I have proof they were deliberately poisoned there's nothing I can do. For all I know they might've eaten something and died in their sleep."

"But if you suspected foul play, you'd get the vet yourself, wouldn't you?" Jack returned calmly, for all that he was seething at the lanky young detective's lack of initiative, and then he went on to explain about the footprints and the huge coincidence that all three had died on the same night.

"If you think I'm going into that field getting my shoes covered in shite, you have another think coming!" snapped the Kid, turning his eyes down to his shining black oxfords, as though it was sacrilege to even suggest that they should be soiled just to look at some silly old footprints. "As far as I can see, there's no sign of foul play. The stables haven't been broken into –"

"You wouldn't have to break in if there was no lock on the door, would you?" Jack cut in.

Save for a slight raising of an eyebrow at Jack's pointed remark, the detective continued with his summing up: "In my opinion no crime has been committed, and unless I have a veterinary's report on my desk tomorrow morning, confirming that the animals were deliberately poisoned, my hands are tied. So, I'll bid you good morning."

Stifling the sarcastic retort that sprang to his lips Jack walked to the gate with the detective, his eyes following in his wake as he pedalled away, and if wishful thinking ever became reality somewhere on his way back to town the Brylcreem Kid would fall off his bicycle and break his neck. Still, he had thought it prudent not to mention Paisley, for if anything should happen to his person or property, he would be the prime suspect.

Although the finger of suspicion pointed at Paisley the footprints were far too big, even for him, and yet, instinct stronger than reason kept telling him that if Paisley hadn't done it himself, he was behind it. He must think, do nothing without careful consideration. There were several ways of getting back at him, devious ways, starting by sabotaging his machinery and transport, and his old charm: 'there's a path which no fowl knoweth and which the eye of the vulture hath not seen', was suddenly alive again. Still, such action would prove nothing, and the police would soon put two and two together. To gain any real satisfaction he would have to expose Paisley and seek retribution through the courts. Someone else besides Paisley knew, and when two people knew something, it was no longer a secret, although it now seemed that his day of reckoning would have to wait. Perhaps if England was kind to him...

Somewhere in the background of his mind, without hardly being conscious of it, he knew that the dilemma he had been struggling under, whether to stay or go, was at last resolved, and yet, the thought of pulling up stakes with all its implications struck deep into his dulled senses with the grim finality of a death bell sounding. He had Eileen to think of, the crops had to be sown, he had the turf to cut and countless other jobs to attend to, and there was no guarantee he would ever earn enough money to come back and turn the tables on Paisley. Perhaps if he waylaid him late some night and beat him senseless with a pickshaft, he could steal a bicycle and cycle to Athlone fifty miles up the track, and from there, catch the Dublin train and be safely across the Irish Sea before anyone noticed his absence. On the other hand, if it wasn't Paisley...

Still, there was much to be done before he was in a position to take any steps in that direction and, as his thoughts returned to his dead horse, he felt the lump in his throat tightening as he recalled with increasing desolation the companionship of their years together, toiling in wind and rain, cultivating his clapped-out acres with scarcely a crumb to show for it at the end of the day, the pigs and the tinkers which always upset him, and his capers in the blacksmith's shop while he was being shod, memories in a host of other memories that had suddenly turned sad.

Later that evening he buried Charlie's remains at the back of the stable, so deep that no predatory animals or birds would ever taste a morsel of his flesh, and he snarled at Jim Madden for suggesting he should sell his carcase to the master of the hunt, although he accepted the pound grudgingly offered for the dead cows. As he heaped the last of the soil on the grave, a sob that would not rise caught his throat with a cruel hand, while the hollow reverberations of the top part of the stable door banging to and fro in the wind kept reminding him of his loss with heart-rending clarity. Finally, with his chest tight with tears that would not come, he turned away, knowing that if he stayed a moment longer, he would lose all control.

Living in some borderland between reality and nightmare Jack's days dragged by. The sun came up, the sun went down, he rose every morning and lay down at night, weary with a weariness that comes when all hope is gone until the merciful adjustment nature makes when what cannot be cured must be endured gave him the strength to go on.

A week later Jack was a man with his mind made up, and Eileen, quick to sense his intention, remarked gloomily: "I suppose you're off to England now, leaving me here on my own. But you don't have to go really – we still have the pigs, the calves, the fowl, and that young heifer'll be soon ready for the bull. We could manage with the donkey and cart for a while, and you can always borrow the horse off Paddy Keane."

"Borrow the horse off Paddy Keane!" Jack exploded, cutting Eileen short. "In the first place Paddy Keane wouldn't give you the scaldings of his taypot – you know how stingy he is yourself. Isn't that why I put him in charge of the booze at the Stations and, as for giving me a loan o' that ould nag of his, I'd have a better chance if I asked him for a loan o' the wife, he thinks that much of him. It was bad enough running a one-horse farm without even thinking about running a one-ass farm – where's your pride? And besides, I won't have another horse on the place – when I come back, we'll have a tractor."

"It's all right for you to say, come back with a tractor, but say you don't come back at all, what's going to happen to me?" asked Eileen, her tone full of self-pity, for Jack's plans were striking at the very foundation of her security.

"You'll be well looked after," returned Jack reassuringly. "And remember when I said I'd never let another dog inside the house after Brownie got run over? – well, I've changed my mind. Now that I'm going away, it's different. I've seen Michael Joyce, and he has a nice black-and-white dog for you, six months old – that is, if he stays with you. So, I hope you treat him better than you treated me. I've made arrangements with Murt Burke and the Moores to do the field work and cut the turf till I come back, and to keep an eye on you. So, you've got nothing to fear."

"What'll happen if they come back again and kill the pigs and calves?"

"You'll still have the donkey, won't you? – and you can fly into Egypt on him!" snapped Jack, rolling his eyes to emphasise his perseverance. "The Lord save us, what I've got to put up with in this house – it must be worth at least twenty plenary indulgences – it's no wonder I'm off to England. For Christ's sake, Eileen, will you ever think of something cheerful to say. All this doom and gloom is getting to me – you're like Wednesday's child. Did it ever cross your mind that I might be worried too?" he went on, and he was worried, far more than he was letting on, for now that the tightrope of life on which he had been precariously balanced had slackened, he was facing the abyss of uncertainty into which he had always been afraid to look, and Eileen's petty fears were nothing compared to the difficulties he felt lay ahead.

When it suddenly struck her that she was only thinking of herself, Eileen forced a smile, for really she had nothing to fear. Intuitively she knew that Paisley presented no threat, for her rejection of him would keep him away. Her greatest concern was the thought of living alone, easy prey for Mike Cullinane who was sure to come calling once he heard Jack had gone, especially if he never came back. The thought of laying for Cullinane stirred in her a spirit of protest, for she could never force her flesh to consent to a surrender it did not desire. But Jack would come back, if she knew Jack at all, and suddenly repentant, she recalled the many times he had pulled the rabbit out of the hat when it was most needed and his sardonic grin that had a way of reducing troubles to their proper proportions. Even his jeers, which had so often stung her to angry retort, had always made sense, and though his words were mostly barbed, they were the barbs of truth. "What part of England are you thinking of going to?" she asked, concern replacing the self-pity in her tone.

"London and soon," returned Jack, without deliberation. "When a plunge has to be taken, it's no good lingering on the bank. A man once told me that no matter which country you go to, you should try the biggest city in it first, and if you don't make your money there, it's unlikely if you'll make it anywhere else either – it makes sense. Imagine a man coming to Ireland to make his fortune – perish the thought – he wouldn't come around here, or Dunmore, or Cloonfad, would he? He'd try Dublin first – big eejit that he'd be in the first place. But seriously, Eileen, you've got nothing to worry about. As I said, the neighbours'll do most o' the heavy work, and keep an eye on you as well. As soon as I get settled, I'll send you a few quid, but for the love o' jasus don't hang around the house and mope. Go out a bit – it's not the end o' the world, you know."

Over the years Jack had built around himself an invisible wall against setbacks, a wall of sangfroid that he could hide behind, and even when beaten, he could always steal a little victory by laughing at defeat. But now that this unexpected tragedy had breached its battlements, the laugh he attempted to bring some light-heartedness into the conversation was bitter and utterly lacking in humour. "I'm the one who should be worried," he said, feigning a carefree air. "It's all right for you. You have Sergeant Driscoll and the law on patrol, and the whole village on the lookout, not to mention Michael Joyce's dog – you're better defended than England was during the War."

On the night before his departure Daly's kitchen was bursting at the seams. Jim Madden and Mick Moore were among the first to arrive, followed by Murt Burke, Tommy Fogarty, Peter Costello, Michael Joyce, John and Rita Quinn,

Kathy Moore; Tom, Jimmy, Martin and Ann Kennedy, Silver Walsh with his tin whistle, Paddy Keane with his accordion, and Granny Mulhaire with her little bottle of holy water from Knock Shrine for Jack to take with him.

"Mind you don't lose your religion over there now, Jack," said Granny, her words a blessing more than a caution.

"That's about all I've left to lose, Granny," Jack laughed, accepting the holy water reverently so as not to hurt her feelings, for he believed the time for holy water had passed. Poor old Granny, her skin as brown and wrinkled as a dried parchment, was one of that dignity of grandmothers to whom age is its own embellishment and, as if he was seeing her for the last time, memories of his childhood came flooding back, after-school memories when he used to hurry to Granny's on his way home, and how Granny had always found little jobs for him to do, jobs that he later realised didn't need doing at all so that she could pay him a penny. Other little kindnesses too began to obtrude, as if someone had just wiped clean the mirror of his memory, until he was almost reduced to tears – the little things in life that are never appreciated until it's too late.

Despite the music and the forced air of joviality, the kitchen was enshrouded in gloom, unlike other nights when it was animated by political arguments, backbiting, even blasphemy, and had resounded to the lilting strains of THE FLOWER OF SWEET STRABANE and the patting of dancing feet on the concrete floor. In the light of the tragedy that had befallen the Dalys the neighbours were profuse in their offers of help, whether in the form of labour or goods, and Jack was pleased with their support and to know that he had friends.

All too soon it was time for the final farewells, and one by one Jack shook hands with his well-wishers as they took their leave. While he was opening and closing the door, he noticed that Kathy Moore was hanging back outside as though she wanted to have a word with him in private and, when a glance around showed that no immediate departures were imminent, he gently closed the door behind him. "Well, this is it, Kathy. It might be long time, no see, if you know what I mean," he said, sensing rather than seeing her agony of embarrassment in the darkness.

Kathy wasn't as bashful as Jack had assumed, and he was taken completely by surprise when she threw her arms about his neck and kissed him passionately, forcing his lips apart with the tip of her tongue. There was lust and demand in the kiss, everything but tenderness, and instinctively he responded, running his hands up and down her lissom body which was rapidly developing in softer, rounder curves, while she kept pushing a knee forward provocatively until he was sexually aroused. Even then, she didn't ease away, and Jack was first to break from the embrace, the suddenness of it all leaving him lost for words, although Kathy immediately broke into what seemed to be rehearsed lines.

"I hope you don't think I'm too forward, but if didn't do that, you'd never know the way I feel about you," she said. "I've felt this way for some time now, and I know you think I'm a bit young, but when you come back, I'll be grown up and waiting. Please don't say anything – just think about it. And don't worry about things here – I'll look after Eileen."

The blurted words flowed out as if she was reading from a letter, and before Jack's mind had time to digest the evidence of his ears she was gone. Astonished, though pleasurably so, he stood rooted to the spot until the latch lifting revealed Peter Costello and Michael Joyce standing in the open doorway, the lamplight sending their long shadows stretching into the night. Kathy was right – it was something to think about.

Early next morning, after a quick breakfast Jack smiled sardonically as he donned his overcoat, wondering if the threadbare garment would hold together long enough to make the return trip. Murt Burke was standing silently on the hearth, his back to the fire, waiting to accompany him to the railway station, while Eileen was making much to-do about clearing the table, although Jack wasn't fooled by her casual air, for he perceived that she too was fighting back the tears. Having no wish to prolong the agony he kissed her on the forehead, picked up his suitcase, and turned towards the door. It was only when he opened the door and a gust of cold wind swept the kitchen, fluttering the curtains and fanning the fire, that the realisation struck him that he might be closing it behind him for the last time, like so many others who had taken the same road.

Outside, the stars were beginning to fade, and from force of habit he stood for a moment checking the sky for signs of rain. The wan glow from the street lighting over Castleford, magnified at intervals by the brighter lights of the early morning traffic, was flickering in the distance like the aurora borealis and, without a word passing between them, they stepped out briskly for the station, a loose steel tip on the heel of one of Murt's hobnailed boots making a hollow ring on the tarmac road like a badly-shod horse.

When they reached the first bend in the road, instinct demanded that he should stop, and when he looked back at his birthplace, nestling among the trees in the false dawn, lamplight still showing in the kitchen window, he was taken by a pang of desolation, the type of desolation that perhaps a newly-weaned animal might feel at being parted from its mother, the urge to turn back struggling with the necessity to go forward.

Fighting against the churn of powerful emotions the scene evoked he set off down the winding road, feeling the silent reinforcement of his neighbour keeping pace by his side, the odd barking dog heralding their approach as they hurried past dark houses which were still wrapped in slumber. Although the road was as familiar to him as his own mind it was only now that the full significance of the deserted cottages along the way came home to him, their collapsed roofs, lifeless windows, and gaping doorways peering out from the shadows. Overgrown with briars and silent as a graveyard they had a haunted look about them, haunted not by ghosts but by a powerful absence, for never again would the ring of laugher echo within their walls, a frightening reminder that one more stroke of misfortune and his own cottage could be joining them.

When they reached Castleford, the glow from the streetlamps was fading in the increasing daylight, and they kept up a steady pace, past Grogan's Bar, Pudding Joyce's eating house, the marketplace, and the Phoenix, the lump in Jack's throat, that had been rising ever since he bade a silent farewell to his home, finally turning to tears when they reached the last uphill stretch to the railway station, a short walk which down through the years had been the Calvary of thousands – the lonesome road.

Although the train wasn't due out until seven it was already standing at the platform, its steam spread low in the misty air, and when he failed to recognise a face in the scattering of travellers, Jack turned to his taciturn friend, right hand extended. "So long, Murt – see you at Christmas, please God," he said, as casually as the constriction of his throat would allow, and though his farewell, reinforced by a smile, was both a promise and a prayer, it was said with a confidence he was far from feeling, unlike the optimism of so many men setting out for so many wars – all over by Christmas.

"God bless you now, Jack, and a safe journey. And don't be worryin' about Eileen – we'll look after her," said Murt, returning the handshake, and for a moment Jack thought he detected tears in his opaque eyes.

The minutes ticked by slowly, one by one, like mourners passing in a funeral possession, until the engine whistled dolefully and dismally, as though it was in concert with Jack's mood, trolleys clattered along the platform, and doors banged as the last of passengers stepped on board. A final few seconds of farewell followed through the open windows, necks craning out, hands extended, hands reaching up barely grasping, until a longer, more shrill whistle blast sent the connecting rods on the engine's wheels pushing and pulling, and the train chugged out, leaving the platform shuddering in its wake.

Soon the miles were dropping behind them, the silent telegraph poles speeding by faster and faster, the clickety-clack rhythm of the wheels beating out an ominous message: *'you'll never come back – you'll never come back – you'll never come back',* as they steamed through pastures mantled in new green and lonesome tracts of bogland, its black water looking cold and depthless in the early morning solitude. Absently twirling a tiny gold bell with his fingers, something he had picked up near his front gate after the detective had cycled away, Jack's thoughts returned to his dead horse and cows, and for the umpteenth time he went through the process of eliminating his enemies.

According to Madden, who had slit open one of the cow's stomachs, it was the work of strychnine, administered by person or persons who knew what they were doing. Besides Paisley, Cullinane had a motive for getting him out of the way and so had O'Hara, and yet, he found it hard to imagine either of them clambering over stone walls in the darkness, or perhaps they had paid someone to do it. However, getting someone else to do their dirty work would leave them open to blackmail, which narrowed the field down to Paisley, and no matter which way he set the compass needle of his deliberation, it always returned to point at him and Big Jimbo Maughan, the tinker, one of the tribe who was with him in Grogan's on the day Grogan had shown them the road. The footprints were big, and they were made by wellington boots – Jimbo had big feet and always wore wellingtons with turned-down tops. Paisley could have driven him there in his car. There were tracks farther up the road where a car had turned, and there would be no fear of blackmail, for Jimbo's word wouldn't hold water in a law court even if he swore on a mountain of Bibles, Korans, and Books of

Common Prayer. So, the only way to get at the truth would be to hammer it out of Jimbo –

Jack's train of thoughts stopped abruptly when he was reminded again of the uncertainty of the future, for this was no time to truckle to small problems when greater ones lay on the horizon. Presently, his worldly goods totalled seven pounds, some loose change, and the sandwiches Eileen had made to take with him, enough to keep him for a week if he was lucky, and if he wasn't lucky, he could easily wind up sleeping under the stars like the tinkers he so despised. His aim was to reach Camden Town where there was a large Irish community and play it from there. He had no contingency plans – he was in at the deep end and all he could do was swim with the tide.

As the train rattled along, his thoughts kept rotating from his desire for revenge, to the uncertainty ahead, and back to Kathy Moore's outpouring. Although she was scarcely sixteen her kiss was adult and provocative. If she went around kissing men like that, it was only a matter of time before someone took advantage of her, and yet, it would have served no purpose to reveal the love that was still bottling up his heart, despite all his disappointments, a love that was now living on hope alone.

It was almost noon when he alighted in Dublin and, as the ship wasn't due to sail until nine o'clock that night, he spent the day wandering up one street, down another, from Capel Street to O'Connell Street and back again in a criss-cross pattern, stopping for tea in dingy cafes and browsing in shop windows, until he felt he knew the price of every garment, every pair of shoes, every joint of meat, and every fish in the city.

Yet ironically what he failed to notice was the image that stared back at him from some of the windows, which was a fair depiction of a male Irish emigrant of the fifties setting off for London to make his fortune: young, clean-shaven, hair parted at the side and combed back in waves, a resolute lift to the chin, and sharp inquisitive eyes. His dress too: a tweed overcoat, belted loosely at the waist, grey single-breasted suit, the twenty-four inch bottoms of the trousers almost covering his shining black shoes, white shirt, starched collar, and maroon tie, typified his emigrant status, and to complete the picture he was carrying a brown millboard suitcase, which he kept under such careful surveillance every time he put it down, that no one could be blamed for suspecting it contained the crown jewels, and not a pair of hobnailed boots, his second suit, an old jacket and trousers, a few working shirts, some items of sentimental value, and a razor.

Finally, when it was time to embark on the second leg of the journey, he made his way to Dunlaoire where the *Princess Maud*, looking cold and uninviting in the gathering darkness, towered over the dock, and the dark water lapping about its hulk could hardly have sounded more desolate had it been lapping about Charon's boat. Although there was still two hours to go before sailing time a queue of men, women and children had already formed, four and five deep, lengthening with each new arrival until it rounded every pillar of the embarkation hall like a giant anaconda. The patient faces, silent, looking quietly ahead, had no elation in them, no shine of hope – Ireland's spare parts fleeing to purgatory to escape from hell. The children too seemed to sense that it was no excursion, a trip across the sea and back, but a journey that would take them away from all they knew for a long, long time, perhaps forever.

When the gangways were lowered, the resolute band, most of whom were carrying suitcases of poor quality, some of which were girdled with belts, ties or twine to keep them from bursting open, shuffled forward in short measured glides like the moves on a chessboard, their fate written in the grim lines of their faces as others have it written on their palms. All were heading for the land of the fish and chips, a land of uncertainty, yet a land of hope, the women hoping to go into nursing or find work in the factories, the men, in the booming construction industry, while the disenchanted might perhaps weep there, weep with bitter loneliness, for many of them would never see their homes again. Only a few would return with the fortune they had their hearts set on, but perhaps everyone counted themselves in that few – like Jack Daly.

After a fanfare of whistle blasts, followed by the wail of a foghorn, the deck began a slow graceful rolling and the emigrant ship ploughed out to sea on its three and a half hour journey, a short voyage that would change forever the lives of all on board. Standing at the stern, looking back at the harbour lights winking dimly in the darkness, Jack felt an icy shiver running down his spine, as if someone had just stepped on his grave and, shrugging deeper into his overcoat, he felt with each heave of the waves a slow detachment from the land of his birth.

Starlight as bright as a ballroom covered the tranquil sea and sparks flew up from the chimney stacks, vivid in the darkness, but quickly gone like his shattered dreams of things that might have been. It was hard to go forward with his heart full of aching memories, so he set his thoughts against the past, but his thoughts kept escaping, chasing one another back over the waves and back over the years. Memories, both fond and bitter, came suddenly alive in his mind, milling on top of each other, as though he had reached another milestone in his life's cycle and, his first romance on Bundoran's strand, his bewitching night on the high headland overlooking the Atlantic, and other sentimental moments, flashed before his eyes like the visions of a drowning man, until Mary O'Hara's angelic smile put the brakes on the roller-coaster ride.

It was easy to say forget her, but the exciting tingle of her kisses still lingered on his lips, for it seemed that there was no regular path for getting out of love as there was for getting into it. A vague sadness weighed on his soul, which set him to wondering if it was a conflict of fates, a crossing of loves, or perhaps it was destiny that was driving them apart just to bring them together again in a new deal. The thought lingered until the scowling face of old O'Hara put a damper on his optimism, rekindling his bitterness, and when inevitably it conjured up, like a genie from a bottle, Bull Paisley's big head, he cursed the system which allowed such wickedness to prevail. It now seemed that the Bible was just another masterpiece of fiction, for in the common world of fact the wicked were not struck down as in the story of Sodom and Gomorrah, nor the good rewarded. On the contrary, success was given to the strong, failure thrust upon the weak, which suggested that if there was to be any striking down, he himself would have to wield the axe.

Finally, when the cold wind forced him to go below, Jack was made to suffer the reality of the cliché: 'the *Princess Maud* never leaves anyone standing on the quay'. Passengers were squashed together everywhere, sitting on the stairs, on the floor, or on their luggage, and women tended to children in conditions that fell far short of even basic standards, which left him with no choice but to squeeze into room among them.

Chapter 2

Next morning at seven, when the mail train coasted to a halt at London's Euston station, Jack yawned and stretched out of his restless slumber and, suddenly realising his whereabouts, he came quickly to his feet, dragged his suitcase from the rack, and stepped on to the platform, the shrill whistle blasts and the slamming of doors all along the length of the train startling him into full wakefulness.

Hanging back to let the more impatient passengers through he joined the shuffle towards the ticket barrier, and though he had heard tales of mighty London, he was totally unprepared for the tide of humanity sweeping through the station. Streams of men and women, dropping from trains that had just stopped, were surging along under the steel-girdered roof like an underground river towards an open sluice gate and dispersing fanwise to their various destinations. Following tentatively in their slipstream he reached the street and, as he was about to ask directions, he spied a road sign for Camden Town.

At the first main intersection the streets exploded into life. Trams, buses, lorries, taxis, horse-drawn drays and bicycles were swishing, honking, clip-clopping and tringing along in a never-ending procession, and the pavements on either side were thronged with people from all walks of life: elderly women who looked frightened to cross the street, fashionably-dressed young ladies with expressions on their beautifully made-up faces of such intensity that they looked as though they were in pain, men in pinstripe suits and bowler hats carrying briefcases and umbrellas walking side by side with workmen in donkey jackets, cloth caps and boots, uniformed municipal workers, charladies, darkies, turbaned Sikhs, Indians and Chinese, all in such a hurry that they hadn't time to bid one another the hour of the day.

When he reached Camden Town, he stopped to check his bearings and, as he had just enough money for the fare back to Castleford, he felt somewhat uneasy about straying too far from Euston station, his escape route if things didn't work out. The idea of returning home, which had taken root the moment he set foot on the platform, was growing stronger all the time, even it meant borrowing the horse from Paddy Keane, for it was indeed a rum bevy of society in which he found himself, nothing at all like what he had been expecting. Their accents too were as varied as their appearance, and the combination of pinched vowels, cockney twangs and brogues, mingling with Urdu, Chinese and the strident choruses of the street traders that fell on his ears would defy even the phonetic capabilities of Henry Higgins to classify.

Considering all the refined English people who came to Galway on their holidays he was disillusioned by it all, from the weather-beaten old men wearing white silk scarves and half-fingered mittens selling vegetables from barrows, to the men in pinstripe suits and bowler hats, and any notions he might have had about London being a posh place were quickly evaporating in the polluted air with the exhaust fumes of the bumper-to-bumper traffic and the pungency of horse-piss, dogshite, and rotten fish.

Now that he had arrived in Camden Town, he was out of ideas, and unless he found work and a place to lay his head all in the next twenty-four hours, it was back to Castleford for him, although the thought of returning with his tail between his legs had the effect of stiffening his spine. Others had faced the same uncertainty and survived, and so would he, even if it meant sleeping on a park bench.

In a more resolute frame of mind he stood awhile at a street corner taking in his new environment until the smell of frying bacon reminded him that he hadn't eaten since finishing the last of Eileen's sandwiches on the ship and, with his nose leading, he found its source – Mack's Café, a greasy-looking establishment with a small frontage squashed between a grocer's and a newsagent's, the rancid smoke billowing from the open top sections of its grimy windows a smelly reminder of Pudding Joyce's eating house.

With his paucity of purse fighting a losing battle with his hunger pangs, he ran an eye over the menu board outside. The full breakfast for a half-crown looked good value, and he slipped through the doorway just as a group of four men were leaving. The inside mirrored the outside, inasmuch as it was small and cramped, and its tubular chairs and tables were so tightly-packed together that there was barely room to move. Behind a short counter a tubby balding man in a black-and-white striped apron was busy scribbling down the orders, pouring the tea, and taking the money and, as he joined the queue for the counter, he noticed many Irish faces among the rough-and-ready, all-male clientele. Still, none of them acknowledged his presence, not even by a nod, for all their attention was focused on the short-skirted blonde waitress who was bustling back and forth, hips swinging, from the kitchen to the tables, calling out the contents of each plate in a shrill cockney accent: "Egg, bycon, sausage and beans, two 'oly ghost – dobble egg, bycon, and bobble, two slices – egg, bycon, bobble and squeak, and a fried slice – dobble egg, bycon and two o' drip – one dog sandwich."

When he ordered and paid for his breakfast, he threaded his way through the aisles of tables, his tea in one hand, his suitcase in the other, his eyes searching for a place to sit, until a man at a single table nodded to an opposite chair. Flopping down on the seat he ventured a tentative good morning and sat silently while the man made a comprehensive study of him over the rim of his teacup with that wily proficiency of appraisal which all Irishmen seem to share.

After a few moments of awkward silence the man left down his cup and lit a cigarette. "You look like a man who's just after docking," he remarked, in the distinctive brogue of Southwest Ireland.

There was something about the man that held Jack's interest, something in his laid-back attitude, which was totally at variance with the general acceleration he had encountered so far. Somewhere in his middle twenties he was solidly built, angular-featured, and clean-shaven. His short brown hair, which showed traces of a side parting, was tousled as if he had been wearing a cap and, though the hands cupping the match he was holding to his cigarette were swarthy and toilworn, they weren't cut and bruised and twisted out of shape like so many hands that do manual work for a living. From what he could see of his dress – a navy-blue donkey jacket and check shirt open at the neck – it was clean, although it took a second perusal to reveal what had attracted his attention – his hazel eyes, which were mild, with perhaps a trace of cynicism in them, as if nothing ever surprised or excited him. Now those eyes, brow unfurrowed above them, were waiting patiently for him to explain his presence, although the wry twist to the smile that was hovering on his lips seemed to say, for what it's worth.

Satisfying the curiosity of inquisitive strangers wasn't in Jack's nature. Yet the man had asked no questions except with his eyes and, feeling that it might be in his interest to unburden himself and perhaps get an inkling as to the lie of the land, he nodded a greeting. "Yes, as you say – just after docking, and I'm looking for digs and work in that order," he returned. "If you can wise me up any, I'd be obliged."

The man grinned, showing off a compact set of tobacco-stained teeth. "I don't think the digs'll be much of a problem as long as you have money, but the work – it all depends on the type o' work you're looking for," he explained. "There's plenty o' the hard type to be got, the type you don't get rich on and puts a hump on your back before your time. I suppose I don't have to tell you about that type o' work."

"No – you don't have to explain about that type o' work, but any kind o' work at the moment'd be a godsend."

"I know the way you feel – believe me," said the man, grinning again, this time almost pathetically. "If you're interested, there's a fella called O'Donoghue that might suit you. He picks up men outside the door here every morning, but I feel I must warn you that it's hard work, a lot different from what you were doing back yonder. At the moment, all over the country, they're taking the electricity down off the poles and putting it underground. Cable work, it's called, thick work, digging trenches for heavy-duty electric cables, and when the cables are laid, filling them in again, all day, every day. He pays three quid a shift to some – fifty bob to others. It's all up to how you perform. The shift is a long one – half-seven to six, with just two short breaks. If that's any good to you, be outside here in the morning."

"What time?" asked Jack.

The man hesitated just long enough to pull hard on his cigarette, and then he smiled, a quick smile that flashed and disappeared as swiftly as a trout crossing a knife of sunshine in a pool. "The work is out near Luton, and the lorry pulls away at half-six – sharp, and you won't be back till well after seven at night," he explained. "It's a long ould pilgrimage, and it'll take a lot more out o' you than doing Lough Derg or climbing Croagh Patrick, and there are no indulgences to be gained either, only plenty of abuse. So, don't say I didn't warn you. I'm working out there myself, but I missed out this morning."

"I can see nothing wrong with that," returned Jack. "I'm not fussy what I have to do. And you mentioned digs."

"No – I didn't mention digs. You mentioned you were looking for digs," the man returned matter-of-factly, and there was no more expression on his face than in his voice.

Taken aback by the somewhat snappish reply Jack felt that he had stepped over a forbidden line, or perhaps there was something perverse in the man's character and, considering all the tales he had heard of England, it was possible that he was being led up the garden path.

When Jack failed to comment, the man grinned again, this time apologetically. "If you're looking for a lie-down, there are three houses side by side, numbers 76, 78 and 80 in Brecknock Road belonging to Widow Kilbane – good digs, fairly clean, and she's got rooms to let as well. When I say, fairly clean, I mean the blankets won't walk – no lice, that's your best bet," he explained, without any prompting. "And, if you want a start, be outside here tomorrow morning at six – dressed for work. Don't mind that it's Thursday – every day is the same to O'Donoghue. I should be there myself, that is, if she doesn't lie on my shirt-tail again in the morning."

"Thanks, pal," returned Jack, scribbling down the address on the inside of his cigarette packet. "Anyway I'm Jack Daly from Galway."

"Jack will do – first names only in this town, mate," the man explained. "I'm Pat, and it doesn't matter what part of Ireland you come from, not to me anyway, but to some people it means everything."

The conversation was interrupted when the waitress arrived with Jack's breakfast, and Pat, with a curt nod of farewell, picked up his cap from under the table and headed for the door.

Digesting the man's advice with his food Jack decided it was worth putting to the test, although later, when he was back on the street, he realised that Brecknock Road could be on the moon for all he knew.

"Op by the Brecknock pob, moite," a hurrying passer-by called over his shoulder when he asked directions, although the man at the street corner selling papers was more explicit. After trudging uphill for almost a mile he found the public house and then the road, which had terraces of three-storeyed brick houses on either side, steps leading up to the front doors and down to the basements, with nothing but low walls of crumbling brickwork between them and the pavement.

Climbing the short set of steps to the well-weathered door of No 78, the middle house of the three, he let the brass knocker fall a couple of times and waited. He was about to knock again when a lady in a loose housecoat opened the door and stood silently on the threshold appraising him, one hand on her hip, the other on the jamb of the door, her bare insteps shining in the opening of her furry slippers. Tall for a woman, she had long auburn hair which was smoothed back from her high forehead and held together by a chequered silk scarf, her grey eyes were wide apart and slightly slanted, her nose was straight and pointed, and the only flaw in her features was her mouth, which was wide because her lips weren't quite full enough. Her skin, even in the gloom of the doorway, looked pitted and flaky, as if the constant use of make-up was taking its toll, although her figure beneath her smock looked trim and nicely rounded and, considering it was early morning and she was without cosmetic artifice, she looked to be in her early forties.

"Well?" she said, sliding her eyes over Jack, as if she was reading a page of type, all the way down to the footnote of his scuffed suitcase without once anchoring on his features.

Feeling somewhat uncomfortable under her gaze Jack looked down at his toecaps. "I was told I might find lodgings here," he said, stuttering slightly.

"Were you now?" returned the lady, with more than a little hauteur.

Jack had been warned that green Irishmen were always the butt of jokes in England and, certain the man in the café had played a trick on him, he picked up his suitcase and turned away.

"Wait!" the lady called, and when Jack looked back, she was halfway down the steps, making as if she was about to follow him. She had almost reached the pavement when she stopped, and when a sudden whip of wind caught the flimsy material of her housecoat and sent it swirling and wrapping about her legs and thighs, accentuating their shapeliness in every detail, nothing short of a heart attack could have quelled the surge of virility coursing through his body.

"You're an independent one – I never said I hadn't lodgings," she said, and this time there was no impertinence in her tone. "So, why the sudden hurry away?"

"I'm just after coming over from Ireland, and I thought someone sent me here just for a lark," returned Jack, suddenly feeling foolish, as though the joke was still on him.

The lady's face lost some of its coldness. "I can give you full board for three pounds a week, or I've got rooms to let at thirty shillings a week where you'll have to fend for yourself, but I must remind you that the rent has to be paid in advance," she explained, smiling for the first time, her upper lip curling away from her even set of top teeth, the crow's feet on the outer corners of her eyes wrinkling prettily, a smile that took years off her appearance.

"The full board'll be fine, ma'am, if that's all right with you," said Jack and, after a quick rummage in his wallet, he produced three one-pound notes.

"Thank you," returned the lady, the blandness back on her face. "But I must have your name."

When Jack gave his name, he scraped his shoes on the grid, wiped them on the mat, and followed the lady, whom he presumed was Widow Kilbane, into the dark hallway. It was only when he took in his surroundings that he could understand her scarcely perceptible smile, for the hall was as dingy as it was musty-smelling, and the linoleum was so worn in the centre that the boards were showing. A bare bulb dangled from the ceiling on a frayed length of flex, and the walls, from which the paper was peeling, bore a pattern of dirty hands. Holding his head upright, as if he hadn't noticed its shabbiness, he followed her up endless flights of stairs until they reached an open door on the top landing.

"I'll let you have this single room so you'll have a little privacy," said the lady, ushering him into a tiny sparsely-furnished room which smelt of DDT and mothballs. "The bathroom is just down the hall – you can't miss it. Dinner is from seven on, but you'll have to fend for yourself in the morning – I'll explain it all to you later. But by the look of you, I'd say you want to catch up on your lost sleep. So I'll leave you to it."

When he heard the lady's retreating footsteps on the stairs, Jack threw his suitcase on the narrow iron bedstead and took stock. Besides the bed there was a wardrobe, which had a panel missing on one of the doors, a chest of drawers, a washbasin, a wooden chair by the bed on which a polish-tin lid gave the idea of an ashtray, and a cracked mirror above the washbasin was reflecting the sunlight from the only window.

Once he had unpacked he slipped between the sheets, certain that the lady was Widow Kilbane, having made his final deduction from the weight of gold and diamond rings on the fingers of her left hand and, with his mind locked tightly against the cacophony rising from the street below, he closed his eyes and crashed into oblivion.

When he awoke he felt refreshed, and though he had no idea of the time, the angle of the beam of sunlight streaming through the window suggested it was late afternoon or early evening. Swinging his feet to the floor he lit a cigarette and sat awhile counting his money, making separate piles of the coppers and silver on the chair by the bedside, which was just about enough to pay for another week's lodgings. The next step was to find a job, no matter how little it paid, for it would be folly to depend entirely on Pat's suggestion, Still, his advice had been good so far, and where else could he look for a start unless he asked at some of the building sites he had passed on the long trek from Euston.

The clip-clopping of a horse's hooves and the sound of a bell floating up from the street attracted him to the window, and the unintelligible singsong call of a junkman brought people hurrying from doorways, carrying chattels of every description to his cart. As it was a first-time experience, he watched somewhat curiously as they formed a queue, reluctantly accepting what the man grudgingly offered, and by the time the horse had trotted off with his load of odds and ends, with it went the last of his illusions of London being a city of plenty, for its denizens seemed to be every bit as hard up as the ones he had left behind in Castleford.

Without actually being aware of it, Widow Kilbane had invaded his subconscious, for the moment his thoughts returned to her, unbidden his hand began to stroke his two-day growth of stubble and, after bathing and shaving, he returned downstairs.

When he reached the ground floor, he was startled by a voice from the shadows, saying: "You're feeling better, I take it, after your sleep?" And, when he turned, the landlady was standing in an open doorway, which he could see led to a basement.

Speechless for a moment Jack had to blink twice to convince himself that it really was the lady of the morning, for she had undergone a complete transformation. Her hair, neatly tied up in a ponytail, highlighted the perfect symmetry of her neck and the attractive jut of her collarbones, and her bright-blue jumper, which had a plunging neckline, hung so loosely on her shoulders that both bra straps were visible, an indecorum which she quickly corrected when it fell under Jack's admiring gaze. Her black skirt, which reached just below the knee, was so tight-fitting that it looked as if it had been put on wet and then allowed to shrink around her figure, and in the gloom of the hall her creamy skin glowed and her eyes sparkled, a sparkle that had been missing earlier, a lack of sparkle peculiar to women in the flowers.

"This way," she said, leading Jack down the steep stairs to the basement. "I'm sorry my manners weren't all they should have been earlier, but you'll soon find that I'm not at my best first thing in the morning, and I was so disconcerted over being caught in my déshabillé that I completely forgot to introduce myself. I'm Teresa Kilbane, although I'm quite aware that most men who have sought accommodation in my modest hostelry refer to me as Widow Kilbane, especially the ones who skipped without paying the rent. But to be called 'Widow' lends an air to propriety rather than the contrary and I take no umbrage. So, come into the kitchen and I'll have the cook make you a cup of tea," she went on and, though her accent was clipped and high-toned, her pronunciation was too correct and lacked the careless certainty of the born lady. More puzzling still, everything about her was at loggerheads with the mundaneness of the establishment.

The kitchen, which had been knocked through into the adjoining basements on either side, ran the full length of the three properties, and a row of small windows, which were interrupted at intervals by boarded-up doors, looked out at eyelevel on an enclosed backyard. It had its full complement of cookers, sinks, stoves and kitchen furniture, and the round-the-wall shelving was neatly stacked with all types of crockery. When he was seated at one of the long kitchen tables, she introduced him to Mrs O'Neill, the cook, a plump elderly Irishwoman with a round pleasant face. "As I said earlier," the landlady went on, "you'll have to fend for yourself in the morning, but as you can see, everything is laid out, and I'm sure you're not beyond boiling an egg or grilling a rasher of bacon. Besides, there'll be plenty around to help you, so don't be too shy to ask."

All questions answered and two cups of tea later, the landlady led him to a spacious sitting room, which had as furnishing two couches in opposite corners, the stuffing showing through the upholstery, an untidy semicircle of armchairs of similar quality, a jumble of high-backed chairs, all of different framework, two mahogany tables, which were littered with magazines and newspapers, and a nest of smaller tables. The only occupants were two elderly Irishmen, who were slouched in armchairs watching television, whom she introduced at Mick and Martin.

Although television was new to Jack and he was fascinated by it, nothing short of being struck blind could have stopped his eyes from following the rhythmic swing of the widow's hips as she left the room, and Martin, lifting his cap with a forefinger and thumb and scratching his grey mop with his remaining fingers, could hardly have characterised her more aptly if he was a writer of prose – "She's a fine woman surely, the widow is."

From six o'clock onwards the other lodgers, all Irishmen in working clothes and boots, came thundering down the stairs, their heavy tread on the bare boards almost shaking the building, and one by one they flopped down wearily on every vacant seat, as if they were on their last legs. It was easy to see now why the linoleum was so worn, and why it would be folly to do anything about it, just as it was folly for parents to go in for expensive furnishing and decoration until their children were reared. Eyes glued to the television or heads buried in newspapers, scarcely a word passed between them as if they were total strangers meeting for the first time, and for all that most of them were in their teens or early twenties they were a taciturn, surly lot, as if some inner affliction had robbed them of the blitheness of youth.

Save for a more mannerly man with a Northern-Irish accent who introduced himself as Bob Little, the only man to venture his surname, Jack was quick to notice that this was a different breed of Irishman from the easygoing type he was accustomed to, and their boorishness was seen to greater effect when Mrs O'Neill called them to the dining room for dinner.

The dining room, which was on a par with the sitting room in size, had four long oil-clothed tables evenly spaced out on the quarry-tiled floor. A mound of potatoes, boiled in their jackets, were stacked in pyramid fashion in the centre of each table, and when Mrs O'Neill had heaped each lodger's plate to prodigal fullness with beef stew, the potatoes were attacked from all sides with forks until the mounds crumbled almost to nothing. There was no grace or friendly banter, just snap, grab and elbow, scowls instead of smiles if someone hogged the condiments. There was no sign of the widow – there was something catchy about the name, Widow Kilbane – although the redoubtable Mrs O'Neill was well capable of dealing with any squabbles.

His appetite catered for, Jack tilted back his chair, lit a cigarette, and watched silently as the others dispersed. So far so good, he thought, for the meal he had just polished off, which was served in such proportions that it left him chair-bound and belching, made a mockery of all that was being said in his homeland about the food in England being scarce and of poor quality. Now all that remained for him to do was follow the rest of Pat's advice and present himself outside Mack's Café at six next morning.

He was about to rise from the table when Bob Little, one of the few remaining diners, dropped into an opposite chair. "Is this yer first day in England, or did yez just move here from some other degs?" he asked, in a drawly Northern-Irish accent.

Early or mid-twenties Little was of medium stature, square cut, and blunt of feature, and his high forehead was made to look all the more prominent by his receding sandy hair. His blue eyes were sharp and intelligent, and there was something of perhaps bitterness about his mouth when he smiled, and Jack's first impression was of one who had seen better days.

"Yes – it's my first day in London," returned Jack readily, pleased to have someone to talk to, even if meant answering questions.

"I suppose yez'll be looking for a start on the buildings now yez are here."

"If I can get one," said Jack. "A fella this morning told me where to try."

"I'm working in a factory myself – making parts for cars. The money isn't a lot – ten qued a week, take home pay – but it's regular," explained Little. "But, if yer start doesn't work out, I'll put in a spake for yez with our gaffer."

"That's kind of you," returned Jack, although the pay he mentioned, when comparing it with Pat's three pounds a shift, wasn't very encouraging for a man hoping to save enough money to return at Christmas and pick up where he had left off.

After swapping small talk for a few minutes Little excused himself, leaving Jack alone in the dining room save for one latecomer at the next table, who had obviously been eavesdropping on the conversation and, just as he was about to return to the sitting room, the man made signs that he wanted to have a word in his ear.

When Jack leaned forward, the man said in a undertone: "You'd do well to steer clear o' that man you were talkin' to – he's an Orangeman. I don't know what he's doin' here among all us, Irish – he'd be better off in an English lodgin' house among his own."

Although every Irishman was bitter about the manifold wrongs the Catholic population of Northern Ireland were suffering at the hands of the totalitarian, British-backed Protestant regime: segregation, inferior accommodation, second-class education, prohibited from taking up posts in the civil service or joining the police force, and the dreaded B-Specials terrorising and burning out whole communities like the Ku Klux Klan in America, Jack found it hard to associate Little with such atrocities, and he would be sinning against one of his own commandments if he judged a person on someone else's say-so. Believing it to be in his best interests to mind his own business, rather than getting mixed up in petty malice, he made no comment, and after a few moments of awkward silence he returned to the sitting room.

Chapter 3

Next morning, the first traffic sounds below his window and the shuffling tread of feet on the landing outside his door brought Jack out of his restless slumber and, dressing quickly, he sped downstairs. When he opened the kitchen door, the animated buzz that hit him was like the lifting of a roof off a beehive. Men were rushing hither and thither, tripping over one another in their urgency to get something into their stomachs, hurrying from the dining room to the stove and back again to the dining room, tea slopping from over-filled mugs, toast burning, kettles boiling over, frying pans spluttering hot fat, a confusion that could be compared in a milder form to Judgement Day, a day henceforth when there would be no time even to go back for one's coat, a day when the first would be last and last would be first.

A glance at the clock showed quarter-past five and, helping himself to a mug of tea from one of the huge enamel teapots, he gulped down two hard-boiled eggs and a thick slice of bread and butter before joining the stampeding surge through the door, leaving the dining-room tables littered with half-empty mugs, crusts of bread, eggshells, cigarette ash, and the floor swamped in tea spillings, as if a cyclone had swept through it.

Pulling up the collar of his working jacket against the cold April wind he sped down Camden Road to Camden High Street, the pavement ringing beneath the heavy tread of his hobnailed boots, and when he reached the main intersection, he stopped dead in his tracks, awestricken by the scale of the activity at such an early hour. Hundreds of men had already congregated and were milling around the long lines of lorries which were parked bumper-to-bumper on either side of the street, stretching as far as the eye could see in a rainbow of colours, most of which had Irish names on their cabs: Murphy, McNicholas, Lowery, Rahilly, McGinty, Kennedy and others. To provide shelter from the elements the backs of the lorries were rigged with canvas canopies, and each lorry had its own entourage of workers, waiting as it seemed to be ordered to climb aboard by the more authoritative men who were pacing back and forth, counting heads, scribbling in notebooks, and barking orders like sergeant majors on parade.

When he reached Mack's Café, he recognised Pat in the gang of men standing in the footpath two green Thames Traders which had 'O'Donoghue Contractors' on their cabs, a motley gathering in which all age groups were represented, the fresh faces of the younger ones, some no more than boys, shining like mushrooms amid the stubbled ones of the more toilworn. Bareheaded or wearing caps, their dress was as varied as their age and stature. Jackets of every cut and colour, most of which were tattered, hung from shoulders broad and narrow over open-necked shirts, and their trousers were either baggy-arsed and hanging down, or tight-fitting and torn at the knees and crotch, while one man was turned out in a suit, shoes and tie, as if he was on his way home after a night on the tiles. The majority were wearing hobnailed boots, others, wellingtons with turned-down tops, and yet, despite the disparity in their ages and appearance, they had one thing in common – they were all keen and wide-awake.

Pat was standing with his back to the café window, peeping over the headline of a tabloid newspaper he was making a pretence of reading, as if he was ashamed to be associated with the gang, most of whom were unruly and noisy, their coarse, somewhat vulgar banter bringing the odd reproachful frown from some of the passers-by.

When Jack smiled a greeting, Pat nodded in the direction of a tall elderly man wearing a donkey jacket and cap. The man had ganger written all over him and, as his back was turned, Jack was at the disadvantage of having to tap him on the shoulder. "Are you looking for any good men?" he asked, when the man spun round.

"Am I lookin' for any good men?" the ganger returned, repeating the question verbatim, his weather-beaten face screwed up in a scowl and, looking Jack over from head to toe as if he was a beast for sale, he shook his head slowly in feigned bewilderment, "Am I lookin' for any good men? – what a question to ask – sure I'm always lookin' for good men – why? – d'you know any?" he asked, in a nasty-nice tone, giving Jack a more comprehensive appraisal with a wily eye and, perhaps satisfied with what he saw, he forced a laugh. "How stupid of me – sure it's yourself you mean," he went on, rapping his temple with the knuckles of his right hand, as if he was chastising himself for having taken the question in the wrong context. "Well, you can never let it be said that Harry Tobin isn't a fair-minded man, and to prove it, I'll give you a start, but if you're no good to me, I'll sack you before the day is out."

Unbidden, a smile came to Jack's lips at the ganger's candour and, when he threw a glance at Pat, he was smiling too. This time his smile seemed to say – I did warn you.

As the clock above the paper-shop window neared six-thirty, there was a sudden lull in the chatter, and when the ganger looked meaningfully at his watch, in one headlong rush the ragged band scrambled on to the backs of the lorries, Jack among them. When all were on board, the double-tapping of hobnailed boot against the tailboard, like the double-ringing of a bell on a bus, gave the driver the cue to be on his way, and soon they were weaving through London's early-morning traffic, the men who couldn't find room under the canopy hanging out dangerously over the sides. All were grim-faced, with scarcely a word passing between them, as if they were on their way to face a fearsome foe, the surly silence broken only by the flapping noises of the canvas on the canopy and the humming of the wheels on the tarmac road.

An hour later, when Jack felt the urgency leaving the rhythm of the wheels, instinctively he knew they were nearing their destination, and not long afterwards the lorry ground to a halt beside two wooden huts. Immediately the driver applied the handbrake the men, showing unbelievable alacrity, vaulted over the sides in a life-or-death manner, as if they were rats abandoning a sinking ship, and began to flock round the ganger, who had travelled in the cab of one of the lorries. Holding a key aloft for all to see the ganger opened an enormous wooden toolbox with the same ceremony as if he was Michael Miles, the host of *Take Your Pick,* a programme Jack had watched on television the night before. Literally, there was something of take-your-pick about it, for the box was crammed with pickaxes, shovels, forks and grafts, basic tools which would shape each man's destiny and determine whether he went up or down in the world, although it was hard to imagine many levels below their present status.

Across the street, an open trench, fenced in by pole barriers, mounds of earth and road lamps, ran along the footpath. On a nearby grass verge a reel of heavy-duty electric cable was quickly jacked up, and under the ganger's abusive goading the men proceeded to pull the cable off the reel into the trench. When the cable was laid and covered with sand and marker slabs, the in-filling commenced, and when the trench was filled and compacted, the paving slabs were replaced and the leftover soil swept up and shovelled on to the backs of the lorries. When everything was back as though it had never been disturbed, the ganger, like a military commander, moved ahead, marking out separate lengths of trench for each man to dig, and the gang spread out. As the sun climbed the sky, jackets, pullovers and shirts were discarded, and sweat glistened on foreheads as forks and pickaxes knocked sparks off the stony ground.

The singling out system induced competition among the men to gain the ganger's favour, as he paced back and forth, like a giant bird of prey commenting vulgarly on the slowness of the progress and swooping on any slackers. When another length of trench was ready, another reel of cable was laid, and the backfilling and clearing up began all over again, as morning turned to afternoon and then to evening with just two short breaks in between.

Mercifully, six o'clock came, quitting time, and when Jack, with muscles he didn't even know he possessed aching and every movement of his body bringing sharp pain, was about to climb on to the back of the lorry, the ganger called him aside. "I suppose you'll be wantin' a pound or two sub now that the shift is over?" he asked, in a totally changed attitude from that of the morning. "Three quid a shift I'm payin', so there's two in case you're broke. I'll square you up tight tomorrow evening – Friday is pay day. So, what name do you want me to put down in the book for you?"

"Jack Daly."

"I'll just put down JD for now, in case you have different ideas later," said the ganger, winking meaningfully, and no more was said.

Although Jack couldn't understand the hugger-mugger about his name he pocketed the two pounds as most of the others were doing, and on the journey back to Camden Town the mood was more high-spirited and general conversation broke out, mostly about public houses and dance halls. Every so often there was an explosion of yoo-hoo-hooing at passing women, and some of the signs they made, piston-like motions of rigidly-upheld forearms and clenched fists, were crudely explicit. Although he was puzzled by the system and bone weary he was pleased that he had come through the day, and later, as he was making his way back to his lodgings, he heard a voice in the background calling in his wake: "You'll never go back now!"

'You'll never go back', was a catchy saying among the workers, and for all its drollery it bore a cynical ring, as though it could easily come true. The more he tried to dismiss it, the more it kept repeating in his subconscious: *you'll never go back – you'll never go back'*, like a parrot that knows only one phase, something like the message he had deciphered in the rhythm of the train's wheels. Yet, back he was determined to go, and in the following days he stuck to the backbreaking process of bed to work, work to bed, save for Sunday morning when he attended eleven o'clock Mass at the local church, hoping to bump into someone from home.

Except that there were two collections instead of one, he could see no difference from the service in Castleford, the men standing at the back, shuffling impatiently, clearing their throats and looking at their watches, the families and the women occupying the pews. Yet, there was a marked difference in the mainly Irish congregation – they were all young and healthy-looking, with scarcely a grey head or stooped shoulder among them.

Afterwards he dallied outside until the crowd had dispersed and, considering all the returning expatriates who gave Camden Town as their place of abode, it felt somewhat odd that he failed to recognise a face. It could hardly be that they had all lost their religion, as Granny Mulhaire had warned against, or perhaps they had attended earlier Masses.

By being thrifty he was saving over half his wages, some of which he sent to Eileen. However, despite the optimism he put in his letters, the light at the end of the tunnel was moving farther away all the time, and no matter how much he tightened his belt his goal seemed unattainable. He needed a break, and breaks never come to people who sit around and mope. He wondered where he had heard such philosophy, perhaps in some film about Depression-era America, but it made sense, and anything that made sense always appealed to his practical nature. Making money wasn't associated with academics alone or connected with knowledge, for even the most ignorant of bog-trotters had made vast fortunes in England, America and Australia – and in so few years. The answer must lie in determination and persistence, like a good salesman could sell merchandise to people who had no possible use for it. Pat might be the man to put him on the right track, and for all that he had chosen such a menial occupation he had earlier perceived that he was college-educated, well-spoken if the occasion demanded it, and fly.

Now that the weather was warming up, throats needed slaking after the day's work, and in the evening, as soon as they alighted in Camden Town, the gang dispersed hotfoot for the various public houses, but unlike the others who stuck to certain bars, Pat was unpredictable. Some evenings he went to the Mother Redcap, the next evening it could be either the Halfway House, the Brighton, the Elephant's Head, the Windsor Castle, the Stores, or the Mother Redcap again, and discreetly as he thought, Jack kept on his heels.

One evening in the Brighton, when they teamed up in the round, Pat looked him straight in the eye. "I know you're following me around, mate," he said, quite frankly, his face as unreadable as the back of a playing card. "And what's more, I know why."

Caught on the back foot Jack was tongue-tied with embarrassment, and he stood silently taking in the scene over Pat's shoulder. The Brighton, its oak-panelled walls embellished with ornate mirrors, framed illustrations of olde worlde London, and the usual advertisements for beverages and tobacco, was a typical London public house. The bar area was arranged with the usual public-house furniture, and a long brass-railed counter, bristling with beer-pump handles, ran the full length of one wall, the rows of shelves at the back glistening with neat arrays of wines, spirits and glasses. Yet, for all its big city characteristics, most of the customers were Irish, and their various brogues became more distinguishable as alcohol turned up the volume of their conversations and arguments, which were spattered with quick wit, four-letter words and raucous laughter.

Listening to the coarse banter it would be easy, Jack thought, to close his eyes and imagine that home was just down the road and not five hundred miles away, and certain now that Pat had taken offence, his mind was back in Knockrush with Eileen and the neighbours, wondering how life was going on there without him, missing it too in a way that he could never have imagined while he was living there.

Still, it wasn't the first time as far as Pat was concerned that Jack had read the cards wrong and, as he was beginning to find out, his disposition was as changeable as a woman's mind. Smiling sardonically he took up the conversation again. "You want to get ahead in this town so you can save enough money to go back and pick up the pieces of whatever you broke before you left and, by sticking close to me, you think you might learn something. Well, maybe you might or maybe you might not, so let's take a leaf out of the book of people we left behind in Ireland. Over there, they give away what they need most themselves –"

"What's that?" interjected Jack, purposely falling into the trap he felt certain Pat was baiting. "I never knew they gave anything away over there, except maybe the odd grain o' tea or a saucer o' flour to the tinkers."

"Advice!" returned Pat, beaming in the belief that he had put one over on Jack. "Advice is the name o' the game. It's one o' the few things in life that's really free – for blessed are the advice-givers for they shall be called arseholes."

"They'd wear out a rosary beads too, praying for you," returned Jack. "But presently I'm in the market for advice, if you can wise me up any."

Pat took a swig from his pint and meditated for a moment. "Now listen here to me – you'll get on a whole lot better in this town if you don't rock the boat," he began. "Don't be a rebel without a cause and start arguing that everyone is born equal – the natives don't like it. It's taking the piss out o' their kiss-arse system – their right of privilege and all that. If you ever read David Copperfield, there's a prime example in it as to how you should behave – be humble. You've got to pretend it's right that you should bow down to your betters – yes m'lord, no m'lord, three bags full m'lord – all that kind o' shite, and, as for mentioning a republic to them and getting rid o' the Queen – that's a mortal sin. The people here are conditioned into the system they were brought up in – Queen first, country second, kissing arse and the like. You won't change them, no more than you'll change the crowd back in Ireland. Over there, they're brainwashed into believing that the Pope's word is law, and that it's a sacred duty to go on their knees to the clergy and take off their caps to the people in authority, although it's not generally conceded by the world at large that our civil liberties should be the endowment of monarchs and bishops."

"Surely it's not the same here as at home – class distinction and all that?"

"Worse, if any, and remember, it's their country and we're just living in it," returned Pat. "So, act the way they imagine the Irish to be – thick and illiterate. Let them think they're doing you a great favour by allowing you to come here at all, and that you're grateful when they hand you a fork, a shovel, and a pickaxe, tools to put a hump on your back – 'see what you can to with these, Paddy', and your hole open all day, shovellin' out o' some trench – 'good on you, Paddy boy – that's the style – you'll never go back now'. Let them believe that you're over the moon to be even allowed to do the work they're not able to do themselves, work that nobody else wants except us or maybe the Poles – you'll get on better that way."

Jack found it hard to accept Pat's characterisation of the English. In most of the films he had seen they were portrayed as gentlemen, tolerant and refined, with a sense of fair play second to none, and the ones who came to Galway on holiday were impeccably mannered, for all that they were still being castigated for their barbaric deeds of the past.

Pat was quick to read the scepticism in Jack's eyes. "You don't believe me – I can see," he said, shaking his head as if he was just after wasting his breath. "Well, take it from me, we're only here because we're needed to make up the shortfall in labour and, as for being welcome, you'll soon find out yourself. I'm only trying to put you wise as to what to expect, because the English try to give a different image of themselves to the world. But at the back of it all, they're every bit as crooked as the border they put around Northern Ireland, and that's crooked. As the Red Indians say: 'they speak with forked tongue'."

This wasn't the first time Jack had heard the contentious issue of Northern Ireland coming up in conversation, unlike his homeland where the subject of partition was completely ignored. It always seemed to burrow its way into every discussion between the English and Irish, although usually light-heartedly, culminating in the compromise: 'If you give us back the Six Counties, we'll give you back Camden Town'.

Although there was a certain amount of logic in Pat's advice Jack could find nothing in it that might turn a penny into a pound, and so he took it with a pinch of salt, but gradually as he began to mingle more in the cosmopolitan world of inner London, a community in which the English, whether they were born Londoners or from farther afield, displayed an arrogant air of superiority, he could see what he meant. It was as if they were the chosen people, the saviours of the human race, and whenever two or more Englishmen met in a public house, one of their first questions was sure to be: 'What did you do in the War? – Alf, Bill, or whoever', and from then on, Dunkirk would be spiritedly refought and over-exaggeration would find a platform, drink magnifying the events – 'we stood alone – the French let us down – the Yanks came in when it was all over' – twaddle, like Jim Madden magnifying the Troubles in Ireland.

So much too for one of the dogmas of his homeland: that you would meet better Englishmen than Irishmen in England, or was it just propaganda on their behalf to discredit the character of the emigrant, to portray him as a blackguard or a man of low intelligence, or perhaps the phrase was coined to bolster the conviction that it really was the sweepings of the country who emigrated to England.

Still, he felt that his best option was to stick close to Pat, and on the following Saturday night he found him in the Halfway House dressed immaculately in a suit and tie. Sitting on a high stool at the counter he was in the company of a sharp-faced, gangling young man.

"Jack, this is Reg from Bolton – a convert to the Irish cause," he said, introducing Reg with a supportive slap across the shoulders. "And Reg, this is Jack – we work in the same trench for O'Donoghue. Even though we, Irish, only use first names, Reg likes to be introduced properly. So, for what it's worth, Ashton is his surname."

After the handshake Jack's discreet once-over showed that Reg was down-at-heel, an observation that was strongly supported by his crumpled navy-blue suit, the collar of the jacket peppered with dandruff from his receding fair hair, a white shirt gone yellow from poor washing, and a limp red tie and, if the purpley little tentacles creeping out from his nose to his cheekbones were anything to go by, he was very much a tosspot.

Pat was in an exceptional good mood until eight o'clock came and the piano began to jangle and, as the night advanced and the pianist's accompanying chorus grew more raucous, the whole bar joined in the old cockney favourites: *Roll out the Barrel – On Mother Kelly's Doorstep* – and many others, which wasn't at all to his liking. However, when they crashed into *The White Cliffs of Dover*, he really showed his annoyance. "That song is definitely taking the piss," he swore bitterly as he mimed the chorus.

"Tomorrow when the world is free," he repeated, his irritation increasing. "Tomorrow when all the countries in the British Empire are free would be more like it. The ignorant shower that are always singing about a free world are the very people stopping it from being free – Kenya, Malaya and God knows how many other colonies. To make matters worse they're conscripting young men under the guise of national service and sending them abroad, brainwashing them into believing they're fighting for Queen and country, when really all they're doing is terrorising and killing the people who are fighting to free themselves from British oppression, and they can't see it, nor do they want to see it."

"Calm down, Pat – it's only an ould song!" interjected Jack, surprised that a man as self-contained as Pat could lose his cool over a sing-song and equally surprised that Reg hadn't taken him up on it.

"It might be only a song, but for people to be singing about a free world that'll never be free until they allow it to be free is the height of ignorance," countered Pat. "And look at the misery they brought to the world down through the years – if it wasn't for Hitler's Third Reich, they'd still be the villains of the piece. They were the Hitlers before Hitler. You've only got to look back to Kitchener, the first modern-day war criminal, to see what I mean, starving thousands of Boer women and children to death in concentration camps, and Churchill bombing civilians in the Middle East, just to see the effect. Isn't that where Hitler got the idea, modelling his Third Reich on the British Empire."

"Before you go on to Northern Ireland, Pat, and how it was partitioned without a referendum, let me get a word in!" Reg cut in, still unperturbed by Pat's outburst. "I'll have to agree with you – it's somewhat of a paradox to be singing about a free world if you're the cause if it not being free, especially when you're not entirely free yourself, or to preach about democracy when you haven't got democracy yourself. If that shower, as Pat referred to them, doesn't realise that they're still chained to a semi-feudal system of master and serf, it's poor lookout for them. But where Pat and I differ, Jack, is that he talks about the past, looking back all the time to Hitler and Kitchener and so forth, which only inflames old animosities, whereas I look to the future, to the day when we shake off our shackles and get rid of the class system, this right of privilege, for once and for all. However, as I can see that music isn't going to soothe the savage breast, it might be a good idea to get out of here and have a ramble towards Chalk Farm and try a few pubs along the way. What d'you say to that, Pat?"

When Pat, who was still agitated, grunted his agreement, they set off, and though the streets were quiet, the public houses were crowded and noisy. As the night advanced and they moved from one to another, the chatter and laughter spilling into the street through the open doorways grew louder and more raucous and, as if to keep pace with the rising volume of the din, policemen were appearing at street corners, inconspicuously at first and then more noticeably.

"Straighten yourself up, Jack – walk like a soldier on parade," warned Reg, as they passed a group of policemen who were standing across the street in the shadows, eyeing them speculatively. "There's a Black Maria parked up that alley behind them – I can just about make out the square front of it from here. So, it looks like they mean business."

"I see it!" said Pat. "They're on the prowl tonight for sure. Once they take out the paddy wagon, as they call it, they never go back empty-handed. It's like the Coiste Bodhar [death coach]. It doesn't matter whether you're drunk or not, if they haven't got a full load, they'll take you."

"And that's not all, Jack," added Reg. "When they get you inside, they'll steal most of your money. They won't take it all – they'll leave you enough to pay the fine Monday morning and perhaps the price of a few drinks, depending on how much you have. If you make a fuss about it, they'll beat you up with batons and say you were resisting arrest – you can't win with them."

Jack smiled to himself, dismissing it as blarney, like the tale of the Catty Odha taking away small children who hadn't filled their pockets with stones, or one of the silly pranks played on green Irishmen, or like the Englishman – Irishman joke, which ran: 'Well, Paddy,' explained the Englishman, when Paddy asked naively about the functioning of the traffic lights, 'when the lights are red all the Englishmen cross and when the lights are green all the Irishmen

147

cross' – 'Begob,' says Paddy, 'that's not leaving much time for the Orangemen to cross'. Still, there was something ominous in the manner the police were sizing them up, like wolves stalking their quarry and, taking a tentative glance over his shoulder, he hurried to keep pace with his friends.

By the time they reached Chalk Farm Reg was well under the weather, and by the time they reached the Caernarfon Castle on the way back he was beginning to stagger. "It's best we get him off the street before the cops see him – I know where he lives," Pat suggested and, taking an arm each to keep him upright, they set off for his lodgings in Inverness Street. They had scarcely travelled a hundred yards when they were suddenly surrounded by police, as if they had been watching covertly from the shadows.

"We'll take care of your friend from here!" ordered one of the group of four constables.

"We'll manage him all right, officer," returned Pat, with exaggerated politeness. "He only lives a few minutes' walk from here."

"If you want to look after him, Paddy, you'd better come with him – you're obstructing a police officer in the course of his duty!" snapped the constable sarcastically and, grabbing Pat by the arms, he frogmarched him round the corner and bundled him into the back of a Black Maria, a blow of a baton across the shoulders from one of his colleagues helping him on his way.

Jack, who was left holding Reg upright, could hardly believe his eyes, and before he had time to object the other two constables were pushing them both towards the van, prodding them in the ribs with batons to hurry them along.

Besides Pat, there were four others in the Black Maria, young Irishmen, one of them protesting that he had a date, although his pleas fell on deaf ears as two of the constables, batons drawn, took up seats one on either side of the back doors. Uncertain as to what was in store for him Jack turned anxiously to Pat, who was sitting on the same bench-type seat, Reg between them. "Keep your mouth shut and speak only when you're spoken to," he whispered, the rumble of the engine starting up cloaking his words, and in a matter of moments they were speeding away. After a short journey the van screeched to a halt and they were herded up the steps of a police station.

"Good evening – gentlemen," the ruddy-faced desk sergeant greeted, his tone cutting with contempt, as the prisoners, seven in all, were paraded before him, and then, raising a bushy eyebrow expressively, he turned to the lanky officer who had made the arrest.

Full of himself, as if he apprehended a gang of bank robbers, the young constable came smartly to attention. "Drunk and incapable – Chalk Farm Road – all seven!" he replied curtly and, moving along the line, he shook each man in turn so that he wobbled for the sergeant's benefit, even Reg who had suddenly come to life. Afterwards, one by one they were called before the desk, ordered to turn out their pockets, and when they had given their names and addresses, all their personal effects were logged, including their money, which was sealed in separate brown envelopes. Relieved of their belts, ties, shoelaces and matches, they were bundled down the steep stone steps to the cells.

"You can talk all you like now, Jack," said Pat, after the constable had slammed the cell door and locked it behind him. "I only warned you because you'd be wasting your breath arguing with that shower – they'd give you a hiding as quick as they'd look at you. You see – it's all one big set-up just to make life as uncomfortable as possible for us over here. If you don't believe me, just look around you and tell me which one of us is drunk, except Reg, and he's sobered up now. The only reason you're in here is because you're Irish – they must've mistaken Reg – but then he does look a bit like a Paddy – isn't that right, boys?" he went on, addressing the others, all of whom nodded in agreement. "All we can hope for now is that they don't pinch too much of our money. I had eight quid and some odd change, but I suppose I'll be lucky if I see half of it in the morning – the fiver is sure to be exchanged for a pound."

"They'll have a job to keep anything belonging to me," piped up Reg, "because I stuffed the only two quid I had down the top of my sock when we were getting out of the Black Maria – all they got was a fistful of loose change. So, the only thing for it is to settle in for the night, and in future I'll have to give more thought to palling about with you, Micks."

Too stupefied to even think of money Jack cast his eyes around the four bare walls of the cell, which smelt abominably of excrement and urine and, after a few sniff-sniffs, he detected its source – a galvanised slop-bucket in a corner near the door. Although their cigarettes had been returned their matches were withheld, not that there was much in the cell that would burn, save for the two piss-stained blankets and mattresses. As Reg had said, there was nothing for it but to sit on one of the two narrow beds and wait for morning and, as he tried to sleep sitting upright on the bed, his back to the wall, listening to the first of Reg's untroubled snores, it was strange that he should recall old O'Hara's words of reproof about suffering his daughter to 'some room in Camden Town – some hovel – to live the rough life of our emigrant brethren'.

Chapter 4

Next morning, it was still dark when Jack, Reg, Pat and their cellmates set off walking in the pouring rain from the police station in Tottenham Court Road to Camden Town, each with a summons to appear before Marylebone magistrates on Monday morning. To add injury to injustice Pat's envelope was four pounds light, and Jack's three. The others too had lost money, and even the silver from Reg's paltry pile was missing, leaving him with just a few brass and copper coins.

"Between us all they had a good night's take – thieving bastards," Reg remarked caustically. "Then, kicking us out just when we were getting a bit o' shut-eye. They did it on purpose too, so we'd have to hoof it all the way back in this downpour – they knew well there were no buses or tube-trains at this hour on Sunday morning. So Jack, now that you've had your first experience of the Old Bill, you can well understand why the cockneys call them 'the filth'."

"It's not much different in Ireland," returned Jack. "If there's any trouble, the cops always put the blame on the tinkers, or on the men home from England on holidays, never on the real culprits."

"Gosh, I didn't know that, Jack," said Reg. "I thought you were all of a kind over there like you are here."

Still, it was an experience Jack could have done without, although his day in court turned out to be something of bank holiday. In the morning, when he entered the solemnity of the courtroom, he was somewhat intimidated by the glowering faces of the magistrates, but Reg quickly put him at ease. "It'll be all over in a minute, like having a tooth out," he laughed, making a joke of the whole affair. "Whores, drunks and anyone caught pissing in the street are always first. This means us, mate, and we'll be tried separately. The arresting constable'll stand up, swear on the Bible to tell the truth, and then perjure himself when giving his evidence. It'll go something like this: 'At approximately 10.30 on the night of etc. etc. I was on patrol with my fellow officers in the vicinity of Chalk Farm Road when I came on the defendant staggering along the footpath in the company of two others, looking the worse for drink. When I stopped and questioned him, he replied: 'What business is it of yours?' His speech was slurred and he smelt strongly of alcohol, and when I asked him again, he made no reply. He was arrested for his own safety, and gave no trouble'. Then, one o' the magistrates'll ask how do you plead to the charge. So, make sure you plead guilty, otherwise they might adjourn your case and you'll be having another day off for your trouble. Regardless of how you plead they'll find you guilty, and don't forget to apologise to the magistrates for any inconvenience caused."

It all turned out as Reg has said, and afterwards, as the financial implications of the magistrates fining him two pounds, the police stealing three pounds, and the loss of a day's wages hit him, he was forced to agree with Pat that it was a set-up, for it was more than coincidental that everyone, save for Reg, who had appeared in the dock that morning on drink-related charges, was Irish.

Back in Camden Town, they made straight for the Halfway House, their newfound friends joining them, all in a mood to make the best of their unexpected day off, and though they were complete strangers before their Saturday-night misadventure, they were now birds of a feather, as if a kinship had been born in the cell. By and by, as drink unsheathed the sword of defiance, Jack sensed that there was a certain bravado attached to getting 'housed', as falling foul of the constabulary was referred to in the vernacular, which prompted him to remark: "It seems to me that the bones of having a good Saturday night out here in London means getting drunk and getting arrested."

"There's more to it than that, Jack," returned Pat. "What about the punch-up, and the ride – the most important thing in a man's life, getting the long-haired one to stack the drapery, whether she's a hoor or not. And don't forget, losing the grip, or pissing in the bed – damping it down, as they call it – it's all in the same equation. Each brings its own particular type of excitement, but if you manage to fit the whole lot in on the same night, it's like having an accumulator up on the horses. You can forget all about getting locked up, that only averages about once a year, like getting hit on the head with bird-shite. We were just unlucky to be in the wrong place at the wrong time, and we can't put all the blame on poor ould Reg either, especially after they mistaking him for a Paddy. So, as you can see, Jack, if you stick with us, you can't go wrong in this town."

Jack felt that sticking with Pat and his mates might present problems, although sitting in his lodgings night after night staving off Bob Little's overtures of friendship was a poor alternative. There was no sign of Widow Kilbane, who lived alone in an apartment annexed to the ground floor, which was out of bounds to all save Mrs O'Neill. It seemed that the running of the properties was left entirely to Mrs O'Neill and her able assistant, Mrs Muldoon, another Irishwoman of the same calibre, although he felt somewhat disappointed that he hadn't seen the widow since the day of his arrival.

Bob Little was a different matter, for his Orange ancestry damned him forever in the eyes of the other lodgers, some of whom had first-hand experience of the apartheid system of Northern Ireland, and yet his manner suggested that he bore none of the conceit and bigotry of his cult. It was in his eyes, as if inside his character there was a better man trying to break out, and there was about him a certain restraint that seemed to hide sadness. Still, his inborn hatred for his breed held sway, although try as he might he could find no justification for shutting him out, for after all, Little was in the same boat as himself – an immigrant in a strange land. This encouraged him to pass some polite conversation with him, and Little, perhaps sensing that at last he had breached Jack's barrier of reticence, went out of his way to pursue it.

On the other hand, there was something about Pat that kept drawing him into his company, for besides having the independent, outspoken air that he liked in men, he always made sense, cynical though it might sound at times. One day on the job, when some of the men were fantasising on what they would do if they won the pools, for the sake of conversation, he asked: "D'you ever do the pools, Pat?"

"Why – d'you think I'd have a chance o' winning," he returned, a sardonic smile flickering for a second on his lips. "First of all take a good look at your workmates. Every man jack o' them is in the tatters, and look at that fella over there with his ould steinbecks hanging down through the crotch of his trousers – no underwear on him and every shilling gone on drink, and that fella over there with the hump – it was O'Donoghue or some other slave-driver that put the hump on him – and none o' them, ourselves included, with a future except to live unknown and die alone in some ould room. Look at their hands – look at your own hands, all cut to ribbons from catching them on the side o' the trench, nails all blackened, and you ask me if I do the pools. Listen mate, if that great ganger in the sky didn't see fit to find us more respectable work than this, I can't see winning the pools being on the cards for us either. You'd have about as much chance of winning the pools as getting your money back off a hoor – and that's some chance."

"You never can tell," returned Jack.

"You never can tell what? – get your money back off a hoor or win the pools? If I won the pools, I'd probably kill myself drinking in a few years, and if I got my money back off a hoor, I'd die with shock – either way, I'd be dead before my time," countered Pat, laughing in spite of himself. "Still, the way my luck is running at the moment, if I bought ducks they'd drown, or if I was in the undertaking business, nobody'd die. Only the other week, this quare wan I was knocking off gave me the road, and I just after buying a large packet o' French letters that very same day – that kind o' luck. If you haven't copped it on already, this is the lowest type o' work in the land – 'the men who dig 'oles in the road', they call us. Even the women won't bother with us once they find out – but let them not bother with us. When all fruit fails, welcome the haws, and when all women fail us, welcome the hoors, that's what I say. They do a great service to mankind – the hoors, and everyone down on them, poor craithers. I think myself the best ones should get an award of some sort from the Queen – WBE – Hoor of the British Empire.

"And why not – she's an adulteress herself, and she gives awards to puffs and perverts," Pat went on, when he saw the astonishment on Jack's face. "I suppose you've often heard the English referring to Ireland as a land of praties, pigs and priests – well, if that's the case, we should look on England as a land of adulterers, hoors and queers – because they're here a-plenty."

Satire was part of Pat's character, and since arriving in London Jack felt as if he had been born again into a new society, the bigger picture taking shape by the day as the scales of naivety fell away from his eyes. For all the rip-tear methods of the ganger he soon found that everything on the job was done for a purpose and carefully thought out, even the money, which was dished out every evening with seemingly such abandon, had its purpose. Considering the money had to be paid but once it was better that the men had it in regularly in case the lack of thrift left them hungry, as only a fool expects a hungry man to do as much work as a well-fed man – and the Irish contractors were anything but fools.

Also, the system of paying cash in hand every day was a double-edged sword, for besides cutting down on absenteeism, it meant that the men paid no income tax or national insurance, and it encouraged them to use fictitious names, which were derisively referred to as 'stage names'. The downside for the men was that there was no compensation for injury, no wet time, nor increased rates for overtime. It was a simple system all round – no work, no money, something like the clergy's system of saying Mass for the dead: High Mass – high money, Low mass – low money, no Mass – no money, the Inland Revenue the loser in both cases.

On the job there was little or no camaraderie among the men, most of whom kept to themselves, as if too close association would be bad husbandry, and it had taken Jack some time to get on speaking terms with them, save for Pat. Pat too could be taciturn if anyone asked direct questions, and yet, he found that he could draw him out by first introducing a subject, saying something controversial about it, and then dropping it. One day, hoping to draw him out on the surly disposition of their immigrant brethren, he remarked quite casually: "They're not a very friendly lot, are they, Pat?"

"I'll have to agree with you there – they're not the kindliest souls. It's just that they keep to themselves and mind their own business," returned Pat. "In this town a man is either a loner or he has a mate. If he teams up with a bloke, they go everywhere together, work on the same job, stay in the same digs, drink in the same pub, go to the same dance hall. The friendship could go as far as riding the same hoor. So, if you're lonely, find yourself a mate. If you're not, go it alone – that's the name o' the game. Everyone here is in the same boat – immigrants away from home. The work in this town might be hard, but at least it's regular, and there's money at the end o' the day. It's a whole lot better than thinnowing mangels or washing sheep's daggings back yonder for little more than a 'God spare you the health' – it's the lesser of two evils, if you get my meaning."

"But what do they do with all the money, Pat? – Do they send it home to Ireland, or what? – because they're always subbing and pleading broke."

"I suppose the majority of them send money home – it helps to keep the clock ticking over there," returned Pat, "But they're not broke, not really broke anyway. This subbing every day is just a stunt to stop people from tapping them. It gives a hard-case image to be broke – hard case, no suitcase, that kind o' style. Anyway, I shouldn't be telling you all this. You'd fare better if you found out for yourself, and besides, there's something driving you – I noticed it the first morning we met in the café. You want to get ahead for some reason or other, and you'll get there too. But what then, ask yourself?"

Although Pat had struck the right chord Jack didn't deem their friendship was close enough for sharing confidences, and he went on minding his own business. This was easy to do, for the only chance they got for airing opinions was at lunchtime in the café or in the evening in the public house. There was little opportunity during working hours, for the ganger kept a sharp lookout for any grouping and scotched any whispered conversations with the remark: "Which one o' ye got the letter from home?' A remark which became irksome from iteration. If he noticed any cliques forming, he would break them up, adding in an undertone, yet for all to hear: "Anyone'd think we had all nancy boys on the job the way ye're always on top o' one another." The sarcasm, in which there was no shortage of four-letter words, was never-ending, but it got results.

There was no winning with the ganger – the ganger was almighty, and he had the power to start, sack and determine the rate of pay. He could galvanise the most shiftless men into energy with a salvo from his extensive repertoire of profane language, and he could see through any excuse, as Jack found out when he returned to work after his day in court. "Don't tell me – you got locked up Saturday night and you had to go to court Monday mornin'," he snarled. "I must be payin' you too much money, otherwise you couldn't afford to be gettin' drunk, and if it keeps up, you'll be havin' a new ganger, and it won't be me that'll be jackin' either. And you!" he growled at another man who was using his bandaged, supposedly blood-poisoned hand as an excuse for missing Monday, swinging his attack on him with the air of a street fighter who, having flattened one opponent, turns eagerly to confront another. "Who d'you think you're trying' to fool – poisoned hand, my arse! It's your mind that's poisoned, not your hand!"

The Irish gangers were a breed of their own, all suckled on the same sarcastic milk, which gave substance to King George's precept that if you want to roast an Irishman get another Irishman to turn the spit, and the immigrant Irish were being roasted and basted by their own, which inspired one wit to add to the myth of St Patrick banishing the snakes from Ireland: 'and he reincarnated them fifteen hundred years later and made gangers of them in England'. Outspokenly offensive and slave-driving they possessed all the bullying qualities of low men elevated to authority and yet, they were no fools, for they always kept a fighting man in the gang for protection in case any of the workers tried to beat them up. When the ganger laughed, everyone laughed, because to lose the job could lead to 'skippering', a slang term for sleeping rough, which had nothing whatsoever to do with captaining a ship.

Not only O'Donoghue, but almost every Irish contractor in London was engaged in some capacity in the vast programme of taking the electric cables off the poles and putting them underground. Thousands of men, mostly Irish, were involved, which lent credibility to the immortal lyrics of *The Mountains of Mourne*.

As a result, gangs of men stripped to the waist, knotted handkerchiefs on their heads, digging up roads and footpaths, became as much a part of the everyday scene as dustmen and postmen and, taking into account the hundreds of miles of streets in London, it was hard to imagine it ever being achieved. It was rough work for rough men, with rough men in charge. Records were broken and, like the laying of the railways across America, many a simple verse was composed about the basic task of digging trenches.

Camden Town, one of the major pick-up points for the construction industry, could be compared in a lesser sense to a boom town in the Wild West. Men of all trades flooded in to be near the source of their employment, and all the lodging houses in the area, even the Routen House, a tenement building of single cubicles let out on a nightly basis mostly to down-and-outs, were filled to capacity. In the evening from six o'clock onwards, the cafés were hard pressed to cope with the droves which converged on its four main streets, and the public houses, once they opened their doors, were swamped in customers, all as dry as if they had spent the day in the Sahara.

As the night advanced and drink added fire to the arguments, fights broke out, which resulted in flurries of kicks helping the losers on their way to the street, black eyes were looked on as mementos of a good night out, and hard-earned money was squandered with such abandon that it prompted one Polish observer to remark: "Pole keep money and throw away pay packet – Paddy keep pay packet and throw away money."

Clannishness too was endemic among the immigrant Irish, and whenever two Irishmen met for the first time, one of the first questions was sure to be 'What part o' the ould country are you from?' which went a long way in determining the depth of any future friendship. Every county had its own association, some their own social clubs. So, it was not surprising that most immigrants stuck to their own, especially the lonely ones, who could almost lead their lives as they had at home on the news gleaned from their local newspapers and letters from relatives. As a result, an affiliation existed between the exiled and the indigenous Irish, which was held together by the glue of postage stamps, for many of the exiles hadn't really left Ireland – Ireland had left them, left them to flounder in a wilderness of bricks and concrete, like the Israelites in the desert without a Moses to lead them and, as comradeship drew them closer, each became a balm for the loneliness of the other.

This clannishness was more noticeable in the immigrants from County Kerry. For most Kerrymen the pot of gold at the end of the rainbow was to work for Murphy, the famed Kerry contractor, stay in a Kerry lodging house, order a copy of the *Kerryman* every week, support the Kingdom, the all-Kerry London football team, drink in a public house which had a Kerry landlord, patronise a Kerry dance hall, marry a Kerry woman, and travel to Dublin every year for the All-Ireland football final, hoping that Kerry would be playing – and win. A stranger with a poor grasp of Irish geography could hardly be blamed for believing there were only two counties in Ireland and Kerry was one of them, for life was homelier in Kerry, the air was fresher in Kerry, if someone had a black cat, there was sure to be a blacker one in some part of Kerry, or if a beautiful woman walked down the street, no doubt there would be a better looker 'back behind in Kerree – boy'.

More clannish still, though less numerous, were the men from Donegal, or 'the Donies', as they were known. All cut from the same piece of cloth there was something sly about them that was discernible at a glance, and once they got a foothold in a job, a lodging house, a bar, or other enterprise, they never relented until they took it over. Although they had a name of being hard-working, which they never stopped boasting about, he had heard one unconvinced gentile speaking out in contradiction: "Good workers at picking spuds, maybe, in Donegal where they eat them skins and all."

Although Pat was from Kerry, Jack noticed that he kept his distance from his county's many functions, and by chance one night, he happened on his surname – O'Shea. On the other hand, where Pat was wary of strangers and taciturn, Reg was loquacious and outspoken, although his five years in London had been ridden by failure after failure, from an aspiring solicitor's clerk down to a dustman, drink being the root cause of his downward spiral. A leftist in the making he never let an opportunity pass without taking a swipe at the stiff-lipped society that had shut him out, and he found a platform among the immigrant Irish, although Jack detected a note of sour grapes in his ideology, that of the resentful class warrior who secretly craves the very privileges he affects to despise.

As for getting ahead financially, Jack knuckled down to the tried and tested method of saving – pennies make shillings, shillings make pounds, and he buried himself in his work, putting in every Sunday shift available. His efforts didn't go unnoticed, and like a scholar impressing his teacher he impressed the ganger and was put to the top of the class at digging trenches, for which he received an extra five shillings a day.

"I see you're going up in the world – joining the elite," Pat remarked, rather derisively, when he heard about the raise. "But take it from me, there'll be more expected of you from now on, and you'll have to set the pace for the rest of us. At least it's something to say you're good at, and the next time I go back yonder on a holiday and they ask me what I'm doing in London, I can stick out my chest and say: 'I'm working in the same trench as that great muck surgeon, Jack Daly'.

"But seriously, it's all right for people in cushy jobs to laugh, but how many of them could do it – schoolteachers and the like, living above their means and grumbling about not getting enough, and then saying they'd be better off digging muck for a living. They'd get a rude awakening, surely. They live under the misconception that the effort entails all brawn and no brain, but you know yourself that it takes more skill than hard work to dig a trench, far more skill than punching a typewriter or delivering letters. First, you've got to learn the knack of keeping the trench straight and not as crooked as a bullock's piss in the snow, as you've often heard the ganger saying, and you've got all the different types of ground to contend with – rock, clay, flint – and which tool to use."

"I'm only doing it for the extra money, Pat," returned Jack, half-apologetically, as they had coined a vulgar name for men who tried to do more work than the others.

"There's more to it than that, if you don't mind me saying so," countered Pat. "There's something eating you up inside that's driving you so hard. If you haven't noticed already, every Irishman in this country has some purpose driving him, whether it's to get even with some girl back yonder who thumbed her nose at him, or just to spite the neighbours and go back someday loaded with money – something like that. You're different, because most of the other's ambitions dry up with time, but yours won't – whatever it is that's troubling you at all. I don't want to know, but I thought I'd mention it just the same."

Again Pat had struck the nail on the head – there was something driving him, and he had changed far more than he realised. He was no longer plastic clay, yielding imprint to every new experience, for ever since the morning he found his horse dead, unknown to him a shell of hardness had formed round his heart, and little by little, layer by layer, it had thickened in the interminable months. He was bitter too, because he had drunk bitterness to the dregs in spite of Mick Grogan's counselling: 'Try not to let bitterness into your heart because it'll find a home there, and remember, the world always pays back it evildoers in its own roundabout way'. But if the world didn't do its work, Paisley would get off scot-free, and besides, he found a certain satisfaction in his bitterness, for every time he drove the fork into the stony ground he imagined he was driving the prongs into Paisley's big head.

As the weeks sped by, Jack heard that there was piecework available digging trenches, but when he mentioned it to Pat, he gave no encouragement.

"Forget you ever heard about piecework, because it's all a con trick to get you to do three times the amount of work for little more than the wages we're getting now," he explained, shaking his head reprovingly. "A piece today and piece tomorrow, that's the kind of piecework I want, or peace at work and not have the ganger shouting at you all day, or be able to drift into that land called peace of mind now and again. Look at it this way – don't ever expect to get rich on what you knock out of your own frame no matter what job you've got. The most you can expect is to live comfortably – it's only wages. To get rich, you've got to use other people's money and have men working for you, and you've got to have that element of luck – the luck of money. I suppose you've seen it yourself – men who never did a tap in their lives and they always seem to have money, and you could bring it in bucketfuls to others and they'd still wind up with nothing – that's what I mean by the luck of money. You either have it or you haven't it."

"But surely you've got to push the boat out sometimes and take a chance, Pat."

"The boat is out far enough for me as it is, unless it's the man in the boat you mean," laughed Pat. "But seriously, you go ahead – push the boat out and see how far it gets you. Go on piecework. But you'll soon find that most contractors who let out their work at a price are mushroom contractors – they spring up overnight and are gone before you know it – they don't last. You might be lucky to find a few good weeks' work, but then you're walking around again. You'll find too that most of the pieceworkers are too greedy for their own good, especially the Donies, cutting prices to get the other fella out, so that the contractor winds up with the last laugh. If I was you, I'd stick here with O'Donoghue – the job might be nothing to write home about, but it's regular. Falling for the piecework lark is like falling for the sales talk of the man who sold the magic suit o' clothes to the king."

A negative approach was the last thing Jack needed, and yet, he could see why Pat was mildly content with his lot. Camden Town was like home from home, actually it was better, inasmuch as there was work, wages every week, and every facility on which to spend it on, and it was easy to understand why Digger Nolan and so many others never returned. Perhaps if he could find Digger, he might have a solution, for Digger, with all his wiles, was sure to have got on in this type of society.

On Saturday nights, ever since his brush with the constabulary, no amount of coaxing could entice Jack to accompany Reg and Pat on their pub crawls. Instead, hoping to bump into someone from home who might have tidings of Digger, he attended one of the Irish dance halls, varying his choice each night – Charlie Mack's in Victoria, the Garryowen in Hammersmith, the Banba in Kilburn, the Galtymore in Cricklewood, the Blarney in Tottenham Court Road, the Gresham in Archway, and many others, so many that it would take at least a year to get round to them all.

One Saturday night in the Halfway House, as he was excusing himself to go to the Shamrock in Camden Town where he had arranged to meet Mick and Tom Burke, two brothers from Castleford, who had promised to have news of Digger, Reg frowned his disapproval. "I know you want a woman, Jack, like every other man, but why go through such a rigmarole in a smoky dance hall, getting refused left, right and centre by the thick skivvy-type women who frequent such places," he remarked, mistaking Jack's purpose. "Why don't you do as we do and go down Bayswater Road for a whore? They're all lined up there – all good-looking, and it only costs a couple o' nicker for a short time. I'll wise you up as to how it works. When you pick out the one you fancy, whistle for a taxi – the cabbies know the score. He'll pull down the blinds and drive down Park Lane, round by Hyde Park Corner, and drop you off again at the same spot. By that time you should've hammered the job on her, and all you have to do is pay for the taxi. You're only wasting your time the other way, and the end product is just the same."

Reg wasn't on his own in his logic, for on several occasions others in the gang had drawn his attention to the advertisements in newsagents' windows for drama lessons and other misleading notices which, they had explained, were a cover-up for prostitution. Still, the idea of paying for it brought a sickly feeling to his stomach, which prompted him to say: "You'd be better off, Reg, if you went to church now and again, instead of the hoorhouse."

"Yes, Jack, I agree, but we've got to look at both sides of the coin, because the church and the whorehouse aspire to accomplish the same thing," returned Reg who, like Pat, was seldom stuck for an answer. "The hymns, the sermons and the prayer help to relieve us of our worries about the next life, while the whores help to relieve us of our worries in this life. So, off with you to the Shamrock, but you'll soon find that I'm right."

The Shamrock, for all its small frontage, was lofty and spacious, and it was as Irish a setting as one could imagine so far from home: bunting of green, white and gold criss-crossing the ceiling in looping festoons, murals of O'Connell Street, Dublin and other Irish scenes on the walls, and a traditional ceilidh band entertaining.

When Jack entered, there was an impatient buzz in the air as the crowd waited for the next dance to be announced, the women huddling together on one side, the men on the other side, as alert as prowling cats waiting to pounce, a no-man's-land of empty dance floor between them. At the first tuning notes of the fiddles the throng of jostling men, like racehorses coming under starter's orders, began to advance towards the women, while the women retreated as far back as their surroundings would allow, not unlike the early Christians in the amphitheatre before the lions were released, and the instant the band struck up there was a first come, first served type of charge across the floor.

The women were just as unmannerly as the men, and they picked their partners as they pleased and, when tendering their refusals, some shook their heads sullenly, while others never bothered to answer at all and just stared into oblivion, perhaps waiting for Errol Flynn to come along. This type of rudeness seemed to be part of the culture, which was so different from the Phoenix, the Astaire and Seapoint, where courtesy was shown to all comers. There was an utter lack of gaiety, for it seemed that the men's sole purpose was to get the women's knickers off, stacking the drapery as it was called, while the women seemed determined to keep them on until perhaps it suited themselves to discard them, a conflict of intentions at which the women seemed to have the upper hand. It was once bitten twice shy with Jack, and reluctantly he had to agree with Reg – jostling in a smoky dance hall with nothing to show for it except deflated ego and sexual frustration.

Standing in one of the wings Jack watched until the music stopped, and when there was no sign of the Burkes, he climbed the carpeted stairway to the balcony tea bar and took in the scene from aloft. When a Siege of Ennis was announced, again there was a mad scramble for partners, while the bouncers in their green blazers lined them up, four facing four, in four uniform lines. Finally, when the head bouncer gave the cue to the bandleader to commence, the drone of the fiddles, backed by the louder, sharper accordions and concertinas filled the hall, and the lines of couples advanced towards one another in perfect formation, the nimble patting of three thousand or more dancing feet resounding like castanets as they beat out the rhythm of the reel on the waxed and polished floor.

Looking down on the colourful spectacle, the men in their well-tailored suits, all young, clean-shaven and spry, many with looks that some film stars would envy, and the women all youthful and pretty, their dance dresses floating out as they whirled in perfect timing to a selection of traditional reels, Jack symbolically saw the flower of Ireland's youth below him, the children who had followed the Pied Piper, a lost generation destined never again to return except for a holiday or a funeral. Still, like the ill wind blowing good for someone, Ireland's loss was England's gain, a transfusion of blood into her flagging race, which was depleted and debilitated after two world wars. It was a transfusion of courage too, for like the pioneers of old it took courage to tear up roots, although it now seemed that in spite of his country's hatred for her old adversary, England had again stolen the oyster, perhaps unwittingly so, and left behind the shell.

In the past, and justifiably so, Ireland could lay the blame for her lack of prosperity on England's doorstep, but on whom could she lay it now? And it was hard to believe that these young people tripping so blithely below him were the sweepings of his country as the indigenous Irish so scornfully claimed – the rubbish which they so wanted to be rid of – the depart from me, ye curseds.

Finally, when he returned downstairs, he cast his eyes about, hoping to raise at least a smile from one of the women, for he still found it hard to believe they were all as ill-mannered as they appeared. "Take a leaf out of the Englishman's book and tell them plenty of lies," Pat had advised. "Lies are part of the establishment here – they think that putting together a good lie and getting away with it is the equivalent of telling the truth. Tell them anything that comes into your head, but for Christ's sake don't tell them you're digging trenches for a living." Still, to resort to lying to enhance his chances of getting a date held no appeal, or perhaps he was too thin-skinned, an odd man out, and like so many other nights he felt all alone in the world, for sometimes there can be no lonelier place than in a crowd.

Chapter 5

When summer, with its hot panting days, slipped in, making it impossible to stay indoors in the evenings, Jack took to rambling with Bob Little, exploring the streets off the beaten track, a wilderness of mean terraces of two-up, two-down houses, railed-in enclosures of shrubbery, tatty greens and parks which reeked of dogshite.

"If they ever run short of anything in this town, it surely won't be dogshite," he remarked, one evening as they made their way towards Finsbury Park, wrinkling his nose as he sidestepped to avoid a fresh dropping. "People come here from all over the world expecting to see streets paved with gold, and what do they find? Streets paved with dogshite. What d'you say to that, Bob?"

"Dogshite, dogshite everywhere and all the parks did stink, dogshite, dogshite everywhere, nor any drop –" returned Little derisively, pausing when no suitable rhyming words came to his lips to put the finishing touches to his verse. Finally, he gave up, saying: "If only dogshite could be drank, it'd be easier to complete my piece of doggerel – doggerel, I like it. Perhaps, I'll drop on the right words when I give it more thought. But I'll have to agree with yez, Jack – if every piece o' dogshite we saw this evening was a gold nugget, we'd both be millionaires before we got back to the degs, and they say that dogshite and a woman have something in common."

"What's that, Bob?"

"The older it gets the easier it is to pick up," returned Little, the faintest trace of a smile crinkling his lips. "But I hope yez don't mind me saying this, Jack – but yez're a different stomp of a mon from the crowd in the degs."

"How d'you mean – different?"

"Well, yez're the only one there who takes me at face value and doesn't resent me. Don't say they don't, because I can sense it – they don't want me there. They think that I, being a Protestant from the wee North, should find degs in some English house."

Jack smiled wryly as he tried to anticipate Pat's response to such a statement. It was sure to run in the vein: 'What did you expect? – it was your crowd and the English that put the border round it in the first place. Was the country that big that you had to split it up against the will of the majority and then set up a Protestant state for a Protestant people?' However, sensing that Little's intention was to be friendly, he just nodded, saying: "You're right there, Bob – they're a sour lot, surely."

"I can't say as I blame them, considering the great divide between Catholics and Protestants in our part o' the country," Little went on. "But I've had a change of heart since I came to England. I'll be quite candid with yez, Jack, at home we were brought up to despise Catholics and look down on them as inferiors. But now that I've mexed with the English, I'm having second thoughts. They don't treat me as an equal, and they look down on me in the same manner as they look down on yooze, just like the ads yez see for degs in paper-shop windows: 'No Irish, Blacks or dogs'. Well, that applies to me too, and I a Unionist from the wee Sex – the Queen's most loyal subjects. As far as they're concerned, I'm as Irish as yooze are."

"But there's nothing wrong with being Irish!" Jack cut in, slightly huffed.

"That's all right for yooze to say," returned Little. "But when I tried living in Irish lodging houses, the other lodgers knew what I was without me even telling them, and they either shunned me or took the pess out o' me by drawing my attention to the pecture of Pope Pius XII, which seems to be a fexture in every Irish lodging house. They looked at me as if I was a fiend, as if it was me who was persecuting the Catholics and burning them out o' their homes. On top of that, at work I'm treated as a lackey. I get all the shite jobs to do and they call me Meck or Poddy, anything but my name, as if I didn't have one – I'm seck of it. But at least in the wedow's degs, yez hear nothing of religion or the Pope."

"Would it not be better for you to go back home, Bob, where you'd be among your own people?" Jack suggested. "Or maybe you're planning to go back someday?"

"That's just it – I can't go back. Yez see, this black cloud came over one day and I left under it," returned Little, a harsh laugh turning any mirth in his tone bitter. "I've shet on the eggs over there, if yez know what I mean – my boats are burned behind me. It's like this, I was accused of putting a woman up the pole and the shotguns were out for me. That's why I envy yooze lads when I see yez all going home for Christmas, and some of yez having dreams of going back for good someday."

"And did you – put the woman up the stick, I mean?"

"It's hard to tell – I rode her all right and there's no doubt she was in the club. But then it was easier to count who didn't shag her than who did. No matter, I was the one she pointed the fenger at, and it was either marry her or go. Yez know the saying: 'Yez've made yer bed and now yez'll have to lie on it'. I never had any intention of lying on it, so I sold a few o' the ould fella's cattle unbeknown to him and hit for London. That's two year ago now, and I've heard nothing since – they could all be dod over there for all I know."

Perhaps feeling better now that he had unburdened himself Little gave a short cynical laugh. "So you see, Jack, I have no nationality. To the English, I'm Irish, and to the Irish here I'm classed as English or worse than English, and worse still I can't go back home," he went on, and though his summing-up was meant to be light-hearted, his tone was completely lacking in humour. "So, what do I do now? – I wonder would changing my religion make any defference?"

"It can hardly be as bad as all that surely, and I can't see religion being an issue in such a godless city as London," countered Jack. "You should come out with me some Saturday night. I have a couple o' mates who wouldn't care if you were the Devil's own disciple as long as you liked the crack – hoors, drink and the like."

"I can see nothing wrong with that – men after me own heart," laughed Little, and on the following Saturday night in the Halfway House, when Jack introduced him to Reg and Pat, they came up against a cynicism that matched their own – everything to grumble about, nothing to be positive about.

One humid evening shortly afterwards, when Jack went to the kitchen to make a cup of tea, he was surprised to find the landlady there, going through the motions of clearing up, although the clearing up had already been done.

"Hi, Jack," she greeted, her lips parting in a seductive smile, a hand shooting up to tidy an imaginary loose strand of her hair. "Sit down – it's the first opportunity we've had for a chat since the day you arrived. I'm making a cup of tea, if you care to join me."

The widow's flirtatious body language wasn't lost on Jack, and in the act of pouring the tea she leaned so far forward that he found himself staring down her cleavage. Tongue-tied with embarrassment he dry-coughed to clear his throat. "I must say this, you're doing a fine job here – Missus O'Neill looks after us like we were her own children," he returned and, prurient though his thoughts were, it was a pleasant change to talk to someone as well-spoken as the widow after the coarse, somewhat simple-minded conversations which passed between his workmates.

Smiling at Jack's attempt at flattery the widow made a few fanning motions with her hand. "It's stiflingly hot in here – I must open the window," she said and, as she stretched upwards over the table to unfasten the hasp, the outline of her bra straps and knickers were plainly visible through the gossamer material of her white summer dress.

It took all of Jack's willpower to tear his eyes away, and he didn't look again until she was seated in an opposite chair, the table between them.

"Tell me about yourself, Jack?" she asked, "You can call me a nosy cow if you like, but I've been worried about you ever since the Saturday night the police called, making enquiries about you – are you in some kind of trouble?"

Somewhat disconcerted to learn that the police had called on the night of his arrest, perhaps to verify his address, Jack felt it merited an explanation and an apology. "I'm sorry about the police," he said. "It's something that should never have happened."

Whether or not it was put on, something akin to relief showed for an instant in the widow's smile. "Do you have parents, Jack?" she went on. "I hope you don't mind me calling you Jack, and do feel free to call me Teresa."

Unknown to himself Jack was becoming as taciturn as his immigrant brethren, and when he felt himself being drawn out, he sensed an ulterior motive in the inquisition, although the only motive that crossed his mind was the obvious, which he dismissed as absurd. Since his arrival in London he had heard his fair share of tales of earthy relationships between landlady and lodger, grossly exaggerated, he believed, but so far he had heard nothing on those lines about the widow, save for the macho intentions of some of the lodgers if the opportunity arose and, encouraged by the concern in her tone, he replied: "Both my parents are dead."

"Do you have other family – brothers and sisters?"

"I have a sister. We have a small holding back in Galway. Times got hard, so here I am."

"Oh, how sad," said Teresa, her voice taking on a matronly tone. "I hope you don't mind me prying, but do you keep in touch with your sister?"

What Jack had earlier dismissed as absurd was fast becoming the obvious, although he could see no harm in satisfying her curiosity, or any other part of her body that needed satisfying. Either way, it wasn't as if she was stealing from him. "Yes – I write now and again," he returned, after a few moments deliberation. "It's a hard world we're living in. There's no certainty in it only death, and the only good thing about death is that we're all booked for the same trip someday, rich and poor alike."

"I wish you wouldn't talk so morbidly, Jack," Teresa tut-tutted, her pencilled eyebrows coming together in a frown. "You should look on the bright side of life too, for Christ's sake. Death'll come in its own good time – it frightens me even thinking of it. But what an outlook for a young man to have – 'there's nothing certain only death'. Enjoy life – that's my motto. Who can tell what's waiting round the corner. After all, tomorrow is another day, as Scarlet O'Hara said in *Gone With The Wind*."

The name 'O'Hara' evoked memories of Mary just when he had disciplined his mind against drawing her up, and unwillingly the whole episode of his confrontation with her father, his hatred for Paisley, his dead horse and cows rose to his memory. It was all in the same equation, an insipid cocktail of love, bitterness and revenge, for it was hard to dwell on one without the others encroaching, and it had the effect of souring the cream of his surprise encounter. He needed a distraction to stand between him and the past, something to keep his mind off his desire for revenge. Perhaps Teresa might be the one to fill that particular void in his life, and though she was old enough to be his mother, she had about her a sultry seductiveness that appealed to the carnal side of his nature. Still, his vanity rebelled at the idea, and the timeworn cliché 'what will the neighbours say?' added its own discouragement.

Finally, pushing all thoughts of Castleford into a darker chamber of his mind, he forced a grin, saying: "I'm sorry for being so morbid – Teresa, and I do appreciate your concern."

"Oh, that's all right," returned Teresa. "When you came into the kitchen, I could see you had a distant look in your eye. If there's ever anything I can do –"

A discreet masculine cough interrupted the conversation, and when they looked to the door, Martin was shuffling towards the stove, muttering to himself. Annoyance flashed for an instant in Teresa's eyes, and then she smiled. "Goodnight, Martin," she greeted. "I've just finished tidying up for the night and I was having a cup of tea with Jack – there's still some in the pot."

When Martin grunted something incoherent under his breath, Teresa rose from the table and, turning the full beam of her smile on Jack, white teeth gleaming, cheeks dimpling prettily, she excused herself.

Jack's eyes followed the provocative swing of her hips as she turned towards the stairs, and when he recognised the invitation that any male could read, he glared daggers at Martin, as if he was to blame for her hasty exit. It might be weeks before he bumped into her again, although next time he vowed not to be so reticent.

On the following Saturday night, as he was returning earlier than usual to watch the late-night movie on television, he was surprised when Teresa appeared in the gloom of the hall. He was about to call a greeting when she placed an index finger on her lips and beckoned for him to follow her into the dark interior of her apartment. At the flick of a switch the room sprang into light and, gently closing the door behind them, she indicated one of two leather armchairs. "Grab a pew – make yourself at home," she invited. "I hope you don't mind me waylaying you like this, but we were only halfway through our conversation last time when we were rudely interrupted by the barbarians."

Mouth agape Jack's mind could scarcely keep up with his eyes as they sped over the spacious room, astounded by the luxury in which he suddenly found himself. It was as if someone had said 'open sesame' and he was in a modern-day Aladdin's cave. It took more than a glance to absorb it all, from the neat arrangement of bookcases, cabinets, tables and chairs, all in polished oak, to the tapestries on the walls which were interspersed with mounted paintings depicting biblical scenes, and the carpet was of such quality fabric that he immediately stopped in his tracks when he felt his feet sinking into the pile. Never, if he hadn't seen it with his own eyes, could he have imagined that such opulence could be hidden behind such a drab exterior.

Teresa, a smug smile on her lips at Jack's astonishment, rested a hand lightly on his arm and guided him to a flat-top cabinet which, at the touch of a button, opened into a bar containing such a glistening array of bottles and glasses that he almost jumped back at the suddenness of the transition.

"Name your poison, buddy, as the Yanks say," she laughed, indicating the goodly display with a flourish of a hand. "Scotch?"

Jack, his mind still at sea, nodded absently, for it could easily be a scene from a movie – Teresa in a black, ankle-length dress of shimmering silk, which was split on one side, a full thigh peeping through at the slightest movement of her body, her hair knotted in a chignon so heavy that it was keeping her head erect, the creamy skin of her neck and bare shoulders glowing in the wan light cast by the shaded wall-lamps, and he, a poor stranger off the street who had just rung the wrong doorbell.

Bringing to bear all the charm of smile and glance she possessed Teresa poured the Johnnie Walker Black Label into crystal glasses with careful intensity, filling one and handing it to Jack before topping up her own. "Ice?" she asked.

"No, thank you," Jack replied, rather formally, his voice unconsciously modulating in keeping with his surroundings.

"Oh, come on, Jack – unwind, for Christ's sake! I'm not going to bite you. I'm just lonely and need someone to talk to," said Teresa, in a wheedling tone, easing closer and bringing her delicate perfume into play. "Come – sit down," she went on, leading him by the hand to an armchair, and when he was seated, she sank into the opposite one, crossing her legs in the process. "As I said, I need someone to talk to, and you seem to be a cut above the other lodgers."

"How d'you mean – a cut above the other lodgers?"

"More refined, and I can sense too that you've got problems," returned Teresa, "I noticed it the first day on the doorstep. But judging by the stubborn set of your jaw, I'd be willing to gamble that you're no man's lackey. But who's the girl?"

"What girl?"

"The one you're tearing your heart out over."

For the second time that night Jack was taken completely by surprise, and whether or not she sensed it, Teresa had plucked at the one heartstring that could be made to twang. While she was waiting for him to respond, she re-crossed her legs, saying: "I suppose you're wondering about me, and asking yourself: 'what am I doing here?' So, I'll put you in the picture. You're here to talk, and you're free to leave any time you like, but first let me tell you about myself. I'm not a widow really, not even a grass widow – I've never been married before. I just put on the widow guise to give me status, as I've already explained. I loved a fighter pilot many years ago, but alas, he was killed in the War, and there are some women who can love only once."

Allowing her words to trail off Teresa averted her gaze, as if she was trying to stifle the emotion the memory evoked and, holding her glass aloft, she toasted: "The dead are dead, so here's to the living, and why should the dead rob the living of any happiness they can grasp?"

The drama was somewhat overdone, Jack thought, for a game of 'will you come into my parlour said the spider to the fly', and to complete the charade she lifted the lid on a radiogram. Seconds later, the romantic strains of STRANGER IN PARADISE were floating over the room, rekindling a memory of a long-ago night at the Phoenix, which set him to wondering if it was intuition alone that had prompted her to select that particular record, or was it a favourite she used for seducing her fancy men? – for now that his logic was back on straight lines, he could perceive no other purpose.

"Let's dance – I want us to be good friends, that's all," she said, taking both his hands and easing him to his feet, and when she pressed a switch on the wall, the lights dimmed almost to darkness, swathing the room in a romantic glow. "Now I won't look so old – so just imagine you're dancing with the girl you left behind in Galway."

In the soft glow of the lamplight the lyrics carried Jack back over the waves to a night that was still strong on his mind, make-believing as Teresa pressed her body closer. Drifting more and more into the world of fantasy he closed his eyes, while Teresa took the form of his partner on that memorable night, her bare arm encircling his neck, her breasts tight against his chest, their cheeks brushing lightly, her perfume tantalising his nostrils. As round and round they crept, he wondered if life would ever be perfect, or would there always be a yearning for someone out of reach, a certain someone with whom the supreme happiness alone could be shared? – Or were all lovers' dreams destined to dash hopelessly on the rocks, like the Atlantic's wild waves?

Still rapt in dreamland his fingers loosened the zip on the back of Teresa's dress, and like a blind man feeling his way he slipped a hand inside the waistband of her knickers. The sudden thrill of fondling soft bare flesh knocked him out of his romantic reverie and, as if a demon had taken control of his senses, he grabbed her roughly by the hair, forced her head back, and kissed her hungrily on the lips, his tongue probing her mouth until he felt her breasts stiffening. Still locked in the embrace he cast his eyes about until they fell on a chaise longue which was conveniently positioned for the purpose he had in mind and, summoning all his strength to his aid, he lifted her off her feet and plonked her unceremoniously down on the cushions, dragging her dress up to the waist and forcing her thighs apart with his knees. It didn't take much in the way of strength to quell her feeble attempts at pushing him off, and yet, the more she struggled and kicked in the air, the more she worked herself into a compromising position, making it easier for him to remove her flimsy knickers, the last obstacle in his feverish quest for fulfilment.

"No – don't rape me – stop, you'll kill me, you big brute! Oh- oh!" she cried, her pleas giving way to a sharp intake of breath as he entered her, and a gasp of what seemed pain, as if he had just stabbed her with a knife. However, once he had consolidated his position astride her, forcing her knees up to her ears, she responded with such vigour that it derided her earlier protests.

After a spate of shorter, more urgent stokes, which immediately brought fulfilment, Teresa wriggled out from beneath him and led him to the bedroom, and before the anticlimax of disillusionment and disappointment that men feel after ejaculation had time to set in – the disillusionment a child might feel when it opens a beautifully-wrapped package and finds nothing inside, and the disappointment that perhaps had made Adam hide in the bushes when he realised that he had traded paradise for just one taste of the forbidden fruit – her articulate fingers roused him for the second time, and thereafter, nature took its course again and again until sheer exhaustion claimed their bodies.

When the early-morning light streamed through a gap in the curtains, Jack yawned into wakefulness. Teresa was still asleep, lying on her back beside him, the sheet pulled up to her chin, her make-up flaking off in scales. Lighting a cigarette he took a few meditative puffs, his thoughts wandering back to another night of uninhibited pleasure on a high headland overlooking the sea. Comparing the two nights he failed to find a common denominator, for his latest adventure was rugged, earthy, and almost nymphomaniacal on Teresa's behalf, and lacked the tenderness, selflessness and fulfilment of the other night, and he found nothing to cherish from it, save that it reminded him of his first dabble in the waters of fornication down Poke Lane with Biddy Dooley, a woman twice his age with varicose veins on her legs as big and blue as duck eggs.

Dozing and awakening he felt Teresa leaving the bed, and some minutes later, the smell of frying bacon wafting from the kitchen stoked up his appetite. When she returned, she was wrapped tightly in a dressing gown, and she was carrying a breakfast tray. "Breakfast in bed for his majesty after raping me, I don't know how many times, and taking the virginity I had kept intact for the last ten years. Really, I should be cross with you for taking advantage of me," she said, reproach tinged with jocosity in her tone. "But somehow I'm not, and when you've eaten, it's bath time."

While he was eating, Teresa sat on the edge of the bed, stroking his hair back from his forehead. "As I've said, I should despise you for having your wicked way with me against my will – I pleaded with you to stop, but you took no heed. It's been so many years, and you were so masterful that I was forced into responding," she went on. "Now that we've gone this far, I want us to be good friends, nothing more, and I do hope you get that girl you're carrying the torch for. But in the meantime, if you ever feel like talking the matter over, you can always tap on my back door. I say the back door, because I like to be discreet. I like to keep my self-respect and good name, not like other landladies who boast about – I'm going to use a rude word here – who boast about having a cock-lodger, and we'll have to ignore each other when anyone is around. So, let's be sensible about it – you're twenty-one and I'm on the wrong side of forty. Relationships like ours have only one way of ending – so, it's better that it's realised in the beginning."

When he had eaten, Teresa wiggled off with the tray, and shortly afterwards the sound of running taps reached his ears. When she returned, she draped a king-size robe over his shoulders, and like a boxer on his way to the ring she led him to the bathroom. When he was fully submerged in the bubbly bath water, she washed him thoroughly like a baby, and then, towelling him dry, she led him back to the bedroom. "Now lie on your back on the bed and close your eyes," she ordered, an authoritative note in her tone, and when he did as he was bidden, she took the lid off a jar of cream, opened the bathrobe, and began to massage the fragrant cream into his thighs and groin in slow rhythmic strokes.

Stretched out, eyes closed, Jack relaxed until Teresa's sensual lips found his, and when he became sexually aroused, she climbed astride him, her rhythm quickening with each thrust, until finally, in one feverish lunge she came down viciously on his upward surge of passion. As her sharp fingernails dug into the tender flesh of his buttocks, an orgasmic sensation compounded of ecstasy and pain shot through his body, and she never relinquished her grip until her frenzy fizzled out. "You'd better go before you kill me," she said, slithering down breathlessly beside him. "But be careful in case anyone sees you leaving."

For the remainder of the day Jack's thoughts kept returning to his surprise adventure, examining it from every angle, from her lonely spinster guise, to her capitulation, in which her subsequent desire far outweighed her earlier resistance, and lastly, her final vigorous thrusts astride him – like a jockey on a beaten horse trying to steal the race on the line. The whole episode smacked of sham, like the thirteenth stroke of a crazy clock, and such acting on her behalf, had it been done in a Hollywood movie, would surely have merited an Oscar. It was hard to believe her story, harder even than the tale that Adam and Eve were Irish, and their names were O'Toole and O'Hare.

On the other hand, perhaps she was telling the truth – innocent till proven guilty, and what had he to lose? She had said she wasn't possessive, and he had carte blanche to call whenever he pleased. Vanity too came into play when he realised that if it ever leaked out he would be the envy of the lodgings, and that night, with his whole body aching in an agreeable way, he slept like a dormouse.

Now that he had found his distraction, it quickly developed into a habit which became harder and harder to kick. Teresa was so understanding, so easy to sit and talk to, and one night, under the strange influence which sometimes prompts a person to confide in the newfound friend rather than the old, he poured out his story.

"So, you believe this Paisley guy had your horse and cows poisoned and you intend to exact revenge?" questioned Teresa, showing keen interest. "And this girl – this Mary what's-her-name, you believe when the two years are up, she'll come running?"

"Something like that – not as clear-cut though. I'll have to go back."

"I'm not going to laugh because I know how serious you are, but if someone told you the same story, what advice would you give? Still, everyone must have a goal in life, and all I can say is, I hope you make it. But first of all I feel I should give you an insight into women's logic – this is something I know about, for only a woman knows what a woman can do – which button to press to get a man going either way. It takes one woman to see through another, just as I'm sure it takes a man to see through another man, for in most cases people in love cannot see even the most obvious of their partner's shortcomings. They're dazzled like jackdaws – dazzled by the glitter, not the gold."

"Whether you're right or not, it's all I have to keep me going," said Jack, happy to continue with the subject now that he had broached it.

"By what you've told me, this Mary you mentioned is well-to-do and you're just a small homesteader," Teresa went on. "So, let's look at it from a woman's viewpoint. Once that adolescent ideology of everyone being born equal wears off, there's a vacuum in a woman's mind, call it a transition period from girlhood to womanhood in which she becomes conscious of social standing for the first time. It's then she begins to look at every suitor's prospects, not that she means to be mercenary, but because it's in a woman's nature, and to satisfy the rules of convention – are you with me?"

"I don't know, but go ahead anyway."

"I'll put it like this, a gypsy and a nobleman's daughter could never hit it off no matter how much they were in love – the rules of convention would never allow such a relationship to gel. I'll give you a few instances. Handsome young man from the right family background, rich, with prospects – every girl's dream. Handsome young man with prospects only – worth stringing along, and so on, down to the lowest level of society. So, a not too handsome young man, without money or prospects, but from the right family background, is the end of the range. A handsome young navvy who digs holes in the road for a living, I'm afraid, is not on the list of eligibles."

"Surely love comes into the equation somewhere, Teresa?" countered Jack, Tim Kelly's advice on the subject coming back from the grave to haunt him.

"Don't take me up wrong, Jack – I'm not trying to put you off. I could just as easily tell you what you wanted to hear, but I'm being cruel to be kind. If this Mary is in love with you, she'd have followed you to the ends of the earth while she was still in the idealistic stage of her life, but now, with every month that passes, she'll make excuses to herself, and the longer it goes on, the harder she'll find it to make that leap. It's quite obvious that she's under her father's influence –"

Teresa stopped abruptly in mid-sentence and stared curiously at Jack's hands. "What's that little gold thing you're twirling round in your fingers?" she asked, her eyes fixed on him intently, as if she would read his mind. "Did she give you that?"

The little gold thing was the little gold bell he had picked up at his cottage gate on the morning after the killing of his stock, and he had developed a habit of twirling it with his fingers whenever he was in a pensive mood. "No – she didn't give me that," he replied, wondering why she was so interested. "It's something I found – I keep it as a good-luck piece."

"You're going to need it – the luck I mean. But have you any photographs of Mary to show me, or any photographs of home?"

"No – nothing like that. But I have it all pictured in my mind's eye."

"All I can say is that life doesn't begin with 'once upon a time' and end with 'they lived happily ever after' as it does in fairy tales, and it's under no obligation to give us what we expect," Teresa went on. "The horse you fancy seldom wins the race and rarely the guy gets the girl – at least, not the girl of his dreams, but it's comforting to know that as often as not the placed horse pays more than the winner. In most cases money is a redeeming factor for the lack of looks, as most women are prepared to ignore all types of shortcomings in a man if there's a healthy bank balance to paper over the cracks, which in itself is a mild form of prostitution. But they say it's better to have loved and lost than to have never loved at all. That more or less sums me up – loved and lost."

Such conversations became regular, and Teresa, for all her claims of disinterest, never let an opportunity pass without slipping in a few home-made truths and paradoxes, as if she wanted to steer him away from his purpose. Why? he wondered, for she had made it quite clear that there was no future in the affair and he was free to break it off whenever he chose, or perhaps he was reading too much between the lines.

Chapter 6

Now that six months had dropped behind him, Jack realised that there was no quick fix for his situation, no short cuts to reaching his goal unless he got into the cut-throat business of subcontracting, which like all ventures required capital. Even then, he would need contacts and, hoping to bump into someone who might put him on the right track, he began to fraternise more with his fellow immigrants. However, he soon found that getting information out of them was like bleeding a stone, and though their dispositions varied from amiable to surly and some made disagreeable drunks, he noticed that they all had one thing in common – loneliness, a carefully-concealed loneliness that didn't sulk or complain, but nevertheless peered out from behind their smiles and coarse humour. Most were generous with their money, true to their word if they gave it, and though they condemned with a mixture of yearning and anger the priest-ridden society they had left behind, they rushed to defend it any time it came in for ridicule from outsiders.

This loyalty to the old sod was very much in evidence one Saturday night in the Halfway House when Reg had in his company Ron and Bill, two associates from his days in the legal profession. At a glance Jack perceived that they were the sneering pretentious type, their haughty manner oddly at variance with the easygoing nature of the mainly Irish regulars, and for all that everyone was dressed in their Saturday-night best they stood out like magpies among crows. Although nothing offensive was said there was an uneasy atmosphere, a veiled hostility, which found vent in short barbed remarks on the contentious issues of nationality and social standing.

Whether or not Reg sensed it, he continued with his habitual ribbing of Pat. "How is it that most Irishmen here in London claim to be farmers' sons?" he asked. "If there are so many farms over there, why do they have to come over here to make a living?"

"They come here to make up the shortfall in labour – you've only got to look at all the ads in the Irish papers to see what I mean. Also, there's an arrangement between the two governments to counterbalance the influx of immigrants from Africa and the Caribbean," countered Pat, in his own inimitable style. "And don't be getting up on your high horse thinking you're doing us a favour by having us here, because I saw more poverty in this country than I ever saw in Ireland. And another thing I'll say, at least when we come here we don't begin by kicking you out of house and home, like you know who."

The battle of words raged between the pair, each giving as good as he was getting, until Bill, Reg's friend, butted in. "Is it true that the Irish keep the pigs under the bed?" he asked, rather contemptuously, his sarcastic smile barely crinkling his pencil moustache.

As if a bomb had exploded, the chatter ceased, and Jack was surprised to see the hot blood of anger that rushed to the faces of Pat and his friends mirrored in Bob Little's, and it would have immediately come to blows if Reg hadn't intervened, for what Reg could say to Pat and what other Englishmen could say to him were horses of a different colour. "He didn't mean any offence, lads – honestly," he said, in an attempt to defuse the situation. "Isn't that right, Bill?"

When Bill nodded an apology, Pat, perhaps perceiving that he was anything but repentant, countered with a similar-type smile. "No offence taken, but if we're going to take the piss out o' one another, let's do it in a gentlemanly fashion – flattening noses and blackening eyes never solved anything," he returned. "Now, to answer your question about the pigs, first let me say that a pig is a very intelligent animal, a lot more intelligent than a bulldog, but like all your countrymen you've got the story wrong. We don't keep pigs under the bed – it's not practical, but years ago we use to hide some of the litter under the bed when the English landlord came round to value a tenant's assets, which no doubt would result in an increase in rent if they were discovered. Also, if there were English soldiers in the vicinity, there was every chance they might be stolen.

"This shouldn't be too hard for you to imagine, considering they stole everything else we had, even the crockery off the dresser – and the trees. Everything had to be red-hot or nailed down when your lot was over there – even the Sacred Heart lamp wasn't safe. Stealing is in yeer blood – the country you boast so much about was built on the proceeds of slavery, famine and theft, and no doubt your mates showed you some of the stuff they rifled out of dead Germans' pockets during the War – rings, watches, cigarette cases and other sentimental stuff, and your police, stealing money from the people they arrest. Reg can bear witness to this –"

"I don't know why yez're always trying to ridicule us, Irish – on about pegs under the bed and all that!" Bob Little cut in, again surprising Jack. "I'll have yez know that every English house I lodged in had a cat pessing in a tray by the cooker – giving a bit o' flavour to the steak and kidney pie, you might say. Cat's pess and steak and kidney pie is good for the health, I suppose – no wonder so many of yez have that wishy-washy colour."

When Reg made as if he might say something, Pat beat him to it, rounding again on Bill. "You seem to enjoy taking the piss out of other nationalities, but like Mrs Brown's dog, ye can give it, but ye can't take it. I often heard ye saying that the only good German is a dead German, and hey presto, here they are ruling ye, and the Queen's uncle a Nazi to boot, not to mention her sister-in-law married to a colonel in the Gestapo. But if you dare open your mouth about it, you could easily wind up in the Tower o' London for treason, which means you've got to kiss arse. Like a leopard changing its spots, the monarchy changing its surname doesn't alter the fact that it's German and, as most people are proud of their ancestry, you can never be really sure where their loyalties lie. So, the next time you join in the chorus of GOD SAVE THE QUEEN, remember you're singing for God to save the Kaiser's first cousin – twice removed."

Pat kept on, a deceptively smooth tongue covering any sarcasm, and it was delivered in such a droll tone that it didn't actually cause offence, save for some uneasy shuffling. He seemed to take sadistic pleasure in deflating the pompous, and he could no more resist pricking conceits and hypocrisies than a small boy could resist sticking a pin in a balloon. He did it subtly too, by first drawing out his unsuspecting victims by seeming to agree with them, and then pulling the carpet out from under them, and they were never quite certain what had happened until they found themselves standing out as prejudiced, jingoistic, toffee-nosed and slightly ridiculous.

Reg quickly brought the party back on an even keel with a few bawdy jokes, and yet, for all his charisma, his friends looked far from comfortable, which was a grim but true reminder of the chasm between the two races and how utterly impossible it would be to bridge. There was hostility under the surface ready to break out at the least provocation, no matter how much they went out of their way to be friendly to one another, Reg's friends perhaps believing in their superiority of intellect and right of privilege, Pat's friends believing in God-knows-what, perhaps in being anti-British.

Later, when they were alone in the toilet, Pat explained: "The English like to be top dogs; that's why I took them down a peg, and it seems to me that they spend half their lives making up nice things to say about themselves – how noble they are, and all that kind o' shite. At the back of it all they're bad losers, and let's not forget the Englishman's sense of fair play we hear so much about. As you know yourself, fair play is the last thing you should be expecting from them and, if we delve deep enough, I'll bet we'd find that it was one of their own who coined the phrase. It definitely wasn't an Irishman, a Zulu, an Indian or the wife of a Boer farmer. They can see no wrong in themselves, because they're blinded by their own conceit. Even if they committed murder, they'd try to put the blame on the victim. They're a thankless shower too when you think of all the Irishmen who fought and died for them in both wars, big eejits that they were in the first place, because they never give them a mention, not to mind erect a memorial to them like they did for the Poles."

"I thought you were a bit rough on them," said Jack. "Did you see their shocked faces?"

"No, Jack – I wasn't half rough enough. They believe they're on a higher plane than the rest o' the world, and they have such high opinions of themselves, especially for subjects hardly a generation out of serfdom, as if they could talk about the pigs under the bed and they having damn all, not even a pig, if it came to that. One word could sum up the lot o' them – 'stout'."

"What do you mean by 'stout'? I thought 'stout' meant solidly built and fat."

"In this town, among our own, a stout man is a man who's either thick or ignorant and doesn't know he's thick or ignorant," Pat explained. "When you get to know them better, you'll find that they all suffer from the same sickness. A type of blindness that won't let them see themselves as they really are: arrogant, conceited and ignorant, and they're never happy unless they have something to grumble about."

"I don't altogether agree!" interjected Jack. "I've met some nice English people too."

"Yes, there are some nice English people, but most o' them are refugees from reality," countered Pat. "They make such big issues out of small things and ignore the real problems that it makes me wonder sometimes how they ever got an empire. 'Immigrant' is a dirty word with them, and they're down on immigrants of every nationality, whether they were born in the Empire or not. They can't see that without the immigrants productivity would suffer and the whole economy would contract, and it never seems to register that they were, and still are, illegal immigrants in half the countries of the world themselves."

"That's a bit strong, Pat – it's wrong to condemn the people of today for what their ancestors did, now that they're committed to democratic rule," returned Jack. "And didn't they keep the War going against Hitler until the Yanks and Russians came in?"

"And how I often wish they hadn't, because they never stop going on about the War," countered Pat. "If you ask me, Hitler did them a great favour, because there was no difference whatsoever between the Third Reich and the British Empire, save to say that the British Empire endured longer. That's why they keep showing you the scale of the atrocities committed by Hitler, hoping that it'll take the edge off their own atrocities, something like a man who keeps pissing in the bed every night, and then drawing attention to a man who keeps pissing and shitting in it every night – highlighting the greater of two evils. If there was no War, they'd have nothing to talk about, and this democratic rule you mentioned – that's an English joke, because all they know about democracy is how to spell the word. Explain this democratic rule to the Catholics of Northern Ireland – herded into ghettos, disenfranchised, getting second-class education, banned from the civil service or holding high office, and a system of monarchy imposed on them. Even the MPs have to take an oath of allegiance to the monarch and her heirs, and not to the people they represent, which means that their right to freedom of speech is shackled from the very beginning – where's the democracy in that? Yet, they never stop preaching democracy, but to me, if patriotism is the last refuge of the scoundrel, then democracy should be the last refuge of the mendacious politician."

"That's just their system of government and, as you said yourself, Pat, it's their country and we're just living in it."

"True, but what about all those toffee-nosed magistrates who have no judicial qualifications whatsoever, dishing out prison sentences to anyone they don't like the look of, especially to us, Irish – the rich sitting in judgement on the poor, religious discrimination, race discrimination, no bill of rights, no constitution, just the outward show of democracy – no democracy please, we're British, but we've got to seem to be democratic. Look at the statues of all their famous men dotted all over the city: Nelson, Wellington, Kitchener, and not a republican among them, a liberty, equality, fraternity republican, I mean. To me, an English politician preaching democracy is like the Hunchback of Nôtre Dame telling someone to stand up straight. I suppose you've seen the notices in paper-shop windows for digs – no Irish, Blacks or dogs. Well, it's a good job the darkies are here, otherwise we'd be copping all the prejudice."

Pat was seldom short of an answer, and repartee sprang to his lips like fragments of metal to a magnet, which left Jack with no choice but to leave him with the last word.

When they returned to the bar, Reg was still pouring oil on the troubled waters, and he immediately drew the attention of the company to Jack. "What's this I hear about you knocking off your landlady – what's her name – oh yes, Widow Kilbane – you sly old side-shafter, you," he laughed. "So, this is the reason we're not seeing so much of you lately, and you know the saying – nobody misses a slice off a cut loaf."

"Cut – how d'you mean cut?" interjected Pat. "It must be down to the last few crumbs by now, considering all the men she stacked the drapery for."

"If her big mouth is anything to go by, yez can imagine what to expect in the downstairs department," chimed in Bob Little. "It's like 'alas poor Yorick' – everyone knew it well, and yez all know the saying: 'if one man isn't enough, twenty wouldn't be too many'."

The laugh ran round the bar and, as others added their comments on the widow's lack of virtue, Jack felt himself blushing. Although London was a vast city it seemed that gossip travelled through its smoky environs faster than the speed of light, which brought up the question – how did they know so much about the widow? Although he shuddered at the picture his imagination evoked he smiled smugly, for he knew that he was the envy of every man there, which again highlighted the difference between the immigrant and the indigenous Irish. In his homeland for such pursuit he would be ostracised by the polite society and threatened with excommunication by the Church, and perhaps by way of atonement charged with a series of sackcloth and ashes penances until his soul was purged of the evils of the flesh, while among the Irish in Camden Town, it was all a joke, so much so that it dispelled the earlier discord.

Invariably, it was left to Pat to have the last word on the subject. "You've come on in leaps and bounds in this town, Jack," he laughed. "You made a name for yourself digging trenches, you fell foul of the law, you went before the magistrates, and now you're riding the landlady of the digs, all in a few months – what next, I wonder?"

When Jack saw the admiration in the eyes of the group, as if he had just passed all the tests for a knighthood, he straightened to his full height, vanity replacing his earlier embarrassment – he was cock-lodger, although it also unveiled the duplicity of women when he realised that Widow Kilbane had been round the track more than a few times.

A week later Jack was dealt a devastating blow – Jimmy Murphy was back in Castleford and Eileen was planning to marry him. *He's changed*, her letter said. *He's got a job in the new textile factory opening in Galway. He worked for the same outfit in Manchester, so he got priority, and he's buying a house near the factory. I'll be locking up the place here, and I'm selling the hens and pigs and what little stock we have. I need the money for the wedding. I suppose it'd be no good asking you to come home for it. But you have no need to worry, Murt Burke is going to graze the land and keep the thistles cut, and Kathy Moore is going to light a fire in the cottage from time to time to stop it from getting damp.*

Kathy sends her regards. She's very clever. She's just passed her exams and she's starting a good job in Moon's department store in Galway. She's planning to stay with myself and Jimmy when we get settled and go home at the weekends –

The letter ran on in the same vein, and though he detected excitement and happiness in Eileen's scribble, his bile rose at the thought of Murphy as a brother-in-law. He's changed, she had said. It was hard to believe, and where had he got the money to buy a house in Galway? Murphy was the type who would rather starve on a penny than work for a pound and never had more than two halfpennies to rub together. According to Eileen, he had saved it over the years, although she failed to mention from what type of employment, for other than his gift for getting women to drop their knickers, he had no conceivable talents. Few women could see further than his good looks, another discernible flaw he had detected in the female character: some had a penchant for picking up stray cats and dogs and birds with broken wings, while others picked up superficially attractive men, mostly rakes, with a view to reforming them, useless men with no grit, who were sure to quit when the going got tough.

Murphy fell easily into the category of the handsome good-for-nothing, and now that he had returned to claim Eileen again – like a fox for his kill – what next? "Of all the women in the world he had to pick my sister," he mused, as he tried to see the funny side, recalling Humphrey Bogart – play it again, Sam, and all the gin-joints. Still, it was hard to see it working out, especially if Murphy got the sack for giving one to the factory manager's wife, and what of Kathy Moore? If her provocative kiss was anything to go by, she could easily fall for Murphy's charm. On the other hand, why should he be worried about Kathy's chastity, or did she mean more to him than he cared to admit?

For all its disturbing news he read the letter over, as if it would bring Knockrush and the neighbours closer and, as loneliness gripped his heart, he formed a picture in his mind of Eileen locking the door behind her, another cottage perhaps destined to join the other tumbledown dwellings and succumb to the blackberry brambles, briars and nettles. It was as if the lid on a coffin was being screwed down, the body abandoned and left alone and, enshrouded in the sad sweetness of remembrance, he almost could see the clock with its weights and chains, the dresser full of shining crockery, the oil lamp on the wall, the plaque of Blessed Martin, and the pigs' pot hanging over the empty grate, all staring back at him reproachfully, as if they were accusing him of desertion in the face of that uncompromising enemy – emigration. The memory lingered, fanning the flames of his nostalgia until the simple lines of *The Old Woman of the Road,* a school day poem, brought a tear to his eye:

The plaintive verses reminded him how lucky he was to have a house, and it had the effect of bolstering his determination to go back. However, when the reason for his misfortune filtered into his reverie, his nostalgia turned to anger and he cursed Bull Paisley who, for no other reason than spite, had cut his lifeline, forcing him out of his home. Nevertheless, his day of reckoning would come, for Paisley had made a fatal mistake – he had depended on others to do his dirty work, and in the fullness of time tongues were sure to wag. A face too kept intruding on his train of thought, a beautiful face, and next year she would be twenty-one. Dare he venture a letter on the pretext of having left without saying goodbye? No – it would serve no purpose, for according to Widow Kilbane, Mary might walk with him through the golden land, but would never trudge with him through the one of hardship and uncertainty. It would be better to wait, and though life with Mary was a far-off magnificent dream, it seemed that most people lived on dreams – and hope, or perhaps fate might lend a hand and send him back a rich man.

As winter set in, Jack's dream of going back a rich man was soon shattered by the slave conditions of the construction industry. As the days got shorter, so too did the wages, and travelling to work on the back of the steel-bodied lorry in the icy weather was almost unbearable. Nevertheless, the job was pushed on relentlessly, regardless of hail or rain, and 'grumble and go' was the name of the game.

As Christmas neared, one evening as Jack was returning from work Teresa was waiting in the hall. "Can you call tonight?" she asked in an undertone, and later, when she opened the back door to his coded knock, he sensed something out of the ordinary in her behaviour. Flopping into an armchair he sat silently while she took an opposite seat. "I was wondering if you'd like to spend Christmas with me?" she asked at length. "We could stay in a hotel by the seaside – Brighton is nice this time of year."

As Jack was about to voice his objections, Teresa cut him short, saying: "I know you're trying hard to save money, but this trip will cost you absolutely nothing. I simply dread spending Christmas alone, and if I went to relatives, it'd be nothing but inquisitions and advice, and my advice to you on relatives is, keep them as far away as possible, especially the poor ones, because they'll only drag you down to their level. We could pretend at the hotel that you're my nephew. So, what do you say?"

Sensing that Teresa had detected a soft spot in his nature Jack felt it was pointless to argue. "In ordinary circumstances it should be me inviting you, and it doesn't seem fair that you should be paying," he returned. "It's going against the grain and makes me feel cheap. Anyway, what choice have I got? If I don't agree, you'll keep nagging me till I do."

Brighton was chosen, and Teresa made arrangements to travel on the day before Christmas Eve. On the morning of their departure, Jack sifted through his scant belongings and, save for the suit he had bought for Galway races, he had nothing presentable to wear. When he tried to squeeze his full reflection into the cracked mirror above the washbasin, it jogged a memory of the races: the music, the hullabaloo, his night with the strange lady, and the wily fortune-tellers who were always on safe ground whenever they foretold the crossing of water in any young Irishman's coulter of destiny. Shaking himself out of his reverie he reached for his overcoat, which was hanging on the back of the door, limp and out of shape like a wilted horse blanket, and when he fingered the threadbare material, he cursed profanely – cold or no cold, he would have to face the outdoors without it.

When he reached Victoria Station, Teresa was pacing back and forth by the departures board, her brown leather luggage at her feet. She was fashionably turned out to combat the weather in a three-quarter-length suede jacket, beige flared skirt, and tan leather boots; a tartan cashmere scarf had its tasselled ends bobbing at her waist, and a white tam-o'-shanter sat rather precariously on top of her pinned-up hair. Feeling somewhat drab in comparison Jack picked up her luggage and followed her through the hurrying throngs of Christmas shoppers to the train. Fortunately, they had a first-class compartment to themselves, and they were hardly disturbed until they arrived in Brighton.

The Grand Hotel wasn't exactly the type of hostelry Jack had envisaged and, somewhat disconcerted by the luxury in which he suddenly found himself, he followed at Teresa's heels as they were ushered up to their suite on the top floor overlooking the sea. When they were behind closed doors, he turned the full glare of his scolding eyes on Teresa. "The Devil roast you anyway – you should've realised that this place is far too posh for the likes o' me. If I'd known what you had in mind, you'd be going on your own."

"It'll be all right, Jack," said Teresa, putting on a penitent smile. "We'll start by having lunch here in the suite and, after we've unpacked, I'm taking you to the shops."

"Unpacked – that's a good one," returned Jack derisively, indicating his brown paper carrier bag which was standing out like an ugly duckling beside Teresa's expensive set of matching luggage. "Unpack what, I ask you?"

"Don't be like that, Jack. Let's have lunch, and then I promise I'll make it all right."

After a four-course lunch, which included lobster, complemented by a bottle of Graves, Teresa pulled out all the stops in persuading Jack to accompany her to the shops, and before he quite realised it he was in Warner's department store, trying on suits, jackets, trousers and shoes. Every time he tried to duck out he was thwarted by Teresa and Warner's avid salesman, until finally she selected an evening suit, a dark grey woollen suit, a black cashmere jacket, several pairs of trousers, a stack of shirts, ties, shoes, socks and handkerchiefs. Lastly, she added a sheepskin coat to the accumulating pile. Save for the coat, she asked for everything to be delivered to the hotel and, shuddering as he tried to estimate the cost, he wasn't sure whether or not to be pleased.

Perhaps sensing Jack's uncertainty Teresa went immediately on the defensive. "I know what you're thinking, but you're wrong. It's just a Christmas present from me to you – I feel I owe it to you. You've been nice to me, so let me be nice to you – the cost doesn't matter," she explained, and when she noticed that Jack was still unconvinced, she resorted to the blackmail of tears. "Oh, for God's sake, don't be like that, Jack," she sniffled. "Otherwise it's going to spoil our Christmas – I wanted everything to be a surprise."

Jack had yet to find the weapons for fighting a woman's tears, and though he shrugged his acceptance, no word of thanks sprang to his lips. However, the warmth and comfort of the sheepskin coat helped to dispel some of his misgivings, and now that he had it on, it was hard to return it. It was just a loan, he tried to convince himself, until someday he would be in a position to repay her, although the more he thought of it, the more despondent he became, as if he had just taken the king's shilling.

Later, in the hotel suite, when her purchases arrived, Teresa sorted out a dinner jacket, a white shirt with a frilly front, and a black bow-tie. "Wear these tonight – dinner is at seven," she reminded him, before adjourning to her bedroom to change.

Feeling for the first time the comfort of expensive tailoring about his shoulders Jack viewed himself from all angles in the cheval glass and, pleased with the transformation, he felt like pinching himself to make sure he wasn't dreaming, all dolled up in an evening suit waiting to take his Cinderella to the ball. Cinderella indeed! – a woman old enough to be his mother, he smiled derisively, although his derision stuck somewhere between his eyes and Adam's apple when Teresa appeared in her bedroom doorway, turned out like a movie star on her way to a grand premiere. Her evening gown of black chiffon had a daringly low-cut front and plunging back, so that it revealed more than it concealed, and her hair, which was neatly pinned and piled high on top of her head, highlighted to greater effect the swan-like curve of her neck; the crow's feet at the outer corners of her eyes were expertly camouflaged and, when the light caught the diamond pendant round her neck and the sparkle flashed to her eyes, they dazzled like sunlight on water.

Awestricken, Jack swallowed hard, and he was about to wolf-whistle when Teresa placed a manicured forefinger on his lips. "Remember – I'm your auntie," she said, laughing lightly, and yet blushing under his admiring gaze.

The dining room, a shrine to the old order, breathed of convention. Portraits of past dignitaries looked down from the oak-panelled walls like medieval inquisitors on the vast expanse of white linen-clothed tables, silver candelabra, and on the formally-dressed clientele, the men in evening suits, the ladies in a glitter of diamonds and bare shoulders, a few old harridans among them, who were clinging desperately to their painted semblance of youth. Stiff, could only mildly describe the ambience, and when they were shown to their table, Teresa ordered champagne.

When the waiter popped the cork, again for the first time Jack sampled the much-acclaimed drink, and he sipped tentatively until he acquired the taste and then more liberally. After a few glasses its effervescence wafted him into a state of light-headed exhilaration, and the more he imbibed, the younger Teresa seemed to appear. It was as if he was living in a different world, a paradise on earth, and the eight-course dinner of smoked goose, lobster bisque, boiled hake, sorbet crème de menthe, fillet of beef wellington, sherry trifle, a selection of cheeses and coffee, was a meal fit for a king.

"I'll say this for you, Teresa, you certainly pick the choicest places to stay at," said Jack appreciatively. "Even the bishops in Ireland would envy such extravagant living."

"Anything for you, Jack – anything," returned Teresa. "I just hope you enjoy it."

After the meal they sat sipping the bubbly liquid until a stringed orchestra struck up in the adjoining ballroom, and the more the combination of soft sentimental music and champagne began to assert itself, the more they cast aside the nephew and aunt guise, until finally Teresa suggested returning to the suite.

It turned out to be a night as well as a day of surprises for Jack, for the instant he closed the door behind them, Teresa took the initiative. Usually she was modest, not altogether modest, as there was always a touch of carnality in her behaviour, but now she was playing the predator, the hungry cat on the prowl, as though she had lost control of her senses and the animal within her was holding sway. Quickly shedding her clothes, every stitch, she took up a very unladylike posture on the sofa, thighs apart, knees up, her hands grasping her ankles. "Darling, ride the arse off me – that's what we're here for," she cried, almost shrilly, and there was no compromise in her tone.

Still in a state of bewilderment at the suddenness of it all, Jack set himself to the task, the champagne invigorating his libido as Teresa responded feverishly to his forceful thrusts. "Give it to me darling, give it to me!" she cried, her legs shooting up and encircling his neck, the slapping of flesh against flesh growing louder all the time, so loud that Jack became worried in case it could be heard downstairs in the ballroom. Never before had he risen to such heights, until finally he rolled to the floor, gasping for breath.

Still in a demonic mood Teresa followed him to the floor, and soon he was tasting life's feast in a manner that had never before entered his imagination. All through the night she pursued him with her wet sensual lips and, as he lay in a delirium between bursts of decadent passion, he wondered why he should feel disappointed. When finally exhaustion forced Teresa to throw in the towel, they both dropped into oblivion.

Next morning, when daylight flooded the room, Jack opened one eye somewhat laboriously. His throat felt hot and dry, as if flames had scorched it, and two little imps with tweezers were plucking behind his eyeballs. He was lying naked on top of the bed, and when he swung his feet to the floor, the room began to spin like a merry-go-round. Holding the back of a chair for support he juggled with the law of gravity, and every step he took towards the bathroom jounced his head so much that he thought his spine would come through his skull.

To see a naked woman first thing in the morning through the eyes of a hangover can be somewhat revolting, but to see one past her prime unclothed, breasts sagging, skin wrinkled, and the loose folds of flesh that form the spare tyre drooping like the dewlaps of a bulldog, would test the constitution of an ox, and when he saw how ghastly Teresa looked, lying naked on the sofa, her hair dishevelled, her make-up in a mess, he felt as dispirited as if he had gone to bed with Cinderella and woke up with one of the ugly sisters. The more he tried to ignore her, the more compelling it became to look, as if his mind was trying to contradict the evidence of his eyes and, as he picked his steps through her items of strewn lingerie, it was strange that he should recall when as a boy he had thrown stones at women's knickers on clotheslines, not realising at the time that they were the symbol of woman's power over man.

When he returned from the bathroom, Teresa was sitting at her dressing table, wrapped tightly in a robe, rubbing cream on her face. Reddening from ear to ear she turned to face him. "I hope you don't think I'm just a cheap tart after the way I behaved last night," she said, a guilty note in her tone. "You must believe me when I say I never behaved like that before – it must be you. You behaved so masterfully that I just got carried away. Now I feel I should be punished like a naughty schoolgirl. So, do feel free to take me across your knee and spank me – literally spank me, I mean."

Cocking an eyebrow at her kinky suggestion Jack's face split in a sardonic grin. Perhaps he should pay one of the tinkers in Ireland to do it – fly him across and, as he set his mind to imagining Teresa bent over and the tinker laying his stick across her flaccid rump, just as he flailed his ass, it reminded him of the cliché: 'a whiskey glass and a woman's ass made a horse's ass of me'. And, if this combination could do it, it remained to be seen what a champagne glass and Widow Kilbane's ass might do.

Perhaps taking a different meaning from Jack's grin, Teresa smiled. "So, I'm forgiven then, and it doesn't look as though you're going to spank me. So, now that last night's episode is behind us, how about today?" she asked. "You can go wherever you please, with or without me, or we can start by having breakfast here in the suite, and maybe, if you have a mind to, we could explore the town together later. After all, it is Christmas Eve, and we should try to get in the festive spirit."

Chapter 7

In the following days, sensing that there was more than just gratitude behind Teresa's extravagance, Jack adapted somewhat uneasily to the luxury of the Grand Hotel, uneasily because everything looked too pat, like being judged guilty by appearing to be too innocent – vintage champagne and oysters, Parma ham, pâté de foie gras, plover's eggs, lobster and smoked salmon, wine from the vineyards of Louis Latour, Hennessy XO brandy, breakfast in bed, lunch, afternoon tea, cocktails at five, dinner – showing him the life he couldn't afford and that she could provide. Why? he wondered, when he would be content with a lot less, or perhaps she was hoping that he would develop a taste for such gracious living and be easier to manipulate for whatever purpose she had in mind.

The thought stuck like a barnacle, every little gift, every little kindness, fuelling his suspicion. By all accounts Teresa was a wealthy woman – and clever, her three properties all put to their best earning capacity bearing witness of her acumen, and who was he? – an Irish navvy without a future in pursuit of an impossible goal that made sense to no one but himself. It was inconceivable that she would go to such lengths to procure him when she could have any man of her own age group if she so desired, for it was hard to ignore the stares she attracted from the hotel's hoity-toity residents, the men's admiring, the women's somewhat envious.

Grudgingly he had to admit that he found Teresa's matronly instincts, bathing and massaging him as if he was the child she had never conceived, stimulating, and the manner in which she would turn apathy to desire and then to voracity with a touch of her fingers or a brush of her sensual lips was worthy of the highest accolade in the field of seduction, which all went to proving how naïve he had been before he met her, for not long ago if someone had mentioned a dirty weekend, he would have immediately thought of cleaning out the pigsty or some similar chore. Still, at the back of his mind he realised that only a fool would wish away such a life of luxury, a lifestyle that everyone dreams of when they're up to their necks in drudgery. Nevertheless, he was looking forward to the end of their sham honeymoon, even though it meant going back to digging trenches and facing the icy weather on the back of a lorry for three pounds a shift, arriving on the job as stiff with the cold as the unplaned timber seating that splintered and pinched their arses on the thirty-mile journey.

Every time he tried to shrug off his suspicion or searched for excuses to warrant her generosity prudence kept prompting him to tread warily, that there was something false about the affair which had suddenly turned sordid. Although he had long ago accepted that there were many things in life that would be always beyond his reach, including perhaps the woman in his heart, he wanted to be a man in his own right, to find his own level in life, without being moulded into a woman's plaything. Shocked when he realised how far from the straight and narrow he had strayed, he decided it was time to escape from her clutches, even if it meant leaving his lodgings. Perhaps if he found Digger Nolan, they could pool their savings and go into the subcontracting business together.

After dinner, on the night before their return to London, Jack aired his intentions. "That's it, Teresa," he went on, after he had explained his reason. "As I said, I can't go on living like this – I feel cheap. But it's what you must think of me that's the most distressing, and you did say in the beginning that there'd be no commitment."

Perhaps sensing Jack's resolve Teresa smiled bleakly. "All right – I'm going to level with you, buddy, as the Yanks say," she began, an elbow on the table, a hand supporting her frowning forehead. "Yes – I went out of my way to seduce you. I wanted a young man just as an old man wants a young woman. I know I overdid the loneliness bit, and the story about the fighter pilot was all lies. I've had two husbands – old, rich husbands – men who married me for my body only, and if you must know, they made sure they got their money's worth before they divorced me. That's how I got the means to buy the properties. If this is shocking you, I'll stop, but I'd rather you heard me out."

Now that she had admitted to lying, Jack found it hard to believe anything she said, and yet, his curiosity wanted her to go on. "Since we've come this far, I'd like to hear the rest of the story – were there many others like me?" he asked, recalling Bob Little's remark: 'If one man isn't enough, twenty wouldn't be too many'.

"I can see by your self-righteous attitude that you think I'm a slut, a woman of easy virtue like Princess Margaret, but I'm not!" Teresa replied snappishly. "I could get hundreds of men to – to give me one, as you men say. But no – it's you, Jack. It's been you since the morning I saw you standing on my doorstep. It's not just a hot Saturday night with a cold Monday morning to follow – it's more. Sometimes I wish you'd go away and come back twenty years ago. Of course there were others, and yes – I am using you. But I'm not stealing anything from you, and I did say I wasn't possessive. I know someday you'll go back home and right certain wrongs, but what then – ask yourself? Are you going to spend the rest of your days waiting outside the café for O'Donoghue's or some other lorry to take you to work? Think about it, for Christ's sake! Of course you have your pride, but the clothes of pride can be very threadbare. With me, you can have all the comforts money can buy, and you can come and go as you please. If you wait till you can afford it, you're never going to have it – it's as simple as that."

Jack smiled sardonically as Teresa paused to compose herself. What the Yanks said seemed to be part of her vocabulary, and he hadn't to tax his imagination very hard to figure out when she had picked up such expressions, considering the vast presence of the American military during the War, which was simply summarised: 'they're overfed, overpaid, oversexed and over here'. Still, the practical side of his nature demanded that he should hear her out, and Teresa, perhaps encouraged by his silence, went on:

"Everyone in the world is lonely, worried or sorry about something. So, stop thinking about what you've lost and think about what you've got – me and the security I can offer. Say, for instance, you got this Mary you've set your heart on, I'll bet she wouldn't be happy until she turned you inside out, backside over, and hung you out to dry. Then, when she's fed up with you, she'll say: 'What happened to the man I married?' But I won't interfere with you, good, bad or indifferent – you can keep on doing your own thing."

Although Teresa hadn't explained why she had married old men in the first place, or why she hadn't plans to marry again, this time to someone nearer her own age, she made savage and cruel sense as far as his future with O'Donoghue was concerned, a future of near-slavery and abuse with never a kind word, not even at Christmas, except the ganger's vulgar remark: 'A merry syphilis and a happy gonorrhoea to ye, lads, if ye can't stay out o' the hoorhouse'. If by some miracle he managed to save enough to go back and take up where he had left off, nine chances out of ten he would perish on the same rock, and he could almost hear Bull Paisley guffawing as he boarded the emigrant train for the second time.

The answer lay in going back with enough money to pursue his venture without any dependence on the bank, and Teresa might be a means to an end. There was subcontract work going a-begging in the construction industry, supplying men of all trades to the more established contractors at a percentage. All he needed was the initial capital for the purchase or hire of transport and the cash flow to cover the wages for the first few weeks, and with Teresa's help, the problem could be overcome. Now that it was time for compromise, he smiled saying, "That's a very generous offer, Teresa, and I'd be a fool not to think it over. It's just as I've explained – I'd feel bought. It'd be different if we were meeting on an equal footing. Let me think about it. I have a friend in Birmingham I want to look up, and I'll be gone for a few days."

"Go for as long as you please. It's nice to look up old friends, and remember, my door will be always open. But seeing as it's our last night in Brighton, let's go out on the town."

On the morning after New Year's Day Jack boarded the Birmingham train at Paddington and, as the train rattled along, the blobs of sleet sliding down the window were grim reminders of his dreams which were slipping away just as forlornly. Financially, his future was as bleak as the weather, for all that lay between him and the rigours of the world was the twenty pounds in his wallet and another hundred in the post office, the fruits of almost a year of thrift, enough to sit in the poker game as he had once planned. Now, in the light of more adult reasoning, the idea of gambling his hard-earned money on the turn of a card held no appeal. Not long ago it had been his only straw to cling to, until the killing of his stock knocked him out of the rut in which he had been travelling along so doggedly, and yet, if he kept postponing his return, his desire for revenge was sure to wane. Neither could he settle down leaving so many questions unanswered, from his father's disappearance and the shroud of secrecy hanging over his mother's death, to the killing of his animals, or perhaps they were all connected.

Now that his cottage was boarded up, to go back to the same rut, back to the old uncertainty, would take a lot more than a hundred pounds. At least four times that amount, and at his present rate of saving it would take another three years. Even then, he would have to buy two caps – one for doffing to his betters and one for taking off and twisting in his hands when applying for lowliest type of work, which suggested that his only hope lay in going into business with Teresa, if Digger couldn't help.

When the train arrived at Snow Hill station, he took another look at the faded address: 23 Warlock Avenue, Sparkhill, Birmingham, Digger's last known abode and asked directions. A half-hour later, when he alighted from the bus in Sparkhill, he observed that it had a fair scattering of Irishmen among its denizens, which were easily identifiable by their gait as they sauntered along the pavements, heads down, hands thrust deep in their pockets, the seats of their baggy-arse trousers hanging down. After booking into modest bed and breakfast accommodation he went straight to Warlock Avenue, and when the landlady slammed the door in his face the moment he mentioned Digger, reluctantly he decided that the police station should be his next port of call.

There was something unnerving about entering a police station, as if it was tempting fate, and he circled the gaping doorway tentatively in the manner a cat might circle a Chinese takeaway, the memory of his arrest and stolen money rekindling his rancour. Finally, when he entered, the desk sergeant gave him a comprehensive perusal over the rim of his glasses. "And what can I do for you, young man?" he asked authoritatively.

Jack produced Digger's letter. "I'm looking for a friend o' mine, John Nolan, and when I went to his old address, the landlady said he'd moved on, but she couldn't tell me where," he explained. "So, I was wondering if you could help."

Scanning through the letter the sergeant's eyes narrowed suspiciously. "This isn't a missing persons bureau – this is a police station, Paddy," he replied sarcastically. "If this Nolan chap is a friend of yours, you should know where he lives. The post office might help, or you could put an ad in the personal column of one of the local newspapers on the chance he might see it. But have you no idea as to where he might be?"

"If I had, I wouldn't be in here looking for him, would I?" interjected Jack, with equal sarcasm, and he was halfway to the door when the sergeant called him back.

"Don't be so impatient. If you were to tell me you were seeking him on compassionate grounds – if his mother was dead or something – which I can say you are, it entitles me to look in the book," he explained, and when Jack returned to the desk, the sergeant thumbed through the pages of a ledger.

When he found the appropriate page, he gave Jack a rather peculiar look. "The only John Nolan we have recorded here is Irish, age twenty-two, brown hair, medium height and build, two front teeth missing," he said. "He was arrested for being drunk and disorderly last August, and he's of no fixed abode. If he's your man, try the Sally Ann in Sparkbrook, and if you have no luck there, try the Spike in Balsall Heath."

"What's the Sally Ann?" asked Jack, a puzzled frown on his face.

"Salvation Army hostel," returned the sergeant. "Straight out the door, turn right, and keep on towards the city – you can't miss it."

Thanking the sergeant Jack set off walking in the cold afternoon, convinced now that he was on a wild-goose chase. It was hard to imagine Digger being arrested for drunkenness. Digger could hold his liquor, or perhaps he had been arrested so that the police could steal his money, or maybe it was some other John Nolan. Still, save for the missing front teeth, the description fitted Digger to a tee and, taking into account his former landlady's hostility, perhaps he had fallen on hard times. His concern was further fuelled when he was stopped several times along the way by down-and-outs begging the price of a cup of tea, their squalor reminding him of the tinkers back in Ireland, and the very thought of his friend being reduced to such straits brought a sickly feeling to his stomach.

After drawing a blank at the Salvation Army hostel he attracted so many awesome stares when he asked directions for the Spike that he was puzzled as to the type of hostelry he was seeking, until finally a man pointed to a sombre, two-storeyed building with a black slate roof. Set back in its own grounds, dampness showing on its bare concrete walls, it stood out starkly in the murky afternoon, its oak double doors, barred windows, and spiked railings giving it a fearsome look. A wrought-iron gate which led to an arched portico was creaking to and fro in the wind, and while it was in mid-swing, he slipped through and approached the door as tentatively as if Cerberus was waiting inside to savage him, his mind already made up that Digger could never be inside. When he failed to get an immediate response to the sharp rap-rap of the brass knocker, he turned away, and he was at the gate when a voice hailed him. When he looked back, there was a uniformed janitor standing on the threshold of the open doorway, eyeing him speculatively.

When Jack stated his business, the janitor came to attention with a military click of his heels. "Step inside and I'll get the secretary," he replied curtly.

Licking his lips nervously Jack wiped his feet on the mat as the janitor's downward glance intimated, and followed him down a dimly-lit tessellated corridor to a small office.

"Wait here!" was the man's next command, and then he set off down the corridor, the resounding tread of leather on tile the only sound shattering the eerie silence.

When the janitor disappeared round a corner, doors creaked open all along the length of the passageway, and bedraggled men in long nightshirts crowded in the openings, head over head, covering one another like a hand of cards, all eyeing him with bland curiosity, as if he was the latest addition to this weird establishment. The more he tried to visualise Digger among the nightshirted brethren, the more his imagination rebelled, and he was about to tiptoe away when the janitor returned, accompanied by a dapper, bespectacled man in a pinstripe suit.

The man, whom Jack presumed was the secretary, took the seat behind the desk. "Mister Simms, at your service, but first of all I feel I must explain the functioning of this institution," he said, a stereotyped smile fixed on his pale lips. "We provide here for the destitute only, and when I say destitute, I mean destitute, not the poor. They can knock on our door and we let them in. After they're bathed and their clothes fumigated we give them a repast and a bed for the night. For this consideration they're obliged to do a light task in the morning before we give them back their clothes, and then it's out. Although they can return at night, we don't encourage it."

"It seems I was mistaken," Jack replied. "I thought it was some type of hostel."

"Nevertheless, you came here enquiring about a friend, and maybe we can help," said Simms, leafing through a ledger until he found the appropriate page. "There was a John Nolan admitted last October, on the ninth and he left on the tenth. Where he is now, I have no way of knowing, but I feel I must remind you that the people with whom we deal have a tendency to move on to other towns. So, in a nutshell, he could be anywhere."

Jack thanked Simms and the janitor, and when he reached the street, the dull thud of the door slamming behind him sent an eerie shiver down his spine, as if it was shutting out life on all those inside. Out of ideas, he realised that his chances of finding Digger were as remote as winning the pools two weeks in succession, or as Pat had said, getting his money back from a whore – twice. Still, he persevered and, as soon as the public houses opened, he trudged from one to another making enquiries.

He hadn't gone far when he found that their mainly Irish customers were every bit as taciturn as their counterparts in London, and the only responses he received were: 'Try Pig Reilly's café – try Rat McDermot's lodging house – try the Brewer's Arms in Stoney Lane – the Antelope – the Mermaid – I'll tell you where he might be, in Sam Ram's club in Green Lanes – did you try the Ship in Camphill? – a lot o' the long-distance men go in there; they might know where he is' – and other bits of useless information, as if he, a stranger, should be familiar with such establishments as Pig Reilly's café or Rat McDermot's lodging house, and when closing time came round, he was none the wiser.

Back in his lodgings, because he felt sleep was too far away, he sat on the edge of the bed, elbows on his knees, hands supporting his chin, absently taking in his surroundings: a wardrobe, its door swinging on one hinge, a rickety dressing table, and curtains so threadbare that they could scarcely keep out the glow of the street lighting. Although it was a big comedown from the Grand Hotel he felt more at home in this type of accommodation, and now that he had tasted the good life, he felt sickened at the waste and so much poverty about. Still, there were people who would sell their very souls to live in such luxury, but fortunately he wasn't among their number. All he wanted out of life was a chance to pursue his ambition, a blazing turf-fire to warm his neighbours on winter nights, a few pints now and again in Grogan's, and Mary O'Hara for a wife. Not a big dream, yet it was all he had to cling to, for when the dream goes, everything goes. When his thoughts returned to Digger, he put his dream back in mothballs and decided to persevere for another day, and if he had no luck, return to London.

Next morning, after checking some of the suggestions of the previous night without success, as a last resort he questioned the tramps and dossers – the no-fixed-aboders. 'Try the park!' was the usual response, even after he had contributed generously to their slovenly upkeep and he became so nauseated by their filth and the asphyxiating tang of stale urine that emanated from their clothes that he vowed if by some quirk of fate he was ever elected to parliament he would introduce a bill to have all beggars and tinkers steam-cleaned and dipped in case of a cholera pandemic.

Heeding their advice he followed the footpath round the perimeter of the park until he came on a small group of men, all unkempt and ragged, who were standing in an untidy semicircle around a bench on which a cardboard box, necks of bottles protruding, was being held as reverently as the golden calf in biblical days. Still, for all their slovenliness, there was a certain dignity in the manner they were passing around a quart bottle, each taking a full swallow, raising the bottle to the light as if to check the level of the contents and cleaning the neck with a sleeve before handing it on. Even allowing that his back was turned Jack immediately recognised Digger among them, and unsure of his next move he watched the ritual for a few moments, until finally he tapped him on the shoulder, saying: "How's it going, ould stock?"

If Digger looked scruffy from behind, it was nothing to the way he looked when he did an about-turn, and instinctively Jack took a step back with the shock. Unwashed and unshaven, his eyes were puffed and bleary, his face blotched with the purpley hue associated with drinking methylated spirits. His navy-blue donkey jacket had half a sleeve missing and his ex-army trousers was torn at the knees and crotch, the legs as stiff as galvanised sheets from a combination of dirt and dried-out urine.

Still in a state of shock Jack stood staring, and when one of the group asked him if he was a cop, it was only then that recognition exploded like a delayed-action blast in Digger's booze-soaked brain. "He's no cop, boys – it's Jack Daly himself that's in it, bejasus," he grinned, extending a grubby hand. "Pass me the bottle, Joe – this is a friend o' mine, Jack Daly, all the way from Galway."

Offering the bottle to Jack, Digger grinned again, revealing the stumps of his rotten teeth. "Get your mouth round that and get a good slug of it into your guts," he said. "It's the best o' gear – cider, red biddy, and a dropeen o' meths all mixed up together. You couldn't get better to keep out the cold on this winter day."

To be sociable Jack put the bottle to his mouth and made a pretence of drinking, pulling a face as some of the unsavoury cocktail escaped past his lips.

When he saw Jack grimacing, Digger laughed raucously. "Not as good as the poteen back yonder, eh Jack?" he sniggered. "But what are you doin' in this God-forsaken country anyway? You're the last person in the world I was expectin' to see."

"I'm living in London at the moment, and I thought I'd look you up for old times' sake," returned Jack, still trying to come to terms with his friend's fall from society.

"You don't have to go back to London – you can stay here with us," said Digger. "We have a good skipper organised, and if you have any spare shillin's, we could do with them badly – to put a bit o' scaffoldin' under us, as they say in the buildin' game."

It was quite obvious that his old friend had slid a long way down the slippery slope, and Jack was at a loss as to how he should proceed. Certainly he could clean him up, take him back to London, and get him a job. But would he go, or would it solve his problem? After a few moments' deliberation he decided the easy way was the best way out and, taking a five-pound note from his wallet, he squeezed it into Digger's hand, saying: "Have that, ould stock for auld lang syne's sake."

When Digger saw the fiver, his eyes lit up avidly. "You saved our lives for sure," he said, taking the money without modesty or scruple. "But are you stayin' around or not?"

Jack shook his head. "No, I'm going back to London – I've got to be back at work on Monday morning," he said, stifling the disappointment in his tone and, turning away quickly before anyone noticed the tears forming in his eyes, he trudged back to his lodgings.

Another dream had slipped away like the blobs of sleet sliding down the train window and, by taking the money, Digger had lost his self-respect – the last mental prop under poverty. It was hard to imagine that anyone could sink so low, or perhaps there was some truth in the dogma of his homeland that only the sweepings of the country went to England. On the other hand, maybe it was due to the culling system over there which he was now convinced was in operation. Not only was it his own view, but it was the opinion of many immigrants that in all communities in Ireland there was a ruling clique, which included the clergy, and anyone not conforming to their three-bags-full ideology would find employment hard to come by. Then, it was the inevitable trip across the river of no return to become hewers of wood and drawers of water, which brought up the question – why did anyone have to emigrate?

Ireland, with its long miserable history, accepted without question the dictates of an impossible religion of suffering and guilt, darkness and shame, a religion that allowed superstition and ignorance to triumph over science and reason, and that one must suffer on earth so as to enjoy everlasting happiness in the next life, the more suffering the greater the reward. Yet, the ones preaching this doctrine weren't prepared to suffer poverty or be in a hurry to die. On the contrary, they spent fortunes on gracious living and, as one doctor sends for another when he's ailing, so also did priests send for other priests to give them absolution when they were on their deathbeds – something which they had the power to do themselves.

According to the Gospel, Christ raised Lazarus from the dead, although it never explained why Christ should punish Lazarus with more life if he was already enjoying his eternal reward. If heaven, with its many mansions, was as glorious as they preached, such an undertaking was akin to taking him out of the Grand Hotel in Brighton and billeting him in the Spike in Balsall Heath. Also, it made no mention of Lazarus dying again. Yet, he must have died, otherwise he would still be alive, authenticating the happiness in store for all those who had contributed generously to the support of their pastors.

Nevertheless, no one had the courage to question or challenge the Church's dogmatic doctrine, and there was so much to challenge it on, for if Reg Ashton could be believed, Pope Pius IX sent a crown of thorns to Jefferson Davis during the American Civil War, which suggested that he condoned the enslaving of the black races. If Christ's representative on earth was party to slavery and apartheid, did all the black Africans who had been converted to the Faith know of it? Or was religion just one big conspiracy between Church and State to keep the proletariat downtrodden and indoctrinated?

On the journey back to London Jack put away all thoughts of Lazarus, the Pope and the distressing memory of Digger, and put together a proposition for Teresa. If he accepted the help he felt certain she would offer, he would be a fully-fledged gigolo, selling his body for money, and no doubt she would become more demanding. He had yet to come to terms with their night of decadence, and he wasn't fooled by her claim that it was a first-time occurrence, for it seemed to be in a woman's nature to lie about previous sexual experience. Looking at the funny side he tried to concoct a name for the company – Widow Kilbane and Widow Daly's son in partnership – and, as the train rattled along, the rhythm of the wheels rattled out permutation after permutation.

Later that night, when Jack put his cards on the table, at first Teresa was sceptical. "At least you're honest about it, and honesty deserves its just reward. However, I was thinking on the opposite lines myself," she said, sweetening her scowl of disapproval with a forced smile. "I was hoping to consolidate the business here and maybe buy another property, and I need a maintenance man badly. There's so much to keep up with in properties like these: painting, plumbing, roof repairs and so forth, and I was hoping you'd be that man. I'd be willing to match O'Donoghue's wages and throw in full board as well. I have a list of jobs you can start on right away. So what do you say?"

Jack shook his head. "It's a good offer, Teresa, but no."

"Building work is very uncertain," countered Teresa, jokingly adding: "it's all ups and downs – like Princess Margaret's knickers. Yes, all ups and downs, as the knickers said to the panties – I've had my ups and downs but I was never shoved aside yet. But seriously, you've got so many things to contend with in the building game – weather, hiring and firing, cash flow – whereas in the property game, once you have it let, you can sit back."

It was plain to see what Teresa had in mind. If he took the job, he would be under her feet and under her thumb. So, shaking his head, he turned towards the door.

"Wait – don't go!" she called. "I said you could have anything you want as long as it includes me, but there's one condition. If it doesn't work out, we'll drop it – no throwing good money after bad, and I'll need to know every detail."

"Agreed," said Jack, offering his hand to clinch the deal. "I've got some homework to do on it first, but in the meantime I'll start on your repairs."

Chapter 8

The first weeks of January brought snow, followed by a severe frost, bringing building work to a standstill, and Jack, pleased with the arrangement he had made with Teresa, set about her repairs. In his spare time he cleared out an old storeroom at the rear of one of the properties to use as an office, and when he had it painted, fitted out with second-hand office furniture and a telephone, Teresa's accountant had the new company, Dalkan Construction, registered – directors T J Kilbane and J W Daly.

At first it seemed that Teresa was under the misconception that Jack's venture was just a passing whim, which perhaps she hoped the icy weather would wooden-stake before it got off the ground. However, when the enterprise took them to her solicitor's office, she made sure that her interests were well protected, insisting on full control of the company and sixty per cent of the net profit. Jack found it hard to believe she could be so mercenary, especially afterwards at the bank when she instructed that any cheques drawn on the new company account required her signature only.

Now that he was seeing her in her true colours – hard, selfish and devious – Jack found himself feeling sorry for her ex-husbands, and yet, the practical side of his nature made excuses for her. After all, it was her money that was at risk, and he had nothing to lose except perhaps his soul. However, finding subcontract work turned out to be a problem, and for all that he had dispatched letters detailing his services to a dozen or more established construction companies in London, he had yet to receive even an acknowledgement.

As the days ran into weeks, with nothing in the offing, Teresa could scarcely conceal her delight. "You've got to remember, Jack, it's a competitive business," she commiserated, outwardly showing enthusiasm, inwardly perhaps hoping that he would forget the whole idea. "But nothing ventured, nothing gained, that's what I say, and I am pleased with the office. It's something I've always needed to keep my paperwork in order. So, you see, it's a bad wind that doesn't blow good for someone."

Jack was inclined to agree with her, and all he could do was squirm under her I-told-you-so gaze – mother knows best. Redoubling his efforts he drafted another batch of letters and sent them to companies that he had earlier passed over, and when there was still no response, he wondered if he was going about it the right way. Perhaps he should do Bull Paisley on it and grease a palm or two, go round to the offices, drop a few nods and winks. After all, he who has nothing to lose can afford all risks.

The telephone ringing in the office interrupted his train of thought, and seconds later Mrs O'Neill came charging up the stairs towards the landing where he was replacing a newel post. "A Mister McGregor is on the phone for a Mister Daly," she called breathlessly. "Will I tell him to hold, or will I say you'll ring him back?"

Taking the steps two at a time Jack bounded down the stairs, almost knocking over Mrs O'Neill in his haste, and he was greeted by a gruff voice on the other end of the line. "Ah, Mister Daly. I have your letter in front of me, and I'm interested in availing of your services if we can agree terms. But first, let me introduce myself. McGregor's the name, Hamish McGregor – I'm a contracts manager for George Wimpey, Hammersmith," he explained, a slight trace of a Scottish accent colouring his speech. "That said, I suggest we have a meet, if that's all right with you… yes! So, how would nine o'clock Monday morning in our office suit you? … yes! Good show. If you can bear with me, I'll give you the address and floor number."

Later that evening Teresa greeted the news with a burst of feigned enthusiasm. "Here we go – her we go – here we go!" she cheered. "What you really need now is a crash course on how to present yourself at an interview, because in every game first impressions go a long way in determining future relationships. Dress is essential. Let me see, you're looking to get ahead in the building game and winter is coming to a close. Dress to suit the occasion. Wear your brown corduroy jacket and beige trousers, a check shirt open at the neck, neckerchief if you like, brown shoes. Wear your sheepskin coat, but hang it up when you get to the office. Otherwise it'll get too stuffy and you won't be able to think properly. Also, I have a brown leather attaché case for carrying your paperwork. Does that sound like good sense or not?"

"Whatever would I do without you at all," returned Jack, pleased that Teresa was taking such a keen interest. "But I'll have to admit, now that the time has come, I feel nervous, and how in the name o' jasus am I going to bluff him into believing I can deliver the goods?"

"First of all you've got to convince yourself that you can deliver the goods, and after that it should be easy," said Teresa, the wisdom of experience in her tone. "When you get to the office, make a show of being positive, walk erect and confidently, as if you owned the world, don't hurry or charge anyone down, and let the other party do the talking once you've explained your position. McGregor, or whatever his name is, sent for you, so that means he has a proposition to put to you. Think carefully before answering, and if asks you something you're not sure of, stall him. Say you've forgotten to make an important phone call, and then ring me here – I'll be waiting by the phone from nine till eleven. Just mention any kind of rubbish – I'll understand. It'll give you that extra minute to think, and I'm sure I don't have to tell you not to panic."

"Should I ask him out to lunch, or for a drink, maybe, just to break the ice?" asked Jack.

"No – not until you see which way it pans out first. Then, if you do get a subcontract and everything is going hunky-dory, that's the time. If you do it right away, he might get the wrong idea. He might think you're doing it to impress him so that he'll turn a blind eye on your shortcomings, but when you do take him out, do it right – no expense spared in some upmarket restaurant – something he can tell his friends about. I'll show you how it's done – I'll give you your first lesson tomorrow down the West End."

On Monday morning, when the prim lady-receptionist ushered Jack into McGregor's office, he felt as nervous as an actor making his stage debut, although Teresa's advice stood him in good stead. After the formalities he listened as McGregor outlined his programme, interrupting him only when he needed clarification.

Once Jack had caught the gist, McGregor, a tall, gangling man in his early forties, rose from his seat and took to pacing the floor. "Well, that's it," he went on. "As I've explained, work is about to commence on a new housing estate near Maidenhead next Monday morning. As the project progresses, we'll need carpenters, bricklayers and men of all trades, but initially to get us off the ground I need a gang of groundworkers and three teams of bricklayers. Then, when the oversites are in, it'll be all systems go. There are over a thousand houses all told: detached, semis and terraced, so it's a big take on. As I've said, you can have the lot at the rates I mentioned. So, how do you feel about it?"

Jack swallowed the lump of uncertainty in his throat. "No problem – we'll start next Monday, as you say, and pick up from there," he said, regulating his tone so that it sounded confident. "But I'd like a detailed drawing of the whole project, the exact location and, as my men will be working under your supervision, I'd like to have an off-the-cuff word with the men involved on your side. Then, we'll know exactly where we're going. So, I suggest a meeting on site, perhaps sometime on Wednesday – nine o'clock seems to be working out all right. How would that suit you?"

"Good show! But there's another matter I'd like us to agree on before we adjourn. I'd rather deal with yourself personally as regards invoicing, and I don't want our firm's direct labour having to work with yours – it causes friction. Presently the company is plagued by strikes, so the directors are all in favour of the subcontract system. This is our big chance to show them that it can be made to work, and needless to say there should be a good living in it for both of us," explained McGregor, and the slight emphasis he placed on the term 'both of us' wasn't lost on Jack.

The following days were hectic, and for all her earlier scepticism Teresa lent her full support. She immediately got in touch with a second-hand car dealer and, after some crafty bargaining, she talked him into parting with two Bedford vans, in a no deposit, pay monthly, type of deal. Afterwards, to get their full complement of workers, they ran a series of advertisements in the evening papers and the *Labour News*.

Later in the week, when Jack met Pat and Reg in the Halfway House, he explained the pros and cons of his new venture.

"So, you're on your way at last," said Pat. "I had a hunch about you, and I suppose there'll be no stopping you now."

"From what I can gather, Jack, you're going up in the world," Reg cut in, a hint of sarcasm in his tone. "Last week you were one of the proletariat like ourselves, now you're a company director – how could you desert our little circle and go over to the enemy? Yes, human nature demands that scruples should take a back seat when it comes to the acquisition of wealth, even if it means exploiting the downtrodden, and money, the root of all evil, brings out the larceny in the best of us –"

Rather than argue Jack listened as Reg ran on, vilifying the capitalist system, perhaps believing that the world would never be right unless he put it right.

When Reg excused himself, Pat took up the conversation again. "Don't take a blind bit o' notice of anything that gobshite says, Jack – the left-wingers of today usually become the right-wingers of tomorrow," he explained. "But getting down to the business ahead, the first thing you should do is put a good man in charge. He doesn't have to be a good worker, for more times than not a good worker never turns out to be a good man in charge. There are lots o' men, good workers all, who can only put themselves and one or two others to work. They're brainwashed with the idea – if you want something done right, you've got to do it yourself. What you need is a man who can see the bigger picture – the end product, and once you get him, let him do all the hiring and firing, and allow him a bit o' scope to fiddle – let him book in a dead man now and again, or fiddle a few loads o' hardcore – small stuff. This way, you'll keep him keen, but if he overdoes it, stamp on him and stamp on him hard – one warning and then out."

This was contrary to Jack's programme, as he had visualised himself in charge, but when he mentioned it to Pat, he frowned his disapproval. "I'll put it like this, if you have a ganger, you can leave all the donkey-work to him – it's a two-way street. If things are going wrong or the wages are short, you can always throw the blame over on him," he explained, pausing when he noticed that Jack wasn't in favour. "Don't worry, he'll be able to shoulder it – you know what gangers are like yourself – thick-skinned. And besides, you've got to have a free hand – you're the man. You'll be meeting all sorts of head kiddies – contracts managers, engineers, clerks of the works. You'll have the Hurrah Henrys – the ones sniffing the air as if they had bits o' dogshite under their noses keeping them up – you'll have the clever ones, and the stout ones, and you'll have to find a common denominator with each. But this should all come to you when you take them out for a day's drinking. Take them out one at a time, and let them do the talking. Then, you'll get to know their likes and dislikes."

"I was advised not to overdo it on the drink in case they get the wrong impression."

"I'm not saying to overdo it, but drink is a universal currency – a leveller, and sometimes a day on the beer helps to get over a problem, especially with a stout boss. You know the type I mean – the know-alls, the type you have to suggest three ideas to – a good one, a middling one, and a bad one, and opt for either the middling or the bad idea yourself. If he has any bit o' savvy at all, he'll go for the good idea – the one you wanted in the first place. Then, if everything works out, praise him, say: 'Here Mister so and so, that was a great idea of yours', and he'll walk away full of himself. It's a whole lot better than arguing and falling out with him. Remember, the endgame is money, not prestige. So, let the Hurrah Henrys have the prestige, and you have the money."

"Why don't you take charge, Pat?" Jack suggested, now that he could see the logic in his advice. "I'll pay you anything within reason – and a fiddle."

Pat lapsed into a meditative mood. "I appreciate the offer, Jack, but I was never cut out to be in charge," he returned at length. "Besides, if I went working for you in any capacity, there's every chance it'd put an end to our friendship. You'd be better off with strangers, and don't let that soft heart o' yours rule your head – kind words and good deeds never put the world to rights. Above all, keep your distance from the men. Be friendly, but aloof, and the last thing you want to do is go drinking with them in the evening."

"I can't see how getting to know the men personally'd be a disadvantage, and maybe I might be able to help them," returned Jack. "I'd like it to be one big happy family."

"If you go about it that way, you'll have problems," countered Pat. "As Reg said, you're going up in the world – it's them and us, and now you're 'them'. In all walks of life there has to be someone to crack the whip, and if you don't, the men'll play up. Stick to the tried and tested principle 'grumble and go'. Tell them straight out: 'I don't want to hear any grumbling'. If you don't nip it in the bud, grumbling'll do your head in. The English are the worst at it – they never stop. If there was an Olympic medal for grumbling or telling lies, or for throwing shite at other nationalities, they'd win it hands down every time, and now that we're on the subject of grumbling, I was just thinking that if Churchill was ever to make that speech again about 'the few', he should alter it to read: 'Never in the field of human conflict was so much owed to so few by so many who grumble so much about so little'. I think it's here in England the Wailing Wall should be and not in Jerusalem."

For a man who at times had so little to say, once Pat got started on his philosophies, there was no stopping him. "I suppose I've no need to tell you that you'll make enemies," he went on. "But don't take a blind bit o' notice of what people say about you. I'll put it like this, if you did all good deeds in your lifetime, they'd keep searching until they found something bad you did, and if you were a right tyrant, they'd keep searching until they found something good you did – you can't win in life. If you treat a man as he appears to be, you'll make him worse than he is. But if you treat him as if he was already what he potentially couldn't be, you might make him into what he should be."

"I can see what you mean, Pat, so we'll just have to wait and see how it pans out."

In the following days Jack went into meticulous preparation, and by the end of the week there was so much response to the advertisements that he had to take the phone off the receiver. Heeding Pat's advice he hired Martin Carmody to take charge, a man who bore all the qualities of a leader in looks, thought and word and, as the weeks went by, 'in deed' was added to these attributes.

Once the teething problems were overcome, the enterprise settled into something of a routine, and when income tax became an issue, Jack knew from his own experience that deducting the full amount would make him unpopular and less competitive. Again, his old philosophy 'there's a path which no fowl knoweth and which the eye of the vulture hath not seen' came to his rescue and, after consulting a tax inspector, he found the loophole he was seeking – self-employment. In the construction industry any person could be self-employed if the work involved was categorised as piecework, provided they furnished an invoice and declared that all statutory obligations regarding national insurance and income tax would be solely their responsibility. He found too that this system could be exploited for his own benefit, as most of the names and addresses on the invoices were fictitious.

Despite several setbacks the build-up was progressive. Teresa was soon reimbursed and, as the weeks galloped along, Jack found that there was another lucrative side to the business – dead men. At McGregor's prompting phantom names were added to the time sheet and the gain divided fifty-fifty, and to alleviate his guilty conscience Jack reminded himself that in the parable of the unjust steward the Lord had commended the steward for what he had done wisely – fiddling his master. The downside was that Teresa was becoming more demanding. Their romance was now in the open, and she left no one in doubt as to whom the dominant partner was in both the business and the affair, treating him, although subtly so, with the same contempt as if he was a bought piece of merchandise. Although the title – cock-lodger – should flatter any man's ego it only embarrassed Jack, and he searched for a way out.

However, there was no way out unless he liquidated the business, which didn't bear thinking of until he had saved the money he needed to return to Ireland. Still, no matter which way he looked at it, he was shackled to Teresa by commitment as a convict is by his chains – and she knew it and, like a gambler who is ahead in the game, feeling that his luck has run its course and is about to turn, he was always fretful in case she suddenly pulled the plug on the enterprise now that her investment was secure.

The pressure of business kept Jack outdoors more than normal, and one evening when he returned, Teresa was in a vile mood. "I'm sick of being cooped up here day in, day out!" she snapped. "What I need is a month abroad – away from it all."

"That's a wonderful idea, Teresa – where were you thinking of going to?"

"You expect me to go on holiday on my own?" she exploded, her colour heightening, her breasts thrusting out aggressively against the white silk of her blouse. "So, that's how little you think of me! Now you listen to me; we – and I mean we – are going to Spain, and if you try to weasel out of it, I'll go there alone, and I'll let every Spanish waiter who fancies me screw the arse off me – see how you'll like that!"

Although it was on the tip of Jack's tongue to reply derisively, common sense demanded that he should humour her. "Calm down, Teresa – there's no need to shout," he said. "So, let's sit down and discuss it sensibly. I've had a bad day at work, and you just took me by surprise when I came in the door. I was expecting sympathy and understanding, and you gave me the impression that you wanted a few weeks away on your own."

Still bristling with indignation Teresa squared herself for the affray, hands on hips. "Work!" she raged. "Work – that's all I hear, morning, noon and night!

There's nothing at all about me, or how I feel. Well, I want to know what you're going to do about it?"

Jack, his mind on the money rolling in, knew he had to compromise. "Sure, we'll go on a holiday, if that's what you have your heart set on," he said, and when he drew her close and kissed her passionately on the lips, the reek of garlic from her breath brought a ripple of nausea to his stomach. Garlic was her latest fad for slowing down the ageing process and, stepping back out of the range of her breath, he wondered why people were so easily influenced by quack remedies – garlic thinned the blood, too much salt turned it into water, eating too many eggs caused rash, sitting on a cold radiator caused piles, fresh cow-piss on chilblains, strawberry jam on kippers, an apple a day –

Teresa whispering in his ear: "Let's go to the bedroom," brought Jack back to the present. "You know what I want. You've been neglecting me – it's been three whole days and that's too long to go without. I've invested in you – it's part of the deal that you see to me every day – and all this fuss about work is interfering with our love life. So, let's say to hell with it and get away from it all for a few weeks."

In the following days Teresa never let up on Spain, and to keep her sweet Jack agreed to go, although a holiday at this early stage of the project was out of the question. Teresa knew it too, and he wondered why she was being so unreasonable, or could it be that she had sensed what was on his mind and wanted the venture to fail in case he escaped from her clutches?

On Sunday afternoon Jack's suspicion turned to conviction when Teresa drew down the subject again. "You seem to have forgotten our holiday," she said, rising from her armchair where she had been ruffling like a hen all morning.

Jack didn't need a crystal ball to see what was coming next and, stuck between a quagmire and a soft place, he left the question unanswered, behaving as if he hadn't heard, hoping the problem would go away if he remained silent.

He should have known better, for Teresa pounced on the silence with all the suddenness of a prowling cat. "Well, I haven't!" she spat. "I've been to Thomas Cook's and I've booked next Saturday as a provisional date for a two-week holiday in Marbella. I've got to confirm the booking on Monday – tomorrow. Is that okay?"

"That's jumping the gun at bit, Teresa," returned Jack. "In the first place I need to apply for a passport, and if I do go, the business could easily collapse. You know yourself if we don't deliver the goods, we'll be out on our earhole, and I have nobody I can trust to keep an eye on it in my absence – we're dealing with a lot o' money here, wages and all that."

Teresa stood for a moment looking down on Jack, the frown of obstinacy between her eyes growing more pronounced. "How convenient of you to forget to apply for a passport, but you didn't forget your driving test, did you?" she hissed venomously. "And, as for the business – it's my business, and it was my money that set it up. Everything is mine, the office, the transport, the lot, even the clothes on your back, and I can't see why you should be so worried. If anyone is going to lose, it's me, and I want done with it. As we agreed, I have full control."

"If that's the way you want it, Teresa, then we'll just have to wind up the whole caper," returned Jack calmly, for all that he felt like wringing her neck. Women, he had found, could be like cats, not just for the number of their lives or that they liked to lie on their backs. There was no point in arguing that her outlay was safely back in its coffers, and that she was enjoying a healthy return on her investment. "As you said – you're the boss. But it'll take two to three weeks at least to close it down – is that all right with you?"

Jack found it hard to believe that anybody, no matter how rich, would purposely set out to kill a goose that was laying golden eggs, or perhaps Teresa was expecting an entreaty from him over which she could crow and later exact favour. Although all his instincts demanded that he should seek a compromise his stubborn nature prevailed, and he sat silently, waiting for Teresa to confirm her intent.

"So that's it!" she snapped finally, breaking the uneasy silence, disappointment flashing for an instant in her eyes. "And what may I ask are you going to do when it's all over – go back to digging trenches for O'Donoghue, is it? Well, go back then – see if I care! I can't help feeling that you've taken advantage of me and my money – just like a gigolo."

Wincing at Teresa's last remark Jack hung his head, and though the truth was brutal, it didn't make it any less true. Still, to hear it put so baldly brought humiliation. "If that's the way you feel, there's nothing can be done about it," he countered. "And, what I do with my life is my own business. As a matter of fact, you've just made up my mind for me – my gigolo days are over as of now. So, I'll move out this evening."

"Why wait till evening – go now! But you'll soon come crawling back – you know the buttered side from the dry all right –"

Jack remained silent until Teresa's tirade fizzled out, and then he laughed.

"What are you laughing at?" asked Teresa. "To me, it's no laughing matter."

"I was laughing at the difference between what you look like and what you really are."

While Teresa sat sulking, Jack slipped to the bedroom and sorted out his belongings, making sure he left behind all his gigolo clothes, although now that his mind was yielding to the calm that must follow all storms, he silently cursed himself for not being more diplomatic. A few earthy kisses, garlic or no garlic, before fulfilling his commitment in the nether department and he would be still in business. Although his plans were shattered, strangely he wasn't disappointed and, as he gently closed the door behind him, he felt as relieved as a pardoned prisoner leaving jail.

The type of accommodation Jack was seeking wasn't hard to come by and, after spending a few nights in bed and breakfast, he found a bedsitter farther afield in Cricklewood so that there would be no accidental bumping into Teresa, or the men he was about to lay off. Afterwards came the painful task of winding down the business, which was the hardest part after the effort he had made, and his thoughts were echoed by McGregor when he tendered his notice. There was no other way. Teresa had the bank account sewed up lock, stock and barrel, and there was nothing he could do unless he ate humble pie as she had predicted.

After the final payment Jack arranged to meet Teresa at her apartment to wrap up the venture. On his own calculation he would be laying his hands on at least seven hundred pounds, and for the first time he could understand people cursing wasted chances – another twelve months in business and his problems would have been solved.

On the night of the meeting, when Jack turned up at the arranged hour, he immediately sensed an aura of seduction in the apartment. Teresa was wearing white cotton slacks and a frilly pink top which kept falling from her shoulders on to her upper arms and, as she advanced to greet him, the shape of her knees, thighs and crotch were plainly visible and moved rhythmically inside the translucent material. The air was full of the redolence of roast lamb and the table was laid for two, an ice bucket on a stand by its side, from which the neck of a champagne bottle was protruding.

Taking Jack by the arm Teresa moved intimately closer, bringing her perfume into play, her favourite perfume which perhaps up to now had never let her down. "I've prepared a meal, so let's eat before we conclude our business," she suggested. "It's ready now."

"Business first, Teresa," said Jack. "I learned that from you – remember. But I will stay to dinner. You were right in everything you said, and I'll be always in your debt."

When Teresa tried to be overgenerous in the settlement, Jack turned it down, and during dinner and afterwards she did everything in her power to win him back to the fold. "I'm ever so sorry, Jack," she apologised contritely. "I have been naughty, and you know what should be done to naughty girls – they should have their panties taken down and spanked."

"Leave out the dramatics, Teresa," returned Jack. "You think by saying you're sorry that the slate'll be wiped clean. It was all wrong from the start, and to quote your own words: 'relationships like ours don't last...' Now it's time I was on my way."

"Well, what d'you know – hoist with my own petard," countered Teresa, and perhaps sensing Jack's resolve, her entreaties became more impassioned. "Don't go, Jack. If you stay with me, you'll never have to work again," she pleaded, throwing her arms about his neck, clinging and parting her thighs into a position of total surrender.

For an instant Jack felt his self-control wavering, his desire struggling with his willpower, until finally he eased away. Holding her at arm's length he shook her hand, saying: "It's no good, Teresa – words once spoken can never be taken back. They'd be between us forever and ever. You above anyone should know that. We've had a good fling, so let's cherish the good times from it. As I said, I owe you a lot, and I thank you. Now it's time I was on my way."

It was only when Jack opened the door and was about to leave that Teresa, perhaps for the first time, realised that she had lost, and she stood for a moment staring at the holdall carrying the last of his belongings as at an enemy. Then, gathering the rags of her dignity about her, she smiled, saying: "I suppose nothing I say will make you change your mind, but remember, this door will be always open to you if you ever decide to come back."

"You know I won't be back," returned Jack and, as if another chapter in the story of his life was ending, he left a tear-stained Teresa standing on the threshold and walked away.

The settlement worked out better than he had estimated. He had almost a thousand pounds, not enough to return to Ireland and have the security he had his heart set on, but enough to set him up in business in a small way.

It was boom days in the building trade. Stevenage, a whole new town to ease the pressure on the slums of London, was under construction, and van owners for the transportation of workers to the various sites there were in brisk demand. Now that he had passed his driving test, Jack bought a second-hand Austin 18cwt van, and he immediately found work transporting men from Cricklewood to a site in Stevenage.

Ever since Eileen's marriage correspondence between them had trickled to nothing, although her last letter just after Christmas, besides being full of praise for Murphy, informed him of her pregnancy. "He managed that part all right," Jack sniggered to himself, although the news that Kathy Moore had moved in with them after taking up her new job was more disconcerting. *She goes home at weekends,* the letter said. *SHE'S keeping a fire in the cottage, but she's wondering, and so are we all, if there's any fear of you coming home yourself. There's work to be got now in the new Corrib Drainage Scheme, and they're paying a half-crown an hour. Now that I'm gone from the place, you should be able to make a living there easy enough.*

Although Jack didn't begrudge Eileen her happiness he found it hard to stomach Murphy as a brother-in-law, inasmuch as you can pick your friends but not your relatives and in-laws, and now he could understand why old O'Hara resented him. Mary would be twenty-one soon, and if she remembered her promise and was still interested, it was up to her to get in touch.

Chapter 9

The weeks in Cricklewood passed into months, and then into years, the days flying by as though they were being swept along by a gale-force wind, there for an instant and quickly gone, like the underground tube-trains which scarcely allowed the time to get on and off, although every pay packet brought Jack another week nearer to his goal.

The Cricklewood-Kilburn area was rapidly taking over from Camden Town as the number one haven for the immigrant Irish and, as the exodus continued unabated, they arrived there in droves, like the swallows in summer. However, unlike the swallows, they stayed to roost, for no chill autumn wind in the form of discrimination, hardship or racial abuse could force them to return, which lent substance to the cynical saying: *'you'll never go back'*. A God's eye view of the migration would show a constant movement of tiny grains from west to east across a floor shaped like a map, from a dry patch, bottlenecking into a narrow corridor, before crossing a wet patch, to a larger dry patch, and then scattering in all directions. Not only in Cricklewood, Kilburn and Camden Town, but all over England's major cities and towns, Irish communities were mushrooming up, colonising parts of the country which had once colonised theirs, and once they got a foothold, they set about organising clubs and promoting their national games, music and dancing, until many areas were transformed into little Irelands.

Now that he could look back on Ireland with a more distant sun shining on it, like watching a ball game from high-up on the stands rather than milling in the ruck, Jack took in the picture as a whole. Emigration, which was a shot in the arm for his homeland's feeble economy, was dealing efficiently and painlessly with its undesirables, its disgruntled unemployed, and its intellectual dissidents with the same stroke and, as a result, it was a mixed bag of humanity that converged on Cricklewood and the other Irish centres, a multitude that wasn't without its fair share of parasites, villains and thieves. In most cases the migration followed a pattern, the eldest of the family blazing the trail, the others following as they came of age until the full transition was complete.

Taking into account that it was a mixed bag, and from the four corners of Ireland, a mishmash of country folk and townsfolk, there was something about them that told them apart from the more laid-back people they had left behind. It was discernible at a glance, a sense of fatalism hidden behind a devil-may-care attitude and a dry cynical humour, which derided others while deriding themselves, and in the manner they shrugged their shoulders, as though the world could do its worst and they would still remain unruffled.

The new arrivals left little time for the grass to grow under their feet, the vast majority of the men finding work in the construction industry in which several climbed the ranks until the management of many of the established companies were in the hands of Irishmen, and perhaps someday the British media might grudgingly acknowledge that these were the men who had built the vast new towns and the hundreds of lonely miles of motorway without a grumble or a strike. The women made up the shortfall in the nursing profession, and in the factories, hotels and offices, though many of them, perhaps mindful of the male chauvinism of their countrymen, found husbands among England's gullible young men who fell easy prey to the misconception that all Irishwomen are naïve and virginal and the men ignorant and uncouth.

There were mavericks too among them, men who couldn't settle no matter how much butter was put on their paws, footloose men who were treating the exodus as a great adventure, and they roamed to all parts of the country, following up the extensive construction programme of motorways, oil refineries, hydro-dams and pipelines. They became known in the building trade as 'long-distance men' and they travelled to such faraway places as Inverness, Port Talbot and the Isle of Grain, carrying little in the way of luggage, but never without the *Labour News* (the Bible of the construction industry) sticking out of their jacket pockets.

As time went by, Jack found himself agreeing more with Pat as to their status in their adopted society. Although they were badly needed in all walks of life, especially in the construction industry, which would find it impossible to function without them, they were and always would be treated as second-class citizens, and if they needed any reminding, it was all round them, on some factory gates, and in advertisements for accommodation and employment – no Irish. The police used them to fill their cells on trumped-up drunkenness charges, beat them up with batons at the slightest provocation, stole their money, and perjured themselves when giving their evidence, their victims paying the price in sore ribs and empty pockets, a corrupt practice that sowed the seeds of enmity and distrust of the constabulary in the mind of every male Irish immigrant, which no amount of reparation and conciliation could ever uproot.

It was likewise with the magistrates, and nothing seemed to please them more than to have an Irishman in the dock so that they could cast some slight on his nationality, regardless of his guilt or innocence, and then jail him for the least of offences, which made a mockery of the beatitude – blessed are they who hunger and thirst after justice for they shall have their fill. So, it became necessary for the immigrants to grow extra skins as protection against the barbs of racial prejudice, which matured with time until they got so thick that insults hopped off them like hailstones off an elephant's back.

Nevertheless, the immigrants accepted their second-class citizenship with mock deference, countering any ridicule with their own sarcastic type of wit and, with that wily sense of perception that all strangers acquire when they find themselves in a hostile land, they were quick to notice that the citizens of their new society were just as conditioned in the semi-feudalism of the establishment as the indigenous Irish were in the religion of their forefathers. It never occurred to them when they were castigating the Germans that the monarchy which they so revered was predominantly German, no more than it occurred to the indigenous Irish when they were castigating the Jews that Christ, the Apostles and the Virgin Mary were all Jewish, which suggested they were gullible, unbelievably gullible – the first chink in their armour which they felt they could exploit.

The second chink was the veiled hostility between the cynical cockneys and their more pretentious brethren from the Home Counties, which had been festering ever since the general strike of the twenties, and outwardly it appeared to be a class struggle, although in reality it was a struggle for power. The streetwise cockneys soon realised that the Irish weren't as dim-witted as some of the silly jokes about their race suggested and, perhaps believing they could hoodwink them into joining their left-wing trade unions, which were hard at work trying to stamp their authority on the construction industry, they went out of their way to win them over.

However, it turned out that they too underestimated the immigrant Irish, for the entrepreneurs among them, using the bland guile of their race, ran with the hare and chased with the hounds, grovelled to both factions when grovelling was necessary, acted thick when it suited their purpose, and when they found that a heavy purse could tilt the scales of justice, they put money in the right places. Once they got a foothold, they unscrupulously spread their assets into every business that dealt in ready money: public houses, nightclubs, dance halls, lodging houses, building firms and transport companies, until the establishment suddenly woke up to their presence.

During his first weeks in Cricklewood Jack felt that he would be missing out if he didn't go back to Camden Town at the weekends to drink with Pat, Reg and Bob Little. However, as he began to make new friends in Cricklewood, his visits trailed off until a time came when he scarcely recognised a face in his old haunts where once he would have recognised twenty. In London nothing stood still, and perhaps due to the migrant blood in most of its inhabitants, people were forever on the move, although its impersonality, which had once been daunting, now pleased him.

Pat understood, and one night he gave it a fair summing-up. "London is like a dark stranger, because no matter how long you live in it, you never really get to know it. But it grows on you, every blank building, every blank face, because it's the only place you can have anonymity and freedom – real freedom," he explained. "You can have the satisfaction of telling a boss to stick his job up his arse and still get another, because in the building game a man is judged on the nature of his effort rather than on the result. Nobody asks your business, and there's none of this 'do you know who I am?' type of culture, just get on with it, and nobody prays for anything like they do back yonder, where they pray for everything from fine weather to long life."

"Many things are wrought by prayer, Pat, if you listen to the teaching of the Church," countered Jack, just to get him going.

"Yes, Jack, the power of prayer – no chance of a mistake. Just imagine the Queen down on her knees praying for guidance on civil rights issues, whether or not she should grant civil rights to the Catholics of Northern Ireland, the lowliest of her subjects, or the Pope praying for guidance on such controversial issues as birth control, abortion, divorce and eating meat on Fridays, or the magistrates praying before giving judgement, or the doctors praying before prescribing, or could you imagine O'Donoghue up at the altar with his hands joined, hoping to be guided into giving a fair day's wages? Would it work? – no, because the Queen and her establishment would be horrified at the very idea of giving up their most cherished of privileges – the right to look down on other nationalities, especially on the Irish; the Pope, believing himself to be infallible, wouldn't be influenced by prayer; the magistrates would go on judging within the limits of the law, especially when it came to locking up Irishmen; the doctors would go on killing and curing in the same old way; O'Donoghue would still believe he was paying too much, and the men would be still grumbling about getting too little. So, you see, prayer won't influence the way the world goes round, at least not in the way money does."

The Galtymore, Cricklewood's main attraction, was by far the largest Irish dance hall in London, and over a period of time Jack got to know some of its woman regulars. It seemed that once you got to know one, you got to know them all, and they weren't as hard-boiled as they had first appeared. If anything, it turned out to the contrary, for most of them put the blame for their ill-manners on the boorishness of the men, some telling stories of near-rape, vulgarity and insolence. There were practical jokers too among them, the jokes going as far as giving the phone number of some police station as their own to any unsavoury suitors.

However, despite a series of dates and affairs, Mary O'Hara still clung like an albatross about his neck, and no matter how much he tried to shake her off, some romantic film or song came along and jogged his memory. He looked for something of her in every woman he danced with, every woman he dated, and when he found it, his thoughts took flight back to the night of their first kiss, and the lyrics of *Stranger in Paradise*, rekindled the flame.

Nevertheless, a measure of contentment crept into his soul. Cricklewood was home from home, rural-Irish life in a city setting, the same customs, the same music in the public houses, the same St Patrick's Day celebrations and the same Gaelic games in New Eltham every Sunday afternoon, for the immigrants had brought all the old traditions with them, everything except the Stations.

It seemed too that 'time', that great magician and healer, was working its age-old miracle, for his bitterness was waning, and when bitterness loses its savour, people have a tendency to forget, although every time the rag-and-bone man clip-clopped by, chirruping to a horse that was a ringer for Charlie, it all came back to him, almost as clearly as if that dreadful day had returned, fuelling his desire for revenge, for there is something in the loyalty and companionship of a beast that goes to the heart of its master, especially to one who had tasted to his detriment the fickleness and hypocrisy of the human race. Much as he liked Cricklewood, and how the song, *Cricklewood, Oh Cricklewood, You Stole my Youth Away,* could easily become reality, he was determined to go back – just two more years of thrift and he would be on his way.

As life galloped along, new housing estates were springing up, a network of motorways was under construction, and Jack was making a good living transporting men to a site in Welwyn Garden City. One Monday morning in early September he parked his van across the street from the Crown in

Cricklewood, his usual pick-up point and, as it was Monday morning, he dallied that extra few minutes, waiting for the last of his men to turn up. Despite the warm morning and his slight hangover after the weekend he wound up the window, shutting out the profane language of the gangers who were herding men on to the backs of lorries in the forecourt of the Crown, and if ever the tale of St Patrick, the snakes, and the gangers needed clarification, it was there for all to see, not that some of the men didn't need goading, but the degrading scene could easily be a slave market, an insult to humanity. A glance at his watch showed five past six, time he was on his way and, just as he was about to pull out, a tall, grey-haired man tapped on the window.

After four years in London, Jack had become like most of his immigrant brethren, taciturn and wary of strangers asking questions, and he deliberated for a few moments before lowering the window.

"Are you Jack Daly?" the man asked.

"Who wants to know?"

"If you are, I'm Martin King, a friend of your late father," the man returned.

At the mention of his father's name, Jack stiffened, and it took him a moment or two to regain his composure. "I'm your man," he said finally. "I'm Jack Daly."

"Is there somewhere we could meet tonight? I've news I think you should hear."

Still perplexed Jack made a more comprehensive perusal of the stranger. Gaunt and bareheaded, his features were well-weathered, and his casual manner and cynical smile spoke of years of exile from his native land. His double-breasted grey suit, although expertly tailored and of quality cloth, was wrinkled as it seemed from travel, and because he was true to the immigrant code and asked no further questions, he felt a certain kinship with him. "We could meet over there tonight in the saloon bar at about half-eight, if that suits you," he suggested, indicating the Crown.

When the man nodded his assent, Jack drove away, and for the remainder of the day his mind was in a quandary. How had this stranger – this Martin King – found him, and why had he mentioned his late father after so long? However, after his day of musing, he was none the wiser when later that night he turned up at the Crown.

The Crown in Cricklewood, as well-known to the Irish in London as O'Connell Bridge is to the denizens of Dublin, was one of those rough-and-ready, spit and sawdust establishments which catered for all comers, and though its customers were mainly working-class Irish, it wasn't unusual to see men in pinstripe suits and bowler hats rubbing shoulders with them. When Jack entered, it was the time of evening when the men on their way home from work were supping up and moving on and, as it was still too early for the influx of nightly drinkers, all was quiet, save for a sudden chorus of raucous cheers which erupted from a group of men standing at a corner of the long, brass-railed counter when one of them broke wind in a succession of loud reports.

"You're blowin' the stem well, Maurtheen, fair play t'yer ould arse!" came a spirited whoop from one of the group, as if a cup-final goal had just been scored, while the culprit capered about the floor, shaking out his trousers to allow the smell to circulate.

"Mind you don't lose the frame," cheered another. "But I'll bet the ould nappies are a bit rusty all the same."

"You'll surely stifle the quare wan in bed tonight if you keep that up, 'specially after a rally of bacon and cabbage down on top o' the bitter," cut in another, and the uproarious humour continued as more earthy comments were added, while others in the group, feigning disgust, held their noses.

Not long ago Jack would have been sickened by such vulgar antics, which brought to mind old O'Hara's reproof about suffering his daughter to live the rough life of their immigrant brethren, although now that he had accepted this type of coarse entertainment as part of the culture, he took time out from his thoughts, which were still trying to make some sense of the earlier encounter, and joined in the laughter. However, to end all speculation, right on the stroke of half-eight, the stranger appeared in the doorway, dallied for a second and, on recognising Jack, nodded a greeting.

When Jack had seen to the drinks, the man introduced himself again. "I don't know where to begin," he said, returning Jack's handshake. "So, I'll start by sayin' that your father died six weeks ago, God rest his soul – cancer it was – and not the way he was supposed to have died years ago. So, now you're wonderin' why I'm here, and what it's got to do with me. Well, I'm here to fulfil a dyin' man's wish – nothin' more. It's goin' to be a long story, so I suggest we sit over there by the window."

When they were seated at a table out of earshot of the bar, the stranger continued: "As I've already said, I'm Martin King, late of Castleford, but there's no trace of our family there anymore. They've all moved on and the house has fallen in – you've probably passed it thousands o' times on your way to town. But to get on with my business, I was back in Castleford last week lookin' for you. I went straight there from Manchester – that's where your father spent his last days, and it was his wish that I talk to you and explain. In Castleford I was told that you were somewhere in England, and that your sister, Eileen, was married in Galway. When I went to see her, she said she hadn't heard from you in ages, but she gave me this address in Camden Town. So, when I got to Camden Town, the landlady of the digs – a fine woman surely – knew you and asked me to stay, and I'm stoppin' there for a few nights. The landlady seemed to know exactly where you'd be every mornin', and she gave a fair description of you and the van."

When King began again, the words came in a slow drip of emissions, and Jack, sensing that he had something controversial or unpleasant to reveal, interjected: "Say no more until you hear me first. I know you must have great respect for my father if you went all the way back to Ireland and then here to see me. I think I know what you're about to say – my father wasn't my father, something like that. Does that make it any easier for you?"

Some of the tautness left King's features. "It's still a hard story to tell, but here goes," he went on, sighing forbearingly. "Your father never died at Dunkirk, so your mother was never a widow. To begin, I'll have to go back before the War when John Daly married your mother and your sister was born. The Depression was biting hard, and they were findin' it difficult to make ends meet. A young priest, Father Fitzpatrick, came to Castleford and, with the bit of influence he had, he got a job for John on the Council – crushin' stones and quarryin' sand – that kind of job. While John was at work, the priest started carryin' on with your mother, and you're that priest's son."

King's last sentence came in one long gasp of relief, and Jack immediately laid a reassuring hand on his shoulder. "It's all right – I understand! It took great courage to tell it. Just sit there now and I'll get us some whisky. I think we could both do with it."

Still in a state of shock Jack hurried to the counter and returned with two bumpers of whisky. "Drink that now," he said handing one to King. "It's a great job you're after doing. I always suspected something not quite right about my family history, but to be a priest's son is just – just, I don't know – hard to believe that's all."

"Cheers!" said King, tipping back two swallows and, perhaps encouraged by Jack's equanimity, he went on: "I'll put it like this. There's no doubt about it, you're that priest's son, so I'd be grateful if you didn't ask me to go into more detail. The whole village knew, but you know yourself, any time the clergy are involved in anythin' like that, you're supposed to turn a blind eye – hear no evil, see no evil, speak no evil. When John found out, it was too much for him to bear, and so he took the road. But as he got older, he regretted his decision. He meant to go back and make amends, but he kept postponin' it, and you know yourself, the more you postpone a thing, the harder it gets to do. He wanted me to explain this to you more than anythin', so you'd understand."

"It's easy to understand, Mister King, but how did he wind up in Dunkirk?"

"I'm coming to that – I promised I'd tell the whole story," returned King. "Shortly after the matter came to light he set off cyclin' for Dublin, and from there he worked his passage across to Liverpool on a cattle boat, and wound up somewhere in Gloucestershire, workin' for a farmer. Years later, when war broke out, there was big money to be earned makin' and repairin' the runways for the planes, workin' all the daylight hours, seven days a week. They were so short-handed that they went over to Ireland recruitin' labour, and they came over in droves, bombs or no bombs, myself included – no address, just a label round your wrist for some work camp or other.

"So, John left the farm and joined one o' them gangs, and the work took him all over the country. Then, around the time the army was bein' evacuated from Dunkirk, he took a big chance. He was workin' near Dover when the camp came under fire from the air, and when the all-clear sounded, he stumbled on a man with half his head blown off. So, he swapped identity cards and ration books with the dead man, and that night he slipped out o' the camp and worked his way north under his new name, John Ryan. In the end it turned out the way he wanted it. Your mother was entitled to the widow's pension and she was free to marry again, and John was free to lead his own life."

"How did you happen to meet him, Mister King?" asked Jack, finding the story intriguing, yet hard to believe. "Did the people back home know he was still alive?"

"No – just me and him, and now you," returned King. "When the War was over, I bumped into him in Manchester, and for me, it was like 'the dead arose and appeared to many'. But when he explained, I told him his secret'd be safe with me. From then on we became close friends, and needless to say there was plenty of work after the War – our type o' work. I got married, but John never took up with another woman. I used to get the news from Castleford through a cousin o' mine, and when your mother died, he was all for goin' back. But his courage failed him, and he kept puttin' it off. 'Next summer, Martin' he used to say, 'I'll go back and explain the whole story to young Jack. I have a feelin' he'll understand and, with the money I've saved, maybe between us, we'll make the ould place pay'. He always called you his son, and he kept on about goin' back till the cancer caught him. But he was a good-livin' man, and I was always proud to call him my friend."

When Jack made as if he might say something, King interjected: "I know you're burstin' to ask a few questions, but let me get this final bit off my chest first. I have here a copy of John's last will and testament – it's all here in my inside pocket, all signed up with the solicitors. He willed you, as man of the house, his land and cottage – I have the title deed with me. Also, there's a little over two thousand pounds to be divided between yourself and Eileen. He wants you to explain to Eileen and ask her forgiveness – that's why I never mentioned anythin' when I met her. So, that's the story as best as I can tell it, but all those secrets bottled up don't do any good at all. It's not the secret itself, but not knowin' what everyone else knows, and if you try to hush things up, all sorts o' rumours get about which are ten times worse than the truth."

A strange kind of sadness came over Jack, and though he had never known the man, he relived his story in his mind. There was an urge within him to pray or do something, but the time for prayer had passed, and they sat silently awhile, each rapt in his own thoughts. "Thank you kindly, Mister King," he said finally. "You are indeed a true friend of my late father and of mine. And, if there's anything I can do –"

"Everythin' has been taken care of – expenses and such – John made sure o' that," interjected King. "I'm glad now it's all over, and poor ould John can rest in peace, but I'll end on a happier note. There's a young lady in Castleford singing your praises, and if the look in her eye is anythin' to go by, I'd say you're a lucky man. And, before I forget, the landlady at Brecknock Road said for you to call – she said she has a proposition that might interest you."

For all that he was in a sombre mood Jack smiled to himself – a proposition that might interest him, and when his thoughts returned to the lady in Castleford, Kathy Moore came immediately to mind, who no doubt was keeping the home fires burning. Finally, turning his attention to King, he asked all about Castleford, a yearning to be back there again surging faster and faster in his veins, as every scrap of news, every place name, every public house evoked memories of what now seemed happy days.

Oblivious of the chatter going on around them they allowed the past to merge with the present, and the reminiscing continued until the bell for last orders brought them back from their faraway places. "It's time I was on my way, Jack," said King, offering his hand in farewell. "But I'm sure we'll meet again, and I'll give you my address in case you're ever in Manchester. Time goes by so quickly, and before you know it, it's the three score years and ten, and after that the best thing you can hope for is to die in your sleep," he sighed. "But talkin' of sleep, I'll have a good night's sleep tonight now that all that's off my chest, and tomorrow I'll be gettin' back to the wife."

After accompanying King to the taxi rank Jack returned to his bedsitter, and unable to contain himself he sat restlessly on the edge of the bed, grappling with the import of the night's revelations. A priest's son – it was hard to believe and, smiling wryly, he wondered if, as a priest's son, he was entitled to have grapefruit every morning for breakfast, or if he had inherited the supernatural powers of the priesthood, the power to put asses' heads on whom he pleased. If so, they would have to come up with a new nickname for Bull Paisley, one in keeping with his long ears, or perhaps he was a Messiah whose hour had not yet come, or a werewolf who could be killed only by a silver bullet made from a crucifix and fired into his heart by someone who loved him. Who would fire the bullet? – not Widow Kilbane – hardly Mary O'Hara – perhaps Kathy Moore and, recalling Kathy's wistful promise, he tried to picture her again in his mind's eye.

Locking Kathy's image just inside the door of his memory, ready for calling up later, he lay down on his bed, and while he was searching for sleep, his thoughts returned to the deceased John Daly, a man he would have been proud to call his father. What a kindly soul he must have been to bequeath his farm and half his life's savings to another man's son, while his real father was probably still preaching about the evils of the flesh, or perhaps his real father had climbed the ecclesiastical ladder and was now a bishop, complete with red cap and all the power and pomp associated with his station. The man with the red cap, quintessentially a man for all seasons, advocate of the rich when they faced their Maker, a crozier in his hand instead of a sceptre, could open many doors, even the pearly gates, depending on the size of the donation. Perhaps he should seek him out and raise a little dust, but after giving the matter careful consideration, he decided to keep the idea in mothballs until it could be used to his advantage.

Now that his father's story had unfolded, Jack wondered what controversy the future would disgorge about his mother's death, for the truth always came out in the end, no matter how much people tried to distort and suppress it. Finally, before sleep clamped down his eyelids, his thoughts lingered on his inheritance. The extra thousand pounds would bring his savings close to the amount he needed to launch his venture, which meant he could start preparing for his return.

Chapter 10

In the following weeks, now that all the obstacles had been removed for his return, Jack's thoughts began to rewind, and days, long-forgotten, emerged from the mists of the past, as if someone had removed the cataracts from the eyes of his memory. His reverie was full of Grogan's Bar, fair days in Castleford, Pudding Joyce's eating house, the neighbours swapping gossip by the fireside, and the night he walked away from the Phoenix arm in arm with Mary O'Hara. It felt strange that he could recall it all so vividly when he would have found it hard to remember much about yesterday and nothing at all about the day before, or perhaps there was a hand stronger than his own meddling in his affairs.

However, now that winter was approaching, he postponed his return until spring, and in the interim he painstakingly detailed every item he would need to launch his venture down to the last nail, and its cost. The list soon ran into pages and pages and the cost soared and soared until he realised that his savings would just about get him off the ground and, as he began to trim the list, the idea of second-hand equipment began to take root.

A second-hand tractor and trailer and its attachments, which could be bought for a song at one of the farm bankruptcy sales in the rural areas around London, would be a big saving, although the transport costs and import duty would offset any gain. On the other hand, if he bought the items separately and stored them until he was ready to go, he could load them on the trailer and drive the whole caboodle to the Dublin ferry at Liverpool, and from Dublin to Castleford. By proving ownership of the goods for six months or more, which could be overcome by backdating the receipts, he would avoid paying import duty, although the downside was the long haul to Liverpool using by-roads, the uncertainty of the weather, and the possibility of breaking down. The alternative was to take his van and buy the equipment in Ireland, which was sure to cost twice as much.

Heeding Pat's philosophy on fortune and women, it's the bold rather than the cautious man who wins them both, in the following months he scoured the countryside in his spare time, picking up bargains from advertisements and bankruptcy sales, which he stored in a corner of a transport company yard. As winter drew to a close, he found a tractor and trailer at the right price, and when the paperwork was finalised, he earmarked 24th March as a provisional date for his departure – a week after St Patrick's Day.

Now that it was time to say goodbye to his circle of friends, he had nothing but fond memories of Cricklewood and Camden Town. Gone, like the residue of a bad dream, was the memory of the hardship and uncertainty of his first weeks in London, the journey to work on the back of a lorry in all types of weather, the abuse from the ganger, the long hours, the near-slavery, the discrimination, those early days that had tried his endurance to the limit. Still, he had come through the fire, the fire of abuse, resentment and prejudice, and what fire doesn't burn, it hardens.

As his mind wandered back to the resolute faces in the long queue waiting to board the *Princess Maud*, it suddenly dawned on him that he wasn't the only one who had suffered, for every man, woman and child in the queue had to overcome the same difficulties. It was only then he realised that he was leaving behind a better type of Irishman, straighter, more broad-minded, more charitable, survivors of the first rank, and the proof was in their deeds, for not a week went by in the community without a benefit dance being held or a collection taken up for bereaved families, orphaned children, injured workers, and other needy cases, which were always well supported. Furthermore, besides the money they sent every week to hard-up parents, they contributed generously to every relief fund in the homeland, which raised the question of whether or not their largesse would be returned if the shoe was on the other foot, for past experience had shown that nothing was ever done by the indigenous Irish for their exiled brethren in England, except to pour scorn on them, and yet, he was going back to live among them, back to a land swathed in hypocrisy, the characteristic he most despised in the human race.

On St Patrick's Day, when he went to Camden Town to say goodbye to Pat, he found him alone, sitting on a high stool in his usual corner in the Halfway House. Pat, unless he met someone with whom he could argue and get his point across, preferred his own company, but he came quickly out of his reverie when he recognised Jack. "Happy Saint Patrick's Day to you, Jack, and you don't have to tell me – you came to say goodbye," he greeted. "But you didn't have to go to all that trouble – I'd have understood, although now that you're here, let's wet the ould shamrock together."

"Cheers Pat, and a happy Saint Patrick's Day to you too," Jack toasted, when the barman, acting on some type of sign language from Pat, placed a large Jameson before him. "But you're right, I did come to say goodbye – next week I'll be on my way."

"You'll be back, because there aren't many who ever succeeded in doing what you're trying to do," said Pat. "In the first place you'll be about as welcome over there as Judas Iscariot at an Apostle reunion, but a thick skin and a bit o' hypocrisy'll get you over that. The real reason you'll be back is because you'll be lonesome over there – it's hard to believe, lonesome among your own people – and you'll miss the freedom you have here in London. I know – I've tried it. See if I'm right – it'll be great for the first year or so, and then you'll start missing the crack. You won't change them over there – so don't even bother to try. You'll either have to knuckle down to their way or come back."

"I've no intention of knuckling down," countered Jack. "I'll just go along minding my own business and get on with my work."

"What they can't forgive over there is people who do mind their own business," returned Pat. "You've got to fit into their kiss-arse system – be different and be damned. You've got to practise at being a hypocrite, and run England down every chance you get. It's something like the sinners in the Gospel who repent – there's more joy in Heaven over one sinner repenting than for the thousands who need no repentance. So, if that's the case, it could also be argued that there's more joy in Ireland over one man coming back from England running it down, especially if he's broke, than there is for the thousands who come back on holidays, spending money and praising it. Agree too with the also-rans when they say they met better Englishmen over here than Irishmen. You know who I mean by the also-rans – the ones who came over for a few months and went back with their tails between their legs because they couldn't stick a little hardship. Don't forget to go to Mass every Sunday and the sodality once a month, and make sure everyone sees you. Sit among the bigshots in the front pews, because being seen there is the most important part of the exercise – the outward show, and I suppose I've not need to tell you to put plenty on the plate."

"You're taking the piss now, Pat," returned Jack, and yet, he could hardly deny the truth in his words. "I've a good idea what it's like – it couldn't have changed that much in five years. But it's not as bad as you have it painted – there are some salt o' the earth people there too."

"Ah, but those people are poor, and they'll be always poor if they don't wise up to the system, and they're not what you call respected people. Over there, they respect people with money, rather than the honest and the good-natured, and they have a tendency to give money to people who look like they already have money. They praise people because they're cute, 'cute' meaning that they're not beyond tricking someone out o' house and home without a qualm or scruple, or faking an injury just to get that coveted pull o' money from an insurance company. The real name for them is crooks. You know well what I'm talking about – they'd take out a life-insurance policy on some ould bachelor uncle, and if he lived too long, they'd feel cheated. They'd have a look at him every morning, like a pig they were going to kill to see if he was ready for the knife, and if there was no deterioration in his health, they'd shake their heads and say: 'He's fine and fresh yet, God bless him', and they hoping for the opposite."

"I know what you mean, but why don't you come with me and I'll prove you wrong – I'll need someone to help me build up the place."

Somewhere deep down in Pat's throat a cynical laugh rattled like a stone in a jar. "I hope you're joking – me, it is – go back? I know it wouldn't be the first time I went to bed with Lady Luck and woke up with Miss Fortune, but going back would definitely be stretching luck to the limit," he said, shuddering as if at the very thought. "But seriously, could you see me saluting the bag o' yeast, or taking my cap off to the creamery manager?"

"You might have to go back someday," countered Jack. "So, why not now?"

"The only way I'll ever go back is if I'm reincarnated over there – God forbid, and if I was, it'd be just my luck to come back as a tinker's ass," returned Pat, grinning as it seemed at his own imagination. "Just think about it for a minute – all the beatings a man'd get, and the tinker woman sticking safety pins in me to make me run faster. The tinkers must have some kind of grudge against the ass, because they never stop flailing him, the poor bastard. No – London'll do for me. People in London mind their own business. If you dropped dead in the street, most o' them'd step over you as if you weren't there, and that's the way it should be."

"But you must have a notion of going back someday – after all, every savage is supposed to love his native shore."

"You'll find out in the next couple o' years why I have no intention of going back, because you'll be thinking of coming back yourself for the very reasons I mentioned," returned Pat. "You'll get fed up with them over there talking about death all the time, just as you get fed up with the Englishman here talking about his aches and pains, his operation, what he had for his dinner, what he saw on television the night before, and Hitler and the War. They glory in death over there – his last words and all that – just as they glory in talking about Hitler and the War here. On the other hand, you could be doing the right thing, because it's a changing world. Life's way of yesterday isn't life's way of today, and it's doubtful if life's way of today'll be life's way of tomorrow. But we'll say no more on the subject – it's getting too depressing. But I wish you luck. Even if you weren't going back, you're making a wise move getting out o' London now that you have your money made – London is only for people looking to make money. Any man who ever stuck around here after he had it made is now suffering from touchophobia."

"Touchophobia?"

"The fear of being tapped for money. A touchophobic is a man who's afraid to show himself outside the door in case he bumps into any of his old mates and gets tapped, especially by the ones who worked in the same trench as him. The fear of being tapped is worse than the tapping itself."

"Leave it out, Pat."

"Just think about it," Pat went on. "If you have no money, you'll never be afraid of anyone putting the hammer on you. As I said, it's the fear of it that does the nerves in, but saying that, there are these new anti-tapping pills you can take."

"The anti-tapping pills wouldn't be a bad idea, because there are people making a fine art out of tapping, picking the right moment and all that," returned Jack. "But seriously, I just came to say goodbye."

"No – I won't say goodbye, just so long, because you'll be back. Remember the old saying: *you'll never go back, and all the crack you had here – and the women*?

"Yes, I can understand about the women and the crack, if you take the word in a literal sense, because that's all the English talk about, morning, noon and night – women and their fannies, whether it's tight or loose," said Jack. "When you come to think of it, it's a very immoral country, shagging one another's wives and boasting about it – even the papers are full of it. Everyone is at it, from the royalty and the people in high places down to the man sweeping the street, putting it about, as they call it, and making jokes about women's periods – red sails in the sunset and the painter is in town – it seems to be their main topic."

"Did it ever cross your mind that they mightn't know about anything else?"

213

"You've got a point there, Pat, because they are a bit simple-minded."

"But seriously, the day'll come when the born Irishman here'll be as scarce as the Red Indian in America, because the influx of Irish immigrants is sure to slow down in the coming years."

"That's hard to believe, considering they're still arriving in droves. You've only got to look at the statistics – fifty thousand last year alone, not counting the thousands of women coming over for abortions."

"Just you wait and see – immigration from Ireland'll reach a high-tide mark someday, and then it'll start to slow down, the same as it did from Poland," countered Pat. "This new birth-control pill on the market'll spell the end of big families, and the economy over there is bound to pick up. Some clever investors from abroad are sure to see its vast potential, untapped resources and all that, especially if they get into the Common Market, and when a younger generation gets rid o' DeValera's clique and their antiquated policies, it'll be all systems go."

"Much as I'd like to see it happening, I can't see it happening," returned Jack. "In the first place the Catholic Church and the government have outlawed the pill, and it's excommunication for anyone who uses it, and I can't see the ordinary gaum over there doing anything on his own initiative, which is sure to discourage investment from abroad."

"That's not altogether true, because the pill, as we'll call it, is being smuggled in to meet the demand on the same scale as French letters. Take it from me, they have plenty of buyers – it's big business and, where there's demand, there's always supply," Pat went on. "First of all it'll slow down the birth rate and there'll be a drop in the number of single girls coming over here for abortions, and it'll mark the end of orphanages for children born out of wedlock. The threat of ex-communication or that it's a mortal sin'll go in one ear and out the other, but they'll give the outward show of abiding by the ruling of the Church, big hypocrites that they are, and they'll conveniently forget to mention it when they go to confession, so the clergy'll be none the wiser. They'll believe that abstinence or using the so-called safe period is the reason for the decline in birth rate."

"I'll have to agree with you there, Pat – they'll try it out and, as you say, it'll do the world o' good, because a big percentage of the single girls coming over at the moment are pregnant," returned Jack. "But for the life of me, I can't see the scale of the immigration slowing down."

"If you haven't noticed already, all the children of Irish parents here have English accents and English ideas, and you can't tell them apart only by their surnames," Pat continued. "The grown-up ones have become more English than the English themselves, and worse still, they try to hide their Irish ancestry in case the English take the piss out o' them, not like the Irish-Americans who are proud o' their roots. Most o' them marry Englishwomen, so in years to come, the breed'll be crossed beyond identification, and they adopt their kiss-arse culture too – knights and their ladies fair and all that type o' bullshite – which will eventually put paid to our breed. You've only got to look at the Poles, most of the recognisable ones are now over fifty – the ones who fled Poland during the War – and their offspring are already integrating with the English."

"I can see you point, Pat, but as I've already said, it's hard to see it happening."

"It'll happen," countered Pat, who seemed determined to have the last word. "One by one the Irish centres and dance halls'll close down, the GAA clubs'll disappear, and the Irish children'll become strangers to their own parents. All the characters too'll die out – Lady Joyce, Cockney Daly, One-round Callaghan, Elephant John, Mad Farrell, Wide-load Hughes, Horse Kelly, Priest Hillary, and Pony Hyland, to name but a few, and there'll be no one to replace them. It mightn't come in our lifetime, but it's on the cards for sure."

The day sped quickly by, and one morning shortly afterwards Jack set off in his open tractor, the flapping noises of the tarpaulin on the trailer bringing back memories of his days travelling to work on the back of a lorry. Allowing two days for the journey he followed a mapped-out route on secondary roads and, hoping to average ten miles an hour, his target was to reach the outskirts of Shrewsbury before nightfall on the first day.

Despite a favourable weather forecast he was scarcely clear of London when the heavens opened. Nevertheless, he kept on doggedly, hour after hour, mile after mile, every mile an agony, every mile a victory, bypassing Oxford, Gloucester and Hereford until he came to a road sign – Shrewsbury 32 miles. By now the downpour had tired itself into a sullen drizzle, and he continued with renewed enthusiasm until he reached the Saracen's Head, a roadside inn three miles from Shrewsbury where a sign advertising meals and accommodation glowed invitingly in the murky dusk.

Cold and sodden he pulled into the car park, and when he jumped to the ground, his legs were so stiff that his knees buckled with the impact. Fortunately, he hadn't been stopped by the police on the fourteen-hour journey, although he attracted some curious stares from them any time they passed by. Stamping his feet and slapping his hands against his shoulders criss-cross fashion until his circulation returned he picked up a holdall from under the tarpaulin and walked stiffly to the entrance.

An hour later, bathed and shaved, he returned downstairs to the restaurant and, considering it was every Irishman's dream to go back when he had his fortune made, he felt anything but high-spirited. Even the wine and the brandy afterwards failed to kindle any enthusiasm, and yet, he smiled derisively every time he thought of his fortune – a trailer full of bits and pieces and barely enough money to get his enterprise off the ground.

The more he imbibed, the more despondent he became, even when he wound his mind back to the long lonely days he had spent looking into the fire, wishing for the chance to prove himself, to prove that a poor man with capital could get ahead just as well as a rich man, perhaps even better. Now that he had the chance, he wasn't happy, and he fell to wondering why. He had often heard that England held people in her grasp, as if something magnetic kept drawing them back, and now he could believe it. Allowing that he had parted with good friends, there was something else niggling him, something unexplainable, as if he was leaving the good for the bad when the trend was the other way.

On the other hand, perhaps it was the practical side of his nature throwing a spanner in the works, for what was life all about only making a living. He had been making a good living in London, a city without scruples where everything imaginable could be bought for cash and goods fell off the backs of lorries with unbelievable regularity, a city peopled by a cynical breed whose only religion was 'it's the rich wot gets the gravy' and 'dip in the grave when the gravy is 'ot', and he was leaving it behind, the bright lights and the bustle, and going back to a cottage without electricity or running water, to a land that would tilt him into a quietness more than halfway to the quietness of the grave. It didn't make sense, save for the satisfaction of saying: 'I defied the odds and came back', cutting off his nose to spite his face and, after all his years away, he had yet to devise a plan for getting even with Paisley.

On the following afternoon it was past two o'clock when he pulled into the embarkation park across the road from the British Rail steamship terminal at Liverpool docks, and when he had stamped some life into his feet, which were as stiff as a horse's hooves, he turned towards the booking office where a tall man in uniform with gold braid on his cap was standing in the open doorway, eyeing him with bland curiosity.

"Are those yours?" he asked, indicating the tractor and trailer which were standing out among the other vehicles as conspicuously as a tinker's cart among a fleet of royal carriages.

Jack nodded. "I'd like to book passage for them to Dublin, and myself. How much will it cost one way, and how soon d'you think I'll be able to go?" he asked. "I have change of address papers for them here in my pocket, all signed up in the Irish embassy in London."

The inspector's moustache twitched in what seemed bewilderment as he scanned Jack's papers. "You mean to say you drove that contraption all the way from London without a cab or a windshield in this weather?" he asked, incredulity in his tone. "Well if you did, you need your head examined, but I admire your courage just the same, although I must point out that all farm machinery must be steam-cleaned before we can allow it on board. However, everything being okay, we can fit you in on tonight's ten o'clock sailing."

"It's steam-cleaned," Jack lied. "I had it done before I left London. It's probably all the shite from the road on the way up that's making it so rough-looking. But I'll get to cleaning it right away."

"Is it now!" said the inspector. "If that's what it looks like when it's steam-cleaned, I sure as hell wouldn't like to have seen it beforehand – but follow me."

Taking a tape measure from a shelf the inspector strode across to the embarkation park, Jack at his heels, and when he had measured both vehicles and the overall length, he returned to the office and consulted a price list. "I'm turning a blind eye on the steam-cleaning, and it'll work out cheaper if we book them on as two separate vehicles," he said. "One way, it comes to twenty-seven pounds and ten shillings. Embarkation time is eight o'clock, and you'll be last on and last off."

Later that night, as Jack stood at the stern of the ship looking back at the harbour lights winking dimly in the darkness, absently twirling his good-luck piece around in his fingers, the little gold bell that had brought him luck after all, he took up his thoughts exactly as he had left them on his other crossing. The more he reflected, the more the interim seemed to condense, until it could easily have been five weeks instead of five years since his departure, although he felt a dreadful increase in years without seeming to have lived them. It was easy to say turn the tables on Paisley, but how? Harming him physically would be the surest way of winding up behind bars, or perhaps he might find a way of hitting him in the pocket. Mary O'Hara too kept intruding on his reverie, although it would be too much to expect to find her still single – and waiting.

Part 3

Chapter 1

Next morning at six, when the ship berthed at Dublin's North Wall docks, all Jack's misgivings, all his regrets for leaving Cricklewood, even his desire for revenge gave way to an overwhelming sensation at being back again on the old sod, a thrill which could be felt only by expatriates returning after a long absence. Suddenly there was an urgency within him to be home, and two days later, when the spires of Castleford appeared on the horizon like Brigadoon, he felt as if he was just awakening from a long unbroken sleep.

The home air went to his head like an intoxicant, and when he reached the outskirts, he put the tractor in low gear and advanced more slowly, the picture of Castleford which he had logged somewhere in the back of his mind coming alive again, as if someone with a feather duster had just brushed his memory clean of cobwebs: the women gossiping across the open doorways, the corner boys propping up the town hall, the old-timers lounging outside Forde's forge, and the shrill babel rising above the school playground, sights and sounds that took him back and held him hovering over bygone days in a brief moment of nostalgia. At a glance it seemed that nothing had changed, only that the lines of time on some of the faces he recognised were more deeply engraved.

Quickening again when he was through the town he set off on the last lap of the journey, his spirits soaring as he passed each familiar landmark, until he reached the last bend in the road, the one from which he had turned away so bitterly on that long-ago morning. The yearning for home that had been welling up in his breast ever since disembarking in Dublin had now reached his throat, where it was forming a lump, and when the black slate roof of his cottage peeped out through the trees, the lump dissolved into tears. There was no smoke, no glow of life radiated from its darkened windows; only the birds, perhaps disturbed by the noise of the tractor, called warning among the trees, and a colony of starlings flew off the roof and dispersed.

Pulling up at the gate a more comprehensive examination revealed the green fungus on the damp concrete walls from which the whitewash had weathered, the grimy windows, the paint peeling from the woodwork, and the voids in the roof where the slates were missing. At the back of the house the galvanised roof, which had blown off the henhouse, was jammed between an elder tree and the perimeter fence, half in, half out, of the next field, and one section of the barn's double doors had broken loose from its frame and lay where it had fallen, while its brother, creaking to and fro on rusty hinges, looked ready to give up at any minute and join it on the ground. Only the horse stable remained unscathed.

Suddenly apprehensive in case the outer deterioration was just the tip of the iceberg, he approached the front door tentatively, and when he found the key in its usual hiding place under a flowerpot, the floodgates of memory opened with the door and a shiver ran down his spine as if he was disturbing old ghosts.

However, the more the light from the doorway penetrated the gloomy interior, the more it revealed its orderliness and, overwhelmed by a combination of relief, delight and gratitude for Kathy Moore's efforts, he stood for a moment on the threshold unable to contain himself. The kitchen welcomed him from every corner like a faithful dog, as if it had forgiven him for his desertion, a welcome that was made all the more warm when he put a match to the fire which presumably Kathy had laid in the grate and the light from the flames darting up the chimney sent the silhouettes of all objects within its range dancing merrily on the walls.

Opening all the windows, some of which were so rotten that they almost came asunder in his hand, he set himself to the task of making the place habitable again, and while the blustery March wind was purging the mustiness from the rooms, he dragged the feather mattress from his bed, propped it against a row of chairs in front of the fire, and watched judiciously as steam began to rise. Blankets, sheets and pillows came next and, moving from one room to another, he noted all the major defects until his stomach reminded him that he hadn't eaten since leaving Athlone earlier that morning.

He needed so much and, cursing himself for not stopping off in Castleford on his way through, he scribbled a list, paraffin for the lamp and candles among the necessities, far too much to carry on foot. His bicycle was standing against the parlour wall covered with a blanket and, as both wheels were flat, he had no choice but to unhitch the tractor and be in and out of town before dark. Banking the fire he locked the door behind him, and when he reached the yard, it was only then he noticed the sign partly hidden in the shrubbery: Land Commission Property – Keep Off.

Mouth agape, he stared at the notice and, as his astonishment gave way to anxiety, he recalled having heard that the Land Commission had the power to force-purchase any land where the owner was absent indefinitely, especially if the land wasn't being utilised. A glance over the fields showed sheep grazing and the land free of obnoxious weeds, and though it went some way in quelling his anxiety, it was a problem that would have to be addressed without delay.

Determined not to let the setback blight the joy of his homecoming he unhitched the tractor, and when he reached Castleford, some of his earlier animation returned. There was so much to do and so much to catch up on, and like a bewildered bee confused by too many flowers, he didn't know where to begin. Wandering through the familiar streets, picking up his bits and pieces, he stopped several times to shake hands with old friends, although strangely most of their greetings had the appendage: 'when are you going back?' and, when he disclosed his intentions, their smiles turned sceptical, as if to say he should have his head examined.

Strapped as he was for time, he felt that his homecoming wouldn't be complete without a visit to Grogan's, and when he lifted the latch and stepped into the gloomy interior, again he felt an eerie sensation, as if the present was invading the past. Grogan, a little more hunched and wrinkled, didn't need to say he was welcome; it was in his eyes and hearty handshake, and the first drink was on the house. As it was still early-evening, there was only a scattering of customers, mainly youths, most of whom were strangers to Jack, and though they greeted him with cordial nods, he detected something of askance in the odd covert glance cast in his direction. Save for a framed photograph of the Galway football team – All-Ireland Champions 1956 – on the pelmet above the counter, nothing had changed and, promising to be back to renew old acquaintances when he was settled, he finished his pint, his mind calling up bygone days when it was harder to escape from the crack in Grogan's than from Alcatraz.

Later that night, not long after dark, he heard footsteps outside, and when the door shuddered open, Murt Burke appeared in the glow of the lamplight. "Sure it's yourself that's in it, Jack," he greeted, staring intently at Jack as if he was finding it hard to believe his eyes. "I seen the light in the window, and I didn't know what to think – it could be anyone, you know. Is this just a visit, or are you back for good?"

'You'll never go back', was the first thought that crossed Jack's mind, recalling the ominous ring he had discerned in the catchy saying when he first arrived in London. Now it was: 'when are you going back', for he had yet to receive any encouragement to stay. Shrugging off his disappointment he shook hands with his visitor. "Of course I'm back for good, just as I promised," he returned. "I might be a few years late, but what the hell, and I'm sure you've noticed the tractor out in the yard. Well, that's to help me and you do all our work, and the neighbours can borrow it too, if they need it. But tell me this, Murt – what's all this crack with the Land Commission?"

The years hadn't affected Murt in health or habit, and he spat copiously into the fire before taking his usual seat on the hob. "I can't tell you much about it, Jack," he began, somewhat hesitantly, lifting his cap with a forefinger and thumb and scratching his head with his remaining fingers, his regular method of assisting his mental perplexities. "Just before Christmas a couple o' fellas with new suits on them came snoopin' around, askin' all kinds o' questions about you – how long you were gone and all that, and the next thing I knew that sign was up outside. As I promised Eileen, I kept the land grazed and the thrishels cut, and I kept an eye on the house in case the tinkers broke in, and I paid the rates. Young Kathy comes over every Sunday mornin' and lights a fire. But you know yourself, it's hard to keep a house up to scratch when there's no one livin' in it."

"I suppose there's only one way to find out – I'll hit for Galway tomorrow morning on the bus and have it out with the Land Commission," said Jack. "While I'm there, I can drop in on Eileen. Maybe she can throw some light on the matter, and Murt – God spare you the health for looking after the place for me."

Murt didn't stay long, which was unusual and, save for the odd crackle from the fire, the kitchen was as still as a morgue. Later, when he turned in for the night, the sheer silence after the cacophony of London blocked all avenues to sleep and, with every sound magnified, the whispering feet of rats scurrying across the floor sounded as loud as a troop of cavalry cantering across a parade ground. So far, nothing had come up to expectations; even Murt's welcome was lukewarm, considering he hadn't seen him in five years, and it seemed that he knew more about the Land Commission than he was letting on. The Land

Commission would hardly send inspectors about the country on mere speculation, and it was equally hard to believe they had just happened on his homestead and found it unoccupied, especially as the rates were being paid. It seemed strange too that there was no correspondence relating to the matter in the faded pack of mail on the sill in the embrasure of the kitchen window, or perhaps the letters had been purposely returned to confirm his absence.

According to his immigrant brethren in London it was usually small holdings the Land Commission seized, mostly belonging to the exiles from the west of Ireland, poor people who had been forced to emigrate to make a living, which confirmed his belief that it was always the poor who fell foul of every evil in the world, for he had heard too that no dispossession orders were ever issued against the absentee landlords of the vast estates in the Midlands, or perhaps it was part of the organised culling system that he believed was secretly in operation to get rid of the undesirables – the depart from me ye cursed.

As part of the deal he had made with Eileen for the grass keep, Murt was obliged to pay the rates, but had he paid them regularly without having final demands and the bailiffs calling? And what of his neighbours? They were bound to have heard he was back, and yet, not one of them had called, even out of curiosity or to see if he needed anything – milk, for instance. Considering they had turned out in such numbers on the night before his departure, promising all kinds of favours, it didn't make sense, or perhaps they had conspired together, although later, when he had more time to think of it, he dismissed the conspiracy theory as over-wrought imagination.

Next morning, as Jack was leaving to catch the ten o'clock bus to Galway, Mick Moore called and, save to say that Granny Mulhaire's few acres too were in the hands of the Land Commission, he could throw no further light on the issue. Granny had passed away the previous year and, as she had predicted, none of her children or grandchildren returned to look after her in her old age, only just long enough to put her down. Hoping against hope she had left her will open, and in the end there were so many entitled to a share of her smallholding that they left it in the hands of the Land Commission. Perhaps this had triggered it off as Moore suggested, but Jack had his doubts, and though it was on the tip of his tongue to ask how the land was going to be divided, he decided to wait until he investigated the matter further.

When he alighted from the bus in Galway, he went straight to the County Buildings where he was directed to the records office. An elderly clerk, who introduced himself as Mr Griffith, took the title deed and his father's will and, after a quick examination of the documents, he ushered him into a small stuffy office which stank of embrocation, snuff and pipe tobacco. "Sit down for a minute, Mister Daly," he said, indicating an armchair, while he made a clumsy attempt at tidying his desk which was strewn with papers. "I have to do some checking in the main office."

Some minutes later Griffith returned, a folder under his arm. "I've been to the Land Commission department and it seems they've got crossed lines somewhere," he explained. "They were informed that no one had proper title to the land, and that it had been left untended for quite a number of years. Your documentation has cleared up this misunderstanding, and you tell me you're now living on the place."

"That's correct," returned Jack. "But there's something puzzling me – how did they find out? The rates were being paid, and I had a man looking after the place in my absence."

Griffith quickly explained the role of the Land Commission, as Jack had been led to believe. "Once someone reports land left idle, the Land Commission is obliged to investigate, and it usually entails some questioning," he went on. "Your neighbours were questioned, and they all agreed that you hadn't been back for well over four years – they're all listed here."

"Who reported it in the first place?"

"I'm afraid that's confidential," returned Griffith, mopping his brow with a crumpled handkerchief as if he wished to have done with the matter.

"Could I have a look through that folder?"

"You could," said Griffith, "but it would tell you nothing. I can read out a list of the names they questioned if you like – Keane, Joyce, Moore, Burke, Madden, Quinn etc. But these people would have to more or less tell the truth, because eventually they could be summoned to court to testify to your absence if the case was being contested. Listen to me – I just work here. I'm not your enemy and neither is the Land Commission. So, I suggest you put the matter from your mind sooner rather than later. You're now in residence, you have full title to the land, and I can't see you being troubled again on the issue."

When he was back on the street, Jack asked directions to Eileen's address, and ten minutes later, as he approached the front gate of her terraced house, he slowed his step, not quite sure what to expect. His last contact with her had been before he left Widow Kilbane's and, considering her earlier lack of enthusiasm for life, he found it hard to imagine her as being anything but a dowdy drudge, spread out of shape by the rigours of housewifery and childbearing like so many of her gender who had fulfilled their life's ambition – to get a gold ring on the third finger of the left hand. His imagination took him as far as a houseful of brats and an out-of-work Jimmy Murphy stretched out in an armchair by the fire. Yet, on the outside the house looked adequately maintained, white lace curtains were billowing out from the open top windows, and the small front garden had been recently cultivated and was showing the first signs of bloom.

When the door opened at the third rap-rap of the knocker, Jack hoped that his surprise wasn't showing on his face, for contrary to what he had been expecting, it was a rejuvenated Eileen who appeared in the doorway, so untouched by time that it would appear she had drunk from the fountain of youth. Her eyes, which he recalled as being lacklustre, now held a healthy sparkle, her skin had lost most of its swarthiness and stood out creamy in the gloom of the hallway, her hair was stylishly cut and bobbed and, in her grey flared skirt, white cotton blouse, nylons, and high heels, she could, with a push, pass for attractive.

Eileen made no attempt to hide her astonishment and, as she stood staring, mouth agape, eyes dilating, she looked as awestricken as on the day in the Shambles when she had seen all the rabbits.

"Are you going to ask your dear long-lost brother in out o' the cold, or not?" asked Jack, enjoying her consternation, and grudgingly he had to admit that Murphy was seeing to her fairly to have her looking so well, although the real reason for her sparkle wasn't yet apparent.

"I suppose you'd better come in," returned Eileen, leading him to the kitchen, and when he was seated at the table, she answered the question in his eyes: "Jimmy is dead – I'm a widow woman now like mother, God rest their souls. A heart attack he got over two years ago now – it was terrible. I was out doing the shopping at the time, and when he went next door to help young Missus Morris jack up the car and change the wheel, he collapsed with a pain in the heart. Missus Morris managed to drag him as far as the sofa in the sitting room, and then she sent for the ambulance. But by the time they got him to hospital, he was dead."

Jack smiled to himself – jacking up the car. It wasn't hard to imagine what he was jacking up – a fitting finale for a philanderer, live by the sword, die by the sword, live by the –

"You – I know what you're thinking!" cried Eileen, breaking in on Jack's reverie when she noticed his wry smile. "You haven't changed, have you! Now let me tell you this, Jimmy was a different man from the Jimmy you knew. He bought this house, and he never missed a day's work, so he didn't."

"Hold it, Eileen – hold it, for Christ's sake! I haven't seen you in five years and I'm hardly in the door five minutes and you're down my throat. I haven't even opened my mouth."

"No – but you were thinking it just the same!" snapped Eileen. "That's you all over."

"What's it going to be – are we going to have one of those nice long rows you used to love so well, or are you going to put the kettle on and ready me a bite to eat?" asked Jack, still not convinced that Murphy could change, no more than a jackass could change into a thoroughbred stallion. "Why didn't you let me know Murphy was dead – I would've helped, though I can't say I'm sorry after him. But I've got news too, if you'll take the time to listen."

It was destined to be a day of enlightenment, and when Jack related the details of his conversation with Martin King, Eileen confirmed some of the story.

"I sort o' guessed about the priest – I can just about remember him. He seemed to be around a lot, always leaving when I was coming from school, and the other kids, always hinting," she went on, frowning when she recalled Mike Cullinane's later involvement.

"The money'll come in handy, Eileen," said Jack, mistaking Eileen's frown for grief. "But I forgot to ask you how you're managing. If there's anything I can do, let me know."

"I'm managing quite all right, thank you," returned Eileen. "I have two lodgers besides Kathy Moore, I've got my widow's pension, and I'm putting a little aside for young Jimmy's education. Before I forget, I think you should thank Kathy when you see her, and buy her something nice. She's been cleaning the cottage ever since I left, and that's some time ago now."

"Yes – I agree. She deserves more than just a 'God spare you the health'. But leave it to me, and I'll see to it."

Jack had yet to come to terms with Eileen's transformation. The move from the drudgery of the farmyard to the city would account for most of it, but there was more. The worried look that had been so much a part of her character had disappeared, and she seemed to be in full control of her destiny. "I must admit you're looking smart, Eileen – praise where praise is due, that's me," he remarked, pausing until her face lit up at the compliment, and then adding, somewhat derisively: "A big improvement from the days when you were waddling around in wellingtons, up to your neck in cowshite."

"You!" Eileen hissed venomously, her face darkening, her brow lowering. "You couldn't change even if you tried! You could never say one nice word without taking the good out of it."

"Calm down, Eileen – I didn't mean it. And you never asked me what I was doing home, or doesn't it make any difference to you either?"

"Well, what's bringing you home after so long?" asked Eileen. "Is it just for a holiday, or are you back to sell the bit o' land, now that it's yours to sell? If it is, you'd better be getting rid of it soon before the Land Commission get their hands on it. They won't give you money for it either, just bonds – land bonds. I thought when I didn't hear from you that you'd got married or something."

"Married – no," returned Jack. "Why jump in the river just to get a drink o' water, because that's what most young people are doing nowadays, getting married just to get a bit in comfort. But tell me this, what d'you know about the Land Commission? Did you know they'd taken the bit o' land – almost? And how did they know about the missing deeds?"

"I only know what Kathy Moore told me – that they were after it."

"When did she tell you this?"

"I'm not quite sure – about six weeks ago. Yeh, six or eight weeks ago – why d'you ask?"

"So, you knew all about it and you were going to let the place go just like that, so I'd have nowhere to come back to? You're just as bad as the rest o' them. It's a good job I did come back."

"How was I to know you were coming back and not a line from you? It makes no difference now, does it – you're here, aren't you?" interjected Eileen, wishing to have done with the subject so that she could spring her surprise, although she didn't consider it to be the ideal moment to mention that Mike Cullinane knew about the missing title deed, and if he knew, everyone knew.

"You're right – it makes no difference now, but it's nice to know I have friends," said Jack, a sarcastic ring in his tone. "From now on there'll be no more of the old-fashioned farming for me – the few stooks o' corn, the pit o' praties, the scattering of hens and ducks, the two cows and the four calves, the two-pig system – one for killing and one for selling. That's all behind me. Mass production is the name o' the game – pork on the hoof."

"You're daft – I thought you'd have given up on that idea long ago."

"Daft is right, Eileen – if you call making money daft," countered Jack, slightly irritated by his sister's lack of enthusiasm for his venture. Human nature was so consistent, especially in the pursuit of ambition, as most people believed that not to undertake was better than to undertake and come up short. He had seen it in London among the also-rans, and the self-reproach: 'I had my chance years ago and didn't take it', was as hackneyed as the timeworn phrase: 'You don't think I'm that kind of girl', which most women use when defending their virtue.

The sound of the front door opening brought their heads around, and Eileen's son came storming in, checking his stride when he saw Jack. "This is young Jimmy," said Eileen, shy pride in her voice. "Over here, Jimmy, and say hello to your Uncle Jack."

The boy shied away and grabbed his mother's leg, hiding his head under her skirt. "You'd better watch out – Eileen, he's after the skirt already," said Jack, perceiving Murphy in his calculating eyes as he peeped out from the folds of the material. "Nearly four already, your mother tells me – school soon, I suppose," he went on, trying to coax the boy from his hiding place, wondering if he would grow up to be as great a philanderer as his late father and harvest even some of the wild oats he had sown in his lifetime.

The day sped quickly by and, as afternoon turned to evening and Jack was getting ready to go, Eileen dropped her first bombshell. "I'm getting married again soon," she said. "In two weeks' time, to be exact – just after Easter."

"Good for you," congratulated Jack. "Will it be a day out for us all or not?"

"Of course! But aren't you going to ask me who's the lucky man? And I can tell you, you'll be surprised, Jack Daly – hard and all as it is to surprise you."

If Eileen's smug expression was anything to go by, Jack sensed that he was in for a shock. It must be someone he knew, someone from Castleford, and yet, it could hardly be anyone as obnoxious as Murphy. Finally, shrugging his surrender, he asked: "Who?"

"Mike Cullinane."

"What! If this is some kind of a joke, I'm not in the mood."

"It's true, and there's nothing you can do about it!" snapped Eileen. "Ever since Jimmy passed away he has me pestered to marry him. I'm not thinking of myself, I'm thinking of young Jimmy. Mike is a wealthy man, and he's assured me of Jimmy's future – and my own. He's putting it all in writing with a solicitor before we tie the knot – that's the deal."

"You can't be serious, Eileen!" exclaimed Jack, fighting down his revulsion at the thought of the conniving Cullinane puffing and grunting astride his sister. "Cullinane is old enough to be your father – he must be well into his fifties."

Arms folded, Eileen defended her decision. "As I said, Mike is a wealthy man, and you've got to pocket your pride when it comes to rearing a family. And besides, I've got another reason –"

"What family – one child!" Jack cut in. "You're not that badly off, surely. You've got money, a house, and I'll help you if need be. I just don't believe it. If you marry that – that turkey-choker, it's hoordom of the first rank – marrying for money, and you're the very person I heard running down the women who do it openly. Anyway, if the worst comes to the worst, you can always sell up here and live with me back in Knockrush."

"Live with you, it is?" snapped Eileen. "God forbid, if it came to that, I'd sooner go off with the tinkers. I can already see it – me doing all the donkey-work, and you off gallivanting. Anyway, it's my life and I can do what I like with it. Where were you these last couple o' years when I needed you most? – gallivanting over in England and not a line from you. From now on I have my life to lead and you have yours, and it's up to yourself whether you come to the wedding or not."

Jack shook his head in exasperation as he tried to come to terms with Eileen's logic. In the first instance she had married a man who would tip a cat going out a skylight, and now she was about to marry a man with one foot in the grave. Perhaps that was it – one foot in the grave. Clever Eileen! Old rich men were such fools, and they fell easily into crafty girls' hands just like ripe apples when the tree is gently shaken. She would probably love him to death in a few years, and then she'd fall in for all his money. She had mentioned another reason, and a solicitor. So, perhaps it might not be such a bad idea after all – Cullinane with one foot in the grave, Eileen with one foot on the gravy train.

"Why are you grinning like that?" asked Eileen, blushing slightly when she noticed her brother's change of expression and wry grin. "I've seen that grin before. There's something you're not telling me – what is it?"

Eileen's blush confirmed Jack's suspicion that there was more to the marriage than met the eye. "I was just seeing the funny side, that's all, and the two nice brother-in-laws you saddled me with," he returned. "As you say – it's your life, but Cullinane – I just can't understand it, and you know the saying: 'if you want to have steam in the kettle, you've got to have fire in the stove'. But I must be off now, or I'll miss my bus, and in the meantime drop me a line about the wedding arrangements. I suppose you'll be expecting me to do the honours on your behalf when the priest asks: 'who giveth this woman in holy matrimony' or whatever he asks, and tell young Kathy I'm back."

"She's not young Kathy any more – she's twenty-one and engaged."

Chapter 2

On Sunday morning, as Jack was bustling back and forth from the dresser, to the fire, to the table, preparing his breakfast, he was distracted by the front gate creaking open, which was immediately followed by a female voice calling: "Anybody home?" Turning his back on the frying pan, which was sending spatters of hot fat exploding in all directions, he looked to the door, and when it shuddered open, it could only have been divine intervention that stopped him from falling into the fire, for Kathy Moore, as breathtakingly beautiful as a film star, was standing on the threshold.

She was too much for Jack to take in at a glance and, as bemused as a clocking-hen which had just hatched a clutch of ducklings, he stared at her bewilderedly until she blushed. "Come in, Kathy," came a voice from somewhere deep down in this throat, a voice he could scarcely identify as his own, his eyes wandering from her pinned-up flaxen hair down to her black slip-on shoes and back again, more deliberately, over her legs, the attractive outline of her hips and thighs which were leaving their imprint on her navy-blue skirt, her slender waist, the tautness of her bosom against the blue cotton of her blouse, which was partly concealed by a grey woollen cardigan, all the way up to the symmetrical curve of her neck, full sensual lips, slightly-cocked nose, and round, inquiring blue eyes. Eileen had certainly hit the nail on the head; she wasn't young Kathy any more.

Kathy smiled, her upper lip curling away from her even set of white teeth as she made a quick appraisal of her own. "You're welcome home, Jack," she greeted, seemingly satisfied with what she saw. "I always knew you'd come back, and only just in time too – Eileen said you'd straightened everything out with the Land Commission."

Still spellbound, for a split second Jack thought he detected a glint in Kathy's eyes, a coquettish type of twinkle which sometimes betrays a woman of easy virtue. This could hardly be the type of look that Martin King had spoken of and, if he was honest with himself, it was a look he didn't particularly want to see, as it detracted somewhat from the unsullied image he had formed of her in his mind. Shrugging off the thought, he voiced his appreciation: "Kathy, how you've changed – grown up, I mean. If I met you in the street, I'd surely stop and look after you – whistle maybe, but it's unlikely if I'd recognise you offhand. I'm saying this as a compliment, so I hope you don't take offence. It's just that you look so – so glamorous. First of all I want to thank you for everything – without you the house would've fallen in for sure. But you just wait and see – I'll make it up to you."

Jack was so enthralled by the encounter that he had forgotten the frying pan until it whooshed into flame behind his back, and a few moments of panic followed as he bolted through the door and back, the contents of the pan charred beyond redemption. "See what you've done, Kathy. You made me forget what I was doing – coming over here looking all so gorgeous. I nearly burned the house down, and you after keeping it safe for me," he laughed and, drawing her attention to the pan and the remains of his breakfast, he broke into song, parodying the lyrics of the Jersome Kern hit, *Smoke Gets in your Eyes.*

Kathy immediately took the matter in hand. "Sit down there now," she said, easing Jack into the chair at the head of the table and, adding more rashers and sausages to the bits and pieces she salvaged from the earlier mishap, the pan was soon sizzling again, this time under the right amount of heat.

While Jack was eating, Kathy poured herself a cup of tea and sat silently as he sang her praises between mouthfuls of food. "It's a great girl you are, surely. I'll bet you have all the men in Galway running after you. And what's this Eileen was saying about you being engaged?"

Kathy shrugged, a mischievous smile playing on her lips, the twinkle he had detected earlier back in her eyes, as though her engagement was a matter of small moment. "Oh, I'm engaged all right, but only in a half-hearted way. It's safer these days for a woman to be engaged – it stops men from pestering you for dates. All you have to do is flash the engagement ring, and besides, it's got other advantages. Look – that's all you have to do if you want to put a man off," she laughed, flaunting her three-stoned symbol of betrothal. "If you don't, just hide it behind your back until you have a chance to take if off."

When Jack recalled his passionate experience with Kathy outside his cottage door on the night before his departure, he wondered if she had waited as she had promised, and for a moment his vanity soared, only to plummet again when he reminded himself that she was engaged, if only in a half-hearted way, whatever that meant, like being a little bit pregnant. Evidently she knew what life was all about, and the proof was in the manner she kept crossing and re-crossing her legs and smoothing her skirt into attractive alignment with her thighs, making sure that he saw everything she wanted him to see, which evoked memories of his deceased brother-in-law, who would never have let such an opportunity go a-begging, or perhaps he hadn't. However, when he realised that he would be forever in her debt, he put away his prurient thoughts. "Who's the lucky man, Kathy?" he asked. "Is it someone we know, or have you fallen for a stranger?"

"It's Michael McCale," returned Kathy, showing none of the misty-eyed happiness of a bride-to-be. "You know McCale's hardware and grocery shop – he's the oldest son. You should remember him – tall, thin, black hair. He went away to college and now he's back, and he'll be taking over the running of the business next year. I suppose Eileen told you I'm manageress in the lady's department in Moon's in Galway – that's how I met him. He has a car and he gave me a lift home one weekend. That broke the ice and we started going out together, to dances and all that, and before I realised it, he popped the question and bought the ring."

Although he had shopped many times in McCale's, Jack couldn't immediately put a face on the son. If he was the same gangling youth that came to mind, he wasn't much to write home about in looks at least, but perhaps he would be considered a good catch for a woman. On the other hand, women's logic was hard to understand when it came to matrimony, first Eileen, now Kathy, and not a hint of romance from either of them. Men, especially wealthy men, were such fools not to be suspicious of their motives, and the pledge: 'and all my worldly goods I thee endow', was a high price to pay for just a hollow promise of love, fidelity and obedience, seeing as there was no conceivable way of holding them to their commitment. It seemed that Kathy was hedging her bets, making sure that she had a bird in the hand first, which raised another question – why had she gone to such pains to look after his cottage in his absence?

It seemed that Kathy was already inside Jack's mind. "Remember when I promised I'd look after your cottage for you? – Well, I did," she said. "Everyone said I was daft, and that you'd never come back. But now that I've proved them wrong, I feel a certain satisfaction. So, I came over to welcome you home and to tell you that Eileen's wedding is on Thursday week, the Thursday after Easter. She said for you to be there in your Sunday best to give her away. It's at the church in Salthill – eleven o'clock."

"Eleven o'clock in the morning, is it?" asked Jack, somewhat absently, his mind still searching for intangibilities in Kathy's story.

"Of course, goose – surely you don't think it's eleven o'clock at night," returned Kathy, smiling and shaking her head in mock reproach. "And there's a breakfast afterwards in the Banba Hotel. You can either catch the early bus in the morning or come up the night before. So, it looks as if we'll be meeting again soon. I'll be down next weekend, and I'll call over. But I've got to dash now – you know the neighbours and how they gossip," she went on, smiling a farewell and, with a provocative swirl of her skirt, she hurried away.

Still puzzled, Jack tried to make some sense of the situation – it just didn't add up, cleaning a man's cottage, and all for what? Besides, there was her wanton kiss of long ago to consider, much too promiscuous for a sixteen-year-old, and now her engagement, which went a long way in supporting Reg Ashton's conviction that a woman's imagination carried her as far as the altar and no farther. It certainly seemed that way, and perhaps they played it by ear afterwards.

The ponderous tones of the clock striking eleven startled Jack out of his reverie. Last mass was at half-eleven – he'd have to hurry.

Mass on Sunday was the high point of the week in Castleford, especially last Mass, and Jack was born with the conviction that most people attended just to be seen there, or to observe. For days afterwards there would be much speculation and gossip, which usually ran: 'I didn't see you at last Mass on Sunday? – no, I went to an earlier one, the kids, you know'. – 'Happy Gaynor was there, the first time in years – it could only be that the priest said something to him to buck him up'. – 'Did you see Paddy Gannon and the dirty shirt on him? – that lazy bitch of a wife of his ought to be ashamed of herself, letting him off to Mass like that'. – 'And what about that upstart, Callaghan, up in the front seat among the bigshots? – bigshots with a dot over the eye, that is, if you could class the Caseys as bigshots'. – 'And did you see that wastrel, Mick McQuaid, marching up the middle aisle as bold as brass, and he just coming out o' jail'?

Mass was a meeting place, and many topics not pertaining to the Faith, from football to the latest scandals, were discussed in whispered conversations during the course of its solemnity, gossip which continued afterwards as the congregation dallied outside to make sure they gained full benefit from their attendance. As a result, the scene of money jingling on collection plates, farmers haggling with their labourers before paying up, women swapping hatching turkeys and clocking-hens, poteen-makers delivering their product in the safety of the crowd, jobbers discussing the price of livestock, and the covetous eyes of others blatantly breaking the ninth commandment, could in a sense be compared to the debasement that Christ had condemned in the Temple: 'My house is a house of God, but you have made it a den of thieves'. Jack fell easily into this type of hypocrisy, for Mary O'Hara, married or single, was sure to be there, and if he was honest with himself, it was his only reason for attending.

By the time he reached the church, the service had already begun and, easing through the phalanx of latecomers crowding in the vestibule, he found standing room at the back. As it was Palm Sunday, there was extra pomp, the bells for the consecration were muffled, and incense drifted languidly towards the dome as three purple-robed priests, assisted by an entourage of servers in white surplices and black soutanes presided over the great drama of High Mass. The added solemnity had a chastening effect on the congregation, and there was less throat-clearing and restless shuffling.

A glance around showed that the old order was still being maintained, the wealthy and their offspring, representing the Pharisees in the Gospel, appropriating the front pews in the chancel, as if their worldly status entitled them to be nearer in the flesh to their eternal reward, relegating the lesser luminaries to the transepts, and farther back towards the door crowded the rank and file of the faithful. Bull Paisley's presence in one of the front pews, besides rekindling his animosity, evoked a passage from the Scripture of the day when the sons of God came forth to present themselves before the Lord, and Satan came also among them, although the excerpt froze in his mind when the congregation rose for the Gospel and his eyes picked out Mary O'Hara.

Beautifully pregnant in a flowing blue maternity dress Mary was in the pew in front of Paisley, standing beside a stocky, balding man in a tweed suit, whom he presumed was her husband. As his fondest dream drifted away in the incense rising from the thuribles, the wound in his heart, which the years had scarred over, bled afresh, although strangely the pain didn't linger, as if the antidote of time was at last winning the battle. Still, he couldn't tear his eyes away, and in between acts of kneeling and standing he made a more comprehensive study of the couple. Even allowing that he was making his appraisal from sidelong glances it was plain to see that the man was older than Mary, much older. His receding dark hair was flecked with grey and his face, which was screwed up in an expression of solemnity, looked as if it had seen its fair share of summers, although this was offset somewhat by his erect bearing and air of refinement.

After the final three Hail Marys Jack dallied outside, watching silently as the congregation braved the chill spring air, slowly, tentatively, like hens emerging from the coop in the morning, pecking in the holy water stoup with their forefingers and making hurried signs of the cross that didn't look like signs of the cross at all, and now that the mystery of the service had receded, they began to chat cheerily and greet friends. When Mary appeared in the doorway on the arm of her husband, he felt his heart miss a beat and then quicken to catch up, and at a glance he could see that pregnancy wasn't suiting her. Her face was thin, her features drawn, her lips compressed as if she was fighting some inner pain, and the black circles encompassing her eyes brought to mind a half-remembered tale of putting pennies on the eyes of the dead. As she advanced towards him, he ran his eyes over her face, searching for what, he did not know, which he did not find, and for a fleeting moment she held his gaze. Then, without even a flicker of recognition, she looked away as if they had never met.

Her husband, a stranger to Jack, was making much to-do of being the attentive father-to-be, and in the sunlight he looked older than he had first estimated, forty if he was a day. Although he was short in stature he carried himself with an air of authority, and his narrowed eyes bore the unflinching gaze of one whose fortunate lot had always been to command and be obeyed. This characteristic quickly manifested itself as he boorishly pushed his way through the encirclement of scattered groups, guiding Mary by the arm to a blue Jaguar and, as the car accelerated away, the gravel spewing from beneath its rear wheels confirmed the arrogance he had already perceived in his bearing.

Jack continued to stare in the car's wake until it was out of sight, his mind reconciled to the turn of events and, as it had still some minutes to go before the public houses opened, he loitered awhile, shaking hands with old friends, and they were literally old friends – grey heads, stooped shoulders, weather-beaten faces. Others, older still, almost bent to the ground with rheumatism, were hobbling on sticks, with just a scattering of youth among them, their rosy cheeks and boyish faces, some of which had yet to sprout stubble, all the more conspicuous among the wizened ones. To anyone who didn't know that half of Ireland's population was under twenty-one and most of the remainder over fifty, the generation gap would be indeed baffling, like the middle rungs missing on a ladder, although Jack wasn't baffled, for he had seen the missing rungs outside the churches in London, all youthful and healthy, the men, keen-eyed and erect; the women, pretty and vivacious.

Afterwards in Grogan's, he was swamped in the customary gra-mo-chroi adulations. "It's fresh and well you're lookin' ould stock – them few years in England done you no harm at all – when are you going back?" ran the greetings, and their speculation as to whether he had put on or lost weight always resulted in it being for his good. It was only when he set about renewing old friendships that he began to see through the shell of their false welcome, and though they drank his health every time he bought a round, he could feel himself being eased out of the conversation.

As the morning made towards afternoon, the cold shoulder he had sensed earlier was more discernible, so much so that he felt like an alien among them, as alien as if he had come from another planet, speaking a language they did not understand and he not understanding theirs and, lapsing into a pensive mood, his thoughts returned to Mary O'Hara. Save for a glimmer of surprised recognition in her eyes, she had looked through him and beyond him, as if he was some bodiless image from the past, a blink on her memory which, now that he had time to think of it, was a slap in the face for all the years he had spent spinning brightly-coloured fantasies of her that bore not the slightest touch of reality. In his daydreams he had created the perfect woman, dressed her in the finest clothes, told her what to think, to think as he wanted her to think, how to behave, how to smile, how to comfort him, no guiles, no wiles, sugar and spice and all things nice; he went to bed with her every night and woke up with her every morning, fantasies far sweeter than real life could ever be. She had been his Helen of Troy, although now that the years had taken their toll, she would be lucky if the remnants of her beauty launched a rowing boat, not to mind a thousand ships.

"And turning away they're sour, says he, such trash is not the food for me," he quoted to himself and, smiling sardonically, he turned away like the fox in the fable and wended his way homewards.

Later that night when he returned to Grogan's, he was made to swallow several doses of the same two-faced medicine and forced to listen to the old-timers rambling on about the good old days, a topic that had become tiresome from repetition, for seemingly forgotten in the mists of wistful reminiscing were the good old days when they had washed sheep's daggings for just a few coppers' worth of wool, or went from door to door collecting jam jars, or mixed dried cowshite with the tobacco to make it more plentiful, or the days when they had slaved in all kinds of weather just to keep body and soul together. It was hard to imagine that those were the days the old-timers wished to bring back, or perhaps they were just pining for their lost youth. It was no different in London where many were still claiming that the War years were the best years of their lives, when they spent their nights in damp, overcrowded air-raid shelters and woke in the morning to face death and near-starvation.

Sitting alone on a high stool at a corner of the counter he tried to make some sense of it all. Perhaps he was looking for too much out of life, or perhaps life might be different in another town, and yet, when it was time for the dance and he stepped out on the short walk to the Phoenix, some of his earlier animation returned, the years rolling back as the music blaring through its open windows reached his ears.

The addition of neon lighting around the sign outside gave the Phoenix a nightclub type of façade, and when he entered, the whole hall was swinging to the Buddy Holly hit *I GUESS IT DOESN'T MATTER ANY MORE*. It was darker and noisier than in the old days, so dark that he couldn't find the cloakroom which had been resited, and so noisy that he had to shout when asking directions. The guitar and keyboard lead, which had replaced the trumpet and saxophone, gave the music a different tone, and the crowd was younger, so young that he failed to recognise a face. Still, in the midst of the hustle and bustle, noise and smoke, it seemed somewhat ironic that he should recall his remark to Eileen when she was making her comeback after a lapse of the same number of years: 'it's the creaky gate that always gets oiled'.

Now that the roles were reversed, Jack felt like the creaky gate among the younger generation, although whether or not he got oiled was in the lap of the gods. The dancing too lacked discipline, all bumping and shoving, and every time he took the floor he was asked if he could jive, at which he made clumsy attempts.

It was only when the tempo slowed that he could see any semblance of the old days. The revolving coloured lights reflecting on the glitter balls still spun their magic, and couples danced cheek to cheek, locked in wonderland, a wonderland that he himself had once known. It brought back memories, so many memories that he found himself looking back, back to the good old days like the people he ridiculed, sinning against one of his own commandments. If he was ever to go forward, he would have to set his mind against the past, for there was no bringing back the past, no more than there was of changing it, and if he kept looking back, he would do nothing else but look back. Strangely, for the first time he could see the moral in the story of Rip Van Winkle: life moves on, the young soon become the old, the future – the present, the present – the past, and now that another of his dreams was shattered, a long unbroken dream of things that might have been, it was time to lock away his reminiscences of the Phoenix in his memory chest with his other sentimental souvenirs.

Next morning Jack was up with the birds. It was decision time. The big question was, did he have to go ahead with the piggery, and if so, what then? Was there a future? Would he find the happiness that had so far eluded him? Common sense told him to play it by ear for a while; no one knew of his plans, save for Eileen, and she could be silenced.

Still, even with all that was on his mind, Mary O'Hara kept intruding on his reverie, and if for nothing else, she was an incentive for him to make a success of his venture, just to show her that he had it in him. He had discreetly found out that her husband was Henry Cooke, a solicitor from Mayo, who was practising in Castleford with her father, and she was expecting their third child, which would account for her lack of sparkle. Cooke looked the possessive type, and by adhering to the proverb: *keep her belly full and her feet bare and she'll never leave you,* he was making sure that she didn't sparkle in case she escaped from his clutches. It was a typical case of the young wife and the older, wiser husband, the professional marriage in which there is no room for stars in the eyes. Although he had expected at least a nod of recognition from her he wasn't bitter, just slightly annoyed at his own obstinate blindness that refused to see her as she really was and the years he had spent being miserable over her, or as Pat had once philosophised: 'you can convince a fool of anything but his own folly'.

Still, he had another option, something Eileen had unwittingly mentioned – he could sell up and return to London, although the idea struck a disagreeable chord. The piggery was his brainchild, the ambition that had kept his hopes alive through so many dark days, and now that he had overcome most of the obstacles, throwing in the towel would be akin to a jockey pulling up a horse before the winning post when he had the race at his mercy. He could always set about the basics, the defects that needed putting right even if he decided to sell, and the neighbours would be none the wiser as to his intentions.

While he was giving the matter its full measure of deliberation, it seemed odd that Widow Kilbane's advice should filter into his reverie – a prudent businessman always keeps his ideas private until it serves his purpose to make them public. Over the weekend he had called on most of his neighbours, and though their greetings were cordial and full of encouragement to stay, hypocrisy exuded between the lines. Strangely, none of them mentioned the Land Commission, which suggested they had something to hide.

The initial stages of his project entailed making one field of his nine acres, and he began by loading the stones from the dividing walls on to the trailer and stacking them in the yard for use later in the building of the pigsties. Afterwards he planned to plant oats, barley and potatoes to supplement the pig meal, and use the straw for bedding, although most essentially he needed electricity, a pump for running water, and a new septic tank. Also, the cottage needed dry-lining, the roof needed attention, and the outer walls needed rendering. It wasn't long into the morning before he realised he would need help, permanent help, if he was to keep to his schedule of having his first sows littered by October and his first consignment of pigs ready for sale in the following spring.

His train of thought was interrupted when he spied a lone tinker woman approaching Murt Burke's cottage, which was in his field of vision. The cottage, because it was in a hollow, looked low and stunted, and there was no sign of Murt or any telltale smoke spiralling from the chimney, although this was no cause for concern as Murt seldom rose before nine. The tinker woman, who seemed to know her way around, wasn't slinking, and he followed her progress with his eyes until she reached the front door. After a succession of loud raps the door opened, and it remained open just long enough for him to catch a glimpse of Murt standing on the threshold in his bare feet, holding up his long johns with one hand and scratching his arse with the other and, as soon as the woman slipped through, the door closed behind them.

Burning with curiosity he moved down the slope towards the gate where the woman would have to pass on her way back and, as the minutes ticked by – five, fifteen, thirty – he waited patiently. He was about to return to his work when the door opened, and the woman came hurrying towards him, checking her stride when she noticed his presence. "The top o' the morning t'you!" he hailed jovially.

"And to you, sir! I just called to see if the good man o' the house wanted anythin', poor craither," returned the woman so readily that it fuelled Jack's suspicion as to the real purpose of her visit. She was young, twenty-five at the most, stoutly built, blunt of feature, smoky of complexion, her eyes shifty, her face unwashed. She was shabbily clad in a loose-fitting grey dress which was dappled with grease stains, and the few wisps of her hair that peeped out from under her plaid shawl were mousy in colour, reminding him of the curtains in his bedroom that had once been brown but which had hung on the window so long that most of the colour had been bleached out of them by the sun.

"And did he?" asked Jack, wrinkling his nose at the whiff of smoky stench from her body, the same stench which perhaps made horses bare their teeth.

"No – not today, sir," she replied and, allowing her shawl to hang loosely to show that she had no ill-gotten goods on her person, she hurried away.

"Isn't Murt the sly ould bastard now – so the rumours were true all along," mused Jack, and he was so cock-a-hoop that he felt like heading for Galway and confronting Eileen with his evidence. Still, at the back of his mind, he knew that Eileen, even if she had seen it with her own eyes, would search and search until she found a plausible reason for the visit other than the obvious.

Later in the morning, when Murt arrived to drive off his sheep, he was his usual taciturn self and made no mention of his visitor. "God bless the work, Jack – you must've been at it early," he hailed, when he noticed the progress.

"And so were you – at it early," returned Jack, in an undertone. "As you can see, I'm making one big field out o' the lot – this way it'll be easier to turn the tractor. I'm going to sow all corn, and maybe a few spuds. The soil should be better now after its few years lying fallow."

"You'll have a job to make a livin' out o' just that, Jack."

"Who knows, I might do up the whole place and sell it, and besides, I've got another idea in my head."

Not long before Murt made his appearance Jack had fought a decisive battle in his mind – should he stay, or should he put the place up for sale? If he sold, he could make a pretence of returning to England and, after a few weeks when everyone believed he was across the Irish Sea, he could come back some night and give Paisley a good hiding with a piece of lead pipe – London style. However, he had decided that this wasn't his way. To gain any real satisfaction he would have to find Big Jimbo Maughan and hammer the truth out of him in front of witnesses which, if it did nothing else, would put the skids under Paisley, make him sweat, and perhaps later he could figure out some way of hitting him in the pocket. An opportunity was sure to present itself, and besides, he had Kathy Moore to think of.

Chapter 3

In the following days, in order to keep to his schedule, Jack found himself working from dawn till dark and, as for company, he might as well have been on Crusoe's desert island. The tradition of going visiting at night had all but died away, save for Murt Burke and Jim Madden, who went to Michael Joyce's, now that the last of Joyce's family had taken the well-trodden path eastwards. Emigration had almost completed its grim task, Peter Costello, Ann and Jimmy Kennedy, and many others of the younger generation having fallen before its blade, while the other, more deadly reaper was stealthily making inroads into the older generation, so much so that it was now possible for the whole community to congregate in Joyce's kitchen.

Nevertheless, like the ill wind blowing good for someone, the exodus had inadvertently eased the burden on those left behind, and the money coming from their offspring in England brought the first signs of prosperity to the village. Scarcely a week went by without the postman calling, until even the most ardent advocates of the dogma that the best son stays at home, the next best son goes to America, and the sweepings go to England had to grudgingly admit that the stamp bearing the Queen's head was a far more reliable harbinger of money than spiders or itchy palms. Any time the older generation came up short, all they had to do was write to someone or other of the family in the land of the fish and chips and subtly hint at hard times – the hard-up parents who had worked their fingers to the bone for them – and their entreaties would not be ignored, although little did the exiles realise that in the event of anything coming up for grabs in the family, their largesse would be as past tense as water under the bridge.

Almost every home had electricity, some had cars, new houses were springing up, the old ones left to fall in, and many of the old establishments, including Pudding Joyce's eating house, were giving way to more modern enterprise. In growing up Jack had developed a love of poor people which he could not have conceived if he had not been poor himself. He had learned that when people are poor, they still have the impulse to give, to share with those in the same circumstances. However, in the new prosperity brought about by mass-emigration, he noticed that his neighbours had become more cagey and aloof, and the camaraderie of the old days was gradually disappearing, never to return.

After a night or two listening to Murt Burke grunting and Jim Madden telling the same old tales Jack spent his nights in Castleford, mostly in Grogan's, where he put the word about that he was looking for a helper. The type he had in mind was an intelligent youth, someone whom he could mould into something of himself, and in time be capable of taking on responsibility. What he didn't want was a malingerer, someone who had to be driven, someone who would lie awake all night concocting excuses rather than getting on with the job. Nevertheless, even in a country on its knees from endless recession, he soon found that the latter category was the only type available, usually the shakings of the bag left behind in the cull, mammy's boys who were bluffing their parents with sham threats of joining the exodus, while the parents, fearing that they might be left alone in their old age, surrendered to their every whim. Driven to desperation, one night he brought the matter to Mick Grogan's attention.

"It's all the parents' fault," Grogan explained, holding up the glass he was polishing to the light. "Most mothers have developed a habit of hangin' on to the youngest of the family like a pet lamb, mollycoddlin' them until they're good for nothing. Others try to live their own lives again through their children – don't make the same mistakes as I made – mother knows best, and the more pretentious ones nag their sons into joinin' the priesthood so they can show off in front o' their neighbours – we have a priest in the family. So you see, Jack, when it comes to holy orders, it's really the parents who have the vocation; that's why there are so many Irish priests and nuns in the world, not to mention the money that's in it. They have themselves brainwashed into believin' that their own children are somethin' else – they live on expectations, and the ones who have influence push them into top jobs that they're not fit to do. So, it would appear that whoever said that children should look up to their parents, not as an example, but as a warning, wasn't far off the mark. That's what you're up against and, as for mentionin' a shovel to them, forget it."

"Is it as bad as all that, Mick?"

"Yes – but I'll see what I can do."

On the following Saturday night Grogan introduced Jack to Martin Finnegan, a young man from Baronsfield cottages on the outskirts of Castleford. Tall and loosely-built Finnegan looked the type who was used to hard work, although his boyish face showed only the barest trace of stubble. He had a thick mop of ginger hair which overflowed his ears like a tea cosy, and he was so pale of complexion that it seemed his hair had drawn all the colour from his face. His small blue eyes were set closely together and were considerably at variance with his broad angular features, high forehead and full lips, as if God's attention had been distracted for an instant during his creation, and though he was neat of appearance, his hand-me-down navy-blue suit, which hung loosely on his bony frame, a white shirt, frayed at the collar and cuffs, and scuffed, down-at-heel black shoes, told the tale of his means.

Taking a leaf from the Irish ganger's book Jack explained what was expected of him, pulling no punches. "Well, that's it," he said. "So, what d'you think – have you any questions to ask?"

"I could do with the job badly, sir," returned Finnegan, his eyes alive with enthusiasm. "That's if you'll have me."

"But I never said what the wages were," said Jack. "I don't expect you to work for nothing – but next to it will do."

Finnegan laughed, exposing a gapped set of strong yellow teeth. "Give me what I'm worth," he said. "Mick said you were a straight man and that's good enough for me."

"What do they pay these days for a week's work, leaving out all the praise and the 'God spare you the healths'?" Jack asked. "For instance, what would the likes o' Bull Paisley pay for a five and a half day week?"

"About seven quid a week, I suppose. But I don't want that much, sir – just whatever you think I'm worth."

Jack stifled a smile, certain now that he had found his man. "You can have the job, and I'll start you off at seven quid a week, eight till half-five Monday to Friday, and a half day on Saturday, and I'll pay you extra for overtime," he explained. "But don't think I'm doing you any favours, because you'll earn every penny of it. The only snag is, I don't need you till Monday week, if that's all right with you."

"Jasus, that'll be mighty, sir," returned Finnegan, rubbing his palms together vigorously as though he intended to produce a spark from them, and yet, Jack discerned a shade of scepticism in his eyes, as if he thought it was too good to be true.

"So, let's shake on it, and we'll say no more till I see you at eight o'clock on Monday morning week," said Jack. "Just one more thing – I'd prefer if you called me Jack. The 'sir' word is a bit too strong, seeing as I've yet to be knighted. In the first place I'm not rich enough to be a knight, I don't take drugs, I don't perjure myself in court, I'm not a thief, I don't associate with prostitutes, I'm not a flasher, and I have yet to kill a wild boar with my bare hands, not to mention committing buggery, although I sometimes wonder how many knights and their ladies fair would be left if they were disqualified on those grounds. Still, a knighthood is no load to carry, for the simple reason that a judge in a law court'll always give you the benefit of the doubt. Your word is sacrosanct, as if it came from the lips of Christ Himself, because a knight of the realm isn't supposed to lie – it's against all the principles of the Order of the Garter. So, now that we've sorted out the business end, what are you having to drink?"

Although Finnegan was a likeable chap Jack decided to keep him at arm's length, as familiarity might defeat the effort and, after they had toasted the success of their future relationship, he moved on to the Royal Hotel.

Standing out prominently at the convergence of streets in the centre of town the Royal Hotel was a popular haunt for Castleford's bourgeoisie and, as it was Saturday night, the carpeted lounge was crowded with their pretentious presence. The men, all smartly turned out in suits and ties, were standing in groups at the bar, while their wives, wearing the latest fashion, were seated at the surrounding tables, their forced gaiety and high-pitched laughter paraphrasing their conceit. The air was full of the scent of expensive perfume mingling with cigar smoke, and when space was grudgingly yielded to him at the counter, Jack ordered whiskey, his intention being to knock it back and move on. As he was about to put the glass to his lips, he felt the hairs on the nape of his neck prickling, and when instinctively he looked around, his eyes were drawn to a group standing in the centre of the room, Paisley obtrusive among them, his big head sticking up like a castrated old tup among a flock of young wethers.

Save for the odd glimpse he had caught of him at Mass, he hadn't seen Paisley since his return and, making a discreet perusal of him over the rim of his glass, he observed that easy living had taken its toll on his once muscular frame, which was now fat, whiskey was showing on his face, and the hard line of his jaw was obscured by an unhealthy bloat. Although he looked as odious as ever, wealth is always respected, and though he was out of earshot, his body language suggested he was argumentatively dominating the conversation.

When inevitably their eyes met, the contempt in Paisley's stare sent Jack's nerves humming with hate, just as they had hummed on the day in Grogan's when he had slighted Eileen's virtue, and a whole volcano of vengeful feelings erupted in his breast. Unable to contain himself he felt like having it out with him there and then until a warning voice whispering in his ear hinted at prudence. Knocking back his drink he turned to the door, and when he reached the street, the cool night air brought a measure of calm to his turbulent mind.

Easter brought the sun, and the spring madness in the air had as an accompaniment the blithe chirping of the songbirds, a chorus which was discordantly disrupted by jackdaws squawking, horses whinnying, and donkeys braying, their desire in harmony if not their refrain. Jack too was suffering from spring madness, for ever since Kathy Moore's visit he was finding it hard to keep her off his mind. However, as if there was some truth in thinking of the Devil as there is in speaking of him, on Sunday afternoon, as he was dozing in his armchair, he was startled into wakefulness by the gate creaking open and a shadow in the doorway blocking the light. When he recognised his visitor, he came quickly to his feet. "Come in, Kathy," he greeted, blinking the sleep from his eyes.

The draught from the open doorway was wrapping Kathy's light-blue dress round her legs and thighs, accentuating their outline in every detail, and she lingered on the threshold longer than was necessary, as though she was conscious of its effect, while Jack, his covetous eyes glued to her seductive pose, drooled over her, like a half-starved dog would water over a haunch of meat in a butcher's window. Finally, he took a small gift-wrapped package from the mantelpiece, saying: "I have a present for you, Kathy, just a small token of my appreciation for all you've done for me."

"Oh, you shouldn't, Jack!" exclaimed Kathy, carefully stripping the wrapping from the package, and when she saw the gold chain and ruby pendant, she rushed forward and planted a kiss on his lips, lingering just long enough for her perfume and feminine fragrance to work it sorcery. "It's beautiful, but you shouldn't – there was no need to go to such expense."

"It's the least I could do, Kathy," said Jack. "I owe you a lot more than that, and nobody knows better than myself – I'd have nothing to come back to if it wasn't for you."

Putting the pendant back in the box Kathy pulled up a chair, and in the act of straddling it back to front, hobby-horse fashion, the edge of the seat caught the hem of her dress and dragged it halfway up her bare thighs. Even when she noticed Jack politely averting his gaze, she made no effort to correct the indecorum. "I suppose you're all set for the wedding next week, Jack," she said, smiling in a manner which suggested there was more to read between the lines.

"Yes – it looks as if it'll be the wedding of the year. But tell me this, Kathy – what's that cheolawn of a sister of mine thinking about at all, marrying that – that ould – no, I won't be vulgar?"

"Why does any woman marry? She's in love, of course – goose. But I suppose if you believed that, you'd believe anything."

Kathy, her skin unblemished save for a few freckles on the arms and shoulders, was a picture of health, and when she rose from her chair to do the washing-up, Jack followed her every movement as she flitted from the dresser, to the back-kitchen, to the table, her dress swirling, wrapping and clinging, his imagination running riot, until the provocation became too much for him to bear. "Here – let me give you a hand," he said, and in one false stumble she was in his arms.

It was as if the clock had been turned back five years, and before he quite realised it Kathy's tongue was halfway down his throat and she was kissing him passionately on the lips, exactly as she had done on that long-ago night. Again, he found his hands sliding down over her hips, fondling and squeezing, gently at first, and then more forcefully. Opportunity was knocking for the second time, and the more his fingers dug into the soft flesh of her buttocks, the more desire took control of his senses.

Easing breathlessly from the embrace Kathy cast an uneasy glance at the open doorway. "The door, Jack – put the bolt on the door. You never know who might walk in," she cautioned, and when Jack did as he was bidden, she allowed herself to be back-pedalled to his bedroom where the inevitable became reality on top of the feather bed.

Even after nature had taken its course there was still lust in Kathy's kiss, and she persisted, kissing and fondling, until Jack was aroused for the second time. There was no modesty, and the natural way she positioned herself, knees up, thighs apart, betrayed a wealth of experience in the field of sexual pursuit. When he was astride her again, he set his mind to wondering where it was all leading to, or was this what Martin King meant when he said that he was a lucky man?

"I know what you're thinking, Jack, but you're wrong," said Kathy, breaking in on his reverie. "I know you're thinking I'm a fast piece – a good trotter, as you men say – but I'm not, not that fast anyway. You see, I saved myself for you like I promised."

The deceleration in Jack's rhythm, as if he was having none of her overtures of fidelity, forced Kathy to pause. "Not altogether," she laughed, "because it's hard for a woman to keep her virginity and all the men trying to get inside your knickers. But I was faithful to you in my mind, and I feel I owe myself this for waiting so long. You were always the man in my dreams ever since I found out what women were put on this earth for. There was something about you that always attracted me, because I'm like you – I don't believe in all this religion lark either – it's too hard to digest. It's something like the wise old owl that lived in the oak and the more he heard the less he spoke – the older I get, the less I believe."

"You shouldn't live your life in dreams, Kathy," returned Jack, now that he could speak from experience. "Nothing ever comes of dreams only disappointment."

"You're wrong, Jack. Everyone should have a dream, and you were always mine," countered Kathy. "You might well ask yourself why I'm doing this and I engaged and, but why shouldn't I sow my wild oats like you men do before I get married and, if you're wondering why I'm going to marry Michael McCale and not one of my own class, I'll put it like this. I saw what being a small farmer's wife did to mother – a child every year and old before her time. Can you blame me for that?"

"No – I can't say as I blame you, but don't you think you're being unfair to your fiancé?"

"No – if he had the chance, he'd be doing it too behind my back," returned Kathy, breaking off in a long gasp and bringing her knees up into an even more compromising position as Jack's rhythm quickened again, more forcefully now. "Oh-oh – o-oh – I'm enjoying this; phew, phew! – you're powerful," she panted, as he grunted his way to his satisfaction.

Lying side by side on top of the bed, the draught from the doorway soothing the parts of their bodies where they had earlier cooled their passion, Jack wasn't sure whether or not to be pleased, although Kathy, whose thoughts seemed to be on the same wavelength, quickly put his mind at ease.

"I know you, men – you hate to be tied down. So, don't feel under any obligation. As I've told you, I'm engaged to Michael McCale, but I never let him do this to me – you can believe me there. But the manager of Moon's – yes – sometimes. If I let Michael do it to me, he'd never marry me – he wouldn't have to then," she explained, giggling as she set about arousing Jack for the third time without success.

"It's like flogging a dead horse," laughed Jack, when Kathy finally threw in the towel.

"Whoever heard of anyone flogging a dead horse?" returned Kathy, the mischievous twinkle in her eye confirming that there would be another day. "But I have to go now, otherwise we'll have the neighbours talking."

Jack perceived from Kathy's behaviour that she was determined to get the most out of life like some women he had known in London and, as he watched her pulling up her knickers without a modicum of bashfulness, he found it hard to believe. Kathy Moore – sweet, innocent Kathy, as he had once thought.

Before she left Kathy planted a quick kiss on Jack's lips, saying: "I'll see you at the wedding on Thursday. If you come up on the early bus, you can stay over on Thursday night at Eileen's. As you know, Eileen won't be there – just yours truly and her two lodgers – and maybe I'll let you in on a secret when the wedding is over."

After the wedding Eileen moved into Cullinane's farmhouse in Aughamore, across the bog from Jack. Although Cullinane looked as suave as ever the addition to his years had lessened considerably the spring in his step, no matter how much he tried to conceal it, and yet, as if it was a peculiarity of nature, the eye quickly adjusts to the new image until all memories of the old image are obliterated from the mind. One happy family, Kathy had laughed: Cullinane and his son, Trevor; Eileen and her son, Jimmy. Trevor, who was about the same age as his new stepmother, had always walked in his father's shadow, taking more after his mother who had been rich, beautiful and empty-headed, and though up to now he had been his father's sole heir, he didn't seem to resent the marriage. If anything, he seemed pleased, for he got on well with Eileen, as if she was the sister he never had. He was placid more than simple-minded, although many would argue that he was a card or two short of the full deck.

However, if the wedding reception was anything to go by, it was far from a happy family, at least not on the groom's side, for Cullinane's brothers, sisters and their offspring could not reconcile themselves to the fact that he had married beneath him, and at every opportunity they turned their resentful eyes on Jack, as if his scheming was to blame. In sadistic fashion Jack went out of his way to exacerbate their displeasure, adding insult to injury by shaking hands with Mike and Trevor more times than would be considered normal, as if to cement the unification of the families, underlining the handshakes with sly grins and winks.

In the following weeks Kathy called regularly at Jack's cottage, mostly on Sunday mornings before last Mass to give her visits the appearance of a continuation of her old routine. True to her word about letting him in on a secret, she disclosed that Eileen was pregnant by another man at the time of her wedding, a handsome stranger who had lodged with her for a few weeks and moved on, and she was planning to pass the child off as Cullinane's. Now that the real reason for her marriage had come to light, Jack could see the funny side, and what a dark horse Eileen was to have thought of it.

Kathy was an intoxicating mixture of temptress and angel: temptress in the manner in which she flaunted her natural attributes, angel inasmuch as she was kind-hearted and selfless, and yet, for all her pretences of gentility there was a wild streak in her. She was forward, almost too forward, and she was outspoken on matters which most people would consider to be immoral. Usually women were secretive about their sexual affairs, and a stack of bibles wouldn't get them to admit that there had been more than one man in their lives. Even then, it was always something that had happened when they were very young, at a time when they didn't know what life was all about, and they were always at their hottest when defending their virtue as cowards are their courage, and liars their veracity. Still, it was a relationship without romance or love, from which the novelty soon wears off, although for Jack it saved him from having to jump in the river just to get a drink of water, as he had earlier remarked to Eileen.

Kathy, for all that she was nice to look at, was intelligent too, which suggested it wasn't for her looks alone that she had been made a manageress of her company. She seemed to have a finger on the pulse of things, and by and by she explained all about the Land Commission. No one in the village knew who had reported his absence, one suspected the other, and when statements were required, they had no option but to tell the truth, especially when telling the truth might be to their benefit. Now they were burying their heads in the sand.

Although Jack was pleased to know that the community as a whole wasn't involved, there was still a Judas in their midst, but now that he had put the wheels of his enterprise in motion, it wasn't important any more.

Martin Finnegan, his assistant, surpassed all expectations, and he worked silently, patiently and competently. Nothing seemed to excite or surprise him and, as he had worked on and off for farmers, he had first-hand knowledge of pig breeding. He was easy to get on with because he had so little to say, and yet, he was an understanding listener when Jack explained the end product of their labour. He was astute too, and for all his air of indifference Jack sensed that he knew all about the killing of his stock and that he was holding Paisley responsible.

Despite the progress being made on all fronts another problem kept obtruding, a problem that would not go away until it was addressed: the housework, and if for nothing else, Jack missed his sister for her culinary proficiency. The days when he could rely on one of his neighbours to send a daughter to help had long since passed, although it never occurred to him that his neighbours hadn't a daughter left to send, and so he was forced to spend more and more valuable time on the domestic chores, besides doing the cooking.

"This'll have to stop, Martin," he grumbled, one lunchtime as he tried to get his teeth into a tough piece of steak, while Martin, sitting at the opposite end of the table, kept chewing and chewing without comment. "I asked Hopkins, the butcher, for the best, and this is what he sent out – cow steak – the yellow fat on it is a sure sign. They say he buys ould cows and drives them into the slaughterhouse in the middle o' the night so no one'll see them – then he mixes the meat with the prime stuff. That's why he always asks: 'Is it for boiling or roasting you want it'?" he went on, cursing Hopkins. "And I'm sure you can guess where the good beef and steak goes – to the doctors and solicitors and up to the bishop's palace and the presbytery."

To add to his burden his cottage was becoming dirtier by the day, and so disagreeably familiar were the stains on the curtains, the grimy windows, the dust, and the smell of sour milk that he felt something should be done about it besides taking a wife as Martin's expression seemed to suggest any time he drew down the subject.

The last straw came next day when a lump of soot came thundering down the chimney, hopped off the hearth, and landed smack in the middle of the pan as he was frying the steak. "That's it! We'll have to get a woman to do the cooking and tidy the place up!" he exclaimed, flicking the fragments of soot out of the pan with a fork. "Have you any ideas there, Martin? And another thing I'll say while I'm at it – if someone ran off with the frying pan, the two of us'd die with the hunger for sure."

Martin, who wasn't one for answering a question without first giving it its full measure of deliberation, aided by a scratch of his ginger mop, was silent for a moment. "I don't know anybody that'd suit," he said finally. "If it was in the town, it'd be different. You see, you've got the two-mile journey to think about, and you know yourself what they're like in the town – the first shower o' rain and it'd be an excuse for them not to turn up."

"What if I put an ad in the *Herald*, a box number so no one'll know who's doing the hiring, and explain that it's two miles from town?"

"It's worth a chance, and you've got nothin' to lose only the money for the ad."

"I'll scribble out the ad now before I forget, and Martin, finish early this evening so you'll get to the *Herald* office before it shuts, and then it'll be in this week's edition.

There were two replies to the advertisement: a Mrs Fox and a Mrs Regan, and when Martin couldn't throw any light on either of the applicants, Jack took them in alphabetical order. On the morning of the first interview, expecting some skivvy type with housemaid's knee and nylons hanging limply, he nearly choked on his tea when a tall, slender lady appeared in the doorway. Middle or late twenties she had sharp imposing features, olive skin, green eyes, and her short jet-black hair was smoothed back so fiercely from her forehead and so sternly repressed by hairpins that no vagrant tendrils escaped. Her grey three-quarter-length skirt, white blouse, and black cardigan gave her a clerical air, and Jack's first impression was of one who had recently left the nuns.

Perhaps perceiving the scepticism in Jack's eyes the lady immediately took the initiative. "My name is Ann Fox, Mister Daly – it is Mister Daly I'm speaking to, I presume?" she said. "I have no previous experience only that of a housewife. But I can wash, clean, cook and sew."

Candour was something Jack admired, although he still found it hard to associate the lady with domestic drudgery. "Sit down for a minute, Missus Fox, and give your eyes a treat so you can see what you're up against," he said. "It means you'll have to run the domestic side, washing, ironing, shopping, cooking – you name it. It's a bit rough-and-ready, as you can see, so if you want to have second thoughts."

"The work doesn't worry me – it's something else," returned the lady. "I'm a widow, and I have two daughters, aged five and six. They're both going to school and I'd like to work hours that would suit their coming and going – would that be a problem?"

Jack smiled wryly – widows seemed to be part of his life, and yet, when his searching glance reached the bottom of the lady's worried eyes, his expression changed, gentleness and understanding coming over his face. "Suitable hours, I take it, would mean that you come here when you leave the children at school in the morning, and then be back in time to pick them up in the evening," he said. "I can't see any problem there if you think you can do the work."

"I can do the job all right, and if I can't, you can always get rid of me," the lady replied matter-of-factly. "I can work from ten in the morning till three in the afternoon, and as long as you like on Saturday, that is, if I can bring the children. I'd like to have Sundays off, and I'm ready to start tomorrow morning."

"For the five days and till one o'clock on Saturday, I can pay you four pounds a week – how would that suit you?"

"Oh, that'll be grand, only I have one more question."

"Fire away!"

"The children'll be getting holidays from school soon, and I was wondering if I could bring them with me for the duration – I'll make sure they keep out of your way."

Jack smiled benignly. "I can't see anything wrong with that," he said. "But one question from me – do I call you Ann or Missus Fox? Jack is my name – Jack Daly, but everyone calls me Jack. I have a helper, Martin Finnegan, but we'll be outside most o' the time."

"Call me Ann," the lady returned, and the sigh of what seemed relief that escaped from her lips wasn't lost on her new employer.

"So, I'll be seeing you tomorrow morning – Ann," said Jack, leading her to the door and, as he watched her cycling away, something in her erect bearing and the determined set of her slender shoulders put paid to the last of his misgivings.

Chapter 4

As the days of spring raced into summer, the new team, a compromise of opposites, went to work, and though everything was going according to plan, Jack was silent, brooding and taciturn. His eyes, which had once held a humorous twinkle, were now hard, and he carried a chip on his shoulder that no one cared to disturb. Turning the tables on Paisley was his only incentive, and yet, even in the event that Paisley dropped dead, he doubted that it would raise his spirits, or perhaps Paisley was just a symbol of the hypocritical society that allowed his ilk to flourish.

Once the wheels of his enterprise were in motion Jack shifted more of the workload on to Martin Finnegan's shoulders, not in a way that was noticeable, but through a telepathy of minds thinking alike. Kathy Moore called every Sunday, and though they used the utmost discretion in keeping the affair secret, Jack knew that even if they were being spied on, she would still run the gauntlet. Nothing tasted sweeter than forbidden fruit, stealth and secrecy adding its own spice, and having the satisfaction of knowing something that no one else knew. Nevertheless, Jack sometimes wondered what had happened to the type of woman 'who had married dear old dad', not in his case, but the homely, long-suffering, brows all furrowed and wrinkled with care type, as in the words of the song, MOTHER NO CHROI, or was it all in a child's imagination. He had seen the earthy side of women's nature, and yet, Kathy didn't play the hypocrite, defending a virtue that she had already lost, like so many of her gender.

Ever since the advent of Ann Fox, Jack noticed a change coming over his cottage, and like a picture being painted, little by little, everything began to fall into place, Ann giving it a charm it never had before until he found it hard to imagine what it had looked like at the outset. The kitchen came first, then the parlour where she polished the oak furniture to such a sheen that it gave back the sunlight which came streaming through the windows now that the grime had been washed away, and gradually the musty smell disappeared under the persistence of beeswax and carbolic. The bedrooms were next to come under her onslaught, and suddenly in a panic when he could find no way to dispelling the lingering scent of Kathy's perfume he took to sprinkling Sloan's liniment on and around the bed.

Ann never relented until the cottage was as clean and tidy as only a clean and tidy person could make it, and Jack spoke his approval. She exercised the same efficiency in the housekeeping, washing and cooking until everything was so transformed that his old slipshod routine, which had creaked along laboriously from day to day, suddenly seemed to move on oiled castors. Still somewhat in awe of her taciturn employer she communicated with him through Martin, not that they had resorted to talking behind his back, but as fellow employees they could discuss matters with less constraint.

According to Martin, Ann had come to Castleford four years earlier with Tony, her husband, and their two babies. Tony, a chemist, had found employment in Shaw's factory until his heart attack some months later had left her bereft, living in a rented house on the Dublin road, supplementing her widow's pension with any domestic work she could find. Jack had already perceived that a sad story lurked somewhere behind the prim image she turned to the world, and now that they had holidays from school, Angela and Mary, her daughters, arrived with her every morning.

The girls, although they were mannerly and well-behaved, never treated Jack with the same reserve as their mother, and as soon as they arrived they rushed to greet him, asking all kinds of questions and running errands for him back and forth to the house. What Martin and Ann were to learn in time the children sensed at first sight that a kind heart lurked somewhere beneath his gruff exterior, and now that he had his first sows inseminated, he found plenty of work for them besides helping their mother which, not only kept them out of mischief, but entitled them to pocket money as well.

One afternoon, Ann called Jack aside. "Jack," she said, still somewhat hesitant at calling him by his first name. "I'd like to have a word with you, if I may."

Hoping that it wasn't a grievance she had to air, or worse still that she was going to quit, Jack nodded for her to make her point.

"I hope you're pleased with my work, and I must admit, I like the job and the children are over the moon," she began, Jack's anxiety waning with her every word. "It's grand for them to be getting all this fresh air, though it's going to be hard to drag them away when it's back-to-school time. But I've got a confession to make. I lied to you when I said I had no previous experience of this type of work – I needed the job so badly. If I said I had other experience, I was certain you'd ask for references, and I don't think they'd be in my favour. I've had several jobs housekeeping for bachelors, but most of them expected something else at the end of the day, I being a widow and all that – I don't have to spell it out for you, do I? So, I told them what I thought of them and left, or in other instances I was sacked – I just wanted you to know."

"I appreciate your honesty, Ann, but it's something I already know, and it wasn't Martin who told me either. It was the two young traitors in your own camp who let the cat out o' the bag, God bless 'em," Jack laughed. "But you gave me a fright – I thought you were going to quit. I appreciate your efforts, and any problems that crop up come to me and we'll discuss them. And, as for the other business you mentioned – about the dirty old men, you can put your mind at rest, because you won't have to worry about that here. You have my word on it – whatever it's worth."

A trace of a smile, barely perceptible, the nearest Jack had ever seen to a smile, played for a second on Ann's pale thin lips. "Do you think I can't see that," she returned. "I don't think you'd bother even if it was handed on a plate to you."

"Now don't you be handing things on plates to me, or you might be in for a rude awakening," Jack retorted, for all that he was taken aback by Ann's uncharacteristic remark and, with a Cheshire-cat grin on his face, he watched sadistically as her olive skin reddened from ear to ear.

Little by little Ann's reserve began to thaw, and the more it melted, the more Jack perceived that she was worried, not for herself, but for her children's future. Her dignity was natural, and when she smiled her wan delicate smile, she almost looked pretty. She was cool-headed and moved about in an efficient and unruffled manner, no matter how unsavoury the task. Even during a short spell of humid weather the flies never seemed to bother her, and the only adjustment she made to her toilet was a little unbuttoning and rolling up of sleeves. Although she dressed plainly and her clothes showed skilful mending and patching, it didn't detract from her deportment, for she was the type of woman on whom simple drapery accorded well. Jack wished he could do something to help her without causing embarrassment or offence, for even the money he gave to the children they had refused initially until he started putting it in pay packets for them, sometimes adding a bonus to make it appear more businesslike.

The summer weather, as it does for most women, worked its magic too on Ann, and one afternoon as she stood in the cottage doorway, arms folded, the slight breeze tugging at her dress gave Jack a fleeting glimpse of the outline of her well-formed legs and thighs, which any man would give his eyeteeth to get between in a carnal compromise, although it was hard to imagine it ever happening. Ann looked so prim, so self-contained that he could never see her tipping back her head in an earthy laugh like Kathy Moore, or being anything but cold between the sheets.

Invariably, it wasn't the first time that Jack had read the cards wrong, for not many years ago Ann had danced and laughed like any teenager, and more than a few men from the affluent set in and around Athlone had sought the favour of the somewhat tomboyish Ann Cusack, the youngest daughter of Walter Cusack, a well-to-do factory owner. In those carefree adolescent days after she had finished her education, life was pleasant for Ann: boating on the Shannon, picnics, tennis, horse riding, and at night, dances and candlelit suppers, until she met Tony Fox, the man she fell in love with, and later married against her parents' wishes.

Tony, who had worked his way through college, was a son of one of her father's employees, and socially didn't come up to standard. But the rebel in Ann had prevailed and she broke with her parents on the issue and, after moving from one temporary post to another, they finally arrived in Castleford, full of optimism. Two years later she was left alone in the world with her children and her grief. There was no going back to her parents, even if it meant putting her children into care, for they would mould them into replicas of their bigoted selves. If only out of respect for her dead husband, she was determined to go it alone, for she believed her parents' obstinacy had contributed to his death just as much as the heart attack.

When she first saw the squalor of Jack's cottage, her heart reached her shoes. "Give your eyes a treat," he had laughed tauntingly, as if the task was beyond her, and it was this lack of faith in her ability that had steeled her spine, turning it into a challenge, although the need of money too added its own incentive. Martin, as if he had sensed her discouragement, went out of his way to put her at ease, but not Jack, who went about his business as though she wasn't there, until her children had broken the ice between them. True, she had heard gossip about Jack, and no doubt there were snide references to her own housekeeper status, which she almost could lip-read: 'There must be more – if they're not careful, they'll have Father Brophy after them'. Under the circumstances she had to agree that a handsome bachelor back from England, who never attended Mass, with a young widow as a housekeeper, were statistics that would raise the eyebrow of even the most ardent advocate of innocent till proven guilty.

Father Brophy, a crusader against drink, adultery and birth control, was the latest addition to the presbytery in Castleford, taking over from the elderly Father Hennelly, and any couples whom he presumed were straying from the Church's dogmatic ruling on contraception would almost certainly be paid a visit, unless they belonged to the wealthy, pharisaic element of the community, a clique which could do no wrong in the eyes of the clergy. Ann felt it was only a matter of time before the priest's attention was drawn to her relationship with Jack. Then, she would be obliged to quit rather than have any doubt cast on her chastity, not for her own, but for her children's sake, as 'trot filly, trot foal', was a philosophy which was still adhered to in the community, and the school playground could be far more vicious than any battlefield. Jack had the name of being a womaniser, which she could well believe, and the proof was in his bedroom, for notwithstanding the embrocation he sprinkled around the bed, the scent of perfume still lingered.

On the other hand, Jack was good to them, for how could she not but appreciate the guile he had used in hoodwinking her daughters into getting involved in the everyday running of the place so that he would have an excuse to give them pocket money, and any time she herself went beyond her commitment, there was always an extra few shillings in her pay packet. The image he portrayed was one of cool indifference, and he seemed to be ashamed of his good deeds as others were ashamed of their sins. Once, when she thanked him for the extra money, he looked embarrassed, and in his eyes she saw the surprise of one who discovers for the first time his own soft-heartedness and is feeling a faint self-ridicule by it.

It appeared that something was tormenting him, or perhaps some romantic sadness had blighted his life and made him bitter. She was convinced that nothing ever pleased him, that he either wanted something badly and couldn't get it, or had never wanted anything and so didn't care about anything. Several times, unknown to him, she had watched him at work, his features grim, as though the thoughts in his mind were not pleasant, and somewhere in the depths of his eyes she had perceived a melancholy that matched her own.

As the green of summer turned to the amber of autumn, the building of the sties neared completion, and all too soon it was time for the children to return to school. For days afterwards the place was enshrouded in gloom, their gay chatter sorely missed as if the birds had suddenly stopped twittering. Jack had to admit that their boundless exuberance had gone a long way in soothing his turbulence of mind, and though they still came on Saturdays, something was missing, as if their efforts at school had sapped all their energy. There was a certain gentility too about their mother that he had grown to admire and, cynical as he had become about women, he placed her in a category far higher than the Mary O'Haras of the world, so much so that he was beginning to feel guilty about Kathy Moore's weekly visits, as if such immorality on his behalf would undermine her respect for him.

However, Kathy's visits were drawing to a close, as she explained one Sunday morning. "I'm getting married soon, Jack – very soon, four weeks' time to be exact," she said. "It's Michael – he said he needs me to keep him warm for the winter. I tried to talk him into waiting till next summer, but he wouldn't have it – I think he suspects."

Jack couldn't understand why he felt relieved. "Congratulations, Kathy – I wish you every happiness," he said, the utmost sincerity in his tone.

"This means I won't be able to call any more."

"True," said Jack. "You can't ride two horses with one arse."

"Who says I can't – but do you think he'll notice?"

"Notice what?"

"Notice on our wedding night that I'm not all I told him I was?" Kathy went on, anxiety creeping into her tone. "I'm getting worried now. Is there anything I can do to make him feel that I am? You were in England – you should know."

"England, Kathy – what has England got to do with it?" returned Jack, trying to keep his tone serious, although he doubted that the English, clever and all as they professed to be, had anything in their book of worldly phenomenon to cover Kathy's situation. "And how would I know? – I'm not an authority on such matters. It all depends on how green he is. The only thing for it is to behave exactly as you did when it was your first night, or get him drunk, the drunker the better, and then say he did it in his sleep – that's all I can suggest. There's not much he can do about it anyway unless he has you examined first, and then you can always say it could've happened on the saddle of a bicycle, or something to that effect. It's no big deal nowadays – you can only lose your virginity once in a lifetime."

Kathy was silent for a moment as if she was digesting the import of Jack's advice. "Yes – get him drunk – give him a Mickey Finn," she said at length. "If that doesn't work, I could keep my legs tight together and let a few yelps out of me – let on he's hurting me. Then, when he's not looking, I could put a few dabs of blood on the sheet – he is a bit of a dope anyway."

"That's a good idea, Kathy – you'll go far," Jack commended, derision back in his tone as he tried to imagine what it would take to make Kathy yelp, or whether or not she knew that it was all down to the depth of her fiancé's infatuation. If he was madly in love with her, he'd believe anything she told him, and if he wasn't, he'd be harder to fool. "You could always buy a pound o' liver on the quiet and take it into bed with you."

"Shut up, Jack – can't you see I'm serious!" interjected Kathy, the closest he had ever heard to anger in her tone. However, seconds later, as if she too was seeing the funny side, she gave a dry ha-ha. "I'm going to miss you, Jack – miss our Sunday mornings," she said. "But it's definitely goodbye – I'll have to be a good girl from now on."

"You were always a good girl, Kathy."

"I suppose we'll think of one another from time to time," she said, sighing wistfully as she made to leave and, after a quick kiss on the cheek, she was gone, leaving Jack in two minds whether to be happy or sad, although what he wouldn't give to be a fly on the wall of her bedroom on her wedding night.

Now that his sows were ready in groups of five to litter on consecutive months, Jack could see the first glimmer of light at the end of the tunnel. Nevertheless, the enterprise was far from complete, the automatic feeding system had yet to be installed, and there were many other irksome little jobs to be done. He had been so engrossed in the project that he had missed Galway races and, save for the odd trip to Grogan's, he rarely ventured out at night. Still, there would be plenty of time for catching up later, although there was no better time to take the first steps in his other unfinished business.

On the last Thursday in September there was a fair in Ballinafad, a small village twelve miles west of Castleford and, as it was an annual event, it was always well supported. The Maughans and the other tinker tribes were sure to be there, including Jimbo, although Jack had yet to decide whether to take the direct route and hammer the truth out of Jimbo, or resort to bribery.

It was past noon on the day of the fair when Jack, dressed casually so as not to attract attention, arrived in Ballinafad in the old Ford 10-cwt van he had bought soon after his return. On any other day of the year Ballinafad would be just a flicker in the eye of a passing motorist, but on this particular day it was like a scene plucked from a scrapbook of yesteryear. Stalls, selling all types of merchandise: bric-a-brac, horse harness, second-hand clothes and reject crockery were squeezed into every vacant pitch round the perimeter of the marketplace, hemming in the animals for sale in the centre, while the clamour of the hawkers peddling their wares, the bargaining hand-slapping of jobbers and farmers, cattle lowing, sheep bleating, and the tinny strains of busker music rose above it in a single sensation of sound.

The whole area was enveloped in an all-pervading stink-sweet smell of cowshite and chrysanthemums, horse-piss and hot dogs and, as Jack had anticipated, the tinkers were there in droves, the women begging, the men drinking in any bar that would tolerate their patronage. For all that he had disciplined his mind against generalising he had perceived at an early age that the tinkers were a thankless breed, the only breed on earth that could turn a silk purse into a sow's ear, or that bit the hand that fed them and, considering it was the public in general who contributed to their slovenly upkeep, they were a prime example of good not always coming of goodness.

As the dealing was all but done, he picked his way through the diminishing crowd and, as there was no sign of the Maughans on the street, he assumed that they were either in Donaldson's or Crazy Joe McKelvey's, the only public houses in the village prepared to put up with the rough antics of the tinkers in their cups.

When he entered the smoky gloom of Donaldson's, birds of a feather was the first thought that crossed his mind, for every disreputable type of character was present: thieves, trickeys, tanglers and tinkers. Conscious of the wary glances his entry had attracted he picked his way through the groups of drinkers towards the back door and, as there was no sign of his quarry or his brothers, he moved on the McKelvey's.

One of the oldest establishments in the county, McKelvey's had fallen into such dilapidation on the outside that it gave a fair indication as to what to expect on the inside. Joe McKelvey, the proprietor, the last in a long line of ancestry, was a bachelor in his fifties, and his outrageous antics, which included eating live mice for a bet, had earned him the soubriquet, Crazy Joe, his psychology in the latter pursuit being that if a mouse wouldn't sicken a cat, it wouldn't sicken him. Once a champion ballroom dancer, over the years drink had caused his slender frame to slip into dissipation, and he was every bit as slovenly, if not more so, as the type of customer his establishment attracted.

When Jack lifted the latch and stepped into the crowded bar, he was immediately stopped in his tracks by the whiff of flatulence hanging in the air and, as if they were attracted by the smell, bluebottles were hovering in droning swarms, some feasting on the pools of spillage trapped in the hollows of the rough-hewn oak counter which ran the full length of the wall facing the door. It was a typical village public house, spacious and low-ceilinged, and it had the usual range of wooden tables, chairs and stools spaced out on the flagstone floor. The customers were mainly tinkers, smelly and ragged, some of whom were sitting on high stools at the counter, others at the tables or grouped round the huge open fireplace which, now that the grate was empty, was being used as an ashtray, a spittoon and a urinal, and it was said that Crazy Joe emptied his bowels there any time he was short-taken, completing the performance by wiping his arse on one of the curtains if there was no newspaper handy. It was on the group round the fireplace that Jack focused his attention – Jimbo Maughan was among them.

Crazy Joe, the stubble above his upper lip stained with porter froth, was standing at the open flap of the counter, his glazed eyes keeping tabs on his disreputable clientele in case of theft, his bulbous nose, which was blue-veined and pitted, sniffing the air, as if he was testing the density of the stink, and Jack attracted only cursory interest as he shuffled into room at the bar. "Whiskey!" he called, rattling a half-crown on the counter when Joe came to serve him.

Sniffing the whiskey in case Joe was up to his tricks, for it wasn't beyond him to top up one of the whiskey bottles with poteen, Jack cast a sidelong glance at Jimbo, who was towering over his cronies like a Clydesdale stallion among a herd of pit ponies, and even among his own breed he was the chief for raggedness. His tattered grey jacket of fabric unknown had lost all its buttons and was held together at the seams by pieces of chicken wire, his ex-army trousers were torn at the droop of the knees, exposing two full moons of bare flesh, his cap, which was set at a rakish angle, was ragged and greasy, and about his waist he wore a wide, brass-buckled leather belt, which represented the one thing solid in his whole accoutrement.

As if some animal instinct within him sensed danger, Jimbo cast an uneasy glance around, and the instant his narrowed eyes spotted Jack, he stiffened, gripped perhaps by an apocalyptic feeling that it wasn't for the good of his health that Jack Daly was sipping whiskey at Crazy Joe McKelvey's counter in Ballinafad.

Until he spied Jimbo in the flesh Jack had no planned strategy other than coercion or bribery, although the idea of bribing Jimbo was as distasteful as paying a thief for returning stolen goods. Finally, as his aroused anger overwhelmed his prudence, in three quick strides he covered the distance between them and landed a murderous left under Jimbo's chin, following it up with a flurry of lefts and rights to his big head before he had time to brace himself. Jack's fighting skills had been tempered in London by many set-tos where all the natural weapons God had given man were utilised: heads, shoulders, arms, elbows, fists, knees, feet and teeth, and a somewhat bewildered Jimbo was driven back until a left to the chin sent him sprawling between the fireplace and the wall. "That's for the stock you poisoned on me some years back!" he cried, raising his voice above the chatter so that all could hear.

Jimbo, his nose bleeding, his eyes beginning to puff, struggled to his feet. "I never poisoned your horse and cows, as sure as God is me judge–"

Before Jimbo had time to finish the sentence Jack drove a wicked left into his guts, impeding the flow of the words, and when compulsively Jimbo's head fell forward, he grabbed a handful of his mousy-coloured hair, pulled the head down, and brought up a knee into his fleshy face. "I never mentioned anything about a horse and cows – how did you know if you hadn't something to do with it?" snapped Jack, and he was about to strike him again when Jimbo threw up his arms in surrender.

"Hold it, for Christ's sake!" he pleaded. "Upon me soul – I never done it. There was a rumour goin' round that you were blamin' me – that's all I was tryin' to say."

"I don't believe you, but was it Paisley who paid you to do it? If you own up, that's the last you'll hear about it."

Perhaps sensing that Jack's anger had run its course Jimbo began to stem the blood flow from his nose with a snotty rag. "No – on me solemn oath I had nothin' to do with it," he swore. "As I said, I heard you were blamin' me. But I didn't do it, and I'll swear it on me children's lives."

Jack wasn't convinced by Jimbo's denials, for swearing on children's lives was fast eclipsing swearing on the Bible, although he shuddered to think of the weeping and gnashing of teeth that was certain to follow if the forfeits were ever called, for the thousands, or perhaps millions of children who were sure to be sacrificed would overshadow forever the massacre of the Holy Innocents and the Holocaust.

McKelvey had now reached the scene, pleading with them to take the fight outside. "It's all right, Joe – it's over," said Jack, anxious to be on his way, as the group of tinkers at the fireplace were staring balefully in his direction when they noticed he was alone, and they looked as if they had enough drink on board to give them the courage to take Jimbo's part. Easing back towards the door to put himself beyond immediate danger he beckoned to McKelvey, who came shuffling over on his gouty feet. "Sorry for the bother, Joe," he apologised, stuffing a pound into his shirt pocket. "That's for the damage, and I'd be obliged if you kept whatever you heard here today under your lid."

For all his slovenliness McKelvey hadn't come down in the last shower of rain and, with a quick stab of a nicotine-stained finger, he pushed the note out of sight. "Don't worry, Jack – my lips are sealed –"

The rest of McKelvey's words fell on deaf ears, for Jack was already through the door, hurrying away from the ragged band which was moving ominously closer, and when he reached his van, he quickly put distance between himself and Ballinafad. Taking into account that Jimbo hadn't owned up it turned out to be a wasted effort, although he was certain that McKelvey would try to make capital out of it. It was common knowledge that for all his antics he was a copper's nark, which was the only reason he was allowed to operate in such an illicit fashion. The news was sure to reach Paisley's ears, and if it did nothing else, at least it would put the cat among the pigeons.

Chapter 5

A few days after his trip to Ballinafad, Jack had a visit from the Brylcreem Kid, who was still one of the kingpins of the constabulary in Castleford. Although he never mentioned Crazy Joe McKelvey or Jimbo Maughan his warning was direct and to the point – raking up old ashes would get him nowhere, his animals were dead and there was no proof that they had been deliberately poisoned. The message between the lines read that Paisley was not guilty, and any attack on his person would land him behind bars. Now that he had shown his hand, he was worse off than ever, and when he looked to his old philosophy for inspiration, he failed to come up with even a ghost of an idea.

As autumn turned to winter and then to spring, Jack's venture began to pay dividends. Thanks to some underhand salesmanship, which entailed greasing the palms of the right people, he had a contract with the bacon factory in Ballyglass, and sometimes to meet his commitment he had to buy pigs, mostly from the nearby farms, many of which had jumped on the bandwagon and gone into pig-breeding on a small scale. This boost to the local coffers, which should have brought appreciation, only seemed to inflame their poorly-concealed envy, and though no one put it into words, it was in their eyes: 'it's wrong – it's against the rules – you're an upstart – you were born poor and you should stay poor'.

In Grogan's too, the atmosphere always changed to one of hush the moment he entered, as if he was John Reginald Christie, the mass-murderer, returning from the grave, and if it wasn't for his loyalty to Mick Grogan, who had in the past allowed him credit when his prospects were about as bright as a goose laying a golden egg, he would do his drinking in Galway, now that he had bought a new Ford Consul.

Grogan understood, and one night while they were having a drink together after hours, he summed it up: "An opportunist is always held in disrepute, Jack, 'specially by those who had the same opportunities and didn't take them. And another thing too – you've broken the myth about England and you're crowin' about it – the natives don't like it. If you'd come back with your heels bare, runnin' England down and sayin' you didn't like the food, or that their beer is like dishwater, or that you met better Englishmen over there than Irishmen, and all that kind o' shite, then you'd be welcome with open arms."

"I can't see what difference that makes," returned Jack. "They all knew me before I left, and they all knew exactly why I had to go. Now that I've come back to take up where I left off, I thought they'd be on my side, especially seeing as I'm putting money their way."

"You've got to remember, Jack, that they have a natural dislike for England and all things English, just as I'm sure the English have a dislike for Ireland and all things Irish – old enemies, you see," countered Grogan. "You're goin' against the grain when you praise it. You'd be better off if you ran it down now and again. Then, you'd be givin' them the chance to say: 'I always said England wasn't all it's cracked up to be – we're lucky to be here in our own country no matter how badly off we are. I'll bet there's many a man over there who'd love to swap places with us – poor craithers'. It's all right to come home on a holiday and flash a few quid; that's taken as bravado – they spend all they have and go back broke – that kind o' style. They'll put up with that and enjoy the free drink, but you've proved there's opportunity over there, and nobody likes to be proved wrong."

"But I'm only telling the truth, Mick," returned Jack. "There's opportunity in England, especially in London – that is, if you're prepared to work hard and put up with a certain amount of discrimination. It's like this, the English in general aren't the adventurous type and seldom take chances. They're inclined to look for permanent employment, no matter how menial, so that leaves a very wide field open to the likes of us, far more than just the crumbs that fall from the rich man's table, as they have themselves brainwashed into believing. It's in the Englishman's nature to bow to authority, so he looks to authority to lead and, if they say, 'jump' – he'll ask, 'which way?' and then grumble about it if it doesn't work out. They're never happy unless they have something to grumble about."

"That's all news to me," said Grogan. "With all their spoutin' about freedom of speech and such, anyone'd think they were the most liberated people in the world."

"They might spout about freedom of speech, but they haven't got freedom of speech," returned Jack. "Whether they like it or not they have a system of monarchy imposed on them, and anyone who condemns it openly could easily wind up behind bars on some trumped-up charge. In the schools the children are spoon-fed with all this Cinderella type o' doctrine – knights and their ladies fair, all dolling up in Santa Claus suits for state occasions, so they wind up looking up to people who wouldn't even allow them to knock on their front doors, not to mind use them. It's easy to convince someone of something he already believes in, and it distracts them from the basic problems of health and housing and gives them an illusion of grandeur for a while, a chance to look down their noses on the world. The monarchy breeds class distinction; it creates too many levels of society – the most decorated looking down on the least decorated, and the poor ould serf having to foot the bill for it all. If they'd just come down from the clouds for a minute, they'd see that bestowing a knighthood has no more material value than giving a candy bar to a child."

"But the system seems to work, Jack, whatever is in it – ours doesn't, and don't forget, we've got our own system of royalty too. The pope is king, the cardinals, archbishops and bishops could easily be the dukes, earls and barons; the canons and priests are the knights and squires, and they rig themselves out in fancy dress too, to con the man in the street into believing there's something in it, so it'll be easier to relieve him of his cash."

"But there's a lot more show made of it in England," countered Jack. "The English believe they're racially superior, that they're the most intelligent race on the planet – Churchill's doctrine, and if a catastrophe occurs, they look for something to blame other than their own incompetence. They're so full of themselves that they can't see that their noses are being rubbed in it by all this right of privilege ideology, which school you went to, and all that, as if all those lords and ladies were some rare breed and didn't have to shite like the rest of us. But the day'll come, mark my words, when someone'll say: 'look at the king', like in the song about the magic suit o' clothes, and pull the carpet out from under all the sham. But if you want to get ahead over there, you've got to let on that you agree with it, no matter how silly you think it is to have royalty and the like. You've got to act the way they expect the Irish to be – thick and illiterate. I met a fella in London who put me wise."

"Their noses are bein' rubbed in it here too and they can't see it," returned Grogan. "You've got to obey the rules – fall out with the clergy at your peril, whether you believe what they're sayin' or not. Take me for instance, if I wanted to give a man a drink early on Sunday mornin', I'm supposed to ask him first if he was at Mass, otherwise they'd pounce on me like a cat on a mouse. You've only got to look at Mick Hanniffy, the builder. He took the bishop to court over some right o' way, which he was quite entitled to do, seein' as the bishop was in the wrong. But he's built his last house around here, whether he knows it or not. The majority of the people are intimidated by the Church, so from now on they'll steer clear of Hanniffy in case they upset the bishop. D'you see what I mean – you've got to conform – when in Rome, do as Rome does."

Jack was forced to agree. It was the old story of travel broadening the mind and not travelling narrowing it, although reading between the lines it seemed that Grogan was trying to tell him something, perhaps hinting that he should start attending Mass, and maybe give a donation to the Church to keep up appearances. Although he realised that Grogan was for his good, the idea of having to conform just to please the community only made him more obstinate, and for recreation he turned to Galway.

Galway, the city of the tribes, had a special place in Jack's heart, for it brought back childhood memories of hot summer Sundays when literally all of Castleford travelled there on the excursion train, the children to swim in the ocean and make sandcastles on Salthill's silver strand, the old people to sun themselves on the Lazy Wall, or steep their corns and bunions in the pools left behind after the tide. There was Galway racing festival too to remember, nights of revelry and dancing into the small hours of the morning – milestones in life.

Furthermore, there was something about the Atlantic that attracted him, something forlorn, as if it had a sad tale to tell and nobody to listen, and sometimes he would sit for hours watching its heaving waves crashing relentlessly against the rocks in its war for possession of the shoreline with terra firma, its natural enemy. Afterwards, when the clean fresh air had purged his lungs and cleared the cobwebs from his brain, he usually took a stroll along the promenade before adjourning to the Atlantic Bar to partake of a plate of oysters and a pint of stout.

The Atlantic Bar, a new structure set back at a short distance from the vast expanse of water from which it had derived its name, was decorated and furnished in the latest mode. A polished mahogany counter, brass-railed and padded, with a matching surround of high stools, ran in a semicircle at the back and completely dominated one corner. The parquet floor was slightly elevated and tilted towards its glass façade, which gave the impression of being on board ship and, whether standing or sitting, the whole panorama of sea, yachts and lighthouse could be taken in at a glance.

As spring turned to summer, one Sunday evening when Jack entered the Atlantic Bar, Paisley was sitting at the counter, arguing with the barman, and perhaps on recognising the voice behind him calling for a pint of stout, he spun round on his stool. When their eyes met, he fixed Jack with a long measuring look that carried in its cold depths something stronger than hate, more insulting than contempt, while Jack, electing not to inflame the encounter, returned stare for stare until Paisley tipped back his drink and stormed through the door.

Long ago Jack had perceived a perverseness in Paisley's nature to do wrong for wrong's sake, and for all Jimbo Maughan's denial he still believed he was behind the killing of his stock, otherwise why had the Brylcreem Kid warned him to lay off? Sliding on to the stool that Paisley had just vacated he sat sipping his drink and, while he was racking his brains for some way of levelling the score without bringing the constabulary down on him, he noticed the barman throwing the odd sidelong glance in his direction, as if he was a vaguely-remembered face from the past. Finally, Jack's curiosity prompted him to ask: "D'you know me from somewhere – England maybe?"

"I don't know who you are, but you certainly put the skids under that fella," replied the barman. "He went out the door like a scalded cat, whatever you have on him at all. He's usually a bit of a bully – arguin' and layin' it down to everyone. I'm just surprised, that's all."

Tall, fair-haired and lightly built the young barman was neatly turned out in the regulation black trousers and white shirt, and he bore the trademark paleness of complexion associated with his station, although Jack discerned a hint of slyness in his sharp features and alert grey eyes. "I suppose he's off now to the Western Hotel to play poker," he ventured, framing the words so that Jack would have to ask the next question.

Feigning indifference Jack waited for the barman to mention the poker game again, before commenting: "It must be a heavy game if Paisley is involved?"

"Fairly heavy!" exclaimed the barman. "If you call a pound a deal and a fiver 'all in' for the last three games fairly heavy – it's fairly heavy. But the man you just mentioned is its biggest loser over the past year or two, and rumour has it that if he doesn't pull in his horns, it'll be the ruination of him."

"That's ridiculous," said Jack, hoping to vex the barman into spilling more. "Bull Paisley could buy and sell this place, and it's hard to believe that a game o' poker would put much of a dent in his fortune. But your remark about him pulling in his horns'd be like a red rag to a bull to him if you can see the funny side. So, better not let him hear you saying it."

Jack's quip about Paisley pulling in his horns was lost on the barman. "Amn't I just after tellin' you that he has a fortune lost," he countered, plainly annoyed that his word wasn't taken as gospel. "You hear lots o' things in my job, and you can take it from me, that game in the Western ruined many a man. There was even a suicide –"

"You're taking the piss out o' me now!" interjected Jack. "If that was the case, the police'd be down on it before they had time to shuffle the cards."

"Do I have to spell it out for you?" the barman returned, mopping the counter with wild sweeps of the cloth to show his irritation. "Seein' as it's all bigshots that's involved the Super turns a blind eye – if you don't believe me, go and see for yourself."

Now that he had his fish on the hook, Jack began to reel him in. "Can anybody sit in?" he asked, smiling an apology.

"You can, if you have the money," returned the barman, good humour restored. "There's no quarter given. If you haven't got the money to continue, you've got to drop out – it's as simple as that. There's no IOUs or cheques – just cash up front. It's draw poker – three cards maximum draw. The rules are simple – a quid a deal, open for a quid minimum, or half the pot if it builds up. But there's limits – the openers can be hardened by no more than double, and when the hands are filled, half the pot is the maximum bet. After that, the stakes can be only raised double – are you wide to what I'm sayin'?"

"They must have money to burn – the highest stakes I ever played for was sixpence a deal."

"Well, that's the truth of it," the barman went on, pleased as it seemed at getting his point across. "The last deal is at two o'clock in the mornin' – sharp. That's Canavan's rules – Tom Canavan, he's the owner of the Western. After that, there's the final three ace-pots – a fiver 'all in'. There's often a thousand quid on the table in some o' them last pots."

Jack whistled through his teeth. "I find it hard to understand Paisley," he said, hoping to learn more. "Anybody with his kind o' money doesn't need to gamble at all."

"Why don't you go and see for yourself. It's like a casino in the function room upstairs, waiter service and all, and there's lots o' smaller games goin' on as well. The only snag is, they charge a half-crown to go in, just to keep out the sightseers."

Over the next hour Jack gathered from the barman that according to rumour Paisley was in trouble with the bank over his gambling losses, which was hard to believe considering he was still showing all the trappings of affluence – Humber Super Snipe car, well-tailored clothes, a thriving business, and a mansion standing in its own grounds on the outskirts of Castleford – established wealth which held far more substance than speculator's wealth. Also, it was possible that the rumour had been put about by his enemies to discredit him, although now that he had heard about the card game, wild horses couldn't keep him away from the Western Hotel, which was just around the corner.

When comparing it with its neighbouring seafront establishments, the Western Hotel was functional and mundane and, as it was situated in a cul-de-sac off the beaten track, it had a name for after-hours drinking, the illegalities of which could be covered by its residential licence. When Jack entered, there was only a scattering of customers at the bar and, after paying the half-crown admission at the desk, he made his way upstairs to the card room, which was on the first floor. When the burly doorman flung open a leaf of the double doors, he was immediately hit by the animated hum of gambling and a cloud of tobacco smoke, and it took a moment or two for his eyes to become accustomed to the change of atmosphere.

The room, which had waiter service, was as the barman had described it, basically furnished with wooden tables and chairs, and there were at least twelve card games in progress, each table having its own entourage of onlookers. Almost immediately his eyes picked out Paisley, who was sitting at the centre table, his back to the door, and unknown to him he watched his play, long enough to observe that he was prone to gambling on worthless cards, repeatedly raising one-card buyers, depending on lady luck rather than playing the percentages, and any time he picked up a potentially winning hand he lacked the necessary guile to capitalise on it.

Once upon a time, if it had been at all possible, Jack would've sold his very soul just to get the stake to sit in such a high-ante game, although now that he had achieved his goal, there was no longer any need to gamble. Still, the slapping of cards and the rustle of paper money was like a drug to his senses, and it aroused in him a passion that had lain dormant since the night he boarded the emigrant ship. The more he watched the bundles of notes swapping about between greedy fingers, the stronger the temptation became to try his luck, for besides his other shortcomings he observed that Paisley was a bad loser. It was sure to get his goat just to see him in the game and it might provoke him into betting rashly, which would increase his chances of winning money from him. Surprise too would be a factor in his favour and, with his mind made up to give it a whirl, he slipped away unnoticed.

All week long, Jack's thoughts kept returning to the game. To go there without a strategy would be tantamount to pouring money down the drain, and when Sunday night came round, he counted out a thousand pounds from the three thousand he had stashed in a niche in the wall behind the fireplace in his bedroom. Splitting the money into five two-hundred pound bundles, he put one lot in his wallet to give Paisley the impression that it was the full extent of his purse, the remainder he spread through the pockets of his jacket. The ruse of splitting his money he had picked up from a Tyrone Power movie, in which he had played a riverboat gambler and, simple as the subterfuge was, it might work on Paisley, provided he hadn't seen the film.

Later that night, when Jack arrived at the card room, the game at the centre table was already under way and, as it had its full complement of six players, he stood silently watching over Paisley's shoulder until a man named Frank dropped out. When he asked for the seat, Paisley spun round, almost choking on his astonishment, making as if he might object as one by one the other players nodded their assent. The rules were quickly explained and the deal commenced, with Jack first to call.

As most of the games were opened on the first deal, the pots stayed relatively small, and Jack picked up a few potentially winning hands which he played deliberately to annoy Paisley, who was enjoying some of the early luck. Although his delaying tactics had Paisley seething, his eyes never left the two hundred pounds Jack had taken from his wallet, which was steadily dwindling.

Finally, Jack lifted a small pot, enough to sustain him without having to delve into his reserve and, playing a waiting game, he picked up two more pots in quick succession.

As the night advanced, the betting grew heavier and, as if to keep pace with the increasing stakes, the faces round the table grew more grim, brows puckering in contemplation, hands gripping cards tightly, almost wringing them, as if it was possible to squeeze one of the spots off a deuce and turn it into an ace. Game after game went by, lady luck see-sawing back and forth, until finally the deal went round the table twice without being opened – jacks, queens, kings, aces: aces, kings, queens, jacks: queens, kings, aces. The deal had reached aces again when John Comer, a man with a florid face and droopy eyelids, opened for five pounds, which Paisley raised to fifteen, and when the play came to Jack, he deliberated longer than usual until the colour began to rise in Paisley's heavy jowls.

"What are you waitin' for Daly? – are you goin' to take the cards home to bed with you or what?" he snarled sarcastically. "If you're goin' to play, it'll cost you fifteen quid."

Paisley's sarcasm scarcely penetrated the outer layer of the second skin that Jack had grown in his term in England and, taking a long deliberate look at his three kings, he made a pretence of folding them. Then, as if by some sudden inspiration, he gathered the hand again and tossed three fivers into the pot. There were three other stayers and over seventy pounds in the kitty, and when Jack drew two cards, he shot a glance at Paisley, whose attention was solely on the money on the table, which suggested he had something good. He had bought one card, and it was hard to tell with one-card buyers, and yet, he would hardly have sweetened the pot if he was just hoping to fill a flush, a straight, or a full house, although a straight flush was possible.

When Comer bet ten pounds, Paisley made it thirty, and when Jack took a peep at his draw cards, which revealed a king and an ace, he shoved ninety pounds into the kitty. "Thirty with sixty," he said impassively, and there was no more expression in his tone than in his eyes.

Such a hefty bet from a man who at one stage was on the point of throwing in his hand forced Comer and Pat Quinn, the other player, to deliberate, and when finally they both folded, Jack focused his attention on Paisley. If expressions were anything to go by, Paisley was riding the crest of a wave, and the speculative glance he threw at Jack's money pile suggested he intended to crowd him out of the game. Counting out a hundred and eighty pounds, he smirked, saying: "Your sixty, and up a hundred and twenty."

Sucking in his breath through his teeth Jack hesitated again, shifting his eyes from his money to his cards and back to his money, which totalled eighty-five pounds, thirty-five pounds short of the amount required to call. A straight flush was the only hand that could beat him, although he doubted Paisley had one, and yet, it was possible.

If Paisley had any virtues at all, patience wasn't one of them, and the more Jack deliberated, the more agitated he became. "What are you waitin' for, Daly?

– put up or throw up!" he snarled. "If you haven't the money, you've got to drop out."

Jack prolonged the drama until finally he drew one of the bundles of notes from an inside pocket, supplementing the money in front of him and, after counting it a couple of times, he pushed the lot into the kitty. "Your hundred and twenty and a hundred and sixty-five more, Mister Paisley," he said, putting added accentuation on the 'mister'.

At the sight of the accumulating pile of notes, which was spilling out to the edges of the table, cupidity replaced the anger in Paisley's face. "Count the pot, someone!" he demanded, his huge bovine eyes dilating in keeping with his nickname, and almost immediately Tom Canavan, the impassive proprietor of the hotel, sorted out the bills in order of denomination, counting and smoothing them into neat bundles.

Sensing a clash of strong hands the onlookers from the other tables began to drift over, forming a semicircle at the back of each contender and, as the tension mounted, Canavan finished his counting. "There's seven hundred and twenty-five quid on the table, including a bet of a hundred and sixty-five to you, Bill," he said, addressing Paisley.

When Paisley lifted his eyes from considering the merits of his cards, the confident look on his face as he drew an enormous roll of bills from his pocket did much in the way of undermining Jack's earlier conviction of his unlikelihood of having a straight flush, which was supported by an apprehensive feeling that his arch-enemy might be cheating, a feeling that was keeping pace with the chill running down his spine as Paisley continued to peel notes of high denomination off the roll. Finally, laying the money on the table, he looked contemptuously into Jack's eyes, saying: "Your hundred and sixty-five, with another three hundred and sixty – that's as near to the limit as I can go."

Worried now, Jack dispensed with his dilly-dallying and, drawing two more bundles of notes from his pockets, he called the bet.

When Jack produced the money, the smugness momentarily left Paisley's face, only to return again when he laid down his four eights. "Beat them if you can, Daly!" he said, confidence oozing from every pore of his bloated features.

A knife could have cut the tension round the table and, savouring his moment of triumph, Jack feigned a look of surprise, and then, without raising a hair, turned up his four kings.

The murmur of awesome disbelief that rose from the onlookers was like the disturbing of a nest of wild bees and, as Jack scooped the money from the table, he met Paisley's hostile stare with a sardonic grin. There was over sixteen hundred pounds in the pot, almost half of which had belonged to Paisley, and yet, in big money terms, it wasn't a significant amount, not enough to add much grease to the slippery slope which, if the barman could be believed, Paisley was already on his way down, but more like what the seagull said when he pissed in the ocean – every little helps.

When the game resumed, now that the high point of the night had passed, it lacked enthusiasm. Endeavouring to recoup his losses Paisley kept raising the ante, while Jack, determined to hang on to his winnings, played only cast-iron hands, and it followed the same pattern until it was time for the last three ace-pots. Fortunately for Jack there was no clash of strong hands and the pots stayed relatively small.

If the sour expression on Paisley's face was anything to go by, he knew that he had been hustled, and he confronted Jack before all present. "You're takin' a fair few quid o' mine away with you tonight, Daly, and I suppose it'll be a prisoner the minute you get out the door with it!" he growled, his jaw shooting out pugnaciously. "But tell me this before you go – am I going to get a chance to win it back or not?"

Nobody likes a quitter, and when all eyes turned to Jack, he shrugged his assent. "You'll have plenty o' chances to win it back," he said, staring Paisley straight in the eye. "I'll be here again next Sunday night."

In the following days Jack never stopped cursing himself for promising to give Paisley a chance to win back his money. Paisley might be a lot of things, but he was no flat tyre when it came to cunning, and he was sure to come with something up his sleeve, although the probability of the other players ganging up on him, he dismissed as unlikely. Paisley wasn't popular, and there was no mistaking the look of satisfaction on some of the faces round the table when the biggest pot of the night was scooped from under his nose.

When Sunday night came round, for all that the pragmatic side of his nature kept nagging him to renege Jack set off for the card game, two thousand pounds spread about his person in case they tried to crowd him out. When he reached the Western Hotel, the game at the centre table was about to commence and, save for one, the faces were the same as on the previous night: Paisley, Canavan, Quinn and Comer, although his suspicion was immediately aroused when the newcomer, Tom Dillon, took the seat on his left.

Playing patiently Jack enjoyed a brief winning flurry and, as the game warmed up and the stakes increased, he detected a cunning gleam in Paisley's eyes. A sixth sense warned him that by some token or other he had telegraphed his hand to Dillon, a shifty-eyed man with a knavish countenance that wouldn't look out of place on Judas.

The conspiracy began to unfold when Paisley bet five pounds, which Canavan called, as did Comer who was next in line. After a glimpse at his own three tens Jack felt obliged to call too, but just as he anticipated, Dillon doubled the ante. When Paisley called Dillon's raise, Canavan dropped out, but Comer raised the stakes another ten pounds. In case it was a bluff Jack went along, and when it came to Dillon, he doubled again. Paisley, without hesitation, upped the ante another twenty, and when Comer dropped out, Jack found himself squeezed between Paisley and Dillon. Stifling his anger he smiled and threw in his hand. Then, with scarcely a moment's deliberation, Dillon folded too, leaving Paisley to scoop the pot unchallenged.

The set-up was as barefaced as it was simple, a three-cornered conspiracy: Paisley, Comer and Dillon, and for the remainder of the night the game followed a similar pattern. Every time either of the trio had a decent hand, the other pair kept pushing up the ante before dropping out, although it didn't always work in their favour, for Canavan and Quinn turned the tables on them several times, and more than held their own.

It was raining outside when Jack emerged from the smoke, noise and tension of the card room, poorer of purse and lower of spirit, and he stood awhile in a shop doorway, reflecting on the night's events. No matter which way he looked at it the game was crooked, but who were the losers? – there had to be losers. Contrary to the barman's enlightenment it wasn't Paisley and his clique, hardly Quinn and Canavan, who seemed to have come out ahead and, with the question unanswered, he returned to his car.

Chapter 6

While Jack was driving back to Castleford in the pouring rain, the windscreen wipers flicking back and forth could scarcely keep pace with the idea that was forming in his mind, a daring plan of beating Paisley at his own game, and he knew the very man to help him – Ray Power, for if there was a shrewder man on earth he had yet to meet him.

In his younger days Ray had been ostracised by his well-to-do parents for marrying beneath him, and because of ill health he found it difficult to hold down a regular job, which turned him to gambling, supporting his family on winnings from horses, greyhounds, cards and snooker. As is often the case when a person has a deficiency, nature makes an adjustment, and consequently Ray was gifted with keener than average intelligence and an uncanny sense of perception. Somewhat of a cynic, he believed the human race was divided into two categories: winners and losers, and that there was always a hand to slap you down, never one to pick you up.

Jack had first witnessed Ray's carefully-concealed talent in the county snooker championship in which he had much show of being knocked out in the first round. However, a week later, he played the winner for twenty-five pounds and beat him, hustling him with such guile that everyone believed he was just lucky, although anyone who believed Ray was just lucky and put the matter to the proof soon found that there was no luck attached to the wafer-thin man with the wry smile, sallow features, and a consumptive cough reminiscent of Doc Holiday. If Ray could be persuaded, between them they could manipulate the game to suit their ends. Initially, it would mean staking Ray and sending him ahead for a few nights to get the lie of the land, and then they could both sit in without arousing suspicion. The burning question was – could he trust him?

On the following evening Jack drove to Dunhallow, a rundown neighbourhood of mean streets of two-up, two-down houses of concrete and slate where the bad side of Castleford's character lived, for it seemed that every thief, ex-jailbird, harlot, tricky and dropout found refuge there. Ironically, it was the townland where Paisley had been brought up, and yet, even among all that was bad, needy respectability found a home, for under many roofs lived poor but honest souls whose presence there was due to the uncompromising hand of privation. It was in one of these abodes that Ray had been forced to live ever since falling out with his family.

For all that the evening was warm and sunny, an air of gloom hung over the area like a pall, hopeless washing darkened on clotheslines, and ill-clad children were carrying pails of water in an endless procession from a communal pump. Parking at a distance from the houses he locked the car and approached a little girl who was sitting on a wall, clutching a rag doll to her breast. "Can you tell me where Ray Power lives, young lady?" he asked, in a wheedling tone, squeezing a shilling into her little fist.

When the girl opened her hand and saw the shilling, her eyes lit up with both delight and disbelief. "Thank you, sir – he lives over there," she said timidly, pointing to a terrace of houses which overlooked a railed-in triangle of green where a lawn of weedy grass and a few clumps of faded laurel bushes were putting up a brave fight against the smoke-laden and uncongenial atmosphere. "It's the end house – number thirty-nine."

When there was no answer to his knock on the front door, Jack went round to the back door, which was ajar. "Anybody home?" he hailed, peering into the gloom of the interior.

A mumble of furtive whispering and the grating sound of chairs scraping on the floor came from within, and some moments later a thin, balding man appeared in the doorway, squinting against the bright sunlight. "Jesus Christ – if it isn't Jack Daly himself that's in it," he greeted, when his sharp blue eyes became accustomed to the glare. "I've been hearin' nothin' but good news about you, Jack – doin' well with the pigs, they tell me. Well, fair play to you, ould stock – you deserve a bit o' luck. But why are you here – what brings you all the way out to this trick-o'-the loops' paradise?"

Lightly built and sallow of complexion Ray was in his early forties. He had a long nose, pointed chin, hollowed features, thinning sandy hair, and one twinkle of his shrewd eyes confirmed that he knew it wasn't to ask about his health that Jack Daly was standing at his back door.

Jack quickly explained all that had happened from the killing of his stock to the poker game, while Ray, whose sympathies lay with the underdog, listened impassively and, save for a flicker of enthusiasm when Jack disclosed his plan, nothing else was readable in his fathomless features, which brought to mind again the legendary gambler.

"That's an ambitious plan for sure, Jack," said Ray, after a few moments' deliberation. "You'll be riskin' a lot o' spondulicks. But if you've got that kind o' money, I can't see any reason why it can't work."

"How many nights d'you think it'll take playing there on your own to suss it out?" asked Jack. "And I mentioned Canavan and Quinn. Could it be possible that they're in cahoots?"

The canny smile that flickered on Ray's lips cut Jack short, a smile that said not to try to teach a mother how to change a baby's napkin. "I looked in on the game myself one night, but raising the stake to sit in is beyond me at the moment," he returned, pausing just long enough to put a match to a Woodbine. "Still, I agree with you inasmuch as it's crooked, but don't let that put you off. A crooked game is sometimes the easiest game to win money at and, as far as I can see, you've got it wrong – Quinn and Canavan are the crooks, and Paisley is the goose they're trying to pluck."

Jack was so obsessed with getting even with Paisley that he had hardly given Canavan and Quinn a thought, although it hadn't escaped his notice that they had come out ahead, and now that Ray had mentioned it, he could see what the barman meant. So, why not let Quinn and Canavan do the job for him as Ray's expression seemed to suggest, or perhaps Ray was mistaken. It was hard to believe that two respectable businessmen, one an importer and exporter and the other a reputable hotelier, would stoop to such means to make money.

Again, Ray's streetwise smile interrupted Jack's train of thought. "Take it from me, Jack, the world spews up many a crook, all in different guises. Just because a man goes to Mass every mornin' doesn't mean he couldn't be a crook – a man may smile and smile and be a villain, just as a man may piss in the bed night after night and never admit to bein' a damper. Most people imagine that crooks are like the type you see in the pictures, shady characters that any fool could pick out at a glance, but the reality is different – the man in the suit is far more dangerous than the man with the gun when it comes to stealin'. An accountant can steal more money than any bank robber, and what's more, he has a better chance of gettin' away with it," he went on, taking in Jack's reaction with an all-comprehensive glance. "Take Quinn for instance, he introduces some of his rich clients to the game, and then, in a way that's not too noticeable, himself and Canavan hustle them – they do it over a period of time so that no one suspects."

"If that's the case why don't they play the game in one of the hotel rooms behind closed doors and keep out the rank and file?" asked Jack.

"That's just it. As it is, it's all out in the open, admission fee, the lot," returned Ray. "And look at the business Canavan does after hours, and you can be sure the Super is gettin' his cut. They were all involved that time when Dooley painted the greyhound and hit the track for a fortune – Canavan, Quinn and the Super. As you know, Dooley took the rap and did the time. They're shrewd. They don't cheat in so many words – no marked cards and such, but if you haven't noticed already, Quinn and Canavan always sit side by side at the table every time they get the chance. This way, they know what's in each other's hands, and they're not beyond slippin' a card – d'you follow me?"

Now that it had been explained to him, Jack recalled that Canavan had finished up with good hands more times than would be considered lucky after passing on openers, and so too had Quinn, which meant that besides having Paisley to deal with, a close eye would have to be kept on the others too.

While Jack was pondering on this new twist in the tail, Ray went on: "If it's just Paisley you're after, you should have no problem. He doesn't know about Canavan and Quinn, and we do. Now, about the men Paisley set up to crowd you out – he couldn't have picked worse. Comer is only a gobshite – not only did he lose his own farm over the years to the two gents I just mentioned, but he lost his wife's too. Now his wife, poor craither, is over in England livin' with one of her sons. But where he's gettin' the money from beats me, unless Paisley is stakin' him – a second iron in the fire, as they say, but what an iron. This is Paisley all over – he's clever in some ways, but when it comes to somethin' like this, he's just not at the races. The other geezer, Dillon, is a dark horse, and though he never works, he's always well-heeled, but for the life o' me, I can't see what he's doin' with the likes o' Paisley unless there's money in it somewhere. Still, if you feel like goin' ahead with it, it can be done, but it's got to be done all in one night, because if we turn up at the table together more than once, they're sure to cop us on."

"If we go ahead, as you say, how much money will you need?" asked Jack, his spirit of adventure struggling with his prudence.

"One night playin' on my own should be enough – just to show my face after so long. Now for the bad news – I'll need five hundred smackeroons, but I'll play just to break even."

"Will five hundred be enough if they try to crowd you out?" asked Jack.

Ray smiled, the confident smile of a man at the top of his game. "If you don't know already, poker is a game o' skill, not a game o' chance," he explained. "It takes as much force of character, mental ability, power of decision and insight into motive to play poker as it does to govern a country or lead an army. Wishin' for a royal flush when everyone else at the table have four of a kind is the stuff that dreams are made of, and you'll find that most men who pick up a hand o' cards believe they're the best poker players in the world, which gives the likes o' me an edge, because if they think that way, their own egos'll beat them every time. First of all good cards usually come to good players, natural luck, we'll call it, and on top o' this, a good poker player has to have the instinct to feel where the good cards are layin'. If he thinks that waitin' all night to pick up a good hand is playin' shrewd, he's only pissin' against the wind."

"But you'll need a bit of extra backing if the cards don't run for you," suggested Jack, recalling his own experience of the previous night.

"If the cards don't run for you, you've got to make them run for you, and let your money talk for you," returned Ray matter-of-factly. "Poker is all about figurin' out who has the best hand in each game, where the power lies, and who's bluffin'. If you study the game, you'll find that two pairs or worse win over half the pots. So, knowin' how to bet a hand and how to sucker someone is the name o' the game. Sometimes it's best not to bet a good hand – let them come to you, and then you can catch them twice – call and raise, if you get my meanin'. If at all possible, don't get involved in ace-pots, because they're the last straw for reckless players down on their luck. So, as I said, I'll just suss the game out for a night – I won't push it."

Jack had the money with him and, as he was counting it out, Ray went on: "We don't want to be seen together under any circumstances. So, come out on Friday night week after midnight – say one o'clock in the mornin' to be on the safe side – there won't be many about then. Park your car about a hundred yards on from the end of the streetlightin', and sit in the back seat and wait. If anyone passin' recognises the car, they'll think you're doin' a spot o' courtin'. So, we'll say no more till then."

During the following days, Jack felt anything but optimistic when he realised that it would be easy for Ray to pull a double-cross. He wasn't unduly worried about Ray returning the money – Ray was a gambler and professional gamblers always paid their debts – but he might use it for his own ends, play for himself. He could stall for time, and after a few nights when he had won enough for a stake of his own, he could return the money and say it was too risky. Still, he had a gut feeling to the contrary about Ray, and an equal share of the winnings would present a golden opportunity for him to get out of his rut.

On Friday night, shortly after Jack had parked, lights extinguished, at the arranged meeting place, there was a light tap on the window and Ray got in. "It's all set," he said, surprising Jack who had been expecting a cock-and-bull story. "Actually I had a good night – without hardly tryin' at all, I won a ton and a half. Now, this is the way it looks to me. You were right about Comer, Dillon and Paisley, and Comer is definitely bein' staked by Paisley, which means he won't be carryin' heavy. So, we'll lean on him first until he's forced to drop out. As you know, there's no honour among thieves, and Dillon is the type who'd sell his own mother into the hoorhouse and then be thankful he had a mother to sell. If he sees he's up against it, he'll keep out o' the deep end – he won't follow Paisley in. Then, we'll have Paisley between us – two to one – good professional odds, wouldn't you say," he went on, laughing harshly as he drew the flat of his hand across his throat to emphasise the kill. "The way I see it, they won't allow seven in the game, so we'll need to be there well ahead o' time. Once the game gets goin', only play cast-iron hands, and give me the beck if you want me to raise and you do the same for me. I'll explain all about the tokens to use later – that is, if you're still game.

"I'm game," said Jack, finding it hard to share Ray's confidence and, after he had divided two thousand pounds between them, they went into more detail, perfecting their system of cues until nothing was left to chance. When it was time to go, Ray offered his hand. "Let's shake for luck," he said. "And we'll meet here again on Monday night, same time, hopefully under more – how do I put it? – under more prosperous circumstances."

On Sunday night, when Jack arrived at the Western Hotel, he knocked back two large whiskies to still the butterflies in his stomach before ascending the stairs to the card room. Ray was already seated as planned on Comer's left, his face as inscrutable as the back of the cards he was shuffling with his long slender fingers. Nodding a greeting Jack took the seat between Dillon and Paisley, while Canavan took the remaining seat, leaving Quinn when he arrived no choice but to watch until someone dropped out.

The deal commenced with Comer drawing first blood, but an hour later, after calling some hefty bets from Ray and Jack, he was forced out of the game, and his place was taken by Quinn. Dillon looked ill at ease, and he kept a low profile despite the glares he attracted from Paisley. As the night advanced, the cards were running more and more in Jack's favour, and Paisley, instead of hedging against Jack's remarkable run of luck, kept pushing up the ante. Squeezed between Ray and Jack, his losses mounted, and by the time the last three ace-pots came round he had thrown all caution to the wind.

The ace-pots were Paisley's last chance to recoup his losses, and the deal went round the table twice before he opened for fifty pounds, which Ray, tipping the wink to Jack, hardened to a hundred and fifty. When the hands were filled, the betting commenced at two hundred, doubled and doubled again until Jack folded, leaving Ray to scoop the two thousand pound pot. There was a look of desperation on Paisley's face as he dealt the cards for the next game, which he opened, but after some hefty betting he was squeezed again between Jack and Ray. This time the pot went to Jack, and when the last game went to Canavan on the first deal, Paisley stormed out of the room, only to return some minutes later carrying a small leather satchel.

"There's three thousand quid in that bag, Daly – count it if you like!" he snarled, dropping the satchel on the table. "So, how about one hand o' cards for the lot, just me and you – open poker, that is, if you're not too cowardly to cover it."

Jack was cornered and Paisley knew it. If he lost, he would be back to square one, and if he walked away, it would somewhat blight his moment of triumph. While he was still deliberating, Ray voiced his support for the idea. "If you want to make it fair, I'll deal for you – a new deck," he suggested. "What could be fairer than that?"

Sensing the excitement building up in the onlookers Jack knew he would lose all respect if he turned tail. "All right – one hand for the lot," he said finally, covering the bet.

When Canavan produced a new deck, Ray made much ceremony of breaking the seal, discarding the jokers and blanks, and when he had the cards shuffled to his satisfaction, he placed the deck on the table for one of the participants to cut.

Paisley cut, so the first card went to him, the next to Jack, the flicking of the cards the only sound breaking the silence. The fifth card gave Paisley two pairs – queens and deuces against Jack's pair of fours, and for a breathtaking moment time seemed to hang in the air as Ray flicked over Jack's last card – another four.

The turning of the last card had something of the effect of a slow-burning fuse reaching a keg of gunpowder, and in one long gasp the silence exploded into loud murmuring and exclamations of disbelief, which was followed by the tramping of feet on the bare-boarded floor as Paisley stormed out of the room. This time he did not return.

Shortly afterwards Jack too took his leave, and he was in such a stupor after the tension of the night that he scarcely realised he had driven home until he was pulling up at his gate. For all that it was a warm night and the air perfumed with the scent of new-mown hay and wild flowers, his cottage looked cold and uninviting among the trees, the empty windows staring lifelessly in the moonlight. What it needed was a wife and family to soften its starkness, roses intertwined round the door, a flower garden, and he immediately thought of Ann and her children. The moment he opened the door he could smell its cleanliness, the result of Ann's tireless efforts, and he shuddered to think of the mess it would be in without her.

The night had taken more out of him than he realised, for he felt too fatigued to gloat, although he savoured for a moment the look of dejection on Paisley's face, as if he was about to face the gallows. However, now that he had squared his account with him, he felt no real satisfaction, no sensation, like the kick a man gets out of riding the wife or girlfriend of his bitterest enemy, only the disappointment that sometimes follows an end achieved. It was probably because it had all come about so easily in the end, almost too easily, he suddenly thought, his mind returning to the game and the huge coincidence that most of the winning hands he had picked up were on Ray's deal: full houses, flushes, straights, even four of a kind on a few occasions. It could hardly be that Ray had cheated. No – it was just the way the cards had fallen, lady luck on the side of the righteous.

Now that he had taken Paisley down a peg, he felt devoid of ambition, only to find a wife and live happily ever after and, as he sat staring into the empty grate, not for the first time did the idea of selling up and returning to London cross his mind, for it now seemed that a place where one has lived retains part of him when he leaves, and perhaps if one has lived there long enough, it keeps all of him. Not long ago he had derided Pat O'Shea's words of farewell: 'you'll be back', although now that his prediction was coming true, it was running neck and neck with the cynical saying: 'you'll never go back'.

Once upon a time he had looked on England as a fate second only to death, a place of banishment, a Hades from whose bourn no traveller returns. Now he was looking on it as an escape, a refuge, a place of salvation. Literally, it was an escape, an escape from the hypocritical influence of parents, relatives, neighbours and the clergy and, as if the blinders had suddenly been stripped from his eyes, he could see why so many of his countrymen had got on so well in foreign lands: they were left to do their own thing without any restraining influence from religion or from their less adventurous kindred.

Next morning, when Jack awoke, he couldn't understand why he should be in a downbeat mood. Everything seemed so gloomy, so depressing, as if he was living under a black cloud, and even the thrush in the garden which he awakened to every morning had no song to cheer him, and the feeling persisted until it was time to meet Ray.

When he reached the rendezvous, he hadn't long to wait for the tap on the window and, as they sat in the back seat, sorting out the money, Ray gave a short laugh, saying: "I was worried for a moment in the last game – it's years since I had to pull off a trick like that."

"Like what?" asked Jack, somewhat naïvely.

"Like gettin' that third four up to the top o' the deck."

"So, you cheated."

"I couldn't let him win now – could I?" returned Ray. "That's why I offered to deal, and surely you must've noticed how I dealt to Paisley first – a bit of an advantage to us, partner. And did you see the long face on him when I turned up the third four? – long as a cow's arse, it was, and I'll bet a shillin' he had his shite in lumps this mornin'."

"And all those good hands I picked up during the night – what about them?"

"Use your loaf, Jack," tut-tutted Ray. "I just gave lady luck a helping hand, that's all – I couldn't very well deal good hands to myself, could I? – And besides, the laugh'd be on the two of us if we went all the way to Galway for a poker game and came back broke. It's somethin' like doin' to others as they would do to you – if they got the chance. There's no such thing as fair play or everyone bein' born equal – the rich always have a head start."

Perhaps sensing that he had knocked some of the gloss off Jack's triumph Ray went on in more practical tones: "I hope you're not thinkin' about givin' the money back, or givin' it to the Church to ease your conscience? If you are, forget it. It wasn't cheatin' really, just a little one-upmanship, levellin' the score, you might say. You've only got to look at all the people Paisley cheated in his time – payin' starvation wages and all that. I was just strikin' a blow for the poor. It's no crime if the rich cheat – takin' advantage of the situation, they call it. But when a poor man cheats, it's a felony, a deportation order for England. Forget your conscience, Jack, because conscience makes cowards of us all, and besides, there's nothin' can be done about it now. We can't give the money back and say we were cheatin', and if we give it to the priests, they'll only spend it on high livin' – the last thing they'd do is give it to the poor. Just think of what Paisley did to you. Anyway, Paisley has plenty o' money, and if we didn't take it off him, Canavan and Quinn would."

The logic in Ray's words dispelled the last of Jack's qualms, and the more he thought of it, the more it added spice to his success. To steal from a thief is no crime, and fate sometimes needed a helping hand.

When they had the money sorted, Jack gave an accounting: "Seven thousand, two hundred we won after I took out the stake money – that's thirty-six hundred apiece."

Without bothering to count it, Ray pocketed his share. "Glad to be of service," he said, laughing harshly as they shook hands, and for all that the handshake was meant to be casual Jack felt gratitude in it too. "Maybe this money'll help me to get out o' that shite-hole I'm livin' in, or maybe it'll be easy come, easy go, like so many times before."

On the following morning, when Martin Finnegan arrived for work, he had grim tidings – Paisley was dead. Suicide was suspected but not confirmed. Late on Monday evening he had been found dead in his car, the engine running, the garage doors closed but not bolted from the inside. When Martin hinted that Paisley had been heavily in debt to the bank, Jack was quick to observe that he never mentioned his poker losses, which suggested he knew more than he was letting on and, if Martin knew, everyone knew.

Later that morning, when Ann Fox confirmed the story, she was surprised to find Jack in such high spirits, for at that very moment he was smiling to himself at Ray's unwitting remark about Paisley having it in lumps.

"You don't seem to be too distressed by the news?" she ventured, her eyes searching his face, perhaps for some show of compassion.

"I'll put it like this, Ann. The show is over for Paisley – the fat lady has sung for him at last, and not before time," returned Jack, stifling a smile. "If you look at it realistically, he had to go sometime, and he's every bit as entitled to go as you or I. Just because he's a bigshot doesn't alter the fact, and if you ask me, the world is a better place without him. He wasn't a good man, and the Devil always gets his own in the end. But no doubt they'll put a headstone over him riddled with lies – in loving memory and all that, as if anyone would remember him except for the bad things he did."

Ann frowned, and though she made no comment, her face was primly disapproving.

"Is everything all right, Ann?" Jack asked, when he noticed her frown. "Paisley wasn't a relative of yours by any chance?"

"No, but it's wrong to speak ill of the dead. We're all God's children – that's why we go to Mass –"

As if she had just reached a cliff edge, Ann stopped abruptly in mid-sentence.

"Go on, Ann – say it!" urged Jack. "Say whatever you were going to say before you realised I wasn't a churchgoer."

"I don't mean to criticise, Jack, but it seems so out of character of you to be so callous. As for not attending Mass, that's your own business, but I do wonder sometimes."

"If I explain why I'm not a churchgoer, you'll be at me with a dozen other questions. So, I'm not going to define my position on religion – I wrestle with neither devils nor angels. I'm not one for throwing stones at other people's glasshouses, and by keeping to myself I hoped I wasn't putting up one for them to stone. But it appears I'm wrong."

"But why put yourself in a glasshouse to be stoned? Wouldn't it be easier –"

"To play the hypocrite!" interjected Jack. "Well, I won't. I'm glad Paisley is dead. It's a pity he didn't go twenty years ago, and if the Devil hasn't got him, what's the Devil any good for? I'm so glad that I'm going to have a couple o' days on the booze to celebrate."

"You're wrong, Jack," countered Ann, both disapproval and disappointment in her tone. "You should try to forgive whatever he's done to you."

Jack shrugged his reply, although the surprising indication that Ann cared for him enough to get upset over his attitude to Paisley's death pleased him immensely.

Later in the morning, when he bumped into Eileen in Castleford, he was all smiles. He hadn't seen her since the christening of her son, for all that he had promised to call more often, although he didn't deem his lack of fraternal concern warranted an apology. "And what d'you think of our mutual friend doing Harry Carey on it, just like that?" he greeted. "I'll bet a shilling that's what brought you to town today, just to gloat. If women were allowed into public houses, I'd ask you into Grogan's for a drink just to celebrate, but as it is, we'll have one in the Royal Hotel."

"We'll do no such thing. Still, I'd be too much of a hypocrite if I said I wasn't delighted at the news, but as you know, it's wrong to speak ill of the dead," returned Eileen, echoing Ann's words of earlier. "But changing the subject, how are you getting on with your new business? – good by what I hear, and you have a young housekeeper too, just like the priests you were always on about – and a ready-made family to boot."

Jack struggled to hold back the sarcastic retort that sprang to his lips at Ann's virtue being slighted, seeing as Eileen herself couldn't throw stones, and no matter how much she tried to hide it, she was showing signs of pregnancy again. Still, the day was too good to spoil, and he just laughed. "It's not the same in the ould place without you, Eileen," he said. "So, why don't you leave Cullinane and come back living with me? We could take up again where we left off – it'll be just like old times."

"God forbid!" snapped Eileen. "You haven't changed much, have you – in town in the middle o' the day and some other poor eejit doing the work?"

"Seriously, Eileen, I miss you so much about the place that I'm giving a lot o' thought to leaving the pigs behind, and the priests and the praties too, and going back to England," said Jack. "Once you cross the duck pond, as they call the Irish Sea, you're damned forever in the eyes of your neighbours."

"Oh, shut up, you! Doing James Dean on it – rebel without a cause. Everything'd be all right if you went to Mass every Sunday like everyone else," Eileen scowled. "If you want to live here, you'll have to knuckle down. So, why don't you start by coming out to visit us some Sunday like you promised, and not be keeping to yourself all the time?"

A sardonic smile flickered for a second on Jack's lips, inasmuch as it was turning out to be a day for sermons and not celebrations. "I suppose I could start by going to Paisley's funeral, for all the good it'll do him now," he said. "And you never can tell, I might see you some Sunday soon – then you can bring forth the fatted calf."

"There'll be white blackbirds out when I see the day," retorted Eileen and, leaving Jack alone with his thoughts, she disappeared among the shoppers.

Chapter 7

Paisley's funeral, like all rich men's funerals, was solemn and full of hypocrisy. People stopped to line the streets as the cortège passed, crossing themselves and counting the cars and saying what a fine funeral it was. Everyone who was anyone filled the front pews of the church, the social climbers crowding in behind, jockeying as it seemed for position now that a vacancy had arisen in the ranks of the Pharisees, while the warm sunlight streaming through the stained-glass windows fell gently on the assembly of black clothes and white starched collars, its sombreness relieved somewhat by tweeds and the brighter attire of the children. The bishop, in full mourning regalia, presided over the ceremonial High Mass for the dead, assisted by an entourage of priests in purple chasubles, while chanting choristers swung censers and sprinkled holy water on the coffin with the same solemnity as if a saint was being canonised.

Standing at the back of the church Jack watched impassively as the thuribles tapped out their three-beat praise, his eyes following the clouds of incense drifting languidly towards the dome, as though its fragrance would cocoon the spirit of the deceased against evil influences on its upward journey to everlasting happiness, or from a cynical viewpoint, lending substance to the Irving Berlin song *'there's no business like show business'*. Whichever, if he had any feeling at all, it wasn't one of regret or remorse, for his mind was on another day, a miserable day in the rain, the day they were burying the paupers when there was no such pomp, and his fondest wish was that Tim Kelly could be present if only to witness the type of requiem that only money could buy.

Although the church was crowded there were no tears, not even from the regular funeral-goers, the ones who took a melancholy pleasure from bereavements, which jogged a memory of someone once saying: 'when I die the church might be crowded but the pulpit would hold my friends'. Perhaps in Paisley's case the pulpit could be downgraded to the holy-water stoop holding his friends, for apart from the commendation in the bishop's eulogy he hadn't heard a good word spoken on his behalf. It was all shaking, sprinkling and praying, as if an extra swing of a censer or a sprinkle of holy water could make the difference between salvation and damnation. In view of the character of the deceased, shake, sprinkle and pray might as well be shake, rattle and roll, for if there was any justice after death, Paisley was already supping with the angel with the horns, hooves and tail.

After the service he followed the procession to the cemetery, not altogether conspicuously, but somewhat in the manner that St Peter followed Christ after his arrest in the Garden of Gethsemane, and stood among the crowd as the remains were lowered into the grave, his mind again on the paupers. When he heard the first clods hopping on the coffin, the final dreadful sound that reminds humanity that death smiles on us all, only then did he turn away, overwhelmed not in grief but in self-satisfaction. At least, justice had been done on earth, and for all that the coroner had viewed the evidence favourably and returned a verdict of accidental death, everyone still believed it was suicide. The agreeable fact was that he was down, gone but not forgotten, although time would reduce him to as little dust as that which is sometimes found in a new-born infant's hand.

Afterwards, as he was passing by the Royal Hotel where the pseudo-mourners had congregated, he slowed his step, and though he had no intention of joining them, some evil spirit or some perverseness in his nature which was beyond his power to resist drew him into its carpeted confines. Drinking alone at the counter, eavesdropping on the conversations, he gathered that Paisley had owed a lot of money to a lot of people, and his property was in the hands of the receiver. The general consensus seemed to be that having had money and losing it was a far greater misfortune than having none to lose, and now it only remained to be seen what would happen to all the dogs he had left tied. The thought brought a sardonic smile to his lips: the dogs would have to be loosed, as a man is loosed from his sins when he repents. At least he had left something behind for them to remember him by, a memory to curse rather than cherish, for on the long tortuous road through life one can meet people from all walks of life and forget them, all except the ones who owe you money.

Jack was still smiling when he caught his sister's eye as she entered with her husband and stepson, and to outwardly show that family relations were in accord he called them over.

Sombrely dressed in a grey suit, black tie and hat, Cullinane looked as dapper as ever, and now that he had a pregnant young wife, he was strutting like a barnyard cock, although Trevor, his son, was holding back, walking a pace behind, as if all wasn't to his liking, and he was so pale of complexion as it seemed from pent-up wrath that it was highlighting the pockmarks on his face like piss holes in the snow.

Playing the hypocrite Jack smiled. "A big turnout for the funeral, wouldn't you say, Mike?" he greeted. "The biggest funeral in these parts since ould Sheridan croaked it, if I'm not mistaken. But that aside, what are you having to drink?"

"Yes – funerals have a way of bringing people together," returned Cullinane, favouring Jack with a similar type of smile. "If it wasn't for funerals, there'd be very few community gatherings."

As the afternoon advanced, the conversation rambled from Paisley's debts to the price of livestock, and to Galway's prospects of beating Mayo in the Connaught football final, Jack doing most of the speculating, while Cullinane, as if he felt ill at ease in his brother-in-law's company, kept fidgeting with his watch-chain. Something about the chain, which was weighted down with gold fobs and seals, struck Jack as being odd, something his mind hung on, like a loose thread might catch on a nail while brushing past an old doorpost. He had seen the chain many times before, and yet, there was something about it that kept attracting his attention.

When Cullinane turned his head to have a word with one of his neighbours, Jack took a closer look, and the irregularity he had been searching for came to him suddenly, came with the heart-stopping clarity of glass shattering – one of the fobs on the watch-chain was identical to the one he had picked up at his gate on the morning after the killing of his stock, the little gold ball he was keeping as a lucky charm. Still, there was nothing unusual in the coincidence, for no doubt the company that made the fobs had made many, although another look showed that the bell on the watch-chain was comparatively new and didn't quite match the others in shade, new gold against old which hadn't fined out.

Jack's thoughts immediately took flight back to that fateful morning. The Brylcreem Kid had just left the scene when he spotted the gold bell glinting up at him outside the front gate, which he had assumed belonged to the detective. As his mind recaptured the moment, he recalled that the Kid had been wearing a wristwatch, which he kept looking at impatiently, and now the thought that suddenly struck him was too alarming to even contemplate – perhaps it was Cullinane and not Paisley who had poisoned his animals.

Jack was startled back to the present by Cullinane asking him what he was having to drink, his tone reminding him of the long-ago day at Galway races when he had put the skids under him. Suddenly his retort at the time – 'it's a long lane that hasn't a turning' – took on a new meaning, a hideous meaning and, as his mind worked feverishly, he tried to put together the events of that bygone morning. The single set of footprints leading across the newly-ploughed potato field were large and deeply embedded, suggesting a heavy man with big feet, and no effort had been made to conceal them or replace the stones knocked off the wall or to cover the tracks farther up the road where a car had turned, and Jimbo Maughan had sworn he had nothing to do with it.

At the time Cullinane had been on his short list of suspects with Paisley and O'Hara. However, his hatred for Paisley had distorted his reasoning, for he wanted it so much to be him that he had scarcely given the others a serious thought. O'Hara had wanted him out of the way in case his daughter married beneath her, and Cullinane so that Eileen might fall easy prey to his lechery, or perhaps they had been in the conspiracy together. Questions he should have asked himself then, he was asking himself now, and as if he himself had been the villain, he re-enacted the whole episode in his mind.

The night, as he recalled, hadn't been particularly dark, and from the evidence on the ground it appeared that the man had entered by the front gate and made his escape through the potato field. Why the potato field? – why not the gate again, unless he wanted to throw suspicion on someone with big feet who usually wore wellingtons?

The new slant on the affair sent his eyes darting down to Cullinane's shoes, which he observed were no more than size eight. This seemed to rule him out, but on the other hand, small feet would fit into large-size wellingtons. Look for something out of place, for something that doesn't fit, his mind kept prompting, but the only thing out of place was the fact that the man had entered by the front gate and for no apparent reason made his escape by climbing walls and crossing fields in the darkness. The detective – that was a joke – he was calling the man names – should have spotted this irregularity and checked the depth of the footprints and the length of stride to determine the man's weight and height, but he had been more interested in keeping his shoes clean, and how stupid he himself had been not to have noticed it, for all that he prided himself on his astuteness.

Perhaps there was a bigger picture, a conspiracy orchestrated by the clergy to get rid of him before he found out he was a priest's son. If so, it would explain the detective's lack of initiative, for he could hardly be so stupid not to have recognised foul play when he saw it, considering how quickly he had pounced after his set-to with Jimbo Maughan, warning him to let sleeping dogs lie. Perhaps he was under orders from some higher authority, and the more he reflected on it, the more it reinforced his theory of the culling system which he believed was in operation to get rid of the undesirables, a programme which the English had initiated and pursued down through the centuries, transporting the rebellious and holding on to the kiss-arse kind. Nevertheless, even if his speculation turned out to be true, there was nothing he could do about it. Cullinane was his brother-in-law, Paisley was dead, and O'Hara was recovering from a heart attack.

As Cullinane made ready to go, his cocksure manner, his swagger and snide smile roused Jack's dormant contempt for the man, and though his instinct demanded that he should confront him with the new facts, he shelved the idea until he had a word with Eileen. Eileen might know more than she was letting on, or perhaps Trevor might be the nail that would go. It was obvious that Trevor was at loggerheads with his father on some issue, and if he primed him with drink, he might unwittingly disclose something of his affairs.

When Cullinane and Eileen had taken their leave, Jack wrapped an arm about Trevor's shoulders in a show of family unity. "Now that the others have gone, how about you and me having one for the road, Trevor, ould stock?" he suggested and, before Trevor had time to say yes or no, he turned to the barman, calling: "Two large Powers, please!"

Now that he was no longer under his father's eye, Trevor was in a more talkative mood, smiling from time to time as he sipped his whiskey, a naïve, disinterested smile which was so much the opposite to his father's that Jack found it hard to believe they were father and son. It was possible that for all his cunning Cullinane had been a cuckold with his first wife too as he was with Eileen and, as his wishful thinking sprang into top gear, he listened absently as Trevor poured out his tale of woe. "As I said, Jack, I'm not getting on at all with the old man," he went on. "It's just that he treats me like a child, and I'm well over thirty."

"I can see you problem, Trevor," Jack agreed. "But isn't it the same all over the country – the old-timers hanging on to the reins till they have one foot in the grave?"

"That's not all, Jack," returned Trevor. "In my case there's no reins left to hand over, not to me anyway, now that he has a new family and another on the way. I accept that, but when I asked him for a small settlement so I could branch out on my own, he laughed at me. 'Cop yourself on, Trevor', he said, 'Haven't you got everything you want here'. And when I mentioned about wanting to get married, that's when he really laughed, 'I thought you'd have had enough of women by now', says he, 'all those women who tried to marry you for your money that I had to pay off. The only way for it is, if I make a match for you, and I've got someone in mind – an only daughter with a farm to inherit'. I know well who he means – Big Imelda Brogan, and there are more sets of fingerprints on her arse than they have in Scotland Yard and Dublin Castle put together."

"You don't have to marry anyone if you don't want to," said Jack supportively, raising an eyebrow at Trevor's last remark, for such vulgar expressions he had thought were restricted to building sites in London. "Anyway, matchmaking went out with the penny-farthing bicycle."

"That's all right coming from you, Jack, but you don't know the old man – he devious. If he gets something in his head, he pursues it to the bitter end. I could tell you a few things about yourself that'd open your eyes. While you were away, he reported you to the Land Commission – I overheard a conversation he had with one o' the chaps from the Council. I know it's hard to believe considering he's married to your sister, but –"

"You're right, Trevor – it is hard to believe!" interjected Jack, feigning astonishment. "Are you sure you're not mistaken, taking into account that there'd be nothing in it for him?"

"I don't know, but I heard it with my own two ears, and that's a fact."

"I know you mean well, Trevor, but isn't this carrying things a bit too far – your own father," tut-tutted Jack, hoping to vex Trevor into spilling more, although he should've known better, seeing as Trevor was naïve enough to accept his disbelief as natural.

The pieces of the puzzle, the puzzle that had begun with his father's disappearance, were rapidly coming together, and when Trevor excused himself, Jack sat awhile sifting through the facts, searching for that illusive key piece that would wrap it all up. He needed to talk to Eileen, and if his guess was right – his guess – he could no longer trust his guesswork, considering where it had led him. He had been wrong about Paisley, and no matter how much he tried to justify himself to himself it didn't alter the fact that he had cheated him, which had turned out to be the final push down the slippery slope.

The more he thought about it, the more his conscience came into play, and he set his mind to searching for some form of vindication. He could hardly blame Ray Power and, search as he might, the only mitigation he could find was that Paisley had tried to rape his sister. Yet, the attempted rape hadn't been premeditated, considering he had proposed marriage, and in the light of the two husbands she had chosen there wasn't much difference in character in all three. His loathing for Paisley had arisen from the rough treatment he meted out to his workers which, when all was said and done, was none of his business. If his employees were so invertebrate that they were prepared to knuckle under his insolence, it was their lookout. Jimbo Maughan too was innocent. At least he could apologise to Jimbo and perhaps make recompense, but the other matter was already laying heavily on his conscience.

Next morning, as soon as Martin arrived, Jack drove straight to Cullinane's farmhouse in Aughamore, and when he reached the gate, Eileen was returning from the henhouse, the morning's collection of eggs in a wicker basket. In her years living in the city she had missed her feathered friends, her chickens, ducks and geese, and if for nothing else, she was glad to be back among them.

Shielding her eyes with her hand against the bright sunlight Eileen stood staring until she recognised the car. "Oh, it's you," she greeted. "What brings you here? I know I said to pay us a visit, but this beats Banagher. But come in, and I'll make a sup o' tay."

"Where's Cullinane?"

"Himself and Trevor are gone to Galway on business – why d'you ask?"

"It's just as well, because I was hoping to get you alone to ask you a few questions. I've just found out that it was Cullinane and not Paisley who poisoned the horse and cows," returned Jack, and then he went on to explain O'Hara's motive, his suspicion that he and her husband might have been in cahoots, and Trevor's revelation about the Land Commission, although he was careful not to mention his suspicion of the clergy, not until he heard what she had to say first, for any criticism of the Church was sure to send her into a tantrum.

Eileen greeted the news with a harsh laugh. "I knew all about the Land Commission – I found out from the same source as yourself," she said. "But that's the first I heard about Mike poisoning the horse and cows, and if it's true, there's not much we can do about it now – what's done is done."

"Is that all you can say about it, Eileen? – 'what's done is done'," said Jack. "Here was me blaming Paisley, God rest him, for poisoning Charlie, and the real culprit living under this very roof, and all you can say is: 'what's done is done'. Then, I was kind o' blaming Murt Burke for reporting me to the Land Commission, and you knew all the time and wouldn't tell me. It looked to me that Murt didn't want me back, and he's hardly set a foot inside the door since, only when he wants to borrow something, which is strange considering at one time he was like a dog under my feet. I suppose you heard he got Granny Mulhaire's few acres, whatever good that'll do him."

"So, it's God rest Paisley now, is it! Only a few days ago you were cursing him and saying the Devil had him – that's a big change all of a sudden. But I don't know how you could ever suspect Murt. Sure poor ould Murt would never do anything underhand."

"Will you grow up, Eileen!" Jack cut in. "Poor ould Murt – poor ould Murt, my arse! You'd never recognise the truth even if you met it in the street, and now that you mentioned it, it could've been Murt who put that conniving bastard of a husband of yours up to going to the Land Commission. You wouldn't believe me either when I said he was riding the tinker women. Well, he is – the sly ould bastard. It's true – I saw it with my own eyes, and what's more, he should be ashamed of himself, so he should, and every priest in the country gone hoarse from preaching about the evils of the flesh."

"I still don't believe it, and I won't believe it!" snapped Eileen. "It's all you and your filthy imagination! Well, see if you can imagine this for a change? Years ago my conniving bastard of a husband, as you called him, was our mother's lover – that's how we got by so easily all those years – on Mike's money, and it was a failed attempt at an abortion that caused her death – Mike was responsible. I couldn't tell you before now because I was afraid you'd get down the gun and shoot him. You're always telling me to cop myself on – so I have. That's why I married Mike, to get revenge for mother. You see, the last child isn't his, and the one I'm carrying now is Trevor's."

For the first time in his life Jack was completely lost for words, and he had no choice but to listen as Eileen rattled on. It was more or less the way he had suspected in his mother's case, but the rest of the story beggared belief, and the implications were just establishing themselves when she dropped another bombshell. "Years ago they used to call me a 'good thing' on account of my late husband, God rest him, taking me down Poke Lane and having his wicked way with me. So I thought, to hell, I might as well have the gain as well as the name. It took me a while to see the funny side o' life, as you kept telling me, but I'm seeing it at last. You see, the child I'm carrying now is Mike's grandchild, and if Mike is its grandfather, I'll be its grandmother as well as its mother. Trevor'll see the funny side too – he hates Mike. But I'm looking forward to seeing the look on Mike's face when I tell him someday."

"You wouldn't, Eileen."

"Oh yes, I would!" snapped Eileen. "And I will when the time is right. I often heard it said that it's a great boast for a man to say he had the mother and the daughter, and Mike had. But I wonder how he'll feel when I tell him I had the father and the son. But the last thing I want is you throwing wild accusations around, you and your temper – d'you hear! Leave Mike to me."

Jack could hardly have been more stunned if he had been struck across the forehead with the starting handle of a car, for it was hard to believe that Eileen could be so calculating. Still, his admiration for her grew, and now that all the perplexities of the past had been unravelled, all he could do was accept the cup of tea she had offered.

As the days of summer sped by, Ann's children returned like the swallows – Jack Daly's swallows – livening up the place with their cheerful chatter, something he had sorely missed while they were at school. Children – it was a pity they had to grow up, especially Ann's, who were the epitome of what children ought to be. To keep them away from the danger of being attacked by the sows Jack put them in charge of the newly-weaned shoats, which entailed keeping their pens clean and helping Martin with their feeding, and they set about it diligently and far beyond, washing and scrubbing them until their skins were nearly worn off their backs and their hooves shining like ivory. When there was any disagreement over their names, and there were many: the Mad Hatter, Loppylugs, Billy Bunter and even a few dignitaries: the Pope, Churchill and DeValera, he was called in to mediate. He could just about comprehend Churchill as a name for a somewhat squat, tubby shoat with a short thick neck, but DeValera made his mind boggle. "He looks so sad," they chirped, when finally his curiosity got the better of him.

Nothing daunted them, even when the breeze sometimes veered and whiffs from the septic tank floated over the farmyard, they just wrinkled their noses, and Jack found himself laughing, not the short cynical laugh that had become so much a part of him, but a long hearty laugh, the type of laugh that hadn't escaped from his lips since the days before the killing of his horse. It was innocence personified, and when he recalled his own childhood and the cruelty inflicted on the children of the day, especially on the children from the county home, by nuns, priests and monks, how could he not but agree with the condemnation in the Scripture: 'for whoso causeth one of these little ones to offend, it were better for him that a millstone be hanged about his neck and that he were drowned in the depths of the sea'. There were times when he wanted to reach out and hug them, but he stifled the impulse in case they or their mother took offence, for they were all that was standing between him and his guilty conscience.

As Galway races neared, now that he could afford to go in style, Jack couldn't understand his lack of enthusiasm for the event. Something was missing, the old excitement, unlike the days when he had slaved in wind and rain to have his turf ready for sale, or perhaps it was one of life's peculiarities that there had to be a bad day to appreciate a good day. However, one lunchtime the old spirit was rekindled when he had an unexpected visitor from the past, and he almost jumped out of his skin when he recognised Digger Nolan standing in the open doorway. Ann, her children, and Martin were sitting round the kitchen table, their backs to the door, and when Jack bounded from his chair by the fireplace and made helter-skelter to greet him, they could hardly be blamed for thinking that he had been suddenly short-taken.

"You're welcome, ould stock!" Jack whooped excitedly, the words exploding from his lips like a twelve-gun salute and, oblivious of the consternation he was causing behind his back, he went on, grasping Digger's hand and almost tearing his arm from his shoulder with the vigour of the handshake. "Let me look at you, ould stock! You're back just in time for the races – we'll have one whale of a time, me and you, just like in the old days."

Digger grinned, the shadow of the old grin that Jack remembered so well. And he looked nothing remotely like the wreck of a man he had left behind in Birmingham. Clean-shaven, his hair neatly parted, he was smartly turned out in a brown suit and shoes, white shirt and check tie. But most pleasing of all, the mischievous twinkle was back in his eyes.

Smiling wryly Digger put on display a uniform set of false teeth as he nodded towards the road where a pregnant woman and a young boy were standing beside a black Morris Minor. "No, Jack – my goose is cooked," he said, somewhat ruefully as he indicated the bulge in the woman's midriff and, calling them forward, he made the introductions. "This is my wife, Rita, and my son, Jack – I called him after you. But how about yourself?" he asked, casting a meaningful glance at the group round the table.

"No – that's Missus Fox, my daily help, and her two daughters, and Martin Finnegan, my right-hand man – I'm sure you remember Martin's parents from Baronsfield. But where are my manners – come in, and we'll make a drop o' tea and ready a bite to eat for ye."

For the next few moments everything was higgledy-piggledy, Jack trying to get Digger and his family inside, they refusing to disturb the routine, Martin and the children trying to get out, until Ann took the situation in hand. Seating the visitors round the fireplace she quickly re-laid the table, and when she had fresh tea brewed, she called them up to eat.

Back again at the fireplace, Jack and Digger fell into endless conversation, every sentence prefaced by 'do you remember'. "Do you remember the night, Jack, when we started a fight outside Seapoint to draw the bouncers away from the door so that a few o' the boys could slip in without payin'?"

"No one remembers it better than myself, and a black eye and sore ribs for my trouble – the good old days when we were always broke, the days that most people want to bring back again," returned Jack, he too suddenly wishing for those days to return, for all that he ridiculed people for harping on them. "And let's not forget the day we were picking spuds for ould Dempsey and he dropped dead in the field. I was all for going for the priest and you were all for searching him in case we didn't get paid. I still think it was the height o' blackguarding to take that quid out of his wallet."

"I only took what we had comin' to us, Jack."

"But you never mentioned it or gave it back when his wife paid us a few weeks later."

"How could I? – how could I own up and say I searched him – a dead man?" laughed Digger, and for the rest of the afternoon the light-hearted banter sallied back and forth as the two companions rambled together down *bohareen na smaointe* (memory lane).

When Ann, perhaps sensing that the men wanted to be on their own, took Digger's wife and boy outside to show them around, Jack related his saga.

Digger, serious now, lit a cigarette and blew a few thoughtful puffs at the ceiling. "For Christ's sake, don't let the likes o' Paisley be troublin' your conscience – he's gone, and the quicker you forget him, the better," he said. "But that fiver you gave me in Brum saved my life – that's why I'm here – to return it. When I woke next mornin' in the horrors, I had a wisp of memory that I'd seen you, but I could make no sense of it until I found the fiver in my pocket, and when I put the picture together, I realised what I had become. To make a long story short I kicked the booze and got a job on the motorway. Then, I met Rita, and after that I was freewheelin'. I'm happy now, happier even than the time we used to go to Bundoran together with the FCA. But what about yourself, Jack? You're not gettin' any younger – you're twenty-eight, you know – time to be settlin' down. But what am I sayin' – maybe you're havin' it away with that housekeeper of yours."

"No, I'm not!" snapped Jack, rushing to Ann's defence, slightly annoyed at Digger for suggesting it. "Ann is a widow, a real nice person, and the kids are nice too – I don't know how I'd have managed without her. So, let's go outside and I'll show you all I've achieved – you'll hardly know the place since you saw it last. As I've explained, I've gone into pigs in a big way. There's money in them at the moment, but like everything else that's profitable, there are more and more jumping on the bandwagon, and I was thinking of getting out and getting into something new before they kill the job altogether."

Digger, whose mind seemed to be focused on the relationship between Jack and his housekeeper, wasn't interested in pigs, and if the look in his eye was anything to go by, he was having none of Jack's denials. Yet, he was wise enough not to pursue the matter further and, changing the subject, he asked about Eileen and others in the village.

All too soon it was time for Digger to bid farewell, and Jack walked with him to the gate, waving after the car as it sped away. It was only when the car was out of sight that he released the salty tear that was burning the corner of his eye, although this time it wasn't a tear of sadness like the one he had shed in Birmingham, more like a tear shed when one finds out that there's no Santa Claus and, with Digger's departure, the last puff of romanticism drifted out of his life, like the sudden swirl of smoke from the dying embers of a fire when water is sloshed over it. The fantasy of his youth when he had believed in fairy-tale endings was behind him and he was all alone in the world – and he felt alone. Digger was right – it was time he was settling down, and yet, twenty-eight wasn't old. He had his whole life in front of him, and what better place to rejuvenate his spirits than at Galway races – have one whale of a time, and make it the first day of the rest of his life.

Chapter 8

On the morning of Galway races, when Ann and her children arrived, Jack was all spruced up and raring to go. Ann had agreed to look after the place in his two-night absence and, as he drove away and spied the children in the windscreen mirror waving in his wake, he blessed the good fortune that had dropped them in his lap. It had only come to him of late that Ann was a strikingly handsome woman, a comeliness that would be greatly enhanced if only there was some sparkle in her eyes and warmth in her smile and, save for her one out-of-character remark about handing it on a plate to him, her manner always bore an air of correctness. Yet, for all that his retort had driven a wedge into the wall of her coldness and prised open the door of her reserve, never were two people further apart in behaviour and outlook.

Driving along he fell to wondering what type of man would take her fancy if she ever decided to marry again. Someone cast in the same mould as herself, no doubt, as Pat had once philosophised: 'only when like mates like can there be any chance of real happiness', or perhaps she had a lover? He immediately dismissed the latter as unlikely, otherwise there would be gossip, and yet, eyebrows were always raised whenever widows were mentioned, raised in a manner which suggested that having already tasted the fruits of married life they would always be susceptible to the carnal side of men's advances. Still, it was hard to imagine Ann behaving as uninhibitedly as Widow Kilbane, nor would he believe it, at least not outside the sanctity of matrimony, and if she did marry again, it would be to safeguard her children's future.

He was so engrossed in his reverie that he was on the outskirts of Galway before he realised it, the tinkers camped on the grass verges on either side of the road leading to the city his first smelly reminder. Joining the traffic he was flagged on to the fair green, which was being used as a temporary car park, and from there he made his way through the gathering throngs to the Imperial Hotel. Once he had checked in he gave his feet free rein and, with a feeling akin to intoxication flowing in his veins, he wandered about the streets, soaking up the atmosphere until, as if some invisible puppeteer was pulling strings, he found himself standing outside Fleming's Bar, the music and chatter floating out from the open top sections of the windows enticing him to enter.

When he pushed open the door, the babble of talk became a roar, the music a crescendo and, shuffling into room at the counter, he ordered whiskey. As the music and drink combination worked its magic, he felt a strangeness coming over him that he couldn't quite comprehend, as if the whole scene had taken a backward step to a long-ago day that was still strong in his memory, only this time there was no enchanting young lady gliding through the smoky haze as gracefully as a black swan on a mist-covered lake, shaking her money pouch. It was all so real, yet so unreal, as if he was in some borderline country looking in, present, yet somehow aloof from it all, and though he felt himself acknowledging the nods of his neighbours, clapping for the music, dropping a coin in the musician's pouch, he wasn't part of it, only in his subconscious, or in the shadows of a dream, as if some sorcerer was playing tricks on his mind, leaving an unbridgeable gap between the present and the past. Shaking himself out of his stupor he finished his drink and mingled with the hurrying throngs on their way to the racecourse, amid the clamour of hawkers, trick-o'-the-loops, busker music, and the strident choruses of the hard-faced Dublin women selling race-cards.

Opting for the main enclosure he made straight for the bar, his eyes searching for a friendly face, or perhaps an acquaintance from his days in London. Although he recognised many from Castleford in the crowd he was politely ignored and, with his earlier enthusiasm on a downward spiral, he shrank from joining the elbowing and jostling at the counter and turned his attention to picking the winner of the first race.

After backing losers in the first two races he had twenty pounds on Amber Point in the Galway Plate at ten-to-one and climbed the steps to the top tier of the grandstand. The multi-coloured spectacle was already circling at the post, the tension mounting as the starter called the jockeys into line. At the announcement: "They're under starter's orders," the horses crept closer to the tape, and when: "they're off!" sounded, a tumultuous cheer sent them on their way. Almost immediately the commentator described the action in his faultless diction: "As they race away from the stands, it's Swinging Light, followed by Orange Flute, Prudent Barney, Polar Bear, Come to Daddy, and at the rear of the field I can see Proper Charlie, Slip the Frame and German Queen."

After completing a circuit of the track Amber Point was still in mid-division and, as they raced downhill to the Mooneen, a sharp corner of the course, before turning uphill to face the stiff climb to the finish, the race was developing into a five-horse contest. "And, as they approach the penultimate fence," the commentator rattled on, "Swinging Light, who's been in the lead throughout, is clear, while close on his heels are Orange Flute, Sparkling Flame, and Vulgan Prince, but closing on this quartet and making ground with every stride is Amber Point, and these are steadily drawing away from Proper Charlie, leaving the rest of the field toiling in their wake."

As stride for stride the gallant quintet raced towards the final obstacle, an ear-splitting cheer that started an echo in the distant hills erupted from the stands, drowning out the stentorian tones of the commentator and, as the volume of the cheering increased, spring-heeled these noblest of all beasts rose in unison to meet the fence like ships on a wave, jockeys with whips cracking asking for their supreme efforts as they turned uphill towards the winning post and swept right-handed into the straight, all five almost neck and neck, with first Vulgan Prince seeming to have the advantage, and then Orange Flute until champion jockey, Bobby Beasley, coaxed top-weighted Amber Point to stick out his head on the line.

Immediately the horses passed the winning post, as if by the stroke of a conductor's baton, the cheering broke off, the earlier expectations of most turning to disappointment as the crowd in a slow shuffling movement began to vacate the stand. Carried along in the flow Jack made straight for the bookmakers' ring and joined the queue waiting to be paid out, the realisation that he had twenty pounds on a ten-to-one winner scarcely quickening the beat of his heart, unlike another day when he had two shillings each way on Reuben's Glen and felt like doing handsprings all the way to the tote office. Still, in the midst of the hullabaloo, it felt odd that he should recall Teresa Kilbane's advice: 'If you're ever really down in the dumps, have a bottle or two of champagne if you can afford it, but remember, it's only a temporary cure – like buying happiness for a while'.

Now that his day was turning out to be the direct opposite to what he had planned, he paid the extra money and crossed the barrier to the reserved stand where the cream of the county had assembled and, as he shuffled through to the bar, the almost exaggeratedly well-dressed crowd made room for him, but barely sufficient, as though they were grudging to yield ground bodily as well as socially.

It was easier to name who wasn't there than who was there from Castleford's affluent set, the odd dog-collared priest among them, the men standing in scattered groups, showing off their good-looking wives, the more elderly seated at the tables, some looking askance at him, as if he didn't belong in the same creation, not to mind in the same company, especially when they heard the cork popping off the champagne. Again, the second skin he had grown in his term in England stood him in good stead and, ignoring their stares, he smiled and apologised his way into a seat at one of the tables.

Now that the feature event of the day had passed, there was less toing and froing from the bar, to the paddock, to the bookmakers and, as he sat sipping the champagne, he took in the scene over the rim of his glass. Mary O'Hara and her husband were the first to catch his eye, and now that she had lost most of her radiance, he looked at her as one might look at a flower he had once plucked which had faded, trying to recall the beauty that had enticed him to pick it in the first place, for he found it hard to believe that she was the same woman whom he had once loved to distraction, which lent substance to the saying that memory is the mother of disappointment, for in memory the fruit is always sweeter, the perfume stronger, the wine more heady, and no woman is like the remembered woman, and the picture is sometimes better than the real thing.

The decline in her allure cheered him, and her father's unwitting remark: 'you might thank me in later years', winked back at him from the mirror of hindsight – every cloud had a silver lining. When he glanced in her direction through a gap in the crowd, not even the faintest flicker of recognition showed in her eyes, but not so Kathy Moore, who was clinging to the arm of her gangling husband, a man that only a mother could love, and she audaciously acknowledged his presence with a wink, which set his mind to comparing the two women. Both had reached the same goal: to go through life free from the rigours of poverty, although by totally different routes. For Mary, it was no more than a continuation of the life she had known, the life of the already initiated, of silver salver and etiquette, whereas Kathy, who had mountains to climb socially, had gatecrashed her way, relying on her good looks and charm to vanquish the fate of facing a life of drudgery as a small farmer's wife and the never-ending burden of childbearing.

The champagne was going down a treat, just as it had on the night in the Grand Hotel in Brighton, and he ordered another bottle. The more he imbibed, the more his spirits soared, as Widow Kilbane had predicted, until he found himself looking out on the world through new eyes. When all was said and done, what had life to offer in the line of pleasure apart from a few drinks and a bit of arse, especially a bit of arse. Men had made fools of themselves over it, kings had given up kingdoms for it. Your arse – your arse – my kingdom for your arse, and at that very moment it was all that was on his mind. When he looked again at Mary O'Hara, she glowed into beauty, her dress shot up, her knickers fell down, and in his imagination he gave her a good rough humping, the type of humping on which Widow Kilbane and Kathy Moore thrived, something he should have done years ago when he had the chance.

His mind was so full of sadistic humour that he felt it was showing on his face, for Kathy Moore suddenly looked anxious, as if at any moment he might leap up and announce over the public-address system all the intimate details of their clandestine affair, their Sunday morning romps, and the creaking complaint of old bedsprings, her uneasy smile seeking reassurance that nothing unpleasant would be revealed. Kathy, although she looked devoted to her husband, wasn't the type who made a happy home, and what she looked like and what she really was might be compared to a beautifully-iced cake, cherries and all, but with sawdust for filling, the type used for window-dressing, or perhaps her husband believed that a good-looking unfaithful wife was better than a plain long-suffering faithful one.

It seemed too that the champagne had opened a door of a cell in his brain that had been closed since his affair with Widow Kilbane, for her image kept intruding on his reverie, Kathy's big mouth an earthy reminder of what Bob Little had slyly hinted about women with big mouths. Whether or not it was true there was no denying that the object of his comparison had power, the power to draw a man further than gunpowder could shoot, although the conduct of the species wielding this power didn't always follow the same pattern, for the ones going about with their knees held tightly together were as often as not the ones who could hardly wait to get them apart.

The widow's image would not go away, although he found a kernel of truth in her adage: 'gold glitters, champagne sparkles, but all that glitters is not gold and all that sparkles is not champagne, but they both attract', for it attracted three young ladies to his table. Judging by their sporadic bursts of giggling and body language they were out to enjoy themselves and, without appearing to be too forward, he introduced himself through the bubbly liquid.

Soon, through the enlivenment of the champagne, the old Jack Daly re-emerged, the devil-may-care character who had once thumbed his nose at society, the cool recklessness of the old days back in his face, as though the time-gap he had experienced earlier had been bridged, and Joan, tall, fair-haired and sensual, had the spirit of adventure in her eye.

As the afternoon advanced, he kept the corks popping and, as their laughter grew louder, his little party was coming more and more under the reproachful frowns of Castleford's bourgeoisie, a class-conscious society with iron palings round their houses to keep out the common herd, and the fact that they all had good-looking wives supported Reg Ashton's conviction that a woman's virtue was merely a matter of prices. Now these whited sepulchres were sitting in judgement on him, and he could almost lip-read their disparaging remarks: 'What's the world coming to at all – Widow Daly's son drinking champagne – it's far from it he was reared. That's what happens when upstarts get money, but mark my words, he'll be back in England before long with the rest o' the riff-raff'. When he looked again at Mary O'Hara, he smiled at her as at a memory and, turning away, he surrendered himself body and soul to his three ladyfriends, Joan, Peggy and Maureen, who were sparkling more and more as the empty bottles accumulated.

After the races they left with the last of the stragglers, and on the way back to town Joan accepted Jack's invitation to dinner. To make an impression he chose the fashionable Great Southern Hotel, and for the umpteenth time that day Widow Kilbane invaded his thoughts, the candlelit table evoking memories of the night she had introduced him to a similar ambience solely for his seduction. Every time he sipped from his wineglass he could see her distorted reflection in the wine laughing back at him and, wrestling with his conscience, he reminded himself that life was for living, and according to the catechism all creatures were put on earth for man's use and benefit.

Next morning, when sunlight came streaming through a gap in the curtains, Jack opened his eyes and, struggling with the pain of moving his eyeballs, he tried to get them to focus in tandem. His skull was pulsating, as if there was a bird flapping around inside, looking for a way out, his tongue was on fire, his throat parched, his stomach sourly protesting, not unlike his first morning in the Grand Hotel, although the room was smaller and he was lying partially clad on top of a single bed. There were women's things everywhere, lingerie hanging out of half-closed drawers, a dress hanging on the open wardrobe door, and it took a moment of painful reflection to realise that he was in Joan's hotel bedroom in Salthill where she had managed to drag him the night before when his legs gave out.

After dinner, following a memory trail, they had strolled round the funfair in Eyre Square, and hit the hotel bars all the way to Salthill, although the trail ran out sooner than he had planned, for the last thing he remembered was trying to entice Joan to the headland overlooking the bay where years ago he had enjoyed a magical night.

Jacking himself into a sitting position with his hands he swung his feet to the floor, but when he tried to walk, his legs refused to obey the command of his will, and it could only have been providence that stopped him from going head over heels. Resolutely he tried again, and this time he made it to the door where his jacket was hanging. Feeling somewhat relieved when he found his money intact he opened the door and peeped up and down the corridor, and when all was clear, he stumbled to the bathroom, the floor going see-saw beneath his feet as if he was on board ship.

The cold water he doused copiously on his head seemed to have wet the bird's wings, for the intensity of the flapping slowed almost to nothing and, after washing his face and adjusting his dress, he descended the stairs tentatively, his jagged nerves made all the more jittery by a sudden clatter of plates coming from the kitchen. When he found the dining room, he was greeted by a flurry of waving hands from three familiar figures sitting at one of the tables, their smiles telling a story he didn't particularly want to hear.

"A society for the prevention of hangovers'd be a fine thing," he said, grinning to smother his embarrassment. "But that's yesterday – now how about today, ladies?"

"I suppose you've often heard of the hair of the dog," laughed Joan. "I think it's what you need if you feel as bad as you look."

"A hair wouldn't be enough," retorted Jack. "The way I feel, I'd need at least a tail."

Once again, champagne came to his rescue and, like stoking up the dying embers of a fire, it stoked up the dregs of the previous day's booze and resurrected him from the dead. However, when later that morning they set out for the races, it only went to prove that a chance day's enjoyment can rarely be recaptured, for no matter how much he tried to bring back with champagne the gaiety of the previous day, something was missing, something he couldn't quite put a finger on, as if familiarity had dulled his spirit of adventure or the champagne had lost its magic. The ladies too seemed to sense it, and they left together before the last race, returning to Jack's hotel for dinner to beat the evening rush. Finally, he decided that there was a limit to everything except foolishness and, promising that they would meet again someday, he bade farewell to his ladyfriends and returned to Castleford and Grogan's Bar.

It was only when he was driving home after closing time that he realised he wasn't expected until the following evening and, worried in case his late-night entry might frighten Ann and the children, especially as the cottage was in darkness, he wasn't sure whether he should knock or sleep in the car. He had explicitly warned her to keep the doors bolted, although now that she had probably heard the car, he felt that he should make his presence known, and he rapped loudly on the front door, calling: "It's me – Jack!"

Seconds later, a light came on, and when the door creaked open, Ann appeared in dressing gown and slippers. "You're back," was her only greeting before hurrying to her room, leaving Jack standing sheepishly in the open doorway, his brain so addled with drink that no words of explanation came to his lips. She must be upset, he thought, as he bolted the door behind him and stumbled to his bedroom.

Jack was right inasmuch as Ann was upset, although more disappointed than upset, as she had anticipated him returning sometime on the following afternoon when the children could greet him and relate their stories of how they had overcome all the problems in his absence. Yet, she shouldn't be disappointed, she chastised herself, Jack was paying her for her inconvenience, and the least she could have done was offered him a cup of tea, instead of sitting in judgement on him. What Jack did was none of her business. He meant nothing to her – or did he? If he didn't, how could she explain the warm tide of feeling that always crept over her every time he passed close, bewildering, almost frightening, or why she had felt pleased when there was no longer the scent of perfume on his pillow? There were so many 'whys' in life lately, like why she had searched for excuses for him for treating Paisley's death so irreverently? And why should she be interested in what he had against Paisley, so interested that she had wrung the story out of the tight-lipped Martin that he held Paisley responsible for the killing of his stock?

These were the thoughts tormenting her sleepless hours long after Jack had retired and, as she lay in the darkness, she sensed that his bedroom door was open, for she could hear his snoring, although it felt somewhat reassuring to know that he was close at hand. However, when he began to rave, her feminine curiosity prompted her to creep stealthily to the kitchen and listen. Afraid to go farther than the fireplace in case he might suddenly awaken, incoherent muttering reached her ears, which was punctuated by loud calls for Charlie. Having no idea who Charlie might be she crept closer and peered into the room.

The moonlight falling a little way into the room through the undraped window was painting a paler window on the floor, and Jack was lying on top of the bed, writhing restlessly, his face glistening with perspiration. Suddenly, as if some inner dial was controlling the volume of his raving, his voice became softer, softer than she had ever heard it before, and she had to strain her ears to catch the words: "Mary, you don't have to speak to me when you meet me in the street – I'll understand – it'll work out, you'll see…" the sentence trailing off as he began to snore again. If she was truthful to herself, these were words she didn't particularly want to hear and, castigating herself for her curiosity, she tiptoed to her bedroom. Back between the sheets, she couldn't understand the queer pang of jealousy that jabbed at her heart when she realised there was a woman in Jack's life – someone called Mary, and trying to ignore the prickly thought was like trying to ignore a pebble in the shoe.

Next morning, when dawn crept through the window, ghostlike and silent, sweeping the shadows of the night into the corners of the room, Jack woke with a start. The sheets were wringing with perspiration, the bedclothes on the floor, and for a moment he was in another world where time had no meaning, as if the events of the past couple of days were all in his imagination, jumbled together in a nightmare that had no reality nor reason, although gradually, as the objects in the room became more real to his sight, the episode of the champagne, the ladies, and the races became more real to his mind. It was only a bad dream, which was of no consequence, he consoled himself, for dreams, bad or otherwise, always ended in nothing and left the sleeper exactly where he had lain down.

Rising from his tumbled bed he decided that a drink of cold spring water and a stroll in the early-morning air was the best cure for his ailment and, dressing quickly, he tiptoed to the kitchen and gulped down two mugs of water, gagging on each swallow until his thirst was assuaged. Fearful in case he disturbed Ann and the children he slipped through the back door and quickly put distance between himself and the house. Still in a stupor his limbs were thinking of more positive lines than his head, for he found himself on the well-trodden boreen leading to the vast expanse of bog and turbary that was part of the village, the same acres that Dillon, the TD, had once promised to turn into grassland where cattle could graze to the knee.

Despite his hangover, Jack smiled, for it would be hard to graze anything on it now except snipe, ptarmigan, curlew, bittern and wild geese in the winter, although its solitude came as a balm to his befuddled brain. The mist shawling the countryside was lifting, bringing into light the green expanse of small fields and their criss-crossing of stone walls, and when he reached the end of the boreen, he found a seat on a timber rail between two hawthorn trees where the whole panorama of bog and land fell under his vision.

Struggling against a chaos of nostalgic memories he finally set his mind against the past. The only good thing about the past was that it was past, for it now seemed that everything grows wearisome with time, riches exhaust their possession once it's found they cannot buy a happy ending, ambition, once satisfied, leaves behind only regrets, and it was the way of the world to be wise when it's too late. What to do next was his problem. He could always return to London, although this would mean throwing in the towel at the desire of his hypocritical neighbours.

Perhaps he should conform, start going to Mass again on Sundays, as Eileen had suggested, or why not go a whole hog and give a large donation to the Church, made payable to the bearer in the next world. Then, he might be looked upon as an eligible bachelor, a man of substance, a good catch for a woman. A match could be made for him with some big strong biddy with bad teeth and huge feet, a woman who would thrive on the drudgery of farm life and throw a puttock of a child out of her every year as regularly as sheaves from a reaper and binder, a woman who would be as unloved as the animals on the farm, and no more a wife than the farm would be a home.

As his imagination took flight, he tried to see the funny side. But was there a funny side, for how else could he get a wife? He was past the age for dance halls and getting close to the age when he would be too old to pal about with the youth and still too young to pal about with the old-timers – emigration had made sure there were no in-betweeners. His problem was self-inflicted, Eileen had said, so perhaps he should make one more try.

The peaceful scene of bog merging with land made a picture of contrasts – wilderness merging with civilisation, each striving to claim the other, like sea and shore. If he was a painter, he would paint it, and call it *Nature's Remedy for Stress*, for it felt so relaxing just to sit there, with only the rustle of leaves and the gurgle of slow water breaking the stillness, and watch the world roll by. And, it was rolling by, much too quickly for his liking.

Finally, when the fresh air and tranquillity had worked its magic, he trudged back to his cottage, torn between the idea of returning to live among the English, a race who professed to know so much and knew so little, for whom he had developed a dislike, and the alternative of knuckling down and playing the hypocrite. At first he favoured the former as the lesser of the two evils, although he doubted that he could ever adapt to its system, a semi-feudal system which gave 'sir', 'lord' and 'lady' status to certain individuals, a pedigree not unlike the blue riband at Crufts for the best breed of dog.

However, the sting in the tail was that these awards were given, not to the brave who had risked life and limb to save children from blazing buildings and other hazards, but to music composers, film stars, singers, footballers, mendacious politicians, perjurers, right-wing paramilitary groups, fraudsters and thieves. Nevertheless, these were the people the monarch decorated, whose only claim to fame lay in composing a song, scoring a cup-final goal or making money from exploitation, and yet, failing to mention that many of these so-called pillars of society indulged freely in drug-taking, promiscuous behaviour, and other vices condemned by the law of the land and the law of God, which they, in their elevated status, had a moral obligation to uphold.

On the one hand, in London he would be mingling again with his immigrant brethren, a classless community in which a lack of education was never an obstacle to advancement, as Pat had said: 'I'd rather be in hell with the Irish here in London than in heaven with the crowd back yonder'. Ridiculed on both sides of the Irish Sea, their characters blackened at every opportunity, perhaps in time the immigrants might gain an identity of their own, for there were far more Irish in London than there were in Dublin.

On the other hand, London wasn't a place for settling down, more a type of limbo, a stepping stone where people persevered until they had their money made. His own term there was a typical example, years with no time for looking at them, for thinking of death, or saving the soul, years of almost passionate moneymaking. Now that he had all that life could offer, except a wife and family, and as much security as he could hope for in an insecure world, he could go back to London with none of the anxieties of the past. Still, something perverse in his nature stirred him into disobeying his common sense, or perhaps it was the authoritarian blood of the priesthood in his veins at war with the more submissive blood of the peasantry that was urging him to dig in his heels. Why should he go back just because he didn't agree with the system? As Pat had said, there was every chance that a younger generation might bring about change.

In the following weeks the optimism that a new generation might cast out the feudalism that had his country in a stranglehold found roots, and the idea of staying kept nagging him with the wheedling importunity of a tinker woman on the cadge. Another reason too kept obtruding, much as he tried to dismiss it, and it was never more insistent than on a wet Sunday evening as he sat alone in the kitchen, the usual Sunday evening gloom made all the more dismal by the thought of Ann's children returning to school next morning – he would miss the children.

The first chill of autumn was in the air, the oncoming darkness adding to the gloom, and the monotonous ticking of the clock and its tinny thumps as it coughed up the hours were grim reminders that life was marching on. Turning to the whiskey bottle on the dresser he poured a generous measure and sat staring into the fire, his eyes searching the flames for the image of the idealistic youth who had stared into the same fire nearly a decade ago, wondering what happened to his dreams which had once made his heart beat so warmly. Somewhere along the lonesome road that had led him from his home, the youth had slipped away and there was left a man, bitter and tough, the shell of hardness around his heart thickening with each new disappointment, living in a cynical world of his own making. If he wanted to be accepted, he would have to play the hypocrite, attend Mass, support his pastors, let them see that he had repented. This way, his soul would be shrived, whatever about his mind, and if it didn't do any good, neither would it do any harm.

Chapter 9

It was one of those bright Sunday mornings between autumn and winter when the sun was almost as hot as in mid-July. The withering leaves were clinging forlornly to the trees, and the songbirds' somewhat tired twittering bore a note of despondency either for the coming of winter or to keep in harmony with Jack's mood, for he was on his way to last Mass, the first step in his return to the fold. In case it defeated the effort he had decided against going about it in a flurry, parading up the middle aisle to the front pews and drawing attention to himself. His first strokes back against the current in which he had drifted so indifferently should not be hurried. Better to start humbly at the rear of the church, and after a few weeks when the congregation got used to his presence, ease his way to the fore in position and in the donation stakes.

Although he was late he approached the church door boldly and shuffled through the overspill of men who were standing bareheaded in the vestibule, morally present at a service they could neither see nor hear, their dull piety and the sickly smell of the cheap hair-oil with which they anointed their heads bringing a queasy sensation to his stomach. The air was full of the must of Sunday clothes, and from force of habit he ran his eyes over the congregation, his glance singling out Eileen who was kneeling devoutly beside her stoop-shouldered spouse.

Now that she was in the full bloom of motherhood, Eileen was showing up her husband's age, for he looked very much a grandfather, although now that vengeance was at hand, he found himself looking at him with less animosity. Mary Cook/O'Hara was pregnant again, which suggested her husband was sticking rigidly to the first part of the precept for a secure marriage by keeping her belly full. There was no such luck for Kathy McCale/Moore, who looked the epitome of virtuous womanhood, her gawky husband at her elbow standing out as obtrusively as a gander beside a swan. "Unless he starts pumping harder, Father Brophy'll be having a word in his ear –"

Jack was startled out of his reverie by the bell ringing for the consecration, and though he tried to keep his attention focused on the service, the hard self-honesty that lay at the base of his nature wouldn't allow him. He simply wasn't interested and, with such earthy thoughts flying in and out of his mind, he doubted that he was gaining any indulgences. Nevertheless, he stayed long enough for his presence to be noticed and, slipping away before the final three Hail Marys, he joined the crowd shuffling impatiently outside Grogan's waiting for opening time.

Immediately the door opened, as if by magic, the place was swamped in customers, and for the next ten minutes Grogan and his barman were flat to the boards filling and topping up pints. Now that he was a man of substance, Jack was greeted by a host of 'good morning Jacks' and other salutations, his neighbours chirping mightily like a nest of singing birds. Still, there was a falseness in it – the arm round the shoulder bit – for not long ago they would have divided his few acres between them as the soldiers had once divided Christ's clothes, and perhaps cast lots for his cottage. Even though he had discovered the Judas in their midst, it failed to bring reconciliation, for they were just as guilty as Cullinane for not protecting his interests in his absence as they had promised.

Hypocrites all, he thought, and now he was joining their ranks. The initiation ceremony would perhaps entail giving a large donation to the man with the red cap, and then it would be all systems go and only a matter of time before he acquired the art of saying something nice to someone he hated instead of spitting in his eye, or perhaps praising him to his face and then breaking wind the moment his back was turned. With practice he might become addicted – a hypocriticolic, and if it became really addictive, he could organise a hypocrites anonymous society where each member in turn could stand up and declare: 'I am a hypocrite', and then go on to discuss their affliction with the other addicts: 'I was nice to that horrible Mr Bounderby just because he's rich, and I wishing him dead at the same time'. 'I was condemning my best friend behind her back for having an affair, while at the same time I was wishing it was me, condemning what I secretly desired myself', and so forth.

Invariably, there would be lots to reveal, although he doubted that he would have many members, or perhaps like vampires, hypocrites should be wooden-staked. Then, he could go into the timber business making stakes and, as there was certain to be thousands needed, he could hang out a shingle: 'Jack Daly – Hypocrite Slayer'.

Still, he had only himself to blame – he had joined his country's enemies and crowed about it. The message between the lines was plain – he should have stayed away regardless of the circumstances that had forced him to go in the first place – he was a changeling – he was a likeable lad before he went to England – England had ruined him and warped his way of thinking. Thus, there would be no killing of the fatted calf for those returning from Blighty, no rejoice with me for I have found the sheep that I had lost, and so much for the song *COME BACK PADDY REILLY TO BALLYJAMESDUFF*. For it now seemed that there should be a different message in the whispering coming over the sea – a stay-away message

Perhaps if he went on his knees in the marketplace and repented publicly, denouncing England with all her works and pomps, and swore on the Bible that they lived on nothing but fish and chips, or declare that he had met better Englishmen over there than Irishmen, all might be forgiven. Better still, why not confirm the authenticity of some of the contemptuous verse composed about the menial work undertaken by his immigrant brethren

Suddenly, as if someone had sloshed a bucket of cold water over his head, Jack crashed out of his reverie and, as an icy wind swept through his brain, purging its cells of all such kiss-arse notions, the reality it revealed suggested his only option lay in returning to London and mingling again with his exiled countrymen. They were his people, a race apart, whose generosity knew no bounds where their homeland was concerned, for all that their largesse went totally unacknowledged by its recipients, not even by a kind word, just as their contribution to British society went unacknowledged, booted into the long grass of amnesia by the media. They were and always would be pariahs in their own land, and the selfishness of the children left behind after the Pied Piper had passed through their midst would make sure they had no homes to return to, no chance of fulfilling the dreams they had carried with them when they first set out on the lonesome road.

The bell for last orders, ending the lunchtime session, brought Jack back to the present, and afterwards, as the crowd began to drift towards the door, Grogan called him aside. "Why don't you stay on for one, Jack?" he suggested, in an undertone. "It's quite a while since we had a good chat."

Jack nodded, and when the bar was cleared and the door bolted, Grogan filled two large measures of whiskey, handing one to Jack. "Cheers, Jack – to health and happiness!" he toasted. "But tell me this – is you heart still set on pullin' the pin and goin' back?"

"It's in my head – things'll never change around here," returned Jack. "But the ironic thing about it all is, when I was broke, I wasn't happy because I couldn't afford the things I dreamed about, and now that I can afford them, I feel less happy than I was then. Can you explain that to me, Mick?"

"Not really, but that's the way with life sometimes," returned Grogan. "Still, you have your health, and that's more valuable than all the gold in the world. But if it's only a matter of decidin' between bein' rich and poor, take it from me, rich is the best. On the other hand, you never can tell, this new pope might turn things round."

"I'm sure he will – I can already hear him ringing the changes," said Jack, a derisive note in his tone. "His opening sermon'll go something like this: 'It grieves me to have to tell you, but down through the years we've hoodwinked you. We've taken your money under false pretences and feathered our own nests with it, and all I can say now is – we're sorry. However, in my forthcoming reign as pontiff, I intend to make recompense, first by selling off all Church property, all the gold and jewels, and use the proceeds for medical research and famine relief. Also, I'll nullify the commandment: contribute to the support of your pastors. I'll even go one further and declare that all Masses for the dead, both high and low, are to be said free of charge, so the clergy, bishops and all, will have to fend for themselves by doing part-time work when they're not preaching the doctrine of faith and morals, basic jobs, such as washing sheep's daggings, clearing blocked drains, and emptying septic tanks. Furthermore, I'm going to take the religion back to basics to the time of Christ, its founder, when His disciples walked everywhere and slept anywhere they could find a bed, no chauffeur-driven limousines, no housekeepers, no carpeted palaces, no grapefruit for breakfast, no gambling on cards or horses, no fat bank accounts, and so forth. All these terms will be written into the ordination ceremony, even if it means less vocations'."

"I can never hear him sayin' that, Jack – much as I'd like to."

"Who knows – he might be a radical," Jack went on. "When he studies the facts, he might make a declaration and broadcast it to the whole world, something like this: 'In view of all the new scientific evidence, which disproves our medieval dogma that the world was flat and not round, I apologise to the descendants of all the people we burned at the stake as heretics because they weren't in accord with our doctrine. Also, I find it hard to believe in a life after death, although one thing is certain, we'll all rest in peace when our time comes. In reality all we have to go on is blind faith, and if I doubt it myself, how can I, in all honesty, preach it. You can very well ask what has happened to my divine enlightenment and infallibility, but be assured that in my capacity as the man nearest to God, I've tried to get through, but alas I fear the lines are down – that is, if they were ever there in the first place. And, if I can't get through, what chance has anybody else? So, why fool ourselves! I'm quite aware that it makes people feel good to believe in the life hereafter – the feel-good factor – heaven for the good, hell for the bad, and a place in between for the not-so-good and the not-so-bad. I think the whole world would settle for that. So, here we have the basis for a whole new religion, a popular religion that would embrace all denominations – Pagans, Christians, Jews, the lot'."

"You should be in politics, Jack – even Dillon couldn't draft a speech like that," applauded Grogan. "But the sky'd have to fall first before there'll be any change."

"As you mentioned politics, Mick, I think there should be politics in religion – a two-party system, so that the opposition would have a chance to voice its views on such contentious issues as birth control and eating meat on Fridays," said Jack. "It's far too dogmatic as it is – a one-man dictatorship, and look at the pandemonium there'd be if the Pope went off his head like ould King George. It should be more democratic in keeping with the times: the Pope should come up for election every so often, and the religion should be streamlined – throw out anything that doesn't make sense."

"They'd be cuttin' their own throats if they did that," returned Grogan. "It'd be like killin' the goose that's layin' the golden eggs."

"Religion, as I see it, is a business – a business of believing, and like all businesses it's got to show a profit," Jack went on. "It's part of human nature to believe that anything cheap or free is rubbish, like nobody'd buy anything off a salesman if he was wearing a piss-stained suit and a dirty shirt. That's why the Catholic religion has so many mysteries, to make it appear more powerful, more frightening – frighten the live out o' the congregation by preaching: 'He who believeth not shall be condemned', and then milk the last shilling out o' them with the camel and the eye o' the needle sermon. You've got to remember too that religion isn't always a force for good as so many wars have proved, and the downside is that it's having a damning effect on society in general – men are murdering one another over where they're going to after death, and it's making crooks out o' people who are basically honest. You see, the promise of absolution if we confess and repent is more of an incentive to cheat, steal and lie than vice versa."

"Go on, Jack – you're makin' sense," encouraged Grogan. "I only wish the man with the red cap was here listenin' to you."

"But I'm right, Mick – that's the funny part about it," returned Jack. "What we really need is a whole new religion – bring a touch of reality into it. Go back to the beginning and start with God – give Him a different image. No one wants a vengeful God, or a God responsible for the disasters of the world or for deformities in birth. We need a fair and understanding God, a God who can appreciate the pitfalls of nature and judge sins accordingly, a kind of points system with a grey area in between, especially in sins like adultery. More allowance should be made for a beautiful woman taken in adultery, considering all the men that'd be after her, rather than a plain woman, one who'd count herself lucky if she got the chance to commit adultery. It's something like: 'what does it profit a man if he gains the whole world and suffers the loss of his soul?' so, it should be: 'what does it profit a man if he rides an ugly woman if he only incurs the same penance if he rides a good-looking one?' or 'what does it profit a man if he gives all his money to the priests and winds up in a pauper's grave?'"

"The Lord save us, Jack – you'll get the two of us ex-communicated," tut-tutted Grogan, reaching again for the whiskey bottle.

"Take it from me, Mick, the Faith needs a complete overhaul, otherwise it'll lose support," Jack went on. "It needs to be made simpler – get rid of all the mysteries so that the ordinary man in the street can understand it. First of all I think the Holy Ghost should go – he's far too complicated a figure to explain. I'll bet even the Pope himself couldn't enlighten us on his role in the scenario. It'd be much simpler if they had the Father, the Son and the Mother, as the three divine persons, and cut out all that bullshite about the good sitting at the right hand of the Father; they'd never fit, unless the hand was millions o' miles long."

"The parables too need a few alterations," added Grogan, now that he had grasped the gist of what Jack was trying to get across. "Take the one about the workers in the vineyard – it was surely takin' the piss in a big way givin' the men who started at the eleventh hour the same wages as the men who started early in the mornin'. If it happened in real life, it'd cause ructions, without even considerin' the fact that they were workin' a twelve-hour shift."

"On the contrary!" interjected Jack. "It only goes to prove that Christ was a socialist, a communist, and not a capitalist. By paying them all the same wages at the end o' the day, the weak as well as the strong, the lazy as well as the willing, no favouritism, He was just making sure that there were no rich and no poor, equality all round, if you get my meaning. On the other hand, if He was a capitalist, He'd have a hired ganger, an Irish ganger preferably, and promised him a large bonus if he delivered the crop with the minimum of cost. He'd have given him a free hand to hire and fire and pay as little as he could get away with. As happens in real life, the ganger'd sack the lazy ones and work the daylights out o' the others, and book in a few dead men to feather his own nest – there'd be no such thing as everyone getting the same wages as in the parable."

"You've got a point there, Jack. Still, I think takin' the money from the widow wasn't fair, like robbin' the poor to pay the rich. It'd look a whole lot better if He gave the poor ould woman her mite back, whatever a mite was worth – it'd show kindness."

"I agree, and the miracle of the loaves and fishes should be taken out altogether – it's too hard to swallow –"

"Too hard to swallow – I like it, especially if they had to eat the bread dry and the fish raw, as there was no mention of butter or fires or fryin' pans," Grogan cut in. "And turnin' the water into wine should be done in the mornin' – give them the good wine first and keep the plonk till they were all drunk, when they wouldn't know the difference – take a leaf out o' my book there."

"Yes – I'll bet we could find something wrong with them all," said Jack. "Then, on the other hand, isn't it high time that some kind of move was made to win the Devil back to the fold. After all he was only someone who led a rebellion and lost, which is nothing new if we look back in history. Yet, no priest or bishop can explain what the rebellion was all about, or maybe they just made it up to make the religion appear more frightening. But taking it as gospel, it's hard to believe that an angel would support a rebellion against something good. So, why not extend the olive branch, and hear his side o' the story. It could be done – call a truce, and then get Old Nick and his bad angels round the table. Then, if they came to an agreement, we could say: 'thus on this fateful day, came to an end all evil'."

"And let's not forget all the money that's in religion," said Grogan. "People are bein' brainwashed into believin' that givin' money to the clergy is givin' money to charity. It's time they copped themselves on – they'd be far better off givin' it to the tinkers. Givin' money to priests and bishops should be a mortal sin – it only does them harm if you take heed of the camel and the eye o' the needle bullshite. If they took the money out o' religion, like takin' the gun out o' politics, the world'd be a better place to live in."

"You've struck the nail on the head there, Mick – giving money to priests was condemned in the Acts of the Apostles," Jack agreed. "When Simon, the sorcerer, offered money to Saint Peter, he answered: 'May your money perish with you, because you thought you could buy the gift of God with money'."

"If Saint Peter said that, the priests never mention it in their sermons," interjected Grogan. "So, actually takin' money for Masses is against the teachin' of Saint Peter, and the bit about blessed are the poor in spirit for theirs is the kingdom of Heaven is all a sham, seein' as they glorify the poor, and yet, they're not willin' to embrace poverty."

"It seems so, and if giving money to priests was a mortal sin, Ireland's economy would surely flourish, and the money saved could be spent on building houses for the tinkers," returned Jack. "But I wonder what the reaction around here would be if the new pope pulled the carpet out from under it all and said that believing in the house with the many mansions, the eternal reward and so forth, was the same as believing in Santa Claus. Would they turn on the clergy and ask for their money back? – Or would they kick the grapefruit for the Stations up and down the street in vexation, like the supporters of the monarchy made a football out of Oliver Cromwell's head? If that ever comes to pass, I'll be back, if only to see the look on their faces. But at the moment I think I can safely say without fear of contradiction that in the kingdom of the hypocrites the man with the red cap is still king."

"But just say for instance, Jack, that Christ was never crucified – that Pontius Pilate felt sorry for Him and let Him go – we'd have no religion at all," said Grogan. "If He'd died of natural causes, it'd be awful hard to convince anyone He was really God."

"Just for argument sake, say Christ came back on earth again in His original form, the Second Coming, as they call it, and went riding up to the door of the Vatican on an ass to take over from the Pope, I wonder how would it go down?" asked Jack. "Would the Pope be pleased to see Him and go on his knees and say: *'Hosanna, Hosanna'* or would he deny Him three times like Saint Peter, and say: 'I know not the man', especially if He told him their days of palatial halls and silver salver were over and that they'd have to go back to basics and tramp around the country in sandals and all the trappings of poverty, preaching His doctrine: 'blessed are the poor'."

"I don't think He'd be a welcome visitor," returned Grogan, "especially if He told them they'd have to wash the feet of their flock after Mass every Sunday, like He did Himself at the Last Supper."

"You're right, Mick – I couldn't see the Pope and his cronies accepting it," Jack agreed. "They'd gang up on Him like Pharisees in the gospel and put Him on trial for blasphemy and, seeing as they couldn't crucify Him in this day and age, they'd have him committed to a mental home."

Grogan laughed. "It's good to clear the air sometimes – to get it all off our chests," he said. "But I'd say by the way you're talkin' that your mind is already made up to hit the trail."

"Yes – I suppose it'll take at least six months to sell up," returned Jack. "And, much as I regret it, it'll mean getting rid of Martin and Ann, unless I can persuade the new owner to keep them on. I can't see any other way. But let's have some more whiskey – I'm enjoying the crack at the moment."

Chapter 10

In the following weeks a sudden downturn in the price of pigs twisted Jack's arm into making up his mind, and one morning, finding himself alone with his housekeeper, he decided to air his intentions. Sitting together at the kitchen table over a cup of tea he was doing his best at stringing a few words together to let the axe fall more gently when he heard the front gate creaking open. He always left the hinges of the gate unoiled as a forewarning of intruders, although he was taken completely by surprise when he looked up and saw Father Brophy's wholesome frame darkening the doorway. He eyed the priest with the utmost suspicion, and his first and most natural thought was that he was going to be tapped for money, perhaps the first symptoms of touchophobia.

Before Jack had a chance to invite him in, the priest, a thickset, balding man in his forties, was standing over them at the table. "Sit just as you are – this is not a social call, and what I have to say won't take long," he began, his tone full of the arrogance and authority associated with his station. "It's been brought to my attention that you two are having a clandestine affair, and at times sleep under the same roof, or should I say in the same bed. I came to tell you that it has to stop, and I'll start by hearing both your confessions at the church on Saturday night."

For a timeless moment Jack sat as though poleaxed and, as a slow-burning anger welled up in his breast, he felt as if he might explode, but for Ann's sake, he bit back on the vulgar retort that sprang to his lips. "I won't say you're welcome, Father," he said, quite calmly, for all that he was fuming. "But before we go any further I think you owe Missus Fox an apology."

"I'll apologise to no one!" snapped the priest, cutting Jack short, and he was about to continue with his diatribe when something in Jack's fierce stare froze the words on his lips.

"Hold on, Father – don't get your drawers in a twist. That's some accusation you're after making," he countered, still struggling with his anger. "It's quite obvious that you've been listening to gossip. So, get down off your high horse and sit down for a minute and we'll discuss it for what it's worth, or is that against your religion?"

When Jack pulled out a chair from the table, the priest grudgingly sat down and immediately began to shuffle impatiently and look at his watch, as if he had more important issues to address.

"Now Father, while you're here, why not hear both our confessions together?" said Jack. "It'll only take a second, because we have nothing to confess. Before I explain, I want to point out that Missus Fox is a lady – a very fine lady, and she did stay here for two nights with her children while I was away at Galway races, and we did spend one night under the same roof when I returned unexpectedly, though we didn't share a bed as you so lewdly suggested. It's on account of Missus Fox's children that I'm making this appeal to the better side of your nature, that is, if you have a better side, because you know when gossip like this gets out – a priest taking a woman to task over her virtue – the children are the first to suffer."

"I'm not here to justify –"

"Please have the manners not to interrupt me again in my own house!" Jack cut in, finally giving vent to his repressed anger. "Hear me out – I heard you out! First of all I want you to apologise to Missus Fox, and then spread the word about that the gossip was totally unfounded. If you don't, it'll be like no smoke without fire – do you follow me?

Bristling with indignation, perhaps at being told to shut up, the priest rounded on Jack. "Never before have I been spoken to in such an irreverent manner and, as I said, I'll apologise to no one, and I'll expect you both at confession on Saturday night!" he snapped, his rubicund face turning pale, his heavy jowls quivering. "If you have no more to say on the matter, I'll bid you good day."

When Jack looked to Ann for support, she was ashen-faced and almost in tears, fear and astonishment plainly written on her face, and so stricken that she failed to utter a word in her defence.

Perhaps mistaking Ann's silence for guilt the priest rose to go, but before he had taken his second step towards the door, Jack was on his feet, blocking his path. "You're going nowhere until you've heard my story," he said. "And, you're going to hear it before you leave here, whether you like it or not."

There was no threat in the words, just a quiet certainty, which perhaps warned the priest to do as he was bidden, for he flopped down on the chair, while Ann, sensing that her employer was about to explode, looked on fearfully, mouth agape, her hand flying to her throat, clutching it as though it was torn with pain, the veins beneath the white skin of her knuckles throbbing swiftly.

"I tried to reason with you for the children's sake, but I can see now that I was just wasting my breath," Jack went on, hissing the words through his teeth, his baleful eyes boring down on the priest. "Now that I've been forced into a corner, I have something to say that you should take great heed of. If you don't already know who I am, I'll put you in the picture. I'm not Jack Daly – I'm Jack Fitzpatrick, the son of the priest who broke up the marriage in this house many years ago. So you see, I'm a man of the cloth too by hereditary rights."

"I don't believe it –"

"You mean you don't want to believe it!" interjected Jack. "So, shut up and listen or I'll kick up such a stink that you'll be able to smell it all the way from here to the Vatican, or maybe you think it's something to be proud of, being the bastard son of a priest, the bastard son of some big buffer like yourself, for instance? If you don't know about it, you must be the only priest in the presbytery who doesn't. Now that that's said, it's time for compromise, so here's the deal. First, I want it read out from the pulpit that you've made a mistake by listening to gossip. I want it put subtly with no names mentioned, and yet, leaving no one in any doubt as to whom you're referring. Something like this: 'a grave matter has recently been brought to my attention about a certain widow said to be living in sin. After discreet enquiries I find the allegations totally unfounded, and the scandalmongers should now examine their consciences –' that's the gist. The alternative is that I go to London and give my story to the *News of the World*. I can already see the headline: 'Priest's son seeks father – new genetic techniques to be used', something for the archbishop to read on Sunday morning with his grapefruit."

"This is blackmail, but you'll never make it stick!" the priest replied snappishly. "Even if it's true, who'll believe you? I never heard the like of it before in my life – accusing the Church of impropriety. The Church is infallible – you could be excommunicated for this."

Jack's temper had now reached boiling point, and unable to sit still he took to pacing the floor. "You have some cheek – coming here accusing us of adultery, and nothing at all about your own cronies and their housekeepers!" he cried, his anger fuelled by the priest's assumption that he could be frightened by the threat of excommunication. "I suppose they have the blessing of God, though I doubt it. If I had my way, I'd have the lot o' ye castrated to avoid anything like my case happening again. And you mentioned excommunication. Why bother? – I've already excommunicated myself. I'll have nothing to do with your money-grabbing religion. I want a religion I can look up to, not one that's beneath me, not one that's all about money – selling the Mass and all that."

"That's not true," countered the priest.

"Is it not? Look at all the money you get for saying Masses for the dead, Masses you never say at all – fiddling your faithful flock. If you said all the Masses you get paid for, you'd be down on your knees for the next fifty lifetimes, not to mind the next fifty years. Instead of giving the money to the poor as Christ demanded, you're feathering your own nests with it!"

"That's a lie!"

"If it's a lie, show me your bankbook and I'll judge for myself."

"I'm not sitting here any longer listening to this blasphemy!" the priest replied angrily, his neck reddening to the hue of an agitated turkey cock's and overflowing his dog-collar. "So, I'll be on my way, and don't think you've seen the last of me!"

"You're going nowhere until you apologise to Missus Fox for your filthy accusations," warned Jack, taking an aggressive stance by the door, feet apart, his left shoulder hunched slightly forward.

The intent in Jack's eyes could hardly be plainer, and the priest hesitated, his mind perhaps on the scandal that was sure to follow if Jack made good his threat, or perhaps he believed diplomacy was the better part of valour. Whichever, he turned to Ann, saying: "There's a possibility that I've been mistaken, and if I am, an apology is in order –"

"You are mistaken – there are no ifs or buts about it!" Jack cut in. "And what's more, you should be ashamed of yourself for judging good-living people on just hearsay and idle gossip."

"In that case I'll take back what I've said until I have more proof, and say I'm sorry to you both."

Now that he had his apology, Jack turned on the priest like a rabid dog. "Get out of my house before I throw you out, and don't you dare come here again with your lies," he cried, his tone cutting with contempt. "However, if you want to make your trip worthwhile, go and see the man next door. I don't know what he gives them for it, but he's riding the tinker women who come round begging. It's a holy disgrace to the parish – so why not have a word in his ear while you're in the area?"

Save for the slight raising of an eyebrow the priest completely ignored Jack's comment about his neighbour's immorality, and when he reached the door, he turned for a final sally. "Do you realise the consequences of what you're doing – turning the servant of God out of your house?" he said gravely, in a last-ditch effort to gain control of the situation.

"God had no say in it when you became his servant," returned Jack. "Besides, you're lining your pockets well out o' your so-called vocation. So, if you want to earn your money for a change, ask the man next door point-blank if he's riding the tinker women or not? You came here to confront us on just idle gossip, and now when you have it straight from the horse's mouth, you don't want to follow it up – why?"

Cornered by the challenge in Jack's allegations the priest was lost for words and, as his impotency gave way to anger, he exploded. "I'll see to it that you do no more business in this neck o' the woods!" he spat venomously. "I have friends in high places –"

Before the priest had time to finish the sentence Jack grabbed him by the shirt-front with one hand and slapped his face with the other. "I won't tolerate anyone coming to my door threatening my livelihood!" he cried, and he kept slapping the priest's face with his open palm until it turned pale and tears of pain and humiliation rolled down his cheeks. A dozen times he slapped him, and then, spinning him round, he propelled him through the door, the toe of his boot on his arse helping him on his way. "Be off with you now out of my sight, and let that be a lesson to you and your friends in high places!" he called in his wake. "And, if you have any ideas about going to the cops, just look at the facts. You were on my property making false accusations, and when I asked you to leave, you wouldn't. Then I pushed you out the door, which I'm quite entitled to, and if you say I assaulted you, I'll deny it, and besides, you have no marks to prove it. If you pursue the matter, I'll get the best law firm in Dublin to defend me, Jewish, not Catholic, and I'll see to it that it gets full publicity."

If Ann looked shocked at the outset, it was nothing to the way she looked now, the sunlight falling on her bewildered face highlighting her pallor, and in one surge the hint of tears in her eyes became a flooding reality. Gone was all her composure, and she looked like a lost, frightened child as she turned to Jack as if for support.

Jack's outburst left him completely empty like a shaken sack, and though all his instincts demanded that he should do something, or say something to relieve her anxiety, he felt awkwardly inadequate in the situation. Taking her by the hands he brought her to her feet and, pillowing her head on his shoulder, he began to stroke her hair, smoothing it like a child might smooth the ruffled plumes of a storm-tossed bird. "Now, now, Ann – don't cry. Everything'll turn out all right, you'll see," he said, in low reassuring tones. "I'm sorry for what I've just put you through – I realise now that I should've kept my big mouth shut and my hands to myself."

Leaning against Jack as though her strength had suddenly left her, Ann was so beside herself that no words came to her lips, and it was left to Jack to go on, pouring oil on the troubled waters. "Don't worry about the priest. I'll go after him and give him some money – that should square things up."

"It's not that, Jack – it's the children," sobbed Ann. "As you've hinted, if I get the name of being what the priest mentioned, everyone'll hear it, and it'll be cast up to them at school."

"No – it won't, because I'll get it read out from the pulpit," returned Jack. "I'll blackmail the ould bastard into doing it in spite of himself. I'll go over his head – just you wait and see."

When Ann felt Jack's strong arm about her shoulders, some of the vitality that animated him flowed into her body. "If you do, it'll only make matters worse," she said, her composure slowly returning. "There's nothing for me to do now but go back to my parents, much as I hate to, before the gossip really begins. Everyone'll know that the priest called here today, and you can imagine the rest yourself."

Ann's stricken face touched a soft spot in Jack's nature. "You don't have to go back to your parents, now or ever, if you don't want to," he said, in a burst of kindliness. "There's another way out of this, if you listen to me. You once told me that your children's future was your only concern. Well, I like them too, as you can guess. So, what I'm suggesting is – now don't laugh until you've heard me out – that you marry me. Think about it before you make a decision. I'm serious – deadly serious. We can go to London and start fresh there, away from all the nosy neighbours."

For an instant there was a silence so acute it seemed that neither of them breathed, and Ann, feeling as if a cyclone had just swept through her mind, was devoid of all reasoning, for it was indeed a strange world she was living in. Minutes earlier she had been drinking tea with her employer when firstly she was accused of adultery and now she had a proposal of marriage from a very unlikely source. "You can't be serious, Jack," she said unbelievingly. "You don't have to go to such extremes for me – you have your own life to lead, but it was a nice gesture all the same."

"I was never more serious in my life, and I haven't heard you saying no out of hand. So, don't say no until you've heard me out," returned Jack. "In the old days most marriages were arranged – they believed love came after marriage. Who knows, it could be true – look at the gentry and royalty. I, being a priest's son, am kind of royal myself – Irish royalty, but we can talk about that later. I've known you for eighteen months – my, eighteen months, no wonder people are gossiping – and I do like you a lot, and I don't know what I'm going to do without you. I was just on the point of telling you that I was selling up and going back to London when we were rudely interrupted by the bag o' yeast. I know now that it wasn't much of a proposal – no nice words – but I meant it. So, what can I say now – now that I've messed it up, only that I'd be straight with you as a husband, and the children'll have a good home."

The expression on Ann's face said both yes and no, her eyes saying yes, her frown saying no. "I must say, I am flattered, but it's all so sudden," she said, shaking her head in disbelief. "Maybe when you have time to think about it, you'll change your mind."

"Why should I change my mind? – I'll be getting the best of the bargain, I'll be getting you and the children, and you'll be getting just me," said Jack, laughing in an attempt to bring some light-heartedness into the conversation, wondering why the idea had never crossed his mind before. Here, right under his nose, was the fulfilment he sought, and it had taken the priest's visit to open his eyes. "I know I have my faults, but at least you've seen them all. I'm not going to say I'll change, because people can't change even if they tried, and to know the worst about someone is sometimes the best way to begin. So, what you see is what you'll be getting – no fancy trimmings, and I'll look after the children like they were my own."

"I know you'd look after them, Jack, and me too. But you mentioned about going back to London – is London definitely in your plans?" asked Ann, calmer now, the unhappy shadows lifting from her face.

"There's opportunity in London," returned Jack. "I was just saying to myself the other day, if I made money there starting off with nothing, I'm sure I could make a lot more starting out with capital. And, as for you and the children, it's all right to have them here with you now, but what happens when they grow up? Nine chances out of ten, they'll be forced to emigrate to find employment – what then? You'll be left without them unless you follow them over there – d'you see what I'm getting at. Besides, there's everything in London, and everyone minds their own business, and in later years we can always move to the outskirts."

"I never looked at it that way before, but it makes sense, and I'm sure you know what you're doing," said Ann, laughing lightly. "So, I think I'd better accept your proposal before you change your mind. But there's one question – what'll Mary say?"

Jack had to think – Mary? No name rose to his memory except Mary O'Hara, and it was hardly possible that Ann knew of her. "This Mary you mentioned – can you explain?" he asked at length.

Ann shrugged, certain now that she had been mistaken. "Just a name you called out in your sleep on the night you came back from the races. You were having a nightmare and your bedroom door was open, and you called for Charlie someone too."

"I have it now," said Jack. "Charlie was my horse – Mary must be Mary O'Hara, married now with children. She was someone I thought I was in love with some years back – but I buried that ghost long ago. But what do I do now that you've accepted my proposal?"

"Kiss me, please."

Lifting her chin with a forefinger and thumb Jack kissed her upturned lips tenderly, the sensation sending galaxies of stars exploding in his brain, and when he felt the ardour in her response, it seemed that she too had blundered into the same heaven.

Two cups of tea later, when the stars in their eyes had dimmed somewhat, Jack laughed. "The Lord surely works in mysterious ways," he said. "In later years we can look back and say that it was the priest who brought us together – a marriage made in heaven, wouldn't you say?"

And Ann laughed, a laugh that contained both love and happiness.